TWO RIP-ROARIN' WESTERNS BY T.V. OLSEN, WINNER OF THE GOLDEN SPUR AWARD!

HIGH LAWLESS

"You just shot the wrong man, Landers," Channing said to the hired killer. "You just killed Santee Dyker, the man who sent for you. *I'm* the one you were supposed to gun."

Channing watched Landers' face. When Channing saw the first break of decision, he started his move, beating Landers' lift of arm by a fraction so that their shots did not quite merge. Landers' shot bloomed mud from the street as he buckled backward against the porch column. There was time for only fleeting astonishment to seize his face as he caught the second bullet. He rocked away from the column like a suddenly emptied grainsack and fell full-length on the planking.

Channing sheathed his gun and took two steps forward. He shouldn't have. It was one of the biggest mistakes he'd ever made....

SAVAGE SIERRA

Charbonneau said, "One thing I never figure you for, Angsman, is a great fool."

"But you're too smart to shoot before you hear me out, Charbonneau. The Apaches know you're here and they're set to rampage. When they finish with my camp they'll just be cutting their teeth. Afterward there'll be you. So do we have a temporary truce or not?"

"Why not? I feel generous."

"If any of us ever get out of this alive, Charbonneau, I'll be watching my back with you around. That's one thing never changes where you and me are concerned."

HIGH LAWLESS
&
SAVAGE SIERRA

T.V. OLSEN

HIGH LAWLESS
&
SAVAGE SIERRA

The characters and events portrayed in this book are fictitious.
Any similarity to real persons, living or dead, is coincidental
and not intended by the author.

Published by AmazonEncore
P.O. Box 400818
Las Vegas, NV 89140

ISBN-13: 9781477841860
ISBN-10: 1477841865

∾

Table of Contents

High Lawless ....…...…… 1

Savage Sierra ....…..……… 177

T.V.OLSEN

HIGH LAWLESS

ONE

He stepped from his saddle at the tie rail, wrapped his reins around the weathered crosspole, and had his look at the nearly deserted, noon-slumbering main street. Los Santos was a primitive Mexican-American village nestled in an upper crook of the Rio Grande. The buildings, monotonously white-washed adobe paralleled by dirt paths, were afforded a single rickety relief in the raw, unpainted frame structure of Ranson's saloon. Beyond it and etched against the brassy sky above it, a church flaunted an ironic spire.

With no waste motion he lifted his carbine from its scabbard, pivoted on his heel and headed down the street for the saloon. Picked out in the midday sun, he was compact, not hard, with the relaxed alertness of a cat. His calico shirt and waist overalls were threadbare, worn to a neutral chalk-gray where alkali had not obscured their color. His eyes were brittle amber, without looking to left or right they missed nothing, and the angular surface lines of his face warned a man that he rarely smiled. In his mid-twenties, not quite a small man, he carried himself with a quiet, not-cocky yet uncompromising confidence that usually only bigger and older men could afford. Something, not in his face but in his fluid movements, suggested a sum of thin temper on the edge of violence; a Mexican woman coming from the plaza well with a water *olla* on her shoulder angled discreetly away from his path.

Walking on a long angle, he reached the opposite side of the street where a small adobe store adjoined the saloon, and paused there. Pop Killaine was slacked massively in his back-tilted chair against the store front. Pop was fat, bald and seventy, a local patriarch; he was to be seen here every day, rain or shine, watching the small currents of life that made Los Santos a town—seeing much, saying little. Hooded beneath frosty brows, his eyes probed at the rifle, then lifted to the young man's face.

"Primed for bear?"

"You saw him, Pop." It was a statement, not a question.

"Next door. Buckin' the tiger, drinking up a storm."

"I reckoned he was."

Pop Killaine paused weightily, clearing his throat. "He's with Costello."

"I guessed that, too." The young man's tone was bitter and musing. "What's got into him, Pop?"

"Whiskey, Channing."

Channing nodded once before making an abrupt half-turn and heading on to Ranson's. He shouldered the swing doors open and went through.

The barroom was overhung with stale whiskey fumes and a thinly curling stratum of cigar smoke;at the long bar cowboys rubbed shoulders with feed-lot men, stock buyers, and drummers, for it was shipping time and the saloons of the sleepy village were the center of commerce for this remote corner of the territory. An archway draped with beaded curtains joined the barroom and the gambling hall at the back, and the whir of roulette wheel and keno goose mingled with the murmurs or explosive laughter of many men.

Channing crossed the barroom and pushed aside the beaded curtains. The gambling tables were all crowded, but he thought he glimpsed Lacey's blond head at the back of the room. He moved that way, threading between tables.

A lean body shifted casually across his path, blocking him. He halted, facing Bee Withers. Withers was a foolish, untalkative man of forty in filthy denims. Costello's man. He cheeked a tobacco cud in one whiskered jaw and spat cheerfully at the floor between them.

"Want to buy in?" Channing asked.

Not moving, Withers said nothing, grinning vacuously because he knew that Channing could be crowded a long way.

"Don't," Channing said quietly, just watching. Withers' grin faded as he realized that Channing already considered himself pushed to a limit. He let out his breath slowly, almost delicately, and stepped carefully to one side. Channing moved on without a sideward glance and halted at Costello's table.

Lacey Trobridge's head was hunched between his heavy shoulders as he squinted befuddledly at a fan of cards in his meaty fist.He did not look up. The dealer did, his bland, dark gambler's eyes raising to Channing's. He was a slight, almost ash-blond man in fawn-colored trousers and a bottle-green frock coat. There was a faint, autocratic arrogance about Ward Costello that went beyond dapper airs.

"Lacey," Channing said now, gently.

Lacey raised his head, tossing his blond cowlick out of his eyes. They were a wide, innocuous china-blue, the kind that went quick with pain at the sight of a motherless calf or a saddle-galled horse. His eyes usually held an eager, wagging-tailed friendliness that instantly won both men and women—and masked a score of faults and weaknesses that Channing knew and forgave. Just now the eyes were slitted and bloodshot in Lacey's red face. He recognized Channing, muttered surlily, "Knew you'd be here," and reached for the glass at his elbow.

Channing nudged the glass with the tip of his rifle-oarrel; it shattered on the floor in a dark reeking splash. Lacey's hand froze in arrested movement; behind Channing, the room died into silence.

Lacey tried to dredge up anger, failed, and said plaintively, "No need for that, boy. I'm free, white—"

"And drunk," Channing said. "Do you leave on your own feet or feet first?"

"I'd go easy, Channing," Costello murmured.

"Why?"

They stared at each other for a time-hung space which Costello broke: "Take him when the game's over, then."

"I'll take him now."

"Damn it," Lacey slurred, "don't talk about me like I wasn't here!"

"Shut up," Channing said "Get on your feet." As he spoke he shifted his rifle to his left hand, caught Lacey under the arm and started to lift him from the chair. The brief side-flick of Costello's eyes was enough to warn Channing; he let go of Lacey and wheeled, swung up his rifle and smashed the stock savagely against Bee Withers' down-arcing forearm. Withers shouted with pain, the six-gun he'd swung at Channing's temple falling from nerveless fingers. Without a break in movement, Channing swung his rifle back and forward, the barrel meeting Withers' jaw in a merciless, cracking blow. Withers' legs dissolved; without a sound he slumped to the floor.

"Ed—behind you—"

Lacey's cry brought Channing around, facing back to the table. There was no law in Los Santos; by tacit consent its tough-nut inhabitants settled their disputes personally and a single blunt warning, if that, was as much as a man could expect. He barely caught a single flicking motion of Costello's hand; a pocket pistol appeared in that hand as by magic.

If Costello had meant only to bluff, there was no time now; Channing's rifle was coming to level, and Costello fired as Lacey Trobridge's straining lunge carried him across the table between them. Lacey jerked heavily with the slug's impact; his body plunged aspraddle the table and slid off as it crashed on its side. Cards and chips rained over his inert form.

Costello was already running, heading toward a rear door. Channing, shaking with rage, straightened from the body of his friend. He brought the carbine to his shoulder, tried to bead down on the gambler. But every man in the room was on his feet now; a press of shifting bodies cut off Channing's view. The door swung wide; Costello bolted through and slammed it behind him. Channing elbowed through the crowd to achieve the door. Trying to force it, he saw through a quarter-inch crack that a heavy crossbar had been dropped into brackets.

He flung about and elbowed through the curtained archway into the barroom. Men cursed him as they gave way. He ran the length of the room and the swing doors parted with his hurtling body. He veered hard, skirted the building and pounded up the adjoining alley past the startled Pop Killaine. He found Costello's running footprints deep-dug in the soft earth at the rear of the building. The gambler had cut hard to the right, his steps fading out then on the hard turf.

Channing went down on one knee, tracing the back-springing grass bent by Costello's flight. *You'll find him, the town isn't that big it'll hide him long,* he considered with an icy detachment, and then: *The stable. He'll try to clear out.*

At once he was on his feet, paralleling the rear of the buildings at a plunging run. The livery stable was at street's end, a long, high structure backed by a horse corral. The horses were milling skittishly; between their bodies he saw Costello appear in the livery's rear archway and glance swiftly around. The gambler abruptly pivoted in midstride; Channing caught the sunflash on the pocket pistol, again magically palmed. He dived through the corral poles, lit on his side as the little gun made its spiteful bark; shards of wood bit from a fence pole. Rolling now to his feet, he thought automatically, *That's both barrels.*

The snorting horses leaped away as he lunged across the compound. He reached the archway and hauled up short. In the center of the runway the gray-haired hostler was holding a horse; Costello had a toe in stirrup. His face, pinched with fear, swung toward Channing; he hesitated and then vaulted into leather. Channing lowered his rifle, then hefted it with both hands around the stock as he started forward.

"Come off there or I'll knock you off."

Costello had not spurred away, for Channing could have easily shot him from the saddle. Now, seeing Channing's revised intent, he snatched the reins from the hostler and roweled the animal savagely, driving it squarely at Channing.

Channing swung the rifle back, intending to leap aside and sweep Costello from his perch with a full-arm swing. As he moved his boot skidded on the wet clay of the runway; he flailed his arms, fighting for balance, and then the horse's shoulder smashed him full in the chest. The impact drove the breath from him. His last-ditch effort to keep his footing had arched his body backward and now he plunged helplessly to one side, felt a crashing blow on his skull, and then awareness pinwheeled away into darkness.

He came to with the hostler gently slapping his face with the end of a wet rag. He pushed the old man's hand away. Pain rocked sickeningly in his head as he fought to a sitting position, then cradled his face in his palms. When the dizziness had receded he looked up.

"Costello?"

"Hypered out like the Old Nick was scorching his heels. Evil lick, that. Crown of your hat blunted it or you'd a took a split head, more'n likely...."

Channing turned his head to see the heavy corner post of the stall partition which he had fallen against. With the old man's shoulder for support he got to his feet, swallowed against a roiling sickness, and made his voice steady. "Take my hat, old-timer."

The hostler picked up the mashed Stetson, batted the crown to rough shape and silently handed it to him. Channing adjusted it well forward on his throbbing head, nodded thanks, and walked gingerly from the stable, halting at the front archway.

The gray taste of defeat was in his mouth. Careless overcertainty had permitted the gambler's escape. It would take time, trailing him in the stony hills above town, and meanwhile Costello would put miles between himself and Los Santos. There had to be one sure way to find him, and then Channing had the answer. It quickened his pace as he walked back to Ranson's.

In the gambling room he found a sober crowd gathered around Lacey's body, spread over now by a worn blanket. Bee Withers was propped unconscious and spraddle-legged against the wall and Dr. Alverez, the ancient settlement medico, was kneeling by him and tentatively probing at his jaw with long, bony fingers.

"How is he?" Channing asked.

Alverez looked up and said in his reedy and trembling voice, "You are the young *ladrone* who did this?"

"Replicar," Channing said coldly, sharply.

Alverez sighed with a vague shrug. "The lower mandibular is shattered. It will have to be wired up for a long time. I do not know who will pay. It will be very painful."

Bueno, Channing thought, and aloud: *"¿Cuánto es?"*

The medico blinked his watery eyes rapidly. "Twenty dollars."

"And I'm a *ladrone?* Ten." Alverez didn't object. Channing counted out the silver dollars, clinked them into the withered palm, and walked over to Lacey. He started to reach for the blanket where it covered the boy's face, hesitated and straightened, hat in hand, staring bleakly down. His thoughts left the crowded, murmurous room, ranging back to other days, good days he and the dead boy had known together. He didn't want to see Lacey's face. *He was always so alive,* channing thought *Maybe too alive.* Maybe that was it....

Nine months ago they had thrown in together to hunt wild mustangs in the rocky border hills. Channing had had his own reasons for wanting to temporarily abandon the society of men, and wanting to get Lacey Trobridge away from it too. The kid was not mean-tempered but incorrigibly wild in an easy, free-swinging way; trouble usually found him before he looked for it Channing's problem had been similar; perhaps that was why he'd been attracted to this mercurial boy whose brash, out-going temperament was at odds with his own. It had made him almost paternally protective.

The work had been hard, up in their lonely horse camp twenty miles from Los Santos, their only company the half-dozen Mexican wranglers they'd hired who hung apart from the two Americans. Brutal labor on a thin, monotonous diet of coarse *frijoles* and jerky and over-watered chicory. It meant riding out a hundred miserable vagaries of weather, breaking backs and blisters building horse-traps and driving the animals to them, rough-busting the captured mustangs, finally rolling into their blankets at day's end too exhausted for talk. Lacey had griped incessantly; only his friend's stronger personality had held him from riding off a dozen times.

It's going to be different, Channing had argued; we'll clear anyway two thousand before we're finished... enough for a big down payment on a little ranch north a ways I've had my eye on for a long time. No more pounding leather for thirty and found, throwing it all away on payday. Be our own men...and partners, eh?

Lacey had airily agreed, only half-hiding his indifference. As a token of trust Channing had him drive the first bunch of mustangs to Los Santos to dicker a price; Lacey's friendly ways should fetch a good sum, give the kid a needed sense of responsibility. A mistake. Lacey had gotten a good price...then headed for the nearest gambling room. Dealer Ward Costello had obligingly set up the drinks while he took Lacey for every cent. That had been three months ago.

Channing had hardly castigated the kid; the bitter truth was too plain. Lacey would never bear responsibility if he lived to a hundred: an omission in his nature that could not be filled. The most he could hope was to steer the boy—another futile hope.

Last night after patiently hearing out Lacey's usual tirade of complaints, Channing had announced that they had enough mustangs for a second sale—at least a thousand dollars' worth—and that they'd drive to Los Santos tomorrow. This morning he had rolled out of his blankets to find Lacey gone. Bleakly certain that Lacey had ridden to town to hit the tables again on the strength of his share of the mustang proceeds, he'd saddled up and told the wranglers to follow him with the horses, and then headed alone for Los Santos....

A hand touched his arm. He turned to face the beefy bartender. The man's tough face and voice were gruffly sympathetic. "Sorry as hell. Seen something of the sort coming."

With an effort Channing mustered speech. "There'll be a cost for—"

"Don't trouble your purse, friend; he'll be well buried as a man ever is, here." Brushing aside a word of thanks, he said again, "Sorry as hell Good friend, eh?"

Good friend, Channing's mind echoed. Just a damn fool boy who couldn't keep away from the cards and the liquor and the fancy ladies—and the knowledge changed nothing. He knew how badly he had needed this one friend, and Ward Costello had killed him.

He found himself standing outside in front of Ranson's and there was Pop Killaine crossing the street with his rolling waddle, leading Channing's claybank gelding from the tie rail across the way. Wordlessly he halted, threw the reins.

"Thanks, Pop." Channing stepped to the animal's flank, sheathed the carbine. With the same deft economy of movement he untied the blanket roll behind the cantle and unrolled it. He lifted out a coiled gunbelt and holster. The belt was supple and oiled, the holster-leather purposely stiff and unworked and the inside rubbed slick with tallow. The Colt's .45 it held glided from leather almost at his touch, its weight balanced easily, naturally, in his palm. He spun the cylinder; it turned as though on oiled jewel-bearings.

Pop released a gently explosive grunt. "That bad?"

Channing glanced at him, saying thinly, "Anything you miss, Pop?"

"Not a hell of a lot. Seen a lot of guntippers try to hang up iron, never worked. Don't break the mold now."

The dry sarcasm was felt in his words and not in the old man's tired tonelessness. His eyes were sad with a kindly cynicism. Channing shrugged. "With a reason, anyway."

"No. No good. Boy's dead, it can't bring him back. I'd think on it, son. Hard."

Channing drew an impatient breath, yet his hands hesitated around the belt.

"Might be you'll not need it," Pop Killaine suggested softly.

Channing leathered the gun, wrapped the belt around the holster and returned it to the blanket roll with swift, angry movements. "This won't change things."

"All right, all right, man's got to pay, see he does. But go easy....Seen him ride north. There's law up there. You—"

"Where would he go, Pop?"

Pop shook his head. "Costello, he drifted in, out. Had more money than most sharpers, always wore the finest, ate the best. With the airs of him I'd suspicion him of a fancy background. More'n that, can't say."

Channing nodded, turning away. Instead of mounting he started back toward the stable, leading his horse. Pop Killaine huffed into step with him. "Thought you'd be hell-for-leather."

"I'm a patient man, Pop. I can wait."

"For what?"

"1 cracked Bee Withers' jaw. It'll keep him abed awhile. When he's on his feet...he's Costello's heel dog. He'll head for where Costello is."

"And you'll follow. Streak of Injun in you, Channing. Wager you can hate like one, too."

"No bet," Channing said unsmilingly. He halted, facing the old man. "Do me a favor. My wranglers are coming in with a horse herd. I'll be at the hotel. Sleeping on a headache. Tell 'em."

"Sure," Pop said gently. "I'll tell 'em..."

He stood unmoving as Channing went on toward the stable. Under his frosty brows the old man's eyes were sad and weary and pitying.

TWO

Channing lay bellied at the summit of a long, grassy rise. His eyes were flinty, edged with impatience at last; a two weeks' growth of beard darkened his lower face and his clothing was filthy and sweat-crusted. He watched Bee Withers ride across the ranch yard and dismount. Two men were waiting for him on the main house porch, and he recognized the angular grace in the walk of the one who came down to greet Withers…it was Costello. They shook hands, then entered the house.

Channing rose to a crouch, easing his cramped muscles. His hard face did not reveal the cold surge of satisfaction he felt.

In Los Santos he had waited a week till Withers' broken jaw had mended enough to let him ride. During that time Channing had sold his horses and paid off his wranglers, bought a light grubstake of staples to fill his saddlebags—and waited. He'd stayed successfully out of Withers' sight, yet keeping a weather eye on his movements; when Withers had ridden from Los Santos it was openly and in broad daylight. Channing had followed, holding his measured distance. Withers had headed north, traveling fast and light. When he camped in the open Channing made dry camp close by. When he stayed in a town, Channing camped outside and was waiting each morning to pick up the trail. Withers made a few clumsy efforts to hide his sign, doubling back, making sharp cut-offs from traveled routes, but these gave Channing no difficulty. Withers was never certain he was being closely followed.

Yesterday they had entered the broad basin of the Soledad River in a northeastern pocket of New Mexico. It was mountainous, irregular country, and Channing had begun to worry whether he could hold the trail much longer. Withers had spent the night in Sentinel, a little ranch-center village situated at a bend of the river, and this morning had headed due west from town along a wagon road. At midday Withers rode into the ranch quarters below the rise where Channing now crouched.

Trail's end. Channing came stiffly to his feet and trotted halfway downslope to his claybank, ground-haltered behind the rise. Weeks of frugal meals and lack of sleep, his filthy and unkempt state, combined to hone temper to a tense edge. He mounted and rode to the crest of the rise, forcing himself to think coolly. He took in the ranch layout, missing no detail. The headquarters sprawled impressively in a rolling swale. The main house was solidly heavy-timbered and set off from the working part of the ranch. Costello was down there...no doubt with friends. Friends who would shield a murderer? He didn't know; ignorance gave him pause. To ride in boldly and openly might well place his head in a noose, and yet there was no choice....

He circled the slope, riding up behind the maze of corrals and sheds while keeping these between himself and the combination cookshack-bunkhouse on the west side of the layout. The bulk of the crew must be on-range now, at past noon; he hoped to reach the house without being seen. He put the claybank across an open space, rode up between the stables and carriage shed close to the house and then kneed his mount briskly across the scuffed, hard-packed clay yard to the porch.

He started to swing down, one foot leaving stirrup as the door opened. A middle-aged man wearing a white linen suit and a wide-brimmed Panama hat came out, walked leisurely to the porch edge. Channing finished his dismount and wrapped his reins around the long tie rail. He moved back from the rail to his horse, his scabbarded rifle within easy reach as Costello and Withers edged warily onto the porch behind the older man.

"That's him," Costello said, his low-pitched voice failing to cover its faint tremor.

The older man didn't even glance at him. Watching Channing, he drew gently on the long, thin Havana he held —an arrogant cock of wrist to the way he held it. He was small and whiplash-lean, wearing his white tropicals with a dapper elegance that seemed out of place even in a gentleman rancher. Impressive, yet foppish, till you saw his face. The eyes were pale and colorless, with an icy opaqueness that hid all emotion. The closely schooled set of his face was fine and aquiline. But his thin, incisive lips were bloodless, bracketed with severe lines, and Channing knew that this was a man who bent other men with an iron hand and was bent by no one.

— He exhaled a stream of smoke into the sunlight. His tone was easy, conversational, yet with a toneless inflection that betrayed neither condescension nor hostility: his words said it bluntly. "I know who you are, why you're here, horseherd. I don't underestimate the guts, even the sagacity, of a man who would come this far for your reason. Still, you're a fool."

"I'm listening," Channing said sparely, "but not long."

The man's little finger flicked ash from the Havana. "I'm Santee Dyker. The name means a good deal around here. I can make or break any man who works for me and a lot who don't. Ward, here, is my nephew." His lips twisted faintly, cynically. "A sorry admission, but the truth. He's worth nothing, but I made a promise to his dying mother —my sister. His interests have to be mine."

"That's too bad."

"For you," Santee Dyker murmured. "Ward gave me a story that put the right on his side, which, knowing Ward, I didn't for an instant believe. Your claim doubtless has justice, but I'll not pretend a hypocritical interest in justice. Meanwhile, the killing took place far to the south; you have no friends here. As a man shrewd enough to assess the drift…you'd better get back on that horse."

Channing moved—an unbroken movement that lifted his rifle from the saddle, levered it and brought it to bear on the three men inclusively.

Dyker's relaxed pose did not alter. "Take him with you and my men will overtake you….Shoot him now and you won't get out of the country alive. My country." He paused with a weighted emphasis. "Hopeless, you see?"

Detachedly Channing noted the resemblance between Santee Dyker and Costello: the difference important to him was that Dyker was as strong as his nephew was weak, and Channing knew that no single word was bluff. He faced more than he had bargained for, yet the inflexible stubbornness that was part of him would not let him consider flinching down, he had come too far....

"Step down here, Costello. Keep your hands out from your body."

"Santee," Costello said in a choked whisper.

"Never argue with a desperate man," Dyker said smoothly. "Do as he tells you, Ward; doubt he'll shoot in cold blood, unless you resist. Nor will he get far."

Costello took two halting steps.

"Ease down that squirrel iron, boy. There's two guns covering you." The voice was deep-South, summer-soft. Channing moved only his eyes till he saw a man just coming to view from behind one corner of the house. A second man appeared at the opposite corner. Channing lowered the rifle. The two circled the porch, six-guns steady; the man who'd spoken stopped a careful yard off from Channing and took the rifle from his hands.

"Well-timed, Streak," Santee said.

Streak grinned faintly. He was a slender man of about thirty, not tall; hard and disillusioned eyes still found room for a bright, wicked arrogance in their pale-bleached depths. He leaned Channing's rifle against the porch, jerked off his dusty hat and batted it idly against his brush chaps. A streak of pure white waved back through his wiry chestnut hair. "Yeah. We'd come off fencing, was in the bunkhouse. Saw him crossing between the corrals and the carriage shed. Looked to be prowling, so we circled, come up back of the house....He the one you wanted us to look out for?"

"The one." Dyker stubbed out his cigar on the porch railing, colorless eyes fixing Channing. "Won't warn off, will you, horseherd? Have to be shown my meaning.... Get a rope, Whitey."

The other man holding a gun on Channing giggled. He was twenty or less, rail-thin, with hair so pale it was nearly white. His eyes were slits. A feverish pleasure filled them. "Right away, Mr. Dyker." He loped away, vanishing behind a shed.

Streak drawled expressionlessly, "Sure this is the way?"

"Let him off with a warning, he'll be back. You know these cocky, arrogant brush jumpers. All they own is a self-sufficient pride. Break that and you put the fear of God in them."

Streak rubbed his chin, thoughtfully taking Channing in from head to foot. Channing knew how he looked: a seedy, ragged, and bearded man of less than average height, and light for that. No more than the tramp Santee had named him...yet Streak hesitated. "I'm not so sure...."

Dyker snorted gently as he stepped back inside the house. Whitey returned with a coiled lasso and kept up his nervous, eager sniggering. Dyker reappeared hefting a long blacksnake; he cracked it once with a pistol-shot report."Tie his wrists to the railing. Facing it. Ward, give Whitey a hand."

Streak held the gun against Channing's back while Costello and the thin youth jerked Channing's arms above his head and lashed them to the porch rail. "Not like you expected, eh?" Costello hissed close to his ear.

Channing said nothing, did not wince at the bite of

ropes or the splintered edge of sun-warm wood digging into his wrists, first thinking, *Steady. You've been whipped before,* and thinking automatically then of his father and the savage birchings of his boyhood. Yet the very memory knotted his guts and made his knees go watery and numb. *Don't let them see it.*

"Let me, Mr. Dyker," Whitey said. The crazed giggle again.

"I think not," Dyker said musingly. "The pleasure will be Streak's...."

"No," Streak said flatly. "No pleasure."

"You're like my friend the horseherd, Streak. Proud. Too proud." Dyker spat his words with a flat impact. "There's only one cock of the walk on Anchor Ranch. Me. Remember it." He coiled the rope with a flip of his fist and tossed it. Streak automatically dipped it out of the air and turned it in his hands, scowling.

"Do it," Santee Dyker said coldly. "Fifteen strokes. Lay them on hard."

Channing felt Streak move behind him and grab a fistful of his collar. A savage yank ripped the shirt to his waist and the sun glanced hot against his back. He heard Streak haul a deep breath as he took a few steps back. The blacksnake whistled back and forward, the tip lacing hotly across his shoulders.

"Come now," Dyker said dryly. "We won't count that."

Streak cursed softly and struck again. The lash curled like a burning switch around Channing's side and chest. Once, twice, and three more times. Channing closed his eyes and set his teeth. Streak paused. Dyker's remorseless voice: "That's five. Arm tired?"

Channing stood erect and held the count to nine, then his legs sagged and his senses swam in a painful blur.

The blows fell numbly, yet he felt the hurt with each beat of his heart *Don't. Don't, Pa. I won't touch a gun again, I swear....*

Water dashed wet and cold against his face. He tried to get his legs under him and failed. A hand fastened in his hair, yanking his head back.

"Reckon he won't be able to walk...."

"Set him on his horse."

"He won't stay there."

"Tie him on."

Somebody cut the ropes and he pitched limply down. Hands dragged him up. Images swam blurrily in his vision. He was straddling leather then with his face bowed in a horse's rank, sweaty mane. Again the taut bite of ropes against his wrists.

"Let him go!"

Something cracked against the horse's hip. Channing felt his head snap back, his body arch agonizingly with the animal's leap. Hoofs churned and his body tossed limply with the motion, his chin bouncing against his chest. It jerked him to half-awareness; he fought to hold that vague sentience, though with it the numbness receded and brought throbbing pain. His vision cleared.

The claybank's pace slackened out. He strained against the ropes binding his wrists to the horn till his fingers closed over the reins. Inching slack into his fists, he gradually guided the animal to a halt. Its flanks heaved; froth slobbered from its mouth. He had pushed the animal hard these last weeks, and against his own misery he dredged up pity. His mangled wrists were bleeding, the sun boiled against his back. He steeled himself against a swimming dizziness, threw all his strength into pulling his hands free. Slowly he slipped one hand free of the taut loops, feeling flesh tear; then he was loose.

Flexing circulation back to his fingers, he looked around. The ranch was out of sight. He matched up a swell of foothills to the north with the terrain he'd mentally mapped earlier, as was his habit in unfamiliar country. To the south would be the wagon road that connected Anchor and the town of Sentinel; he pulled the claybank's head in that direction.

Shortly he struck the shallow bed of a clear stream fed by melted snow from the northern peaks. He dismounted and threw reins to kneel by the cool flow gushing over mossy stones. He cupped his hands and drank. The water was icy, hurting his teeth, shocking him to full sensibility. The stubborn, insensate pride that was in him asserted itself; he was reluctant to head for town and a physician's care. No man whipped like a dog wanted his shame exposed to others. Against that he measured the danger of blood poisoning and infection in the burning wounds that laced his back. Gingerly he shrugged out of his torn shirt. He slowly extended his body full length over the stream as he lowered himself on his hands. The impact of the icy water foaming up around his trunk took his breath away. First it blazed wetly against his lacerated back and then a welcome numbness gently encroached. Running water would cleanse the cuts.

Detachedly, almost drowsily, he considered his next move. He did ask himself whether his ends were changed; they were not Get Costello, that simple. The whipping had only hardened his resolve. To the indictment of Lacey's death he could add a pure joy of revenge with no conscience-qualm, no squeamishness about method.

He rose, absently toweled his dripping body with his shirt as, drag-footed, he ascended the bank to his horse. He untied and unwrapped the blanket roll, exposing the oiled gunbelt. He strapped it on, feeling its weight on his hip like an old friend. His smile was not pleasant, a mere tightening of set lips over his teeth. He dug a worn ducking jacket which had been Lacey's from his saddlebag. Oversized on him, its loose folds would not irritate his back. He buttoned it to the neck, discarding his ruined shirt.

In fifteen minutes he reached the wagon road and followed it to Sentinel, riding slowly in his dizzy exhaustion. He met nobody on the road. The ashen pallor of dusk had closed over the town when he reached the slapdash clutter of run-down railworkers' shanties on the east outskirts. He crossed the tracks, rode past the wind-stench of empty stockpens and turned onto the main street. He left his horse at the livery stable with orders for its feed and care, afterward heading for the hotel two blocks down the street, carrying his saddlebags, The leaden exhaustion that pulled at his legs was beginning to hamper all of his movements. His head pounded feverishly. He crossed the hotel lobby and braced himself against the desk as, tight-voiced, he asked for a room and signed the register the curious but discreetly unquestioning young clerk shoved at him.

Up in the narrow and musty cubbyhole of a room he did not light the lamp. He kicked the door shut behind him and paused only long enough to shed the heavy jacket before he lurched to the bed and collapsed across the sagging mattress. Dead, dreamless sleep claimed him almost at once.

THREE

A finger of sunlight hazed through the fly-blown window and across the faded blanket. It touched Channing's face and he opened his eyes. He winced from belly-down to a sitting position, then eased to his feet. His whole body ached, but inspecting his back in the cracked mirror above the washstand he saw that the broken flesh open to the air had already begun clean healing. Mostly the biacksnake had left discolored stripes, not nearly as bad as he'd expected.

Despite his cramps he felt fit enough. He poured water into the basin, carefully shaved and afterward stripped down and sponged himself clean. He changed to his one pair of clean levis and a shirt, then stepped into the hall, locked his room, and went down to the lobby.

The day clerk, a different and older man, glanced up idly. "Mornin'."

"Mornin'. Can I buy a bait?"

"Our dining room's open nine till midnight, back off the lobby there."

Channing went through the double doors into a long room with a heavy oak table running three-quarters of its length. Each place was set but it was an hour before noon and only one old man was eating. He looked hunched and runty, alone at the big table. Channing paused in the doorway, watching with faint amusement. The old fellow was eating as though it were the last civilized meal he expected to enjoy, wolfing it down with scalding mouthfuls from his coffee cup. He looked rawhide-lean, rawhide-tough, in a greasy elkhide shirt and leggings. His freshly clipped hair lay close against his lean skull, but a snowy beard still furred his gauntly hollowed cheeks.

He growled surlily without looking up, "Your pap teach you better manners'n to stare?"

"He tried," Channing said dryly, "real hard."

He skirted the table and sat down opposite the oldster. A fat cook in a soiled apron waddled from the kitchen. "Yours?" Before Channing could reply the old man said in the same half-snarled, uncompromising way, "Grub's all spoilt. Try the ham and eggs though."

Channing nodded to the cook, who gave the old man an unnoticed glare and went back to the kitchen. "Name's Channing."

"Brock." The old man snapped his teeth on the name as if he wanted no more talk. Channing guessed him to be a burned-out, broken-down mountaineer down for supplies, one good meal, one good drunk, and his annual shearing—half-dotty with solitude and distrusting everyone. Yet he caught a brief up-flicker of the bright, still-young eyes, saw their shrewd assessment of him before they lowered. He was odd enough, but sane and no fool, Channing knew then. Brock dropped his knife and fork with a clatter on his wiped-up plate, sleeved his mouth and stood up. He tramped from the dining room with a noiseless moccasined tread, not looking back.

"Where's Brock?" It was a young voice, a brash voice carrying clearly from the lobby.

"Here he comes now," was the desk clerk's reply. "Brock, here's Max and Karl wantin' a word with you."

"I know their word, and this child's got no time."

"You got time for this, dad," said the brash voice,

Channing stood and walked to the double doors, halting there. Two men who were evidently brothers blocked the mountaineer's way in the center of the lobby. One was young and stocky with close-cropped pale hair, and Channing knew it was he who'd spoken. The other was an older man of mournful mien, also light-haired and blue-eyed.

"No beating the bush, dad," said the young one. "John Straker wants to see you—out at Mexican Bit. We was up to your shack yesterday. Nobody there, but found your mule's tracks trailin' for town."

"You rid a piece for nothin'," Brock grunted, and started to walk around the pair.

The youth clapped a meaty hand solidly on the skinny shoulder. "Don't reckon. Karl, get on his other side." The sad-faced one reached out a long arm and caught Brock's.

"Damn your liver and lights! Straker wants to talk, he kin ride up the high country same's the trash he hires," Brock bristled.

"No trouble, dad. Make it easy, all round."

"Let him go."

Channing sidled easily through the doors as he spoke, came across the puncheon floor. He stopped two paces away, weight balanced on the balls of his feet. Half-poised because he could read the way of this in Max's arrogant, wild grin. He sized them up as a salty pair but not hardcases.

Max dropped Brock's arm, rubbed his hands together. "Watch the crowbait, Karl. I ain't had breakfast." He rushed, bulling in with his head down. Channing stepped aside and chopped his right fist in a short, savage arc that ended behind Max's ear. He crashed to the floor, lunged to his feet at once and spun after Channing, who hit him off-balance even as he wheeled. Max back-pedaled, thick legs churning for footing. Channing followed up, belted him under the chest, and when Max straightened, teetering precariously on his heels, Channing brought his open hand up from his waist. Its calloused heel clouting Max's jaw rocked him back in an arching fall. He looked up glassily, wagging his head.

Channing half-turned, leveling his lidded stare on Karl. "You had breakfast?"

"Oh, sure," Karl said mournfully. He walked almost gingerly to Max and helped him to his feet. Max kept his baffled gaze on Channing. He rubbed his jaw, saying with no truculence, "You Anchor? Spur, maybe?"

Channing shook his head in flat negation. "Better get out. Fast."

When the lobby doors had closed behind them the mountaineer's agate-bright gaze swung on Channing. There was no relenting in his snarl. "Who you softenin' me for?"

"You been sizing me," Channing said coldly. "Seen me before?"

Brock dropped his prickly stare to the gunbelt."Wagh, it fits you're hired talent."

"Old man, I don't know about your feuds here. Nor give a damn. Believe that or don't."

Brock fingered his beard. "I believe it," he said with surprising mildness. "Thought I cut your drift, hoss. Even liked it. But you can't never be sure about a man."

With this calm jot of cynicism he turned and padded silently out through the street door. The desk clerk whistled softly. "That's something, mister. Old Brock don't fancy nobody...but he likes you."

"Who is he?"

"Old trapper—mountain man, last of his kind. First white man in these parts...forty year and more ago. Stiff-necked as hell."

"I saw that," Channing said impatiently. "He's got something a lot of folks want."

The desk clerk's sallow face lowered nervously; he aimlessly fingered the open register. "Look...don't know you. You say you're disavowed with Spur or Anchor, fine, but you might take sides. Me, I stay out, clean out."

Channing hesitated and shrugged. It was no mix of his either, no point pushing his curiosity with nothing at stake. He went back to the dining room and sat down to a platter of ham and eggs. He wolfed it ravenously, washed it down with three cups of coffee that was black and caustic. Feeling physically better with himself and the world, he went back to the lobby and selected a leather chair with the horsehair padding leaking out. He pulled it around facing the front window and slacked down, wincing his back to a comfortable position. He stared idly at the saloon opposite the hotel with the sign across its blank, windowless upper story nearly weathered away: JUDD'S—LIQUOR AND TOBACCO.

He toyed with a miscellany of notions on making Ward Costello pay the piper...and Anchor Ranch. His brows knitted in a frown; there were cross-currents in this basin which might prove rewarding to investigate. He at once discarded the idea; he'd lone-wolfed it too long; his ways were direct, not intriguing.

A stutter of hoofbeats pulled his attention to the window again...two riders heading in, leading a riderless horse. He glanced, over at the clerk, who circled the desk and came to the window, peering out."Saturdays some of the boys from the three big outfits come in to see the elephant." He chuckled enviously. "Happen two of 'em crowd in at once, they'll be a town-treein' before nightfall."

Channing stood and walked to the window, hands rammed in his hip pockets. "That's a big fella." He jerked a nod at the tall, bull-shouldered man just pushing through the swing doors of the saloon opposite. Behind him clumped a short, thickset man with an empty right sleeve neatly rolled and pinned above his shoulder stump.

"That's Bob Thoroughgood—Spur foreman. Other's his *segundo*, Shiloh Dawes."

The approach of four more riders from the opposite end of the street drew Channing's gaze. He recognized the pair in the lead—Streak and the kid called Whitey....

"That's—" the clerk began with relish before Channing's flat, "I know them," bit off his speech short.

Channing watched stiffly as they dismounted. He had not been prepared for the cold, feral rage that flooded him at seeing Streak. The man who'd whipped him had been acting under orders, had even been reluctant. It might be the arrogant way Streak sat his saddle or the quiet cocksureness of his lean face—but Channing knew abruptly what he was going to do.

The four riders were scanning the hip-brands on the two horses tied at the rail as Channing stepped from the hotel. He crossed the street as the riders filed into the saloon; he went in on the heels of the last man.

The one-armed *segundo* glanced around, his voice quiet and dry: "Roll out the red carpet, Doc. Streak and the boys are in."

"Man drinks where he chooses, free country," the bartender said tersely. He was a stout man with a head bald as a cue-ball, wearing thick spectacles incongruous with his tough, doughy face.

"So's the air in it," Whitey giggled. "Clean air, up to now...."

"Free inside limits," Doc said ponderously. He grunted over, and came up with a sawed-off Greener which he laid lightly across the bar. "Leave the hatchet in the street or clear the house. The damn lot of you."

"Slack off, Whitey," Streak said irritably. "The usual, Doc."

"The same." Channing elbowed in, crowding the Anchor foreman aside.

"Why, that's—" Whitey began, but Streak made a chopping motion with his hand that cut the kid off. Streak turned slowly, resting an elbow on the bar as he faced Channing, with less than a foot between them.

"You should've been gone, brush jumper, way gone," he said softly, wickedly.

"Maybe you want to argue that?"

Faint puzzlement shaded Streak's bleached eyes; they

flicked down at the bolstered Colt on Channing's hip. "Why—" he hesitated, puzzled but unafraid—"I'm not just sure...."

Channing glanced down at the glasses which Doc was sloshing full. "Maybe this'll make up your mind." He moved one hand to lift a glass in an unbroken movement, throwing the contents in Streak's face. Streak choked, cursed wildly as he backed against the man behind him. Very slowly he raised his arm to wipe the liquor away. He blinked his eyes clear; Channing was now standing well out from the bar facing them all. The violence in Streak's face thinned to wariness. He straightened from his half-crouch, letting his breath out.

"I was right about you," he said huskily.

"It was a mistake."

"A mistake." Streak added wickedly, "I don't back-water. Don't think that!"

Channing nodded unconcernedly as though it meant nothing. "I'm handing my gun to the apron. You do the same."

"That's good, brush jumper." Streak breathed the words, his grin chalk-white. He unbuckled his shell belt and laid it on the bar, not once taking his eyes off Channing. Only when Streak had moved from the bar did Channing shuck his own belt and gun. He tossed it to the bartender and moved after Streak.

"Take it outside, you roosters," Doc growled, but it was too late. Still coming forward, Channing aimed a straight left from the shoulder; it glanced off Streak's cheekbone. The Anchor foreman grunted and bored in. Channing ducked beneath his full-arm swing. He grabbed Streak around the waist, lifted, threw his hip behind the man's right buttock and swung him off his feet. He brought his own weight atop Streak as they crashed to the floor. A wrestling throw learned from a half-Apache wrangler of his, its unexpectedness, had caught Streak off guard.

Channing could feel the straining power in Streak's lean, wiry body as he fought to throw off the mustanger's pinning weight, and knew then that he had a wildcat on his hands. Streak wasn't much bigger than he but the foreman's prideful, near-cocky manner showed him to be used to an easy dominance over tough ones—a right a frontiersman won only by fists or guns, and Streak was no gunhand.

Channing had the hold he wanted now—right hand clamping Streak's left arm, forcing it slowly behind his back while his weight, smothering Streak's side and moving onto his back, was forcing the foreman belly-down where he would be helplessly pinned. Streak's body was set in straining resistance, lank hair falling over his eyes. Then, with the sudden canniness of a tempered brawler who could improvise against unknown tactics, he relaxed, throwing his body in the direction Channing was pushing. The unexpected move carried Channing with it, hurling him off-balance. With a quick twist Streak broke the hold and kept turning his body, rolling Channing off him.

Both men were on their feet at once. Channing knew respectful caution now of Streak's lithe speed and saw a like emotion mirrored in Streak's face. They circled slowly with hands spread and bodies crouch-bent. Streak aimed a lightning kick, his boot grazed Channing's hip as the mustanger moved aside; his hands blurred to grab Streak's foot and twist. Streak spun with the twist to keep balance; he crashed against a flimsy deal table and it fell on its side, carrying two chairs with it. But Streak kept his feet. He took two steps and dived, catching Channing around the waist. The impact carried both backward, the swing doors parting to dump the locked men across the sidewalk. Pain tore across Channing's back.

Streak's head was buried in Channing's shirt-front; savagely he knuckled the mustanger's spine. Channing arched upward, grunting with the pain. He tried to pry Streak away and failed. He grabbed a handful of Streak's long hair and yanked his head back; with the heel of his free hand he pumped three long slogging blows into Streak's jaw. Streak let go and Channing heaved viciously and unseated him.

They scrambled to their feet. Channing started to place his weight, but Streak's wild swing caught him flush on the chin. The world exploded in Channing's eyes, and he was falling...struck the dirt of the gutter on his back. Streak's boot sank into his side and he rolled blindly from the knifing pain. He heard horses snort and prance and choking dust seared his nostrils; he'd rolled between the tied animals.

He sat up as his head cleared, hearing Streak's savage curse. Now Streak was ducking under the tie rail to reach him. It was brief respite, enough for Channing to rally one deep breath. He gathered his feet under him, squatting; then his body uncoiled, as Streak straightened up. He brought the blow from the ground and it glanced off Streak's cheekbone and staggered him against the tie rail. They stood in the narrow space between the horses' sweating flanks, slugging it out toe to toe, the crude science of common experience forgotten in savage abandon.

Channing was jarred back to sanity by the sharp, salty flow behind his broken lips. He gave back a step and then as Streak moved after him, timed a low punch under

Streak's guard and deep into his rigid belly. It was enough to half-double the Anchor man, and Channing brought his other fist to Streak's head in fast combination. Streak tried to counter, but Channing pressed him back to the tie rail, feeling Streak's blows lose force, the dazed shuffle to his movements.

Channing felt the pull of exhaustion weighting his own punches, yet he struck again. Streak's head rocked but he was involuntarily braced upright by the crosspole. Channing let his whole weight carry behind the last blow and his fist and then his shoulder caught Streak's upper body with a bruising force that flopped the foreman over the pole. He went asprawl on his face with legs falling across the sidewalk.

Held wordless during the brutal fracas, the men crowded on the sidewalk broke into talk. It was hushed and murmurous. This had been no whoop-up brawl to release steam; lasting no more than five minutes, it had unleashed a singleminded viciousness that each man felt.

Channing leaned his weight on the tie rail, drawing in great lungfuls of air. A hand fell on his arm. He looked at Shiloh Dawes. "Son," the one-armed man said gravely and dryly, "damned if I know what you were trying to prove. Drive your stakes deep and hard, though. Give you a hand inside? Like to talk...."

FOUR

Channing poured a second whiskey while the first was still exploding tendrils of heat through his aching body. He downed it at a swallow and nodded his thanks at Shiloh Dawes. The Spur *segundo* was seated across from him, a bottle between them, at a rear table. The Anchor men had loaded their beaten foreman on his horse and left. Bob Thoroughgood leaned on the bar, his back to the table.

"Two slugs ought to buy your ears a spell," Shiloh suggested mildly.

Channing eyed him speculatively, seeing a squat keg of a man with white steerhorn mustaches spanning his heavy mastiff jaws. His rough face was tempered with the wisdom of an aging and observant man. "I'm listening."

Shiloh twisted in his chair and motioned with his one arm at Thoroughgood. "Bob, come over here."

The foreman looked irritated, but he started across the room. A large dog lying across his path raised its head and growled. It was a gaunt, powerful beast whose dirty yellow fur blended so neutrally with the sawdust floor that Channing hadn't noticed it. Thoroughgood swore at it but gave it a wide berth as he came to the table and sat down. The dog settled its head and kept up a rumbling snarl.

"Ugly sonuvabitch," Shiloh commented. "He came around one night and Doc Willis, the bartender there, fed him and he stayed on. Dassn't nobody get close to him, even Doc."

Thoroughgood cuffed his hat to the back of his head with a hamlike fist. Despite his thick trunk, his belly was lean as a boy's, his hips whittled horseman-spare. His large Roman head with thick, gray-threaded black hair was sharp-featured as a hawk's. There was an odd sensitivity in his reserve, like a man who'd been deeply hurt; this alone spared him a manner of bitter indifference. He said impatiently, "What is it?"

"Like you to meet Ed Channing."

The two exchanged neutral stares. Neither offered to shake hands. Thoroughgood said, his hard face not changing, "What the hell bug's got you now?"

"Need men, good men, don't we?" Shiloh demanded.

"Damn it," Thoroughgood said almost angrily, "you don't want to hire a hand, you want to hire a gun. No; let them make the first move. Only a damn fool *asks* for trouble. No offence," he added, addressing Channing for the first time, "but you laid Streak Duryea in the dust. No one's done that, and he's not a man to forget."

"Didn't guess he was," Channing murmured.

Thoroughgood snorted softly. "And you don't care a damn, that it?"

"That's it." Channing bridled faintly at this man's surly truculence which wasn't even aware of itself.

Thoroughgood stared at him now with reluctant interest."What's your business?"

"My own."

"Easy, Bob, easy," Shiloh said placatingly, and to Channing: "Just interested in your references. Common practice, you ask a man to work for you."

Thoroughgood frowned but said nothing. Channing toyed with his glass, scowled into it, and then shrugged. "Mostly lately I trapped horses."

"Young man's game, that," Shiloh observed placidly. "Get past twenty-five, your bones brittle up, crack like kindling wood. Couple years you'll be too old to work the rough string."

"Yeah."

"No future there. Man ought to look to his future."

"Spit the meal out of your mouth," Channing said rudely. "No future in what you want me for either. A gun. That's all right. Mine'll cost you triple cowhand's wages."

Thoroughgood looked near-apoplectic. Before he could speak, Shiloh said quickly, "Bob, knock his wages off mine for the next year. I want this fella."

"And trouble," Thoroughgood spat.

"Man, don't be a damn mule! Now the first lease is up, trouble will come faster'n we can handle. Fight fire with fire."

Thoroughgood released his breath explosively, shook his head in resignation. To the mustanger: "What's your grudge against Duryea?"

"Fifteen stripes he laid on my back with a blacksnake."

"How in hell he do that, stand still for him?"

"Not hardly," Channing said coldly. "Rest is my business, let it ride."

Thoroughgood stood, and leaned forward with his palms on the table. "All right. I ramrodded Spur a dozen years, kept it clean of guntipping tramps; never thought to see the day I'd take one on, but that's the way of it Keep that smart tongue in your head and keep your nose clean while you're eating Spur grub." He pivoted on his heel and walked back to the bar.

"He wasn't always this way," Shiloh said low-voiced. "Only after his wife—"

"Not interested. Just want to hear what I'm buying into."

Shiloh summed it up quickly and tersely. Bordering the Soledad basin's north and west ramparts was a long, many-acred strip of the finest grazing land in the Sangre de Cristo foothills. It belonged to an old recluse named Elwood Brock. When the other mountain men of the early days had trapped out this basin, they'd moved on. Only Brock, then a young man, had stayed on, hunting and gold-grubbing, having no contact with other men except for roving bands of Indians who thought him possessed by the holy and left him unmolested. He was an odd One, that was sure, for when government surveyors came through to map this basin thirty years ago, Brock had arranged with them on an apparent whim to buy the whole strip of rich-grassed foothill range that spanned the northwest basin. It had taken all his long-saved fur money and painstakingly panned gold.

The first white settler in the basin had been Custis Thursday, late owner of Spur Ranch. He had developed a thriving outfit south of Brock's strip, but had never succeeded in dickering or threatening the old man into selling him the coveted graze. Later when John Straker had built up his Mexican Bit, a fierce two-way pressure had been laid against the old man. Brock had finally compromised, leasing the land out for a ten-year period to the highest bidder, Custis Thursday. Straker had reluctantly pulled in his horns; Thursday had moved his cattle onto the Strip; and, at first, he had prospered.

Santee Dyker was a shrewd, ambitious johnny-comelately. Unlike his tough predecessors who'd pulled themselves up by their bootstraps, he'd come to the basin two years ago with money enough to start his cattle-land venture in the biggest way; now he threatened to be a far deadlier rival than Straker.

For the ten years were up, the lease had expired, and the three ranches were gathering their forces for a reawakening of the old feud. In the last few years Thursday had put too many irons in the fire, had found out too late that he knew nothing but cattle. A number of bad investments, perpetrated on the aging cattleman by slicktongued frauds, had crashed. Spur Ranch was in a bad financial way—and a month ago Thursday, returning at night from town to his ranch, had been shot from ambush by an unknown rifleman. The killer had not been found, and Spur could not raise the five thousand dollars old Brock had demanded for the original lease, though Bob Thoroughgood had sweated to salvage every penny from the old man's abortive investments.

In spite of himself Channing was interested; it explained the two riders' rough treatment of Brock in the hotel lobby—an attempt to coerce the old man into leasing to Mexican Bit. But Brock's troubles were no sweat of his, though he'd taken an odd liking to the old hammer-head. His job was to get Costello, who could stay on Anchor till doomsday if he chose, protected by Anchor guns. Meanwhile, after defeating Streak, Channing knew he'd be a target for all those guns. He could not afford to lonewolf it in the basin any longer; he needed protection of his own, and Spur Ranch would be a refuge while he made his plans.

Voicing part of his thought aloud broke the silence following on Shiloh's explanation: "Those Anchor boys ...all looked hardcase."

Shiloh swallowed his whiskey and drew his sleeve across his silky steerhorns. "Yeah. Santee started importin' 'em a month ago, getting rid of his old crew for gunnies like Whitey DeVore, Elam Ford, Arnt Chance. All mean-bad. He's buildin' up to take the Strip, even if Brock decides to lease to us or Straker. Puts Brock on a mean spot, but the stubborn old bastard won't leave his mountain shack, though alone up there he's in plenty danger. Santee wants a legal signature on that lease, not carin' how he gets it."

"The law?"

"Hell, son, you know New Mexico Territory. Counties sprawling hundreds of square miles over hell-rough terrain. Sheriff's office is fifty miles away in Cholla, county seat, cut off from this basin by an arm of the Sangre peaks. Even the railroad don't connect us—ours is just a spur line run up through the river pass by the big cowmen here. No deputy here, we never asked for none. No town marshal. Us big ranches always settled our differences amiable, kept the smaller ones in line. Bunch of us—cattlemen, townsmen—sit in on kangaroo court when someone goes coyote, lock him up in a long hut down the street for a spell—or hang him. One lawman wouldn't mean much anyways was there real trouble."

"Seems you got it," Channing observed. "Who owns Spur now? Thoroughgood?"

"No...." Shiloh glanced over at the foreman whose great frame was slumped loosely against the bar, his face in the back-bar mirror scowl-set with dark thoughts. "Bob was a mite peeved when Lawyer Wainwright read the Old Man's will two weeks ago. Bob's been with Cus Thursday eighteen years, foreman a dozen. They worked fine in harness but they was never close...hell, old Cus wasn't close to nobody. Never married, kept to himself in the big house—though he let Bob and his wife live there after Bob married. She died couple years ago."

"The will?" Channing prompted.

"Funny thing," Shiloh mused. "The Old Man left everything to someone we never heard of, a K. Nilssen of St Paul, Minnesota. Lawyer wrote this fella, he's comin' out to take over. Fact we're in town to meet the train...." Shiloh dipped a turnip watch from inside his frayed ducking jacket. "Due shortly. Noon. What's'that name —Nilssen? German?"

"How you spell it?" Shiloh somehow drew a man out with a terse, friendly manner that melted reserve.

Shiloh grunted as he drew a folded envelope from his shirt pocket. "That's the name in the corner...got this letter from him a week ago sayin' he was coming...."

Channing scanned the awkward block printing. "Nilssen. Likely out of Sweden, maybe Norway. Lot of 'em settle that north country."

"That's quick namin'," Shiloh said approvingly. "Never knew none of them."

"Lived with a Scandinavian family up in Montana, few

years back." channing clamped his mouth shut, while knowing the senselessness of his hatred for discussing his past; he couldn't help it.

Abruptly the swing doors parted and a woman stepped inside. Channing glanced at her, as did every man in the room. Each—excepting Thoroughgood—gave her a respectful nod or word of greeting. She smiled and nodded back, her gaze lingering on Thoroughgood. "Hello, Bob."

He grunted without looking up. She shook her head slightly and crossed the room to the back table. Shiloh heaved quickly to his feet, saying awkwardly, "Howdy, Miz LeCroix. Sit down?"

"Hello, Mr. Dawes. No, thank you." Channing also stood as she laid a hatbox and some packages on the table and peeled off her gloves. She was a statuesque woman in a fashionable sky-blue suit that matched her eyes—about thirty, Channing judged. She looked at him as she unpinned a small porkpie hat from her high-coiled hair which caught the murky light in richly dark glints of red to gold. "Hello," she said pleasantly. "You're new."

"Ed Channing, new Spur hand," Shiloh offered sparely. "Anne LeCroix. She owns Judd's place. Judd's dead."

"For a man who talks so much, Mr. Dawes never wastes words." Her curiously direct gaze held Channing's face. "What happened?"

"Ought to see Streak Duryea," Shiloh chuckled.

"Is that so? I've heard these bar heroes talk about cutting Streak Duryea down a notch, never to his face."

Shiloh grinned crookedly. "Channing don't even like to talk."

"I see he doesn't," Anne LeCroix smiled. "What was the trouble, Mr. Channing?"

"Mine, ma'am. Then Streak's."

"I could exercise a feminine prerogative or two and

tease you into telling—why, he's blushing." She laughed then, and gathered up her packages. As she turned, her gaze stopped on Thoroughgood and the amusement was gone, replaced by a deep softening. She said very quietly, "Does he ever stop brooding?"

"Not much," Shiloh said soberly.

"He never was one to laugh much—all the same there was a time...."

Shiloh nodded, a long-ingrained sorrow relaxing his craggy face. "Needs someone to look after him."

A brisk humor stiffened the womanly gentleness which Channing guessed this woman rarely revealed. "And that's you, Mr. Dawes."

"Yes, ma'am," Shiloh said dryly. "Leastways I try."

She walked over to Thoroughgood and touched his arm as she spoke. Thoroughgood gave her a sidelong glance, shrugged his shoulders and grunted something. She turned away, gave Shiloh a self-deprecating little smile and shake of her head and then disappeared through a rear doorway.

"Hard man," Channing observed.

"No," Shiloh said sharply, then lowered his voice. "Just that—a man gets deep hurt enough, he can't feel anything afterward....I talk too damn' much." He creaked heavily around in his chair, raised his voice. "Bob, train's about due."

Thoroughgood nodded and swung out of the bar, Shiloh and Channing falling in behind. A hot, vagrant wind whipped fine dust against their legs as they tramped the long street to the railway depot. The hoot of a locomotive drifted along the tracks. They stood on the dusty platform as the train wheezed in, slowing with a lengthy crash of couplings.

Channing could feel the tense, quickening curiosity of

his companions. This new boss, a Midwesterner fresh to cattle country, could change the accustomed rut of their lives drastically....Channing felt detached by his personal thread of purpose and therefore almost indifferent.

The lank conductor stepped from the passenger car and helped a woman down. Rather a girl...in a drab black dress and straw hat, clutching a shabby carpetbag to her. She faced the grouped men with a prim and unworried, almost childlike serenity.

Thoroughgood stirred uneasily, his boots rasping on the cinder bed. "No one else this trip, Charley?"

"Sorry." The conductor's grin was not quite a smirk.

Thoroughgood looked blank. Shiloh Dawes hesitated, then stepped doubtfully forward, touching his hat. "K. Nilssen, ma'am?"

She nodded soberly and moved a brisk step closer to Thoroughgood, dwarfed by him. She wasn't over five feet in height but not slight—compactly sturdy in the shapeless austerity of her dress. She had a freshly scrubbed look even after hours on a train, though sweat beaded her upper lip and damply tendriled silken wisps of corn-yellow hair against her temples. Her voice was gently modulated, richly accented in a way familiar to Channing, calling back memories of Gunnar Nordquist's farmhouse in Montana...of an immigrant family poor in goods, rich in love and laughter.

"You are Mister Thoroughgood?"

The foreman nodded once, controlling his face with a kind of iron self-possession.

K. Nilssen smiled brightly, looking from one to the other. Suddenly she was no longer prim or drab. "I think we go now, eh, gentlemen?"

FIVE

Kristina Nilssen had not expected the overnight windfall that had made her owner of a New Mexico ranch, but youth coupled with a not-easy past life and a quick-witted curiosity had made her easily adaptable. "Kristina, you'll take the main chance when it comes, you don't give your-self excuses for being afraid. That's the good way," Papa used to say. "Eric, don't put such things in the girl's head," Mama would scold. "A man it is thinks such a way, not a woman. She will grow up, marry a good, solid young farmer. It's the best a decent girl can hope for."

She'd always favored Papa, Kristina knew, and she found no shame in the fact. Eric Nilssen had had his pri-vate dreams, the ones that made life more than just eating and sleeping and having children. He had worked two years to earn his passage to America, not expecting streets paved with gold, only a good fighting chance for himself and his family in a wide-open new land. He had gotten his chance—only to break himself on a gutted dream.

Sitting on the jolting wagon seat, Kristina knotted her fists in her lap, bit her lip in sudden uncertainty. No; she must not think of the past. They were not dead, not Papa or Mama or the dreams, not while she was alive. She had the life they had given her and the hopes and now the main chance and she would rather die trying than live afraid and doubting. What could a woman alone in a strange land do with these things? There was so much she did not know—and she would learn. Kristina braced her spine a little stiffer on the flat hard seat and breathed deeply the pinon-scented air.

Thoroughgood had rented a buckboard at the livery and tied the extra saddle horse to the tailgate with Channing's mount. Channing rode the high seat at her side. Shiloh Dawes and Thoroughgood rode ahead of the team, passing a few words but not many. Kristina's glance fixed curiously on the bull-shouldered back of the foreman, her brows knitted in puzzlement. A strange, gruff man . . . trying to hide the pain he plainly lived with. Yet she thought she liked him. And the old one-armed man too; there was kindness in him.

She couldn't make up her mind about the young one ...Channing. The seat was narrow and their shoulders pressed together. He looked slim and hard and capable, his muscles flexing in easy coordination as he guided the livery team expertly over the rough wagon road. This one would do everything well, she guessed; cold-blooded men usually did. She glanced covertly at his profile, seeing it finely regular but too sharp-planed and brooding. A man with little use for other men, with few human feelings. But was it so? She noted the gentle restraint of his hands on the reins, his occasional low word to the horses. *A man good to animals cannot be bad,* she thought. She sighed a little, half-closing her eyes. She was tired from the long train ride; her thoughts were becoming confused. The afternoon shadows lengthened across the rugged plateau they were traversing, making the shadows of men and horses grotesque moving specters....

"We're here, Miss."

"Oh!" Kristina had been half-dozing, and now she felt Channing's shoulder stir against her slumped weight. Flustered, she sat up, reaching under the seat for her carpetbag. But her hand stopped as her eyes took in the rambling slope. Pinon and juniper darkly stippled the brighter greens of aspen and oak, fading back to grassy meadows and higher wooded benches, hazing away to the serrated purple of snow-tipped peaks. She forced her wondering gaze back to the immediate slope, and downward to the wide clearing with its open-sided hayshed, corrals, blacksmith shop, and ten yards down the yard incline the combination bunkhouse and cookshack. She identified all of these at once and then her eyes moved to the house in majestic isolation upslope against a somber backdrop of evergreens. The main structure was an oblong block of mortared fieldstone with two matching wings of heavy timber, built solidly back against the slope behind. She could guess how here beneath the peaks it would be cool in summer, cozy in winter...a dwelling that fit the country like a glove over a hand.

"Oh," Kristina Nilssen said once more, now whispering it.

Thoroughgood rapid-fired an order at Channing to see to the wagon and horses, then he took her bag from unresisting fingers and led the way to the house, Shiloh Dawes following. She stepped almost gingerly across the veranda and stopped on the threshold as Thoroughgood held open the door. She couldn't hold back a little exclamation of delight.

The leather furniture was well-worn, but choice and substantial. The walls were hung with game trophies and bright Indian blankets and the oak rafters overhead were smoke-seasoned to a rich brown-black. She moved quickly around the room, paused by the fireplace to draw a finger across the dust on the mantle of the huge yellowstone fireplace and frown a little. Then her gaze touched with surprise the window curtains, fine cloth but grime-gray and unwashed in months—or years.

She glanced swiftly at Thoroughgood, seeing the bare patience in his stony face. Pride hardened her thoughts. She was the owner now; she would ask the first questions. "When was a woman here, mister? Long ago, eh?"

"How the devil did you—" He checked himself, added tersely, "My wife. Died two years ago."

"Oh." She nodded very slowly, understanding now. *Poor man.* She smiled at them. "The kitchen—"

"Doorway to your left," Thoroughgood said. "Look— miss—"

"You yust wait. I will make some coffee. Then we talk." He frowned and she said with an edge to it, "I am tired if you are not. *We will not talk until after I have made coffee.*"

Thoroughgood opened his mouth and clamped it shut. Shiloh Dawes glanced at the big man, then turned his face away, but failed to hide his grin from Kristina.

She opened the door and entered the dining room, delightedly taking in the fine oak highboy and the broad, round-topped table. Then her foot struck an empty liquor bottle and it rolled across a floor littered with pieces of harness and heel-ground cigar butts. She made a small dismayed sound, seeing the burns on the table edge where men had carelessly left lighted cigars. She bent to scrub at them with her sleeve, then stopped, gripping the table with her hands. Quite suddenly Kristina felt like crying. She had come a long way, she was very tired...and these stupid men! As quickly, she fought the feeling down. Thoroughgood had come to the open door; he gave a surly nod at the table.

"Old Cus and me ate here nights, went over the ranch books afterward. Guess the place is a little dirty." There wasn't a lot of apology in his tone. "I been livin' on here. Better move my stuff to the bunkhouse...."

"Yah, you better," she cut him off coldly and marched to the kitchen, her back very straight.

Ten minutes later she carried the coffeepot to a low table fronting the leather divan where Thoroughgood and Dawes were sitting. The one-armed man looked at poor ease, but Thoroughgood had stretched out his legs and leaned back grim-faced, plainly damned if he was going to let a dumb immigrant girl get under his skin. Kristina considered this grimly as she carefully set the steaming coffeepot on a folded newspaper. She was about to begin a sharp-tongued comment when the front door opened. Channing stood there, removing his hat.

"Horses are put up, pulled the wagon out of the way. Anything else?"

"Get your stuff to the bunkhouse, pick out an empty bunk," Thoroughgood said. "Crew's out fencing, be in shortly for supper. Acquaint yourself with the place till then." It was a dismissal, and Channing turned to leave.

"Wait," Kristina said sharply. "Have some coffee first, mister. Here…sit down."

All three men stared at her as though she had calmly announced the final Judgment. She shrewdly guessed at the invisible line between owner's quarters and bunkhouse and didn't turn a hair. Let them squirm…. Men! She casually filled four cups and handed one to Channing as he eased onto the edge of a straight-backed chair.

"That looks very uncomfortable," she said sweetly. "Now the divan by Mr. Thoroughgood—"

"No ma'am, no, thank you, this is fine."

In addition to spiting Thoroughgood she'd wanted to break Channing's moody reserve, and now she felt a trifle ashamed of her success. She sank against the sagging cushions of the divan. Sipped the coffee judiciously, nodded and said briskly: "None of you are drinking."

Shiloh gulped the scalding brew. "Oh, it's mighty fine."

"My mother taught me," she said proudly, "though I did no cooking for two years, as a chambermaid in a hotel."

There was an awkward silence, tentatively broken by Shiloh. "That would be St. Paul, ma'am? Take it you met Mr. Thursday there? He was in St. Paul arranging some investments, last year. Figured you might've met him then…."

"Yah, he stayed at the hotel," she said matter-of-factly. "He became sick, very sick. All I could I did for him; poor old man. So lonely and trying to cover it with tough words."

Thoroughgood gave a short, explosive "Ha!" She straightened and glared at him. "I am not surprised now, seeing the company he kept, eh? Do not tell me he was a poor rich old man, mister; I knew it, the same I would do for a dog, even you."

Shiloh coughed hastily. "Just a surprise, you inheriting all this, ma'am. Mr. Thursday never mentioning you and all. Course we knew he had no living relatives...."

"He had a heart, that you did not know. Or care," she said tartly. She set her cup down and said firmly, "Now you fill your boots, Mister Thoroughgood, and get out what you want to say."

She frowned at the severe dark material of her skirt and fingered her frayed cuffs, listening to the foreman. He rattled off facts and procedures of ranch life with dry tonelessness, speaking very swiftly to confuse her. She would not give him the satisfaction of telling him to speak slowly, but she gleaned an outline of the situation, methodically sorted it for the strong points, and said carefully: "This grass of which the old man is the lessor—it is very urgent we need it?"

"We're finished without it," Thoroughgood said flatly. "Your late benefactor made a lot of bad deals, ran Spur into a hole. We're finished anyway, can't raise even a thousand."

"Yah, and it is five thousand is needed," she said musingly, adding: "I have the money."

Thoroughgood spluttered into his cup and set it quickly down. "You got...five...thousand *dollars?*"

"Got ten thousand," she said serenely. "A month ago, I got a package from Sentinel, New Mexico, containing ten thousand dollars. There was no name of the sender, no note to explain. I yust put it away and say nothing, think maybe it must be a mistake and the owner would claim it."

"Ten thousand dollars," Thoroughgood muttered, "Old buzzard must have had it salted away...or got sudden-lucky on one of his fool investments...." She started a frowning objection to his choice of words, but he cut her off excitedly. "You got the money *with* you?"

For answer she reached for her carpetbag and went through her few shabby belongings to produce a neatly wrapped brown paper package, handing it to him. "It all is there."

There was a shining, boyish excitement in the fore-man's eyes that pleased her; he was actually smiling. "This is it...."

"Sure is," Shiloh said phlegmatically, " 'pending how Brock's temper turns."

Kristina put in, "This old mountain man must be strange, more than Mr. Thursday."

Shiloh grinned at her. "Guess it's that living alone."

She laughed, caught up in the half-suppressed excite-ment of the men, knowing she was a part of it now. She sobered with a troubling thought "Just how did Mr. Thursday die? You say only he was shot...?"

Thoroughgood said casually, but almost too quickly, she thought, "Oh, a drifter he kicked off the ranch got drunk and laid for old Cus. Grudge killing. We hanged the man."

Kristina was about to question further when Channing cleared his throat, saying quietly, "Guess nobody in par-ticular's in Brock's good graces. Maybe I can help."

Thoroughgood eyed him narrowly. "How?"

"Gave him a hand this morning when a pair tried to rough him—Max and Karl by name—"

"The Mannlich boys, Mexican Bit," Shiloh nodded. "Tough lads, but not mean-bad,...You thinkin' you might trade on that?"

Channing shrugged. "He liked me some. Maybe, though, he'll think we rigged the other to set this up."

"No matter, worth a try," Thoroughgood clipped out "All right, Channing. You'll ride up to see Brock first thing tomorrow. Shiloh, you make out with the old recluse all right, don't you?"

"Says howdy when we meet, more'n most get from him," Shiloh said dryly.

"Get your sleep. You'll be showing Channing the trail up there."

SIX

Thoroughgood's intensity of mood hadn't abated by the following morning, but his good humor had. He roused Channing and Shiloh out while the crew snored on in their blankets. In the dim light his hawklike features looked fine-drawn and nervous. He paced impatiently back and forth as they dressed.

"Hellfire, Bob." Shiloh's voice was still thick with sleep. "Ease down...."

"*You* step it up," was the irritable rejoinder. "I couldn't much give a damn while it looked hopeless. Now there's a hope, got to strike with hot iron."

Shiloh paused in the act of awkwardly yanking on his left boot. "How far you thinking they'll go?"

"Getting soft in the head? Straker's men tried to grab

the old man off in town in broad daylight. Santee's more cautious but when he moves, man as lief poke a five-foot rattler." He stopped pacing and swung to face them. "Cookie's packed a lunch, it's in your saddlebags. Your horses are outside."

Shiloh stomped his boot firmly on, heaved to his feet and picked up his rifle from the foot of his bunk, sighing, "Well, hearty headaches," as he clumped out of the bunk-house, Channing behind.

As they swung into leather, Thoroughgood stepped to Channing's stirrup and handed up a thin leather billfold. "There's a thousand...dickering money. Dicker damn well."

Channing tucked the billfold inside his shirt. "Sure you trust me?"

"No," the foreman said bluntly. "I trust Shiloh. Get a move on...."

They swung from the ranch yard and, once past the last shed, pointed north toward the blue-toothed arch of the Sangre de Cristos. Glancing back, Channing saw a small figure muffled in an oversized maroon robe on the front veranda of the big house. *Well, she knows, knows what's riding with this and has the sense to be worried.*

But she could not really know—this girl fallen heiress to a great ranch because she had given a loveless and brittle old bachelor his one taste of a woman's unselfish kindness. Thoroughgood had dissembled to her query of how Custis Thursday had met his death, in an attempt to keep her ignorant of the deadly nature of the triangular rivalry; he evidently feared that a woman, once knowing the facts, would not stand the gaff of range war. But she could not be deceived forever. The foreman was trying to preserve Spur Ranch intact for her; though Channing felt strong distaste for the deception, he reminded himself that it was no business of his. Yet he had seen cattle war in the Tonto Basin and in Lincoln County; all the ingredients for pitched warfare were here, and the edged tensions razoring a thin leash. Once one side had cinched an advantage—Brock's lease—violence would break openly...the night-riding, the shots from ambush, the cut fences, burnings and stampedes, and Channing felt the marrow-deep sickness won of experience....

The sun topped the east horizon and slanted warm against their right sides. They mounted deeper into the high country. The land became more rugged, the timber of hardier variety. Belts of fir and cedar were interspersed with grassy benches and meadows. This was old Indian and Spanish country, still unviolated by ax or plow, and the morning was beautiful. Squirrels chattered in the dappled foliage and long-tailed mountain jays flashed through shadow and sunlight. On the open stretches grazed isolated bunches of cattle which spooked from their coming. Old Indian and game trails crisscrossed high into the foothills; these they followed, Shiloh picking the way unhesitatingly.

"Two more hours to Brock's cabin," Shiloh threw back over his shoulder as he humped his whey-belly mare over a deadfall.

"He high up?"

"Pretty deep in the foothills, but short of the first peaks. What you think of Miss Nilssen?" Without waiting for a reply, he chuckled, "Damned if she didn't have old Bob buffaloed. She'll make out. If all Swedes is like her, I'd hate to run afoul of the menfolk."

"Most of 'em," Channing said judiciously, "are like friendly mules...."

"Son, no such thing as a friendly mule." Shiloh guffawed. "She brought luck, that's sure." He added softly and soberly, "Bob was like a kid, last night Haven't seen him this way in years."

"Been with him long time?"

"Sojered under him in the war. Saved my life at Shiloh…where I lost this wing." With pride he told how Lieutenant Thoroughgood had left the breastworks to dash through a hail of fire and carry his fallen sergeant to safety. Grapeshot had riddled Dawes' arm. Shiloh was certain that the lieutenant had saved his life not once, but twice: the overworked Confederate medicos were killing more soldiers from hasty amputation than the enemy had killed outright. So Thoroughgood had commandeered a captured Union surgeon and stood by with a cocked pistol while he'd performed a careful removal of Dawes' arm and fashioned a permanent stump. After the war Shiloh had thrown in his lot with Thoroughgood and had rarely left his side since. "That was young Thoroughgood," Shiloh said meditatively. "Was his wife's death dropped the bottom out of his life. The hurt was two years healin'…then he needed something he could set his teeth in, a purpose. He's got it. Him and me and Miss Nilssen was up till all hours last night. Bob was full of plans…wants to bring a herd of shorthorns from El Paso, throw 'em on the Strip—"

"Shorthorns? Man, they're a short-legged heavy breed. Throw them up in this rough country, they'll break their legs, get hung up in brush…and sure not weather the winters. Graze is too thin—"

"The Strip ain't so high, got rocky bluffs skirting it mostly. Natural fence lines and windbreaks against blizzards. And the grass!…A cattleman's dream, Channing. And it ain't yet been worked to potential. Aside from them fool investments of his, Custis Thursday was too set in his ways. Bob's got his dreams, willing to gamble." Shiloh jogged a way in thoughtful silence, said, "So's Santee Dyker. An honest-to-God gambler from the Mississippi riverboats. And that could...."

It could leave the Strip soaked in blood, Channing thought, and the two men held silence afterward, each with his thoughts....

Short of high noon they topped a rise. Beyond dipped a brushy vale and high on a rocky shoulder of its opposite slope was a cabin of green peeled logs. They paused to blow their horses. No sign of life...the chimney was smokeless; the sun-drenched stillness seemed to brood.

"Brock's?" Channing laconically broke the talkless two hours.

Shiloh's eyes were narrowed. "Could be out hunting, checking a trapline stream," he muttered, but Channing knew he felt it too as the *segundo* grunted brusquely, "Let's get up there."

They dismounted in the bare, trampled clay of the yard and Channing gave the scarred earth one scanning glance. He said quietly: "Brock got more'n one horse?"

"No horses. One old yellow mule." Shiloh cut his speech off sharply, glancing at Channing. "What—"

Channing was already moving through the doorway where the split-log door hung ajar on deerhide hinges, ducking beneath the low jamb. He stopped in his tracks. The room was meagerly furnished with a wooden bunk, a half-log table, a bench and a stone fireplace. Gear, traps, hides, and a Winchester long rifle hung on the walls, all

with an air of tidy economy in ill-keeping with the bed-
clothes wadded in a heap on the packed-clay floor by the
stripped bunk.

"Grabbed him outen his sleep," Shiloh breathed.
"Otherwise they'd never 'a got inside a half mile of the
place without the old mountain man cutting them out."

Channing went outside to decipher the trampled
ground. His mustanger's eyes found the tracks of four
horses and three men who had entered the shack. Inside
of a minute he knew every vital statistic except the
horses' color and the identities of two of the men. He'd
followed Bee Withers for two weeks, and knew that
gimpy, toed-in stride at once.

Shiloh returned from an inspection of the brush corral
at the back, reporting, "Brock's mule's still in."

"They set him on an extra horse," Channing said slowly.
"Bee Withers and two others...."

Shiloh stared at him. "Anything else?—and who the
hell is Bee Withers?"

"One of the others might be Streak Duryea, from what
I saw of his walk—but Withers makes it Anchor sure."
Without more comment, Channing walked to his horse
and mounted, and Shiloh stood for a flat-footed moment,
then cursed and walked grim-faced to his mount. He
yanked his rifle from the boot and checked the action.

"Don't pack a hand gun?" Channing regretted his unthinking words even before Shiloh swung around, bristling. "Handle this kicker better'n any man I've met,
understand?"

Channing nodded mutely, putting his horse into motion.
He realized that handling a rifle one-handed was something personal and prideful to Shiloh Dawes, yet was sur-

prised that the mild-spoken *segundo* had taken his thought-less words as a near-insult.

The kidnappers had struck due west over country that grew progressively more rocky and rugged, laced with long shale slopes and crumbling slides. Channing worked from horseback at a slow pace, frequently dismounting to check an uncertain sign. Often he lost it altogether and had to work the backtrail in concentric circles. It was slow and dogged work; sweat darkened his shirt as much with centered effort as with the rising heat of midday. He held patience; Shiloh did not, fuming with each fresh delay and bridling with the over-all pace.

Well past noon, Channing rose from the ground-check and announced, "They swung at right angles here, cutting south, and the sign's plain. So far it's been the throw-off. Now they're heading for home territory. Doesn't add they'd risk taking the old man straight to Anchor."

"Well?" Shiloh grated.

"You know the lay of the land."

Shiloh cuffed his greasy horsethief hat to the back of his head and squinted at the sun. "We're north of Anchor now. Straight south there's an old line shack, off the beaten way and not much used. Reckon they could hold him there."

"That's probably it."

"Then let's crack it. They got a lead of hours on us. Damn, anything could've happened by now!"

Late afternoon had mellowed to lengthy shadows when they topped a brush-covered ridge which fell away sharply to a small, timbered valley. Wordlessly Dawes pointed toward the trees hugging the base of the ridge. Channing made out the gray roof of the line shack, but little else for the dense trees crowding the building and its corral and outsheds. Wind whipped grimy tatters of smoke from the chimney.

"A hot supper," Shiloh observed dryly. "Maybe Brock's last."

"Unless we work this right." Channing opened and closed his fingers, sweaty against his palms. He knelt and scooped up a handful of gravel, mechanically rubbing it between his hands as he studied the sheer ridge walls that almost ringed the valley. At the far side from where they stood, the cliffs were broken down in a long slide which he guessed formed the only trail down to the valley floor. Trees and underbrush grew sparse between the cabin and that end of the valley. "Doorway on the other side of the cabin?"

"Yeah, and a window."

"Come in by the trail, well be spotted. No percentage in cutting down on 'em from these heights. Be a stand-off, and we might hit Brock."

"So?"

Channing's gaze narrowed down on the almost straight-away fall sheering off from the liprock at his feet "I got to get up by the cabin without being seen. Only chance...."As he spoke, he was turning, lifting the coiled lariat from his saddle. He looped the noose over the horn and threw the coils over the cliff. The fifty-foot rope snaked down the facerock, its tip falling about nine feet short of the base. He took a secure grip on the rope, saying, "Steady him. He'll stand for you."

Shiloh moved to the horse's head and watched worriedly as Channing braced his feet on the rim and swung his full weight outward. The claybank fiddlefooted against the taut rope, but quieted to Shilob's hand and voice. Channing went down the rope hand over hand in a vertical backward walk, knowing his descent would be cut off from the rear shack window by the heavy foliage below. He reached the end of the rope, flexed his knees and dropped to a springy needle carpet. He palmed his gun and moved at a crouch through the trees till the log walls of the shack grew into view. He moved nearer the building and then ran noiselessly the remaining dozen feet. He sank low against the wall beneath the single small dingy square of window, his heart pounding. A smacking sound drifted sharp through the cracked pane.

"Brock," Streak Duryea's nasal voice came drawlingly, "this goes against my grain. Don't make it rougher."

"Hoss," Brock's cracked voice was tonelessly steady, "there's a time us old-timers quartered sonsofbitches like you for lobo-bait."

Then Whitey DeVore's snigger: "Old turnip's still got the bark on. Hell, Streak, he's tougher'n whang leather ...got to soften it."

"Not your way," Streak said in a brittle voice.

"Shooting a man in the back's all right, though?" Whitey sneered. "Man, she's hot. Shoved her in an hour ago. Now look...." There was a grating of iron. Channing yanked off his hat, risked lifting his head to eye-level at the window sill. Brock was tied to a chair, his rock-set face swollen with bruises, nose and mouth bleeding. Streak, hipshot and with thumbs booked in his belt, narrowly watched Whitey fasten a gloved hand around a poker handle protruding from the broken isinglass window of a black potbellied stove. He drew the poker out, the end glowing cherry red. Bee Withers leaned with folded arms against the wall by the door, watching this with a painful, vapid grin through his broken jaw. Whitey straightened, swung around with the poker.

"Be careful where you wave that damned thing!" Streak said sharply.

Still sniggering, DeVore walked to the dirty dishes on the table and laid the poker gently across a chunk of raw beefsteak. The sharp sizzle brought Brock's head up.

Whitey's face twitched frenziedly. "Oh, that got him, that got him. Come on, Streak, they ain't no sweatin' him. Lemme—"

Channing came erect, swinging his fisted gun at the window pane. It shattered; a shard nicked his hand as he thrust it through. In the rage that rocked his mind he gave no order, hoping they'd break. Streak's hand slashed to pistol butt as he pivoted toward the window. Channing shot him in the right shoulder, the slug's impact twisting him with a crash against the wall.

Channing swung back to cover the others: Whitey had already flung the poker at the window; Channing ducked as it cleared his head by inches, sailing on into the brush. He lunged up in time to see Whitey break for the open door, veer sharply outside and out of sight.

Channing wheeled, ran along the wall to skirt the corner as DeVore reached the opposite corner, and they faced each other across the cabin's length. Whitey's gun was out and Channing fired on the instant. Whitey was slammed back, his legs pedaling. His hat rolled off, lips skinned back from his teeth as he fought for footing. Channing held fire, waiting for him to go down. He saw the tightening of Whitey's finger on the trigger. His shot merged with DeVore's. Whitey went down, his legs kicking sporadically. Then he was still.

The shattering echo of a rifle and Bee Withers' stuck-pig squeal brought Channing around. White powder smoke bloomed high on the ridge wall to his right. Turning, he saw Bee Withers leaning far out the window Channing had quitted, his hands clapped to his face. His gun lay on the ground. He had been about to shoot Channing from the side, and now the mustanger looked back at the rocky crest and saw Shiloh Dawes, a stumpy figure against the skyline, lift his rifle and wave it once.

Channing motioned him to come down, and went around to the doorway. Streak was on his hands and knees, gasping his pain as he tried to scoop his gun into his good hand. Channing stepped into the room and sheathed his weapon as he kicked Streak's beyond his reach.

Streak slumped like a tired child against the wall, breathing hoarsely as he stared up with bright-shot and hating eyes. "Damn Indian," he whispered.

Withers was still hunched over the window sill, groaning; Channing grabbed him by the shoulder and turned him, pulling his hands down. Withers' sallow face was bleeding in half a dozen places from thrown splinters chewed from the outer wall by Shiloh's close-laid slug. Otherwise he wasn't hurt, but was too slow-witted to realize it. Channing shoved him over by Streak, pulled his pocket knife and unfolded the blade. He cut Brock's ropes.

The old man stood a little shakily, but briskly rubbing his skinny wrists as he swung his glare about. "Where's that goddamn poker?"

"Take it easy."

"This child lived with the Blackfeet up north in the early days. Learned a trick or so as'd turn that cub's hair white if it wasn't. Where is the bastard?"

His eyes fixed on Channing's face and something be saw softened his piercing glare. "Wagh. Dead, eh?"

"Him or me."

"Don't look to me like the world's nohow ended, fact it's a sight cleaner without that one. Couldn't tell that from your face, though."

Channing's fingers flexed lightly over the Colt butt; he let his hand drop. *You draw lightning once,* he thought, *and you can't turn back.* He had been fool enough to think he could escape it once, mustanging in the lonely hills, only to find himself embroiled again. Once a man drew trouble in this raw country, it marked him. Like the brand of Cain his father had always been fond of throwing up to him.

In his mind's eye he saw that rawboned, black-suited figure—his father—moving for him with self-righteous anger. He remembered clearly that day long ago when his uncle, returning from a hunting trip, had stopped at their house on one of his rare visits. Leaving his gun leaning against the porch outside because the old man wouldn't permit firearms under his root. And he, young Eddie Channing, bare brown toes squishing through the hot dust as he sidled up, fascinated by the shiny weapon. Then the forbidden fruit was suddenly hot and hard in his palms and he was drawing a mock bead on a knot-hole in the porch planking. Somehow the flat explosion of the rifle and a slamming recoil sprawling him in the dust …his father's hand grabbing the scruff of his neck like iron and dragging him to his feet. *I have warned you about these tools of Satan, boy. Now I shall impress the lesson. They that take the sword shall perish by the sword.*

Scripture had always rolled glibly off the old man's tongue; it had been at once his fortress, his book of common law, and his excuse. Fortified behind the zealot's asceticism, he'd had no tolerance for the ordinary weaknesses of flesh. His son was the only scapegoat within his reach, the target for the punishment he couldn't wreak on the great sin-ridden Gomorrah which was the world as he saw it. Dimly the boy had understood this even then; it had not etched the savage birching less deeply in his memory....

"Hoss," old Brock said quietly, the very calmness of the word shocking Channing back to the present. His body felt clammy, trembling with the knowledge that he'd taken another life. His father's words lay on his mind like a cold indictment: *They that take the sword....*

The reaction was brief; he walled it off in his mind, again cold and resolved to the business at hand as Shiloh Dawes came huffing through the door. "All right, Brock? Good....I worked around on the ridge till I could ketch a sight of the shack where the trees grew low." He grinned unpleasantly at Bee Withers. "Had to take a jiffy bead. Too damned....Well, Brock, how d'your notions set?"

The ancient mountaineer stroked his beard thoughtfully. "Looks like you ran out of competitors. This child's tired o' threats from the other two. Cold cash sets easier on a man's sweetbreads than hot iron. That's," he added fiercely, "if ye got the cash."

SEVEN

Brock and Shiloh alternately cursed him for a damned fool; Channing ignored their acid objections as he treated Streak Duryea's shoulder with bluestone and sweet oil he'd found in a cupboard. Streak was silent through the ministrations, face drawn with tight-held pain and a chilling hatred. Once he snarled, "Do unto others, eh, bucko? Oh, I'll remember. *Bueno,* I'll return the favor—with interest."

Channing tore a strip from a cot blanket and bound up the wound. "That'll hold you till Anchor." He ordered Withers to help Streak outside, then went ahead to tie Whitey's body across his saddle. Flanked by the two old men, he watched them head out.

Shiloh began a surly complaint: "We'd of been within our rights—"

"Sure," Channing said harshly. "And Brock wanted to burn 'em a little. Even Streak didn't want that for him before. I just know to me right is right and wrong is wrong. I wonder what the hell's the matter with me."

Shiloh growled under his breath, but Brock's wise and faded eyes met Channing's without wavering. "No one's sayin' it ain't, hoss," he observed mildly. "Only you toss bones to a pack that's tryin' to pull you down. Streak, there, now—no mean *hombre* till things don't go his way. Primed to do wuss'n burn *you* now. Anchor's whole pack of curly wolves'll be lookin' to nail your hide after this. Walk soft, they'll dance on your grave. Keep your primin' dry, hoss."

It was well after dark when the trio reached Spur. They corraled their horses and headed up to the house. Thoroughgood and Kristina Nilssen were waiting for them on the porch, limned in the light that flowed from the open doorway. The old mountain man was half-reeling with exhaustion and the punishment he'd absorbed, but he angrily brushed aside proffered hands as he stamped across the porch. "....Damned molly-coddlin' fools!"

Kristina followed him inside, her eyes flashing and lips set. "You will please take care of your words under my roof."

Brock turned to face her, his cantankerous expression altering sheepishly. "Wagh. Young gel, eh? Fact is didn't see you, Missy. Figured new lady owner these hosses mentioned was some dried-up ole maid friend of Cus'."

A slow smile dimpled the corners of Kristina's mouth. She was wearing a worn and wash-faded calico dress which faithfully outlined two pointed little breasts and a slim waist before it flared into a full skirt. Her blonde hair was drawn to a smooth bun at the back of her neck and she looked trim and altogether Channing. "That is accepted, Mr. Brock. But we had not expected the pleasure of your company…?"

"He decided to come in, deal with you direct." This from Shiloh, who had already warned Brock to say nothing of what had happened.

Thoroughgood cleared his throat. "Better get this lease business settled now."

A little frown pinched Kristina's smooth forehead. She said dryly, "Mr. Thoroughgood is minded of nothing but business, eh? First we eat," and firmly closed the discussion by leading the way into the dining room. Thoroughgood released a resigned sigh, but Channing caught a faint smile on his thin lips. Kristina had won these blunt men with a bluntness of her own more Channing than any feminine wile.

After supper Kristina cleared away the dishes while the men self-consciously fired up some fine cigars of Custis Thursday's which Kristina had found on a top pantry shelf and which she insisted the men smoke up. She sat by and shrewdly offered no comment in men's talk as Brock opened the deal by naming a price well above the expected five thousand. Thoroughgood made his bid well below and worked up to a compromise at five thousand. At seven cents an acre, Spur would again take possession of the Strip for ten years, making all due efforts to keep it clear of rattleweed, larkspur and the like. In the morning they would see Lawyer Wainwright in Sentinel and have the necessary paper drawn up.

Brock was half-nodding before they concluded. Kristina installed him in Thoroughgood's former room for the night. The foreman, Shiloh and Channing took their way toward the bunkhouse. Halfway there, Thoroughgood halted Shiloh with a hand on his arm.

"Let's have the real story. You fooled the girl by saying Brock's face got that way when his horse threw him. Only Brock don't own a horse. Enough moonlight so I could tell he rode in on a strange animal...what happened?"

Shiloh told him gravely, finally adding, "Bob, you sure you're wise holding back the ugly parts? To her this is all just sharp business deaiin'. The truth'll be a shock."

Thoroughgood rubbed his chin. "Maybe you're right. Best she hears it from us. She's got rawhide in her, that girl, reckon she could take it." There was a touch of pride in his voice. He was silent a moment, then brusquely: "Once we got Brock's mark on that lease will be soon enough. Committed so far, she'll be less likely to back down."

"Could be," Shiloh said quietly. "But can't say my mind rests easy for this deceivin', for her own good or no. I'm just sayin' don't wait too long on tellin' her."

Next morning Brock was fiddle-fit, in his own words; he mounted to the buckboard seat by Kristina with commendable agility, taking up the reins and clucking the horses into motion. Thoroughgood and Shiloh Dawes and Channing paced the rig on horseback. Thoroughgood had offered no explanation as to why he wanted Channing to accompany the party to town and Channing hadn't questioned the order. All that remained was the signing and witnessing of the lease; Thoroughgood must believe that Santee Dyker would somehow try to block it.

When they reined up by the two-story business building

where Lawyer Wainwright had his office, Santee Dyker was waiting, lounging indolently in a chair against the clapboarded front. A copperbottom bay with an Anchor brand was tied at the rail; Santee appeared to be alone. Channing flicked his gaze up and down the street: there could be men behind those very windows across the way waiting to cut down on the party. No...Dyker, no fool, would not try wholesale murder in the streets of Sentinel nor would he place himself in the open.

Dyker arose and came to the curb as Thoroughgood assisted Kristina to the ground. With a slight inclination of his head, he doffed his freshly blocked pearl-gray Stetson. He wore a perfectly tailored suit of black broadcloth which didn't show a wrinkle. Even in this conservative garb, in spite of wilting heat and dust, he retained his easy, dapper elegance. His bench-made Justins were polished to a high gloss.

The deep grooves at the corners of his lips twitched in the faintest of smiles. "My new adversary? Well, Bob, something of a change for you, taking orders from a young lady."

Thoroughgood's mouth tightened with the unveiled gibe but he held temper, plainly determined not to betray the depth of the rancor existing here. "Miss Kristina Nilssen," he said shortly. "Santee Dyker...."

Dyker bowed over her hand. "My pleasure, Miss Nilssen. And yours—for you've won."

Kristina smiled, a little stiffly. "I do not want to crow, Mister Dyker. I'm sorry."

Dyker laughed softly. "Crow is what I'm eating, my dear; beak, claws, and feathers. With a side dish of humble pie...not for long, perhaps." His bland gaze found Channing. "Ah, the horsehcrd. Who would have suspected you'd retaliate with such a vengeance? You have Streak nursing a double grudge—as well as his shoulder. He's over at Dr. McGilway's now. And poor Whitey...." Dyker clucked his tongue.

"What is it? Did something happen yesterday?" Her voice was imperative.

Dyker chuckled. " 'O what tangled webs we weave.' And so on, eh Bob?"

"Shut up, Santee!" Thoroughgood rasped. To Kristina he said urgently, "Sis, you don't understand—"

"But I was about to," she said icily. "You will please go on, Mister Dyker."

He told it all, half-smiling and without a shade of emotion, mentioning the brutality of his men to old Brock as dispassionately as Channing's killing of Whitey and wounding of Streak.

"Oh, terrible, terrible," she breathed. "I did not know...." She swung fiercely on Thoroughgood, her small fist striking him on the chest. "What kind of human wolf are you—all of you? Are you animals to tear each other to gorge yourselves on this land?"

"Figured you for more gumption, sis," Thoroughgood muttered.

"Gumption! Brawling and killing, this is to make men of you?" There was an almost hysterical vehemence in her words that made Channing think, *It goes deeper than just this, with her. She's not the type to upset this bad. What could it be?* She abruptly calmed, saying with a despairing, quiet disgust, "I don't want the land. Not at this price. I will sign the ranch over to you wolves...tear it apart, and your Strip too. I don't want any of it!"

Old Brock spoke then, his cracked old voice laying its calm sanity on the tableau. "Don't stampede yet, Missy. Best tally the facts, see which way your stick floats. This

child's an impartial observer, seems to it swings agin
Santee. Shiloh here and Channin' staked their lives...."

She swung to face Channing, fists clenching at her
sides as her eyes blazed at him. "Yes, you—*you killer!*
Go away—stay out of my sight."

Channing's face paled under its deep weathering; swift
and bewildered anger roiled in him and then he turned
and strode away, walking fast. Shiloh clumped up beside
him. "God's sake, boy. She didn't mean it, she wasn't
thinkin'. Don't go off redheaded...."

"She meant it," Channing said low-voiced. "Don't get in
my way, Shiloh."

He walked on and hardly knew when he turned in at
Judd's saloon. He went to the bar and silently raised two
fingers to the bald bartender. One look at his face relaxed Doc Willis' habitual scowl as he moved quickly to
set out a glass and slosh it full. Then he went to the far
end of the bar and seemed absorbed in a newspaper.

Channing stared into his glass without touching it.
Well, what now? Already his rage was evaporating;
though he hated the self-admission, there remained little
but the belated smarting of hurt feelings. Quite suddenly
he felt like a damned fool. He'd prided himself on his
ability to contain his emotions with a limit marked by
independent pride, yet had flared up like a damp-eared
schoolboy at this girl's condemnation. Thoroughgood and
Shiloh would reason with Kristina Nilssen, bring her to
her senses. Maybe....He picked up the drink and
downed it. A stubborn reserve warmed in him with the
liquor. The rest of his personal reaction might be foolish,
but a man's wounded pride was no joke. She wasn't the
begging kind, but neither was he....let her make
the move.

The batwing doors parted and Santee Dyker sauntered

to the bar a few feet away. "Whiskey, and none of your backbar swill....Well, friend, so that's the blow-up? How would you like to—"

"How would you like a dead nephew?" Channing cut in coldly.

Dyker's narrow shoulders shook with silent laughter. "Well, that's my answer. Certainly there's no deceit in you. You could have accepted my offer, then bided your time."

"Some of us are too dumb for you, Santee."

"Don't mistake me," Dyker said pleasantly, watching Doc fill his glass from a bottle under the bar. "I don't confuse honesty with stupidity." He sipped delicately, pale eyes remote and speculative. "Honesty is...shall we say, an untenable luxury for a man of my disposition."

"Along with self-respect, eh?"

Dyker smiled. "One man's tonic is another's poison, my friend. I'm a gambler, not merely with cards—with life. I needed new horizons, new challenges, when I left the Mississippi with a substantial fortune lining my pockets. The great cattle empires, modern baronies erected by men who risked all on a single gutty decision—what better does our fair land have to offer a gambler? I found this area remote and lawless enough, yet prosperous enough, for me to play the house according to my own rules. The Strip is the biggest stake of my lifetime, a key to wealth and power in cattle country. All I was afraid of was a dull game. Thoroughgood has courage and imagination, but his unfortunate scruples might have made him easy prey, if not for you." Santee Dyker raised his glass. "To you, my friend...for making the game interesting."

The brief fanatical intensity of him reminded Channing

incongruously of his father. He felt no fear, but a cold unease that brought realization: in a way the man was crazy—with a dispassionate and unscrupled insanity that made him worse than any poor maniac who could not help himself. The elegant manners were a convenient façade. A woman, friendship, a full stomach, standards of right and wrong which a man could break and regret —the passions of ordinary men did not exist for Santee Dyker. Even the winner's stakes might well turn to ashes in his mouth, for only the challenge was his food and drink, and his bride, and his one friend, and when it was done, what could he have?

Both men faced around to the rear as the door of the back room opened. Anne LeCroix came out, nodded pleasantly to Channing. "Thought I heard your voice." To Santee she said coldly, "You're in Indian territory, aren't you? The Stockman's Bar handles the carriage trade."

Dyker set his glass down, smiling. "Partisanship, Annie? I'd give that a thought. I have a majority interest in the Sentinel Freighting Company now, you know. I can cut off your liquid supplies."

"You have the integrity of a rattlesnake, Santee," she said calmly.

"Good, I like spirited opposition. Channing here provided a bit, but he's bowing out. Too bad." Dyker tipped his hat and walked out

Anne LeCroix came to the bar and crossed her arms on it. She shuddered faintly. "That cold-blooded little...." She looked at Channing narrowly. "You quit Spur? Why? And what did he mean?"

Channing shook his head. "No matter now."

"I've some good liquor in the office," she said abruptly. "Come along." She turned and walked back to the rear door, turned there and cocked her head with a quizzical smile. "Come now, I won't bite."

The yellow dog curled in the sawdust snarled as he passed it following Anne into the office. It was a narrow room furnished with a massive walnut desk and hand-carved armchairs. She walked to a highboy and stood on tiptoe to reach down a bottle and glasses. "Peach brandy. Judd—my husband—favored it."

Channing sat on the edge of a chair, balancing his hat on his knee with a sense of mounting embarrassment. He sensed that this cool and self-possessed woman did not extend an invitation lightly, and it made him wary. He accepted the glass she handed him, nodded his thanks. She leaned back in the other chair, crossing her legs and lightly swinging her free foot back and forth. In a land where women quickly faded, she looked younger than her age, full-bodied yet girlishly demure in a prim white shirtwaist and full blue skirt. From the window at her back sunlight built her shining hair to a red-gold corona. Only the faint, brittle lines around her eyes and mouth betrayed hard experience.

"A friendly bribe," she smiled, "for your confidence. …After how you took Streak apart the other day, I expect Santee had good reason for his words. But there's more, isn't there?"

Channing relaxed a little. He gave her the sparest outline of yesterday's incidents. "Good," she said softly. "All Spur needed was a man who could meet that bunch on their own ground….But you've quit, why?"

"The girl doesn't like killers."

"Doesn't the little fool know the difference?"

There's a difference?"

"You know there is—as in fighting fire with fire. But you're not really leaving?"

"What do you care?"

"I'd like to see you stay." Her eyes were wide and level—blue candor, like Kristina's. But this was no unworldly immigrant girl; Anne LeCroix's candor would mask a personal motive, and he wondered what it was. He watched her narrowly, unspeaking.

"Channing, you're no child. Neither am I. We've both seen life—perhaps more of it than we care to." Her voice held a warm and inviting hint, but he detected a brittle, calculating note. And then, remembering small things he had seen but taken little note of, he understood.

He said softly: "Thoroughgood?"

She drew a quick little breath, rose abruptly and went to the window; stared out at the dingy alley. Her tone was low and brittle. "Of course. It's that obvious? Well... that's right How much of a fool can a woman be? Judd LeCroix took me out of an Albuquerque dive and married me. A love match on his part—it had to be, for he knew my past. He was a good man. I tried to make him a good wife. But he had to come to Sentinel and build this saloon. From the moment I saw Bob Thoroughgood—" She flung out her hand in a little futile gesture. "And I'd thought I'd had all romantic notions knocked out of me. That was four years ago; his wife was still alive, and so was Judd. Yet me, blushing like—a damned schoolgirl...and I haven't changed. That's what I mean. How much of a fool can a woman be!"

"Four years ago," he echoed. "No problem there."

"No?" The word was larded with bitter vehemence. "Why, he's in love with a memory first—then with his

precious damned Spur. To him I'm a fixture around here
—like Doc, or the bar." A faint flush mounted to her
face. "I didn't mean to tell you any of this. All I started
out to do was...persuade you to stay. Bob will fight
Santee to the end, I know...and he might have a
fighting chance to stay alive, with you."

He turned his hat in his hands, looking at it bleakly.
"You can bottle things in too long."

"Are you talking to me—or yourself?"

"Just talking." He clamped his hat on, turned toward
the door. She followed him and laid a hand on his arm.
Her smile was genuine. "I was right. I liked you when I
first saw you."

"Thanks."

"You don't talk much. You seem to think the more."

"A woman has a right to her feelings, same as men."

"But not many men think that way. And...you'll stay
on with Spur?"

"That depends on Miss Nilssen." He added, almost
reprovingly, "She's no fool."

"I see." Anne was smiling as she studied his face.
"Weil, I'm sorry; I have little cause to like women. The
men respect me, they know I run a clean place. But
their womenfolk are certain that any woman who runs a
saloon is one of easy virtue."

"People talk and hens cackle. Morning, ma'am."

"Goodbye, Channing...and thank you."

He stepped outside and headed down the street for the
business building. He hadn't covered half the distance
when he saw Kristina Nilssen coming, holding her skirt a
few inches above her quick pert steps. She came straight
up to him, looking pale but determined.

"I am sorry, mister. I made a mistake."

Channing looked over her head to where Thoroughgood and Shiloh leaned against the tie rail, watching
them. Brock placidly waited on one of the saddle horses.
Some perversity Channing couldn't help made him say
thinly, "They must have made some fancy medicine."

Her head tilted defiantly back. "Listen, they talk me
into nothing. I make up my own mind. I was mad, I think
better. Now I want you back."

He simply nodded. She turned and marched back to the
buggy. Thoroughgood swung her to the high seat, stepped
up beside her with a frosty. glance for Channing. "Deal's
concluded, lease is signed and paid for." He added gruffly,
"Glad you're stayin' on."

Brock leaned from horseback, extending Channing a
horny hand. "*Adios,* hoss."

"Will you please change your mind and come home
with us?" Kristina asked earnestly. "You're very welcome."

"Little lady, no. My stick floats upstream. To them
mountains....Thankee for loan of the hoss. Be bringin'
him in. See you all then."

Jogging back on the road to Spur, Thoroughgood was
filled with boyish exuberance, full of his plans for the
future. "Shiloh, you're going to El Paso...."

"Right this minute?" the *segundo* inquired dryly.

"Tomorrow. You're fetching us back a shorthorn
herd."

"Your pet scheme, eh? You know the old man never
bought it."

"How about you, sis?" Thoroughgood demanded. "You
buying it?"

"Take care of the ranch is in your hands, mister, I'm
just a dumb little squarehead, eh?"

Thoroughgood coughed embarrassedly. "Ahem... you'll be all right." He looked at her intently. "We'll lay this on the line. Santee isn't finished with us by a long shot. Got to be sure you're ready to buy that too. There'll be no turning back."

Channing saw a slow unhappiness shape her mouth; she'd learned something of life and men that morning, and the lesson was not a pleasant one. But her lips tightened. "No turning back," she said firmly.

EIGHT

Streak Duryea was idly pleased that he'd once mastered the trick of building a cigarette one-handed. Expertly he shaped and sealed the quirly, closed his thin lips on it and snapped a match alight on his thumbnail. Exhaling with a grunted sigh, he leaned back on the blankets of his lower bunk, wincing as his bandage-swathed shoulder caught his weight

Damn that brush jumper. For a gambler, Santee should have read the man more accurately. But Santee's very coldness sometimes blinded him to men's natures, as in thinking that force would bend Elwood Brock's mule-stubborn will. Despite his hatred for the mustanger, Streak felt a deep and grudging respect. The man had taken a savage whipping that should have broken body and spirit, yet less than twenty-four hours later had sought out the man who'd administered it, beaten him to a pulp with three of his men present. That impressed Streak far more than Channing's rescue of Brock; the first time Channing had been a man alone in strange country, throwing back defiance in the teeth of Anchor Ranch and all its power. Nobody but a fool kicked at an angry rattler; yet Channing was no fool, and Streak wondered what drove the man....

Lying on his back with the murmurs of the card players in his ears, the rest of the men sprawled in their bunks, Streak turned his head, squinting against the bite of smoke. The bunkhouse was twenty by forty, partitioned for warmth against the high-country chill, with its five sets of double bunks, its battered chairs and settee and the table in the center littered with yellowed, page-curling magazines and an omnipresent Dutch Almanac, and the potbellied stove crackling its warmth through the stale atmosphere. It was like a hundred bunkhouses Streak Duryea had known since his orphaned boyhood, where men came and went, froze and sweated for thirty and found, bare of luxury. and shorn to a minimum of comfort

But there was a difference. The floor here was caked with filth and carelessly strewn with gear, the walls grimy and soot-smudged, violating the working puncher's law of scrupulous cleanliness in his one abode. Streak looked at these men, his mouth twisted. Trash, all of them; the dregs of the chuckline who drifted because no decent place could long absorb their ilk, replacing every honest Anchor man because Santee Dyker had a dirty job in prospect.

And he ramrodded this scum...Streak Duryea felt

an abrupt backwash of contempt Maybe part of Channing's unexpected reaction was a savage capacity for anger against injustice. For Streak himself, lacking the capacity, Channing's way was too unpredictable. He sucked his cigarette, sighting down its glowing tip. A man guided by his own self-sufficient standards had an inner toughness, a drive behind him that would override a man of purposeless cynicism. Where, how, had Duryea lost his youthful lodestar? Too much knocking around in the worst quarters when he'd still had a choice, this leading to one self-compromise after another till there was nothing left to compromise. Savagely he ground out the cigarette. The hell with it. This was his berth, housed with the prideless scum whose wild and violent way of life he'd chosen....

The droned murmurs of the card players had sharpened with an ugly note that caused Streak to raise himself on one elbow. Ward Costello was playing stud with Arnt Chance, a spare, hard-bitten man of forty. Bee Withers straddled the bench by Costello, watching with his foolish grin, the half-healed cuts on his face a sickly color in the sallow lamplight

Chance set his palms on the table, pushing stiffly to his feet. His ax-slash of a mouth was tight. "Like to see you deal that over," he said softly. "Don't usually git fancy belly strippers this far away from the big towns, big casinos."

Costello's slender hands did not move on the table. "You can go to hell, my man," he stated evenly. "Your deck. You dealt the hand—and shot me an ace."

Chance's lean arm snaked across the table, suddenly snatching Costello's right wrist and twisting it viciously. Costello's hand opened spasmodically. A card fell from it. "Figured so," Chance said thickly. "Ace was up your sleeve. Switched this three for it."

He released Costello's wrist and stepped quickly back. At the same time Bee Withers stood, a high, gangly shadow behind Costello. Bee settled his colorless stare on Arnt Chance, and was motionless, waiting. Streak reached to the gunbelt pegged on the wall by his hand, lifting .his Colt from holster. The sound of its cocking broke the smoke-hung quiet.

"Sit down, Withers," he said quietly. "You too, Arnt"

Arnt Chance wavered for a feisty moment, then growled, "Ahhh," disgustedly as he swung toward his bunk. Withers remained as he was, watching Arnt. Costello, scowling as he rubbed his wrist, spoke sharply. Withers slacked casually back to the bench.

Setting his teetji against the pain, Streak swung his legs off the bunk and hunched his narrow shanks to a sitting position. "You're here cm sufferance, nephew. Don't prod your luck."

Costello shrugged, picked up the deck and riffled it His indifference smarted, goading Streak to anger. The men were all watching; two defeats at Channing's hands had already lessened his stature, a loss of face he could not afford. "Goddamn you, Costello, look at me when I talk to you."

Costello gave him a sullen glance. "I don't take your orders."

"Not you, not Santee's coddled nephew," Streak jeered. "But you'll damned well hear me say what we all know. You and your heel dog are laying in here because one man curled your tail. You haven't got the guts to jump reservation while he's inside a hundred miles. One man."

"That's right," murmured Costello. "Took you down a peg or so, though, didn't he?"

Streak leaned forward, lamplight flaring hot and wicked against his eyes. "He did, by God. And I'll kill him for it!"

"Trouble, Streak?"

Santee had opened the door and was lounging against the jamb. His casual query bore the texture of bland steel.

Streak let his breath out. "No trouble."

"Do you take me for a blind man or a fool? Come up to the house. Now. You too, Ward—and Withers."

Streak arose and sidled painfully around the table, preceding Costello and Withers through the doorway. Santee moved stonily aside to let them pass. Streak tramped slowly up the dark slope, cradling his calico-slung right arm in his left hand. The still-green logs of the house oozed pitch, a pungent pine scent carried to Streak's nostrils by a chill wind dipping off the peaks. He shivered. Behind, he heard Costello's quick, nervous breathing. Santee was on the peck and no mistake. The ice-vined little bastard carried no gun, duded himself up and talked like a book read, but foul-mouthed hardcases twice his size talked soft and walked easy around Santee Dyker. Streak, for all his aloof cynic's pride, knuckled under to Santee without shame.

Streak stepped into the front room, shifting his feet uneasily on the deep grass-green carpet. The room was small but impeccably furnished. The fragile-looking furniture, of some tropical wood Streak couldn't identify, had been freighted in; it was perfectly congruous to Santee's casual taste. His fat Mexican housekeeper was kneeling by the brick fireplace, poking at a blazing log. "*Vamos, andale*" Santee said curtly. The woman heaved to her feet, shuffled to the silver coffee service on a low tabaret, picked it up and vanished down a corridor, her *guaraches* slap-slapping the floor.

Santee walked to the highboy and spilled some cognac from a cut-glass decanter into a glass. He walked to the divan, sat and gently swirled the dark liquor. "Now, I am not going to mince words with you, Ward," he said in the casually dispassionate manner that Streak recognized as masking his wickedest moods. "This is the third time in a week there's been trouble on your account Didn't I tell you last time—no more poker with the men?"

"A man needs diversion," Ward said tonelessly. "If they want to play—"

"You have to cold-deck."

"Their idea. Let them prove it."

"Arnt caught him in the act tonight," Duryea broke in mildly. "Had an ace in his sleeve."

Santee exhaled gently. "I see." He let the silence run on till Costello began to fidget. "Ward," he said finally, "just what the hell am I going to do with you? You're no damned use on-range with that lily skin and soft body. Can't handle a gun except for that trick sleeve-rig; you'd crack like rotten ice in a real clinch. You're damned close to it already, afraid. he'll come here—pot you from ambush. You're afraid to leave the ranch, building your real danger out of proportion. Hanging here like Old Man Trouble himself, getting bored, getting in my way, fleecing my crew—"

"No call to talk that way," Costello muttered.

Santee slammed down his glass on the tabaret, sloshing the contents across its varnished top. "Who has a better right?" He swung to his feet, made a turn around the divan, hands rammed in his waistcoat pockets. He halted in front of Costello. "You're a miserable excuse even for a tinhorn," he said contemptuously. "At ibis moment I'd need very damned little to have yon escorted to Spur and turned over to…your friend."

Costello paled swiftly, but wisely held his tongue.

"There was one person I cared for," Santee went on softly. "You're tolerated here for her sake, that alone. I'm sick of the sight of you. Understand? You can't stay here forever, jumping at every sound or shadow. Sooner or later you'll have to face him or run. What are you going to do?"

Costello's hand rubbed his throat; he swallowed, managed a low, miserable, "1 don't know."

Streak had seated himself gingerly on a fragile chair, watching this with speculative amusement Santee had once told him that when he'd worked the riverboat gambling tables, his sister, a regally beautiful woman whom Streak gathered had been as cold and distant as Santee himself, had shilled for him. Her armor has been penetrated only once—by some weasely little drummer named Costello who'd left her with an illegitimate child. After she'd died of consumption, exacting a dying promise, Santee had raised the boy on the riverboats. Young Ward's weak and vacillating nature had been easily molded by early environs—gambling and a transient existence.

Afterward, like a bad penny, he'd turn up occasionally in Santee's vicinity with Bee Withers in tow like a patient dog. The partnership between Ward and Bee, ill-assorted except that neither was any damned good, was perfectly complemented. Ward had no spine, but enough impassioned gambler's gall to maintain them both; Bee was too stupid to be afraid, but responded quickly and efficiently to trouble, handling Costello's difficulties. When the game turned against him, he'd return to loaf off his uncle's bounty for a time, and be off again.

Now Santee was plainly fed up. Duryea almost chuckled aloud, waiting with relish for the rancher's next words. Surprised when Santee curtly addressed Withers: "Bee, you ran with some of the toughest hardcases in Arizona before you partnered up with Ward, didn't you?"

Withers gave a guarded nod.

"Now you've seen this Channing on the shoot, how would you rate him?"

"Right pert, Mister Dyker." Bee's voice was a broken mumble through his wired-up jaws.

"All right, think. You've seen the best of them, who would you pick to face him in a stand-up?"

"Feller from my home-place in the Tennessee hills," Withers mumbled unhesitatingly. "Feller named Landers. We called him 'Brace.' Grease lightnin', dead shot. Gun was a third hand to Brace, Mister Dyker."

"All right, all right," Santee motioned impatiently. "Where is he now?"

"Last seen him five years ago, we was runnin' with the Hashknife outfit in the Tonto Rim country. Of recent years he's hung purty close over Prescott way."

"Would a letter reach him there?"

Withers scratched his tow thatch. "Raickon so. But he'll come mighty high...."

"Write him, let me worry about the rest."

"Cain't write, Mister Dyker."

Santee sighed profoundly. "I'll write him, you add your mark." He swung to Costello. "When Channing's finished, you clear out. For good. Get to your room now, don't let me hear of you around the bunkhouse again."

Flushed with humiliation, Costello walked from the

room with Withers shambling behind. Santee leisurely drew a twisted cheroot from his breast pocket, clipped the end with a gold cutter on his watch chain, and lighted it

"Why a special man?" Streak asked. "I could deadfall him straightaway enough."

"As you did Custis Thursday, yes," Santee said musingly, his eyes lambent through the swirling smoke. "Ambushing Thursday was a job of necessity, not of passion, with you. You might be a trifle overeager with channing, nor is he an old man to be taken unawares even in the dead of night. It must have been he, not that bumbling old Spur *segundo,* who trailed you from Brock's cabin. He's Spur's ace-in-the-hole, a man who's been in this kind of fight before and understands it. And has an uncommon knack of doing the unexpected, what in another would be stupidity or insanity. A successful gambler knows when to cut the odds; having Channing cut down in a stand-up encounter would be certain and impressive. He's the opposition's morale. As Napoleon said, 'In war, the morale is to the physical as three to one'....Meanwhile, there's this herd Thoroughgood is having shipped from El Paso."

Streak nodded moodily. Earlier that day, at Santee's order, he'd dispatched a rider to town to listen to the saloon grapevine. "Yeah. Shiloh Dawes and part of the Spur crew left on the train today, was the talk in town. Ought to be back in a couple weeks."

"The girl must have come here with capital," Santee mused. "Spur was down to a shoestring from old Thursday's clumsy extravagance. I never thought they could pay Brock's price, let alone re-stock their range. They couldn't have much left. If that herd were wiped out...."

"That's half the trouble," Streak observed. "Word's that John Straker and Spur might mend their differences."

"Ah?" Santee said sharply. "You didn't mention that earlier."

"Just talk, Elam said. He overheard one of Straker's crew tell the barber that the Nilssen girl and Thoroughgood were over at Mexican Bit yesterday. They talked with Straker for quite a spell."

"A mutual protection league—against us?" Santee released his breath sibilantly, smiling frostily. "Just possible, yes…and a shrewd move. Have Elam keep his ears open; when we know their next move—we move."

NINE

The men stood uneasily around the parlor, holding glasses of barely tasted whiskey. All were dressed for the occasion. Thoroughgood looked strangely at ease in his black broadcloth, but his near-perpetual scowl had scarcely relaxed. Channing squirmed his shoulders uncomfortably in a suit borrowed from a bunkie, the cravat and choker collar giving htm an acute sense of suffocation.

The two visitors shared their hosts' half-awkward, half-hostile silence. The master of Mexican Bit was a towering, lean man, straight as a rifle barrel, looking the military careerist he'd been. At fifty John Straker's hair was a smooth, dead-white cap which, with precisely trimmed mustaches and brittle gray eyes, gave him a look of steel-willed distinction. He wore a handsome Prince Albert over his ruffled white shirt with string tie. His foreman, Mel Daley, was a quiet-eyed, taciturn man with a long horse face. He rolled a tobacco cut in the pocket of his cheek, and the front of his slightly rumpled and age-rusty suit was already stained by it.

"Come to table," Kristina called from the dining room. The men began a concerted shuffle through the dividing archway. Channing was the last to enter; like the others, he came stock-still to stare at her. He knew she'd spent many hours cutting and sewing on some rich material she'd purchased in town, readying the dress she wore. It was of blue watered silk, low-cut from the milky smoothness of neck and shoulders, bodice hugging her upper body and skirt belling prettily. She had done her hair differently, gathered smoothly atop her small head in a way at once Eastern and alien, yet admirable. Still none of her handsome freshness was lost, rather now taking a man's eye with a soft radiance.

Speaking in her soft, strong accent she directed them to chairs. Channing's eye went over the table with mounting amazement. The fine linen tablecloth and silverware and matched china must have belonged to Thorough-good's wife, but the quantity of food—enough for a Scandinavian banquet—had been prepared under Kristina's direction, with the unwillingly pressed help of the ranch cook. He recognized several Swedish dishes—*knakkebrod, getmesost,* and little rosette fried cakes filled with jam. At each plate was a small glass of mild-appearing liquid.

Kristina took her place at the head of the table with John Straker on her right gallantly stepping up to hold her chair. The men stiffly seated themselves. She smilingly raised her glass. "Gentlemen…?"

Mel Daley lifted his drink suspiciously, giving her his mournful glance. "What you call this snifter, ma'am?"

"*Glogg*. I think you call it—punch?"

Daley's drooping roan mustaches stirred in a grin tolerant of female foofera; he took the drink in a lusty swallow. For a moment he was motionless, but swallowing hard. "By the Sam Hill," he muttered. Kristina laughed heartily. John Straker held a stern face, raising his glass with a respectful, "Your very good health, ma'am," and now with the potent concoction warming their stomachs the atmosphere thawed.

Kristina took little food herself but chatted animatedly as she passed dishes, urging them to sample each. Channing ate in silence, knowing his presence here was by token only, a morale backing to the proposition Kristina had discussed with Thoroughgood and himself yesterday. She had climaxed her visit to Mexican Bit by inviting Straker and his foreman to supper and they were to play their parts. The stage was well-set, Channing conceded with a faint cynicism. All very neat, very Channing. By contrast to Kristina Nilssen's usual candor, this was an elaborate background for her purpose; he found it disquieting. Certainly Kristina was no woman of the world like Anne LeCroix, but maybe a woman knew these things by instinct. This girl's appearance of childish naïveté was deceptive, though not intentionally so; she assessed a situation with a native shrewdness that made up for ignorance. She had stepped smoothly into the reins of Spur ownership from the first, and by now was imperceptibly guiding some of Thoroughgood's own hard-gained lifetime experience. Channing refilled his glass from the punchbowl, dourly thinking. *Well, she knows what she wants, more than you can say.* But through the thought was threaded a nagging sense of disappointment

She laughingly scolded Mel Daley for protesting a third helping of *knakkebrod,* then turned to John Straker, The fitful lamplight played restless highlights on her hair as she leaned her chin on her hand, lips tilted pixie-like. "You are a cold businessman, Mr. Straker, no friv— frivolity, eh?"

Straker patted his lips with his napkin, saying hastily, "I am enjoying every minute, ma'am. An old bachelor never realizes his barren existence except from a delightful contrast."

Her laugh tinkled scoffingly. "Why Mr. Straker, you're a mighty fine figure of a man...and old?"

Only old enough to be her father, Channing thought and took a drink that balled in his stomach with a sour heat.

"That is far better," Kristina murmured serenely. "And . . ." *And now to business,* Channing thought, recognizing the subtle altering of her expression to mulish determination.

Kristina outlined her intention casually, deferring modestly to Thoroughgood now and then by asking him to detail several points. It would involve the throwing together of the crews, wagons and gear of Spur and Mexican Bit to move the shorthorn herd which Shiloh Dawes was now bringing from El Paso onto the Strip. Neither Spur's mistress nor its foreman tried to garnish the fact that this was a protective measure. Thoroughgood anticipated that Santee Dyker would strike at that herd, which represented Spur's big experimental gamble for future prosperity. Without it, the real advantage of Spur's holding the coveted graze was nil. The stringy, half-wild beeves which already constituted the stock of Spur's waning fortunes could be grazed on its range proper with no loss. Santee would be wary of taking on the combined crews of his two rivals, particularly if they posed a powerful retaliatory force. Kristina wanted to avoid bloodshed at all cost, and armed strength was the deterrent she meant to use. Channing felt renewed approbation; there was no shame to her determined refusal to further her ambition at the cost of men's lives.

Straker nodded attentively. "And my stake in this, ma'am?"

She explained that Spur would share the Strip within an arbitrary limit of the number of head that Mexican Bit could graze there at any one time, for a two-year period. Elwood Brock's agreement to this arrangement had already been secured, and she made it clear that after Mexican Bit had helped safely disperse the shorthorns over the graze, Straker's only commitment was to come to Spur's aid in any emergency arising from Santee Dyker's antagonism during those two years. If Straker was satisfied with its conditions, she would dispatch a rider tomorrow to Anchor with a note informing Santee Dyker of the details of their agreement, an oblique warning.

"Hum," Straker murmured, seeming to turn it in his mind; he was quickly decided. "A handshake is considered sufficient in these matters." Kristina did not hide her radiant delight, as, bowing over her hand, he added with a wry gallantry, "Young lady, I've been trapped before, but never so Channingly."

The relief of slacked tension was plain. Thoroughgood unbent so far as to lay a hand on Straker's shoulder when they left the table for the parlor, saying, "John, we've been a sorry pair of mossyhorns not to see it out this way before."

Straker chuckled. "No pretty middleman before...."

Kristina served coffee, and for an hour she was the gay hostess, no longer in a idle. Then Straker stood and reached for his hat. "Thank you for the excellent supper, ma'am," he said, adding forcefully: "I'll call again."

Kristina stood on the porch and watched Straker and Daley ride from the ranch yard, soon lost beyond the long, crooked shadows thrown by the lamplight from parlor windows. Then she turned, wrinkling her nose at Thoroughgood who was lounging in the doorway. "He is a funny old man. But a gentleman."

"See here, sis," Thoroughgood said gravely, "there's a thing or so you should get straight"

"Oh?"

"Wouldn't say you meant to trifle exactly, but he took it seriously. Want to watch you don't stir up another hornet's nest."

She picked up her skirts and stepped past him to enter, saying stiffly, "It was yust an arrangement of business."

"Sure, sure," the foreman said seriously. "But you're a young and pretty woman. Use that fact on a man to get your wants, you'll find he won't stop where you draw the line." He nodded abruptly, said "Good night," and left for the bunkhouse.

Channing finished his third cup of coffee, scalded his tongue in his haste, and started to stand quickly.

"Channing!" She turned to face him with a rustle of skirts, a small frown marring her brow. "Channing, it is true, eh? What he says?"

She was standing close before him, and he sank back on the divan. "Guess so," he said uncomfortably.

Her smile was speculative as she sat beside him, drawing her skirts close. "I am pretty, then?"

He could smell a faint sachet from her skin, and the lamplight laid an ivory sheen on her shoulders. His face felt hot, the high collar choking. "I'd better—"

"Have some coffee!" She bent forward to fill his cup. Looking at the back of her bead, his embarrassment ebbed. She was, after all, competent mistress of Spur or no, a young girl in a new party gown, probably the first she'd owned...gala finery worn for the eyes of an aging rancher and two not-young foremen. And there was him ...a killer near her age, he thought with cold self-castigation. With a faint pity, too, and an akin understanding.

"I'll have that coffee," he said quietly. Their eyes met as she handed him the cup; she flushed slowly. "Thank you," she said low-voiced.

After a moment's silence, he said: "You got it all now. Everything you want."

"Oh," she said softly, looking away. "You see plainly. I am greedy, eh? That's not being a very good woman, I suppose...."

He started to protest, but she shook her head. "No, it is true." She looked down at her skirt, pleating the crisp folds caressingly between her fingers. "This ordering of men's affairs, it's nice to be able to do. But Bob was right, he says I am not fair. And I don't feel so good, hearing it put that way." She turned her head suddenly, her words a vehement outpouring.

"It is not so easy to be fair! My father came to this country to find a good life. The first year on his farm it was corn and potatoes. A drought came and the sun

scorched it all The second year he sowed wheat. Now
locusts like a plague of Jehovah ate away the farmlands.
So neighbors, they quit and said it was no good. But
Papa tried again. He worked in the lumber camps each
winter to support his wife and children and buy seed to
try again. He planted more wheat. It was good this time;
good rains, and no locusts. Standing tall like gold in the
sun. A week before the cutting...."

A dry sob broke in her throat. He wanted to stop her,
but she went on. Hail had flattened the wheat. Her father
had come in from the ruin of his fields to find his wife
Sigrid in labor and terrible pain. He had gone to the
nearby town for a doctor. And had found the settlement
deserted, save for one old man. Some young Sioux braves
had gotten hold of whiskey and murdered a farm family
nearby. The farmer's wife had escaped to tell the settlement. The panicked citizens had fled south to a larger
town. It was as though her father's brain had snapped at
the news. Without a word, he'd rushed off into the empty
night The next morning the old man had gone to the
Nilssen farm. Sigrid and her unborn child must have died
before her husband had returned. In their bed the old
man had found Kristina's two little sisters, their throats
cut. Eric Nilssen lay dead on the floor, his wrists slashed
by the same knife.

Kristina pressed her hands to her temples, her eyes
shining and hard. "I was working in St. Paul...did not
know till I came home for a visit a month later. The old
man told me. So I have everything now, everything—"

She broke down, and Channing, like a sensible man, put
his arms around her and let her sob like a child against
his shoulder. He said gently: "A sight too much remembering. Better to let it go."

She drew away, her tear-stained face serious and abruptly calm. "You know why I hate this useless death, this killing?"

He said humbly, "Didn't before."

"And you have killed," she murmured with no censure to it. "You're not that way, you have kindness. Why, Channing?"

'There's enough hurt for one evening."

"Tell me."

Channing's tongue was sluggish, blurring the words. But her story had shaken him and now he wanted to talk. Wanted to tell her of his father with his Bible and birching rod.

"Your papa was a minister?"

"A deacon or elder in the church, when he was younger. Before Mom died. Heard folks say it was after that he got hard. I was too young to remember anything 'cept being raised by hand. The old man didn't go to church in my recall. Said it was a place for weaklings who had to be told the Word when it was all in the Book, the way a man must live. I'll say this: if he took his own meaning from the Scriptures, he lived up to it."

"There was no word in his Bible of forgiveness, of love?"

"He missed nothing. Forgave the weak fools of the world and showed his love for his boy by raising him in —righteousness. He was a righteousness one, the old man. He hated guns most. Devil's tools for weak, wicked people to lean on...can't say he was wrong, can you?"

She didn't reply, her lips slightly parted as she watched his face.

Channing tugged at his collar with a finger, moved restlessly, "Well, I fooled once with a gun belonging to my uncle, shot it off by accident The old man laid it on, worst he ever had, left me layin' like raw beefsteak. Uncle took me to a doctor, left me there. When the old man came nosin', the doc come out with a shotgun, swore he'd blow him to blazes if he set foot on the porch."

He'd been thirteen then. A scrawny kid with most of the hide flayed from his back. It had been nearly a month before he could leave his bed, the doctor's wife nursing him the while. The old man finally had recourse to the law and got a court order for the return of his son. The doctor swore he'd fight it. Rather than embroil the kindly couple further, young Channing had left in the dead of night. For the next week he'd put distance between himself and the town of his birth. He lived off berries and like truck till he came to a ranch where he was fed and given a charity job of swamping for the cook.

He'd saved his first meager earnings till he had enough to buy a second-hand Colt's and ammunition. It became a ritualistic obsession to stand off in a draw away from the ranch, and, pretending that an old stump was his father's face, blaze coolly away at it. When the scars on his back were fully healed, his bitter hatred had relaxed. But the gun had become proficient habit, deadly habit that made a skinny, undersized kid stand head and shoulders with the biggest man. Backed by a savage vow that he'd be tormented no more.

The ranch crew had laughed, but not too loudly; something in his look softened their taunts. It wasn't till a Saturday night in town that a likkered cowhand strange to him had knocked him down for no better reason than it galled him to see a snot-nosed runt packing a man's weapon. Shaking with rage, young Ed Channing had called him out, let him pull his gun before the kid's smooth draw and speedy bullet sent him kicking in the street The man had lived for two days. When the news of his death came to Channing's boss, the white-haired rancher's comment had been grim and short: "You're a killer, boy. Get off my place."

Eleven years ago. Channing wasn't sure, but guessed that the drifting afterward and the nursing of the new, raw bitterness had really marked him so it showed. No one taunted him again; men gave him one look and a wide berth. He got used to men's cold scrutinies and their curt, "Sorry, no work here." But the railroads were building spur lines out of Kansas; troubleshooters were what they wanted, and he had no choice. The federal government had endowed the railroad with every alternate section of land along their siding, and the squatters had to be moved off. The pay was choice—if you could forget the shamed fright of half-starved hoe-grubbers you shoved back, the loathing in the eyes of their women, the scared cringing of ragged children. But Channing could not forget; when he moved on, it was far north, clear to Montana.

There had been work for a changed man, a brooding and silent stranger who stepped far aside to avoid trouble. But aimless driftings brought only small disappointments that piled up and dogged a man till he came to realize that if he found no meaning in life, he must make his own meaning. His crystallizing purpose sparked by the warmth of his first friendship—with Lacey Trobridge— had been the puncher's eternal dream, a ranch of his own—in partnership with his friend. Then he told the rest: the purpose destroyed, nothing to renew his purpose but revenge.

"Why," Kristina said softly, wonderingly, "you have never had anything! That's terrible...."

"Just life. It goes that way."

His words were almost indifferently matter-of-fact. Yet he was aware of an inward lightening, wondered now if something had left his system like a drained-off poison. Looking at the giri he saw her pale and shaken; the completeness of their cross-shared confidence left him uneasy, a little ashamed.

He gave an abrupt good night as be stood and quickly strode from the bouse. Once only and softly, she called his name; he didn't look back.

Nearing the bunkhouse he saw the cherry-glow of a cigar and the looming shadow of Thoroughgood leaning against the front wall. The foreman stepped out to plant his bulk solidly before the younger man. Channing halted, hearing his angry exhalation that made the cigar's coal flare redly against his frowning features. At the edge of speech, he relaxed with a faint shrug. "Guess you know."

"My place?" Channing murmured.

"Forget it" Thoroughgood dropped the cigar and ground it under his heel, adding with an acrid pointed-nest: "I've got to know you, like you, boy. Don't crowd that fact Lef's turn in."

TEN

Two weeks later Kristina rode out to the branding grounds several miles west of Spur headquarters. The El Paso train with its line of cattle cars had jolted onto the siding at Sentinel late last night. Shiloh Dawes, dirty, tired and whiskered, had brought in the news. Thoroughgood had roused out the crew and had dispatched a rider to notify John Straker. Long before false dawn, the joint Spur-Anchor crews were unloading the shorthorns, starting the drive to the Spur range for the branding prior to the drive up the rugged plateau trails to the Strip.

Kristina capably reined in the buckboard a few yards beyond the branding fires where Thoroughgood and John Straker stood. Men were slapping hot iron on the hip of a bawling whiteface, tied and thrown on the scuffed earth.

Kristina sat for a wide-eyed moment; her eyes stung and she coughed as furling smoke shifted on a hot current of air. Straker turned and saw her. He came to the buckboard and assisted her from the high seat, taking in with approval her calico shirt and leather riding skirt.

"Didn't hear you come, for the noise. What do you think of it?"

She made a wry face. "Looks painful."

His grin broadened. "To save more pain in the long ran. Even then, a baired-over brand at roundup can come close to a bloody argument"

She nodded perfunctorily, her smile an absent one, eyes roving over the milling, dust-moiling herd, the cowboys cutting and bulldogging, a ritual panorama which another time would have held her breathless. She couldn't see Channing. She caught herself abruptly, angry at her unbidden anxiety. Yet her honest reason for coming was to see him—speak to him, she corrected herself. If only to analyze for her own satisfaction the disturbing bond she'd felt between them since that night nearly two weeks ago.

Thoroughgood stepped over, giving her his curt working nod. "It's humming along, sis. With two crews and no hitches, we ought to be on the Strip in a few days."

"That's good." She glanced up at him, hands on her hips. "But Mister Dyker?"

"Mister Dyker knows," Thoroughgood said heavily. "A couple of his boys were hanging around at the depot last night. Likely he has a hardcase or two spotting us from the hills now."

"And?" she prompted anxiously.

Thoroughgood pinched his lower lip. "Anyone's guess. He'll know we got more men than him, that they're armed to the teeth, that there'll be a triple guard on the herd every night, that we ride flankers by day and night."

"They would try to shoot up our herd?"

"No-o," Straker said judiciously. "Stampede them, is our guess. They're not about to ride into our teeth, they'd be chewed and spit out in short order. But a noisy attack well-timed could spook the beeves so they'd not stop till they dropped. If they got pointed for badlands broke up by canyons or *malpais*—these fat stump-legged pets of Bob's would get busted to pieces."

Thoroughgood gave him a grim side-glance. "That's why the flanking scouts, sis. Eyes like Channing's on the lookout, holding our drive to wide-open country, nobody'll edge near enough to start anything."

"It's good they do not," she said gravely. "There are many lives here, men and animals, and money will not buy them back....Channing is on the scout?"

Thoroughgood's lean features sharpened; he opened his mouth, closed it, cleared his throat and said meagerly, "Yeah. South flank. A hundred yards out."

That is not what he meant to say, Kristina thought, and knew a sudden anger. It was none of his business. He thought she was a befuddled child, and she would show him what she thought. Without speaking she swung back to her rig, mounted to the seat and took up the reins. Putting the team in motion, she did not look back.

She guided the wagon over the turf-clumped rolling ground in a wide skirt of the herd, rebelliously urging the team to a pace that threatened to creak the jolting buckboard apart. Seeing a rider sitting his horse in motionless isolation, she headed that way. She recognized him well before she reined the team to a halt that shrouded the parched ground in tan dust. She had not expected the unbidden excitement that now sparked her; she had half-expected his sullen withdrawal. Yet he looked wholly at ease, a cigarette between his sunburnt lips and one leg slung over his pommel. His nod and comment were pleasant if taciturn: "Hot day to push a team that hard."

She frowned slightly at this stolid contentment of a solitary man. *He likes being alone,* she thought, and her tumultuous mood honed her voice with gentle acid: "1 would hate it to bother you, mister."

"Not the least bother," Channing said easily, but the uneasiness mounting in his face gave her satisfaction. She altered her approach to friendly intimacy. "I have seen that you avoid me."

He ground the cigarette out on his boot with a self-conscious downward scowl. "Not aware of it"

"Oh yes. When you see me coming, you find suddenly work to busy you. This, after walking out on me after the party—and talk."

His eyes went opaque and remote. "Nothing else to say. There's a thing about talk—can't be stopped once it starts. And that's no good."

"It is wrong—for friends to talk? This foolish line between bunkhouse and the owner—or maybe it's Thoroughgood you're afraid of."

"Not one or the other. No rule, no man alive, tells me my way."

"Then what?"

"You didn't see Bob's meaning," he said patiently. "He sees what I do. Drop it there."

"No." A strong undercurrent of emotion shaded her voice, and she felt no shame in it

"All right." He looked at the dead cigarette and tossed it away. He said tiredly: "A man like me's no good to anything touching him. Thoroughgood can tell that. Without knowing what you know."

"Why, I think he comes to like you now."

"Nothing to do with this other. Look...Kristina. You're young. Your life's ahead of you. Mine's about finished. Not in years, in the way I've lived them. The things I told you, the reason I'm here. To you it tallies to something romantic-seemin'."

Is that what you think? she thought with, a wondering pity, but held silence in the pause, and he went on: "To Bob and me, it adds to a bullet in the back. Or in the front, sooner or later, don't matter." His voice abruptly roughened. "You're not a fool; don't act one. Keep your distance. Maybe you understand that?"

A hurt anger flared out of her first emotion. She sputtered a Swedish expletive and reined the team into violent motion. She hauled in well away from him. Her face felt burning. *He did not mean that. He meant it for my good,* she thought. *If they are wrong, these thoughts, it will have to be.* She let her mouth tilt in a stubborn and speculative smile.

ELEVEN

The fires of the camp made lone and ruddy beacons in the night's oceanic murk. Each man wolfing his supper in silence felt the communicated knife-edge of unease. The branding had been completed yesterday, and the drive to the Strip had begun that morning. The size of the herd and the progressive roughness of the terrain had held twenty men of the combined crews to a plodding pace. They expected to strike into the Strip lowlands late tomorrow and begin the job of dispersing the shorthorns safely across its immense, open-rolling acreage.

Now bivouacked for this last night on a semi-arid highland meadow which would accommodate the herd bedgrounds a quarter mile away, they all were of the same thought: that if Anchor struck at the herd, it must be

117

tonight. The knowledge marked even John Straker's stern-held face where he sat by Thoroughgood on the tree of the chuckwagon. The Spur foreman forked the food around his tin plate in a bare pretense of eating. The cowhands around the fire ate stolidly if with little stomach; each would be serving long wary hours on a double guard which Thoroughgood had split into two shifts.

Channing, scheduled on the second shift at midnight, scraped up his plate and downed his coffee and was the first to head for his blankets beyond the drawn-up wagons. In a minute Shiloh Dawes unrolled his sugans and stretched out a yard away.

"Shiloh—how'll it come?"

"Law, son," the *segundo* whispered, "got to be a snake with brains to read Santee. *Quién sabe?* The dark could cover whatever he tries. That moon's a sliver, cat couldn't see much a paw away."

"Was thinking," Channing said sleepily, "about the scouts, out there alone. Stranger making to be one of us could ride close, ask one of 'em for a smoke maybe, and—"

A clatter of tinware by the tailgate of the chuckwagon broke him off. Both he and Shiloh came erect in their blankets. In the firelight stood a lean, gangling Spur puncher who'd broken the thick stillness by dropping his plate and cup resoundingly into the wreck pan. The squat figure of the cook faced him truculently. "What the hell was that for!"

"Sawmthin' to drag you awake, gutcheatuh," the puncher said in a long-drawn nasal drawl. "Thet gawd-damn grub's too tumble even for your makin'."

Several men chuckled. Tenseness relaxed like an unclosing fist. Shiloh chuckled, settled back in his blankets. "We all needed that. Let's get shut-eye."

Channing folded his arm under his head. He lay staring at the white star-blaze on a cobalt canopy of sky, tired to where his thoughts raveled into meaninglessness. Thoroughgood had pushed hard these last days, with time for but snatched hours of sleep. Channing tried to sort out his troubled thoughts...regretting his rough last words to Kristina and knowing he wouldn't take them back if he could. It remained as he'd told her and her romantic notions must stem from the disturbing confidences they had shared only once. Cut it clean, forget it, get some sleep. And he slept, his last thought of an empty sense of loss deeper than anything he had known.

He was awakened at midnight by somebody shaking him by the shoulder. He stumbled sleep-drugged from his blankets and moved over to his ground-hitched horse. Shiloh yawned broadly as he swung into leather, a stumpy, half-seen figure in the darkness. The five other riders constituting the shift relief fell in behind as they crossed the flat, bunch-grassed meadow toward the faintly stirring hulk of the herd, held in the rolling open according to plan.

A cold highland breeze trailing across Channing's face pulled him to chilled alertness. He buttoned his jumper to the collar and slacked easily in the saddle.

"Quiet night," Shiloh muttered. "Herd critters get skittish, uneasy, at midnight, though. Never knew why. Strikes me if—"

And suddenly all hell broke loose. Channing took automatic tight rein on his snorting horse, hardly believing his eyes. There had been a single shot—and a vast orange flare out in the night, then a sheet of leaping flames building itself magically into a wide, racing circle of unbroken fire. The whole tableau was highlighted as brightly as day. Etched against high-tossed flames, heads and horns of cattle stirred above the massed black hulk of their bodies, not yet spooked. Spur and Mexican Bit nighthawks were trying to bring their frightened horses under control. And now a second orange burst ignited at the opposite end of the herd, running along an unseen path to meet the other semicircle of flames, now widely surrounding the herd and riders. At the same time, a peppering of shots began from unseen riflemen beyond the fire.

Shiloh Dawes socked steel into his horse's ribs; it squealed and leaped forward with Shiloh's bull-chested roar: "Shag it, you buckos!"

They spurred as one into his lead, heading for a break in the wall of fire on their near side. Channing saw a squatted-down man rise from the grasses and start a panicked run from their path. A rider fired, the roar of his Colt lost in the merged crackle of flames, crash of shots, and cattle-bawling. The man stumbled and went down. Something bulky flung from his hand spurted a gurgling flow. It confirmed Channing's first thought.... coal oil.

Somehow, as he'd half-guessed, the enemy had tolled in close to the outriders, disposing of them in silence. Then Anchor men stationed at pre-planned intervals had worked in silently with their cans of coal oil, sloshing down the dry grass of this waterless plateau in a ring around the herd. Darkness and herd-noises would have obscured their movements from the nighthawks. The signal to ignite the coal oil had been that shot. But it was premature, or one of the nighthawks had seen something in the night and had fired; the running man the Spur rider had shot hadn't had time to lay down his share.

This flashed through his mind as they pounded through the gap in the flames; a blistering wave of heat rode against their bodies and then they were inside. Shiloh bellowed: "Get on the other side, start 'em moving through this hole."

A rider yelled at the top of his lungs, "They'll stampede!"

"No help for it!"

Shiloh lunged his mount up the west flank of the herd, paralleling the rim of fire. The whitefaces were in full panic now, bawling and squealing; their aimless milling prevented a concerted bolt from the surrounding flames. Rifle fire from the invisible marksmen beyond the flames populated the night with steady, withering death; the heavy-bodied cattle at the edge of the herd were plunging to earth crippled or dying. The pile-up of downed steers would make a stampede still more difficult to begin. Yet every man hung behind Shiloh as they raced up the gamut of gunfire, picking up several nighthawks as they rode. Channing had already seen one nighthawk shot from his saddle, and now he heard a yell behind him and twisted in time to see a man spill headlong to the ground and crumple there unmoving.

But there was no stopping; it was ride, ride it out to the end where no hidden guns spoke, and Channing guessed that Santee's limited force was concentrated at opposite flanks. Shiloh's roared orders sent his men careening in a skirmish line across the drag. They blasted the sky with their six-shooters, lashed at the rumps of the nearest beeves with their coiled ropes, screaming at the tops of voices hoarsened to husky whispers as a pungent reek of scorched sod scoured throats and lungs raw.

But the shorthorns were moving. Slowly at first, now with a ponderous shift of movement as the relentless push rippled through the mass to create leaders, and that fore-surge took the rest in its wake.

The gap in the fire-circle could not accommodate the bellowing, horn-tossing mass; those on the outer flank plunged back on their fellows or raced blindly through the flames which were not eating inward on dead clump-grass. A stench of singed hide mingled with oily billows of smoke. The rifle fire concentrated now on the drovers. Channing saw another man topple from his saddle, then stumble to his feet and stagger after his bolting horse. Then the shorthorns were galvanized into a surging jug-gernaut. The stampede had begun.

The riders raced after them, clearing the circle of flames at last, and the shooting fell off and was lost in their wake, and there was only the cutting wind against the face and the powerful surge of horse-muscles beneath. The sea of hurtling beef began to assume the form of a wide-strung crescent with a life of its own, racing down the last flats of the meadow toward the gash of volcanic rock that bordered its west slopes—toward a bloody fate unless its resistless momentum could be turned.

Channing was already spurring sideways toward the west tip of the crescent, the dark forms of unidentifiable riders following his lead. Channing reloaded his revolver with unthinking dexterity before he reached the tip of the flank. He fired, gunflame washing into the eyes of the nearest steers. Then Shiloh Dawes was recklessly crowd-ing nearer still, rifle blazing again and again. The edge of the flank blunted and flattened back on itself like a rising wave, and the riders were firing, swinging ropes, hoarsely yelling like demons.

That side of the herd began to turn, and men relentlessly crowded it and guided it. A bunch split out from the main mass, continued its doomed rush toward the *malpais.* Another bunch followed, and another; but now the millwheel was firmly established. Through the long, dust-choked minutes that followed, the bulk of the herd followed a shrinking circle till the lead steers were eating the dust of the drag. Still the living wheel spun crazily and the men had to hold pace, keeping it bunched till from sheer exhaustion it lost momentum and the stragglers staggered to a stop.

Men drooped breathless and wordless in their saddles; horses heaved their sweating flanks, breath was released in whistling sighs. Channing shivered with the chill biting through his sweat-drenched clothes and lifted his bleary eyes, seeing the distant splash of oil-fed flame dying low against the darkness as it burned itself out The grass was too sparse and short to sustain its artificial life ...so the meadow was saved, and the bulk of the herd.

But men and cattle had died, and Channing thought of his own sinking, weary apathy and in it felt the shattered morale of the others. As though to punctuate his thought, a rider gasped: "I'm through! Thoroughgood can fight his goddamn fights without me!"

And a Mexican Bit man: "Either Straker pulls out of Spur's mixes or I pull out! We didn't hire to get burned and shot down...."

A rider a dozen paces from Channing sharply turned his horse and cantered forward. Channing made out the hulking shadow of Thoroughgood, who'd been on the first nighthawk shift. He was bent low in the saddle. His harsh whisper whiplashed across the rising mutters: "You yellow-gutted nits signed to this drive, you'll see it out. Then you can go to—"

His words trailed off. Without warning he canted sideways in his saddle and fell—limp and unconscious before he hit the ground; one foot still hung in the stirrup.

TWELVE

Doc Willis, the bartender at JUDD'S—LIQUOR AND TO-BACCO, yawned and hoisted his heavy girth from the creaking chair behind the bar to tug his watch from his rusty vest and consult it. "Fifteen to midnight," he said aloud. The yellow dog curled by a table lifted its head. It rumbled displeasure at the sound of his voice in the high, empty room. "Not to you," Doc said coldly. He rolled his three-month-old San Antonio newspaper and swiped at a fly buzzing around a liquor stain on the bar, half-heartedly because the fly was better company than that damned mutt.

Usually even of a week night you could expect a few hands from the outlying ranches. Sentinel was utterly dead tonight, with Spur and Mexican Bit herding up by the

Strip and the smaller outfits, sensing something in the air, keeping close to home. Even the Anchor toughs, a drinking and gambling crowd, hadn't showed. Planning some mischief likely; Bob Thoroughgood had taken a tiger by the tail, bringing in that herd. Doc thought sourly, scrubbing with his bar rag at the liquor stain, that even trouble would be welcome to break this dead tension.

The rear door to the office opened a crack. "Doc.... You can close up now," Anne LeCroix said.

"Yes'm."

The door closed, and Doc started to shed his apron. Cool woman, that Mrs. LeCroix....Likely working this late over her accounts because she couldn't sleep, but you couldn't read it in her expression or voice. Worried over that cold-hearted damn fool, Thoroughgood. Doc shook his head with the profound sigh of a man who had seen it all and could still never fathom the vagaries of humanity. He turned to hang up his apron, checked the motion as he heard the canter of a single horseman coming up the street from the south.

Occasionally at night a rancher or homesteader might ride in to rouse Dr. McGilway out for some family emergency. But this rider was coming without urgency, with almost deliberate unhaste. Doc heard him rein in and dismount before the saloon.

A moment later the man pushed through the swing doors and stood a moment ganglingly, awkwardly, blinking against the light. He stood a good five inches over six feet, wearing a white shirt with a string tie, black trousers with an open vest, a black coat slung over his arm. At first glance his long, homely face was apologetically mild, his thick hands were freckled and large-knuckled, like a plowman's. He might have been an itinerant preacher except for the gun thonged almost invisibly to his thigh in a black, fine-tooled holster. Then there was his jaw set like a trap, eyes flat and pale gray as a blank slate.

His boots struck echoes from the puncheon floor, crossing to the bar. "Mought I borry that rag, cousin?" His voice was gently underpitched, yet it grated like a rusty saw. *One of those Southern hill trash,* Doc thought deprecatingly, but his cue-ball head warmed with a film of perspiration.

The man bent and wiped his dusty boots to a shining black, afterward removed his flat-crowned Stetson and wiped the sweatband. "Thankee, cousin." He laid his hat on the bar and ranged his cold stare over the bottles behind the bar. His sun-faded red hair was long uncut, fantailing shaggily over his ears and collar. "Jis' a leetle finger o' that Kaintuck bourbon."

This one's well-paid, used to the best, Doc thought mechanically as he poured the drink. The stranger sipped delicately and set his glass down. His eyes nailed Doc's like lead bullet-heads. "Mought you say how a man gits to the Anchor Ranch, cousin?"

Just then the dog growled. Doc glanced at the brute in alarm. What the hell ailed him? He'd stretched to his feet and was trotting across to the stranger, hackles bristling. The man only glanced at him with sleepy disinterest.

The dog reached him—sniffed a boot. To Doc's amazement the animal flattened his lean belly against the floor and began to wag his hindquarters. His snarls trailed into a low, puppy-like whine.

Doc said softly, "You're the first he never tried to take a leg off of."

"That so?" murmured the stranger. He gave the dog a careless kick and it yelped and sprang away, settled down a few paces off and laid its head on its paws, watching the man with eyes of love. The stranger cleared his throat rustily. "Ast you a question, cousin."

The office door opened and Anne LeCroix stepped out, her look questioning. "I heard that pet of yours, Doc. Something wrong?"

"No'm. Gent wants to know how to reach Anchor."

"Oh?" Her expression sharpened as she came across the room. "Perhaps I can help, sir. I'm Mrs. LeCroix."

"Brace Landers, mum." The man inclined his towering frame in a quaint, cold bow. "Be obleeged."

She nodded to Doc to refill Landers' glass, then said pleasantly, "I'm afraid there's nobody at Anchor. You see, Mr. Dyker—the owner—is up in the hills with his full crew, moving a new herd on his range. They may be several days, and you may have difficulty finding them. You *are* a stranger to the basin."

"Sure, mum." Landers toyed with his glass but did not drink. "Reckon the barkeep here knows his way around these parts?"

"Why—" Mrs. LeCroix began but the man cut her off with an ice-edged intonation. "Be obleeged he'd ride out and find Santee Dyker—and tell him Brace Landers'll be waitin' his pleasure at this saloon."

Doc's jaw dropped. "In the middle of the night?"

Landers just looked at him, saying nothing, and now the man's still, vicious arrogance pushed Doc beyond fear. He thought of the sawed-off Greener on a shelf under the bar; his fingers twitched.

"Doc was just going off duty," Anne LeCroix said quickly. "I'm sure he'll be glad to deliver your message to Mr. Dyker."

Doc looked at her, his mouth working in speechless anger. Anne shook her head, a single near-imperceptible movement.

Landers tossed down his drink. "Thankee, mum."

"A pleasure, Mr. Landers," Anne said easily. "You look like a man accustomed to having his way." With a nod at Doc, she turned and walked briskly back to the office. Doc followed, muttering under his breath. She closed the office door, shutting off the barroom. He turned wrathfully. "Miz LeCroix, I ain't no errand boy for a goddamn killer!"

"Keep your voice down!" she whispered with sharp urgency. "Listen, Doc. Get my mare at the livery.... Ride for all you're worth and tell Bob Thoroughgood—about this Landers. There's no time to lose.'"

Doc stared at her owlishly from behind his thick spectacles. "Wondered why you told him that Santee Dyker ain't at his ranch. Ma'am, you're playing hellfire. This un's purely skunk-bit mean...."

"I know that," she said impatiently. "The whole look of him is killer. Santee sent for him for...a special reason."

"Like to gun Thoroughgood?" Doc said softly. With the observant but discreet inscrutability of a barman, he'd always avoided even a hint at her feeling.

Her eyes were steady. "That. This will give Bob time. He can come here with men, get the drop on Landers... something. I'll keep Landers here."

"Look," Doc said with difficulty. He cleared his throat. "Don't like leaving you with this fella. Don't know this range much, sure-hell can't find Spur camp in the dark."

"They should be near the Strip by tonight...about ten miles northwest of Spur. It'll be light enough in a couple of hours, till then you can hold to the road—then cut north to the camp." Her hand found his arm almost blindly. "Doc, please. Do it."

"Never said I wouldn't," Doc said gruffly. He turned to a side door that opened on the alley, glanced over his shoulder at her. "I'll ride like hell. You take care now."

THIRTEEN

False dawn had begun to lighten the east to woolly gray as the riders paced into the camp on drag-footed mounts. The cook had left his big cowcamp coffee-boiler on the coals, and each man silently helped himself. They gulped the scalding brew as though to shock themselves from lethargy. Cookie himself was busy patching up wounds and setting several broken bones. The brief flurry of violence had exacted its cost in more than spirit; four men were dead, including one raider. Others were badly hurt Yet Thoroughgood's vehement words before he'd fallen unconscious from his horse had had their sobering and shaming effect. Not a man had said another word about quitting.

Those not on herd duty had gone doggedly to work at

hunting out the bunches that had stampeded into the razor-edged *malpais,* and for the next two hours the rattle of gunfire had pocked the night as they finished off crippled and hamstrung beeves. Channing and Shiloh Dawes had ridden back to the fire-gutted area for a cursory search which had turned up seven soot-blackened ten-gallon coal-oil tins discarded by the raiders, who had long ago melted into the darkness.

Now Channing stood by the fire, filling a tin cup and passing it to Shiloh. He poured a cupful for himself and set the pot on the coals, straightening to face the *segundo.* "It's light enough to ride him in."

Shiloh stroked his white steerhorns absently. His face was worn and drawn with worry. "Reckon. But damn— hate to move him. It's rough trail clear to the nearest road, and that's no easy grade. Could bring the doc here— but it'll take twice the time, and Bob can't stay here. Needs proper nursin'…."

Channing nodded soberly. The bullet had taken Thoroughgood under the heart, ranged between the short ribs and had not emerged. No vital organ had been touched so far as they could tell, but he had not regained consciousness; only a bull-like constitution had kept him in the saddle during those long grueling minutes of forcing the stampede into a mill.

Shiloh turned and walked slowly back to the linchpin wagon behind the chuckwagon, brought to pile the warbags of the double crew. Thoroughgood lay in the wagon bed where they had left him. Cookie had washed the wound with whiskey and tied it up; he couldn't do more. They'd bundled the foreman to the chin with blankets against the chill. Shiloh bent over the wagon box where the linchpin's canvas top had been lifted back, peering intently at the pale, hawkish face.

John Straker came up, batting his dusty hat against his fringed *chaparejos*. He glanced at Thoroughgood. "Hasn't come to?"

Shiloh shook his head mutely.

"He's in a bad way," Straker said, "I were you, I'd waste no time getting him to town and McGilway."

"Maybe you'd do that," Shiloh said softly.

"Me?"

Shiloh humped his sagging shoulders. "A Spur man's got to see out the drive. Bob'd want that."

Straker tugged his mustache in faint embarrassment "Well—"

"He's right."

The startled three of them turned to look at Thoroughgood. His eyes were open and lucid, his words surprisingly strong. "Be obliged if you'd see me to Sentinel, John. Your obligation's ended here."

"What're you saying?"

"Can't hold you to a bad bargain. You can't outguess the devil. I guess we expected everything but fire. We got it." Thoroughgood's first show of energy faded; his eyes closed wearily, voice shrinking to a whisper. "How many men, Shiloh?"

"Two of ours, one of Mexican Bit's," Shiloh muttered. "But they stuck, Bob. The rest stuck."

"No matter," Thoroughgood whispered. "That's three good men too many to lose. And I'm flat on my back. I can't ask you to stay in this fight, John. You may lose everything."

"But damn it, Bob! Spur will lose everything sure— and Miss Nilssen."

A wan smile touched Thoroughgood's lips; his eyes slitted briefly open to meet Channing's. "You say it Will she stay in this fight?"

"You asking me?" Channing said guardedly.

"I got a feeling she opened up to you, you know her mind best. Speak out."

"She'll quit," Channing said unhesitatingly. "After she hears about tonight...three—four," he amended, remembering the Anchor man. "Four dead men. Shell quit, give Santee what he wants."

"Don't blame her any," Thoroughgood murmured almost inaudibly. "About ready to quit myself...."

"Bob!" There was no response to Shiloh's imperative whisper. Thoroughgood was breathing shallowly, but there was a husky rattle to it. Straker shook his head briskly. "Get him to town, Shiloh...fast. I'll stay with the herd, drive it to the Strip and scatter it Least I can do. I'm no quitter."

A muscle knotted in Shiloh's jaw as he pulled worry-fevered eyes to Straker's. "I'll pass that," he said softly.

"Man, I'm sorry," the Mexican Bit owner said contritely. "I know there's more here than meets the eye. But you're half-sick worrying for him; seeing him safe to town's your job....Look, the hell with the bargain! I'm sticking because I want to."

"All right, John," Shiloh said quietly. He raised his voice to bring the Spur crew to attention, explaining the situation and that they were to take orders from Straker and his foreman Mel Daley. He gave two men orders to hitch the linchpin's team.

Channing had started to turn away and scarcely heard him; a sudden thought brought him to a halt in his tracks. The harried violence of the long night had dulled his mind, yet now the thought etched clearly, and shocked him to alertness. An instant backwash of skepticism made htm shake his head, but the notion came back in force and resolved him abruptly. He pivoted on his heel and went to his ground-tethered horse. The clay-bank was standing head-hung and jaded, and he threw off his gear and toted it out to the group of spare horses. He roped out a rangy lineback dun and started to cinch on his rig. Shiloh Dawes came up with his grizzly-roll of a walk and asked a sharp question.

Without turning as he adjusted the latigo, Channing said quietly, "They mant to wipe out the herd. Didn't Know what that means?"

"Want to know what you damn well mean by riding out!"

Channing turned, one arm slung over his saddle swell. "They'll change tactics, hit hard and direct Kristina Nilssen's alone at Spur."

"You thinking—" Shiloh began frowningjy, but John Straker now sauntered up, coffee cup in hand, cutting him off smilingly. "That's nonsense, boy. You're thinking Miss Nilssen may be kidnapped and forced to sign over Spur and the Strip?"

"Santee Dyker's way. Was with Brock, anyway."

Shiloh said worriedly, tugging his mustache, "John, it might be."

"Rot. Even Santee wouldn't dare...*that*. We're a rough lot in this high country, law unto ourselves. But there's not a man in the basin outside Anchor that wouldn't join to tear Anchor down around Santee's ears if he harmed a woman."

"They might have planned it even before hitting the herd. Brock's an old man, they weren't about to stop at torture with him. And she won't browbeat easy, that girl."

"Lord God, that's true," Shiloh breathed. "They'd have to—"

"Only a notion," Straker said with a note of uncertainty.

Ghanning stepped up into the saddle, quartering the dun around as he looked down at them. "That's right So I'll go alone. You watch the damned cattle, Mr. Straker."

A tug of reins turned the lineback's head south from camp and he squeezed it into a trot Behind he heard the two men's strident lift of voices. As men did in a quandary, they might debate away the next fifteen minutes as to what should be done. Channing, with his independent way of incisive thought and action, wasn't waiting.

At a hard pace it would take him over an hour to achieve the Spur headquarters, and Santee had already had hours to make his move. Suppose it was a notion....logic could not shake cold conviction. He remembered the day in Judd's saloon, when he had seen Santee Dyker's ruthless ambition unmasked, and the man's self-avowed lack of scruple. By these old-time cattlemen's rough, stern code, to fight a fight by striking at a defenseless woman was illogical, but Santee would never cavil at means. In any case, he decided, Kristina's safety was nothing to take a chance on.

To conserve its strength Channing held the dun to a disciplined pace for a half hour. A thick ground mist had begun to cloud in swales and hollows, a milk-haze shroud through which upland trees reared like black jagged spires and great boulders were as sleeping cougars. The windless silence was eerie, sharpening the measured *clop* of his mount's hoofs.

He reined in to listen for a distinct sound caught briefly and lost again. Then it picked up once more a hundred yards off to his right. A single rider was passing in the paling murkiness, but he could make out nothing. About to hail the man, he changed his mind...no telling who might be riding this violence-shattered night. Though moving on, he regretted briefly his decision, realizing the unknown's direction was for the Spur camp, perhaps a bearer of some vital news. The thought lent fresh urgency to his certainty that Santee Dyker had only begun to fight. As the rough uplands melted away to the gentle contours of north Spur range, he let the horse out in a run....

In the clearer pre-dawn hours he rode at last into Spur. The main house was dark and still, squatting on its upper bench above the outbuildings. Overhead a storm was slowly building, angrily scudding dark clouds across the pearl-slated dawn. He went upslope to the house and swung stiffly to the ground. As he mounted the steps he had the wry thought: *More than likely you're going to look damned foolish in a minute, trying to explain this to her.* He hesitated, then hammered his fist on the door.

He waited before knocking again, then impatiently opened the door and went in. He moved across the parlor to grope down a murky corridor to Kristina's room. Sharp fear took him by the throat even in his half-expectation. The bedroom door was creaking ajar in a draft; the covers of the empty bed were mussed.

He realized he was shaking with a mingled complex of fear and hate, and he steadied down on it. *Don't go off half-cocked now; be sure.* He swiftly left the house and skirted the yard, searching the ground. There was recent sign of visitors, plenty of it in the soft dirt. The first fat drops of rain began as he crossed the yard at a run to reach his horse.

FOURTEEN

"Mr. Dawes," Anne LeCroix said, her controlled words not quite masking a faint tremof, "will you sit down... please."

Shilob was pacing Dr. McGilway's little waiting room like a caged bear, glaring unseeingly at some dirty lithographs on the wall. The building shook to a reverberating crash of thunder, rumbling off into the steady rattle of rain. He halted, turned to look at her. She was sitting in a sagging leather divan with a faded ducking jacket thrown over her shoulders, shivering a little. Her face was pale and drawn in the saffron lampglow as she kneaded a damp handkerchief between her palms.

"Yes'm," he muttered. The rusty springs of the divan launched a protesting creak as he settled down beside her.

139

He hunched forward, his thick fingers laced together, looking at the floor. Again he retreated within his glum thoughts, unaware of the woman till she spoke again, and gently.

"I'm sorry. This isn't an easy time for you either."

Shiloh rubbed his chin absently. His fist grated over the stubble silvering his mastiff jaws. Finally he shook his head. "It's taking him a sight of time in there."

"The bullet has to come out McGilway is a good man."

"He better be damn good," Shiloh said tonelessly. He sighed, letting his bulk slip loosely back against the cushions. "Bob was a heller in war...a born fighter any time. Outside that he's been mostly a close, cold-like sort. Ruth—his wife—she drew out the other side of him. Me too, once in a while," he added humbly, then with abrupt directness: "You'd be good for him."

"I want to be. I want to know him."

"Maybe you—" Shiloh broke off and got to his feet as Dr. McGilway, his slim, straight figure a little slumped, emerged quietly from the next room. His eyes blinked behind his steel-rimmed spectacles. He gave a jerky nod.

Shiloh released his breath, saying awkwardly to Anne, "I was saying—you'll maybe get the chance. He won't be doing much stomping for a while...."

"Can we—?" she asked hesitantly. The doctor nodded, stepped aside to let them enter. Thoroughgood was stretched full length on a table, half-covered by a sheet. His upper body was bare, the flesh below his deeply weathered face and neck of a startling paleness—not as white as the bandages that girthed his great chest. His eyes were closed and his breathing was deep and regular.

"He's under ether," Dr. McGilway said tiredly, removing his spectacles and tucking them in his vest pocket.

"It wasn't the wound as much as loss of blood. His clothes were soaked with it."

"He stuck in the saddle a good twenty minutes," Shiloh said pridefully. "Time to pump out a heap, wouldn't you say?"

Dr. McGilway gave a low whistle and nodded. "I'd say so. The man's a bull—and a damnably lucky one. That wagon ride here didn't do him any good either...."

Shiloh grunted soberly, eyeing the sleeping man with stern affection. It had been nip-and-tuck for sure.... Long before the linchpin had reached Sentinel, Thoroughgood was out of his head with fever and pain, tossing wildly about in the wagon bed while the *segundo* was torn between the need for haste and his fear of hitting up the team to a fast pace. Before reaching the wagon road, he'd met Doc Willis, the bartender from Judd's, who had blurted out something which was unintelligible because Shiloh had paid no heed.

He'd snarled at Doc to turn his cayuse and make tracks back for Sentinel, tell Dr. McGilway to set up for removing a bullet. Dr. McGilway and Anne LeCroix were waiting as Shiloh had pulled up by the doctor's office and they had gotten Thoroughgood inside, limp and silent now.

Now, as his first overwhelming relief subsided, Shiloh thought of Doc and his gasped message. He frowned, casting back in his wind for its import. He turned to Anne. "Doc Willis started to tell me somethin' when we met. Must have been important, fat gent like him cutting leather that far from town in the small hours."

Anne was bending over Thoroughgood, tenderly adjusting the sheet that covered him. "Have you any heavier covers, doctor? It'll be chilly for hours...." She half turned to Shiloh, gently massaging one temple with her fingers and frowning slightly. "Oh. I'd forgotten.... I sent Doc to tell Bob about that man. Guess it isn't so important now...."

"What man?"

"A stranger...named Landers. A bad one, gunman. He wore good clothes and he'd come a ways. Acted like he owned the place—insisted that Doc ride out and fetch Santee Dyker. Obvious that Santee had sent for him. I thought Bob ought to know right away....I took Doc aside and sent him on to your camp instead."

Shiloh's slow, methodical mind picked at it for a puzzled ten seconds. Santee had imported special talent. To Shiloh's loyally single-routed mind, that meant one thing: Santee was setting a deadfall for the man who spearheaded the opposition: Thoroughgood. Yes, it had to figure. No clumsy attempt, Santee wanted a sure thing. That Thoroughgood had already been laid low by a chance slug would not deter a professional killer. Shiloh's steerhorns twitched now with a grim smile. It might be for the best. A well Thoroughgood on his feet would stand no chance against this gunman in a face-down duel, Shiloh Dawes just might.

"He's still at your place?" Shiloh asked softly.

"When I left, yes. Doc Willis fetched me the back way, ánd I sent Doc home. If Landers knew that Doc was back without Santee, he might do—anything."

Shiloh gave a decisive tug to his hat brim, wheeled and stalked back to the anteroom. He picked up the Winchester he'd leaned against the wall.

"What are you going to do?"

Shiloh turned slowly, facing Anne in the doorway. "My guess, same as yours. He's here for Bob."

She moved quickly to him, her hand fastening on his

Wrist. "You haven't seen him. He's evil——dangerous. He'll kill you without twitching an eyelash."

"Difference is," Shiloh said heavily, "I can handle this kicker better'n most can a six-gun."

"But you're no gunman! Someone else, someone who could face him on his own terms—Channing—"

"Leave it be, missus. You see to Bob." Shiloh pulled her hand firmly away and stepped from the office. He blinked against a vivid fork of lightning splayed whitely across the sky, etching starkly the buildings across the street. As the thin rumble of thunder began, he hesitated.

This face-to-face business was not at all like a soldier's duty in war. There were no personalities on a battle line, civil war or range war. A face-down was different. That difference was a cold-blooded sickness in some men, and in others...he remembered Channing's face after he'd downed Whitey DeVore. It was a thing that could tear a man apart

So Shiloh groped in momentary hesitation. But Channing had ridden off to Spur on a probable wild-goose chase, for so Shiloh had convinced himself in his immediate anxiety to get Bob Thoroughgood to town without delay. *Anyway,* he reasoned with a spine-stiffening pride, *this is your job.* He owed Bob a life and more. Shiloh was not a complex man, and his thoughts swiftly refocused on the fierce loyalty to his friend that centered his life.

Resolutely he stepped off the walk, shoulders hunched against the steady pound of rain. He crossed the street, feeling the hard, cold reassurance of the Winchester against his palm and remembering how it'd been a strange matter of pride for him to master this weapon that other men used two-handed.

He shouldered through the batwings into Judd's, halted in the stifled atmosphere of stale liquor.

The man was sitting at a table in the otherwise deserted room, one arm flung over the back of his chair, his legs outstretched and negligently crossed. He gently set the shot glass he was holding on the table.

"Something, pappy?" he drawled torpidly.

The yellow dog was curled by his feet; it raised its head and showed its fangs at Shiloh. *His friend, one mean cur knows another,* Shiloh thought detachedly, hiking the rifle stock into his armpit, the barrel angling toward the floor.

"Yeah, something. I'm the man you want to see."

"Pappy, your name Dyker?"

"Not likely. You're here to kill a man."

Landers didn't stir a muscle. "You him?"

"No," Shiloh said gently. "His best friend."

"Ole One-wing," Landers murmured, "you're a sorry-lookin' ole bastard, sure enough, but in a second I'm like ter fergit your white hairs, dust your britches."

Shiloh's arm blurred in a movement that cocked the rifle of its lever-spun weight; in an unbroken movement he brought it level and fired. The bottle on the table by Landers' elbow exploded in a shower of glass and whiskey. Shiloh cocked the rifle again—waited. A bitter haze of burned powder stung the air.

Landers leisurely moved his arm from the table, brushed gently at the amber spots on his white shirt-front. "Pappy, you hadn't orter done that." He unwound like a rising cat, coming to his feet with an odd, loose-jointed grace. The dog was rumbling baleful hate at Shiloh. Landers gave it a sidelong kick that sent it slinking iaside, never ceasing its hateful snarls.

FIFTEEN

After leaving his horse tethered in a thick cottonwood grove on the south slope of the dipping vale where Anchor headquarters lay, Channing worked on foot down behind a big hayshed by the rambling maze of corrals. His yellow slicker blended neutrally with the drab, withered grass of the slope, and he took advantage of what scanty cover was afforded by bushes and boulders, though the slashing rain which dimmed the outlines of the buildings alone should have concealed his approach.

Darting in a crouching run, rifle in hand, he achieved the corner of the shed and peered at the shape of the main house through the rain. The curled brim of his low-jerked hat formed a trough that channeled down a stream of water ahead of his face, and he nudged the hat back,

145

its slant then dribbling a chill runnel inside his collar and down his backbone. It shocked away the hot residue of clogging temper.

He sank onto his haunches, the rifle across his knees. Maybe it had been a fool's game coming here alone. His thoughts were a chaotic blur after realizing that Kristina had been taken. He had cut straightaway for the wagon road fork-off that led to Anchor, and short of his goal had made a circuitous swing-around that brought him up by the south. It was a grim reminder that he'd come to Anchor this roundabout way before, tracking Bee Withers. Yet even that time his intention had not approached the dogged, feral determination that drove him now.

With the hot edge of his wrath blunted a little, he could concede the thoughtlessness of this headlong pursuit of the abductors. But now, speculating coolly, he thought that after all it made sense. To have returned to the Spur camp for help would have consumed precious time. Then, mustering the Mexican Bit crews to a mass rescue could only trigger a bloody battle and add to Kristina's danger. This job was for a loner, which was how he thought and acted best.

Still, a sense of aching futility ground his teeth on edge. The storm which gave him cover had its liability; he had no way of telling how many men might be up in the house where Kristina must be, whether any lookouts were stationed at windows. He could have told much from the small sights and sounds of a clear day. The bunkhouse was shrouded in by the pouring storm and a single dim lamp burned in a window there—another in a front room of the main house. If anyone was watching they'd surely spot him if he crossed the open ground near the house.

He rubbed his slicker sleeve across his wet face, hunched his shoulders in a shrug. It was all chance and no choice. He'd make for the rear of the house and the kitchen entrance, let himself in that way. Moving in silence through the darkened rooms to the front, he might be able to surprise them with no risk to Kristina.

He came to his feet, lunged along the east flank of the corrals to the stables and carriage shed close by the house, edging down the foot-narrow alley between them. Ahead lay fifty feet of open yard. He left the mouth of the alley, running full-tilt across the yard, slipping and thrown off-stride by clay mud which balled his boot-soles. He reached a corner by the back porch, flattened against the wall as he edged up the steps and across the porch planking to the nearest window. The kitchen was dark; he made out nothing but a murky gleam of dirty pans heaped in a tub. He leaned his rifle against the wall, unbuttoned his slicker to ready his pistol for close quarters. Then he bent to remove his boots.

Palming up his gun, he moved, weight on his sock toes, to the door and noiselessly opened it. As he stepped into the kitchen and started to close the door, the knob was wrenched from his hand by a savage kick.

A gun muzzle was thrust against his ribs with a savage force that drew a pained grunt from him. But he was motionless; a slight trigger-pressure of a cocked gun was faster than any man's reflexes. The man who'd been behind the door gave a rasping chuckle as he warily reached to lift the gun from Channing's hand.

"We kep' a lookout, bucko. Case some lone fool came hell-roaring in like you. They's men in every room. You'd a been spotted from any side. Move ahead, bucko. Keep your hands out in sight."

Arms half-raised, Channing moved to the vicious prod in his side. Down a corridor leading off the kitchen, through a dining room where two gunnies lounged by the windows. They only glanced passingly at Channing and his guard; one made an obscene joshing comment which the guard returned. In the lighted parlor beyond an archway, the sound of low talk broke off at their approach.

Channing took in the front room at a glance, seeing the three men—Santee Dyker, his foreman, and his nephew ——then seeing nobody but Kristina. She was small and straight-backed in a big armchair, her face deathly pale, matching the white fichu collar of her dark blue dress. A low, almost imploring "No" left her lips as she saw Channing. She half-rose and then sank back resignedly. Her shoulders slumped; he saw some of the courage that sustained her drain away hopelessly.

His guard pushed Channing to the center of the room, and now Channing took in the rest of its occupants. Streak Duryea, leaning against the wall, absently rubbed his cloth-slung arm. He met Channing's stare smilingly, murmuring, "Well, well." Ward Costello gripped the arms of his chair with whitened knuckles, nervous fear shuttling across his wooden features.

Santee Dyker, an elbow propped negligently on the mantel and facing Kristina, tossed his cigar in the cold fireplace and pushed away from it, saying dryly, "Stop shaking, Ward. Your prayers to whatever gods have been answered. Good work, Elam."

The chunky man who'd captured Channing said, "Want I should get back in the kitchen?"

Santee motioned at Streak, who slipped his gun from its bolster with his left hand and trained it loosely on Channing, drawling, "All right, Elam."

The guard left. All of them looked at Santee who had come to stand behind Kristina's chair, his thin fingers softly tattooing its backrest. Channing felt warm sweat mingle with the raindrops on his face and trickle down his neck and chest, saying now, softly: "Didn't miss a trick, did you, Santee?"

"My dear fellow," Santee murmured, "that I enjoy a good gamble doesn't mean I don't believe in cutting the odds as low as possible—by whatever means."

"They hurt you?" Channing asked Kristina, and her lips formed, "Not yet."

"She's a fine, tough-minded girl," Santee observed. "She fought us all the way here—but showed no fear until Elam brought you in. Exactly what does that mean, Channing?"

"You tell me."

Santee smiled. "I won't bother. However, it may be a useful fact, one I'll bear in mind. Just now—how many men came with you?"

"Just me."

"Don't stall me." Santee's smile flattened; he made a slight threatening gesture at Kristina which she could not see.

Channing said huskily, "No stall. I came alone. I had an idea you might do something of the sort, came to Spur to find out."

"Without telling Thoroughgood or the others?"

"They didn't agree with me."

Santee nodded slowly. "Quite possibly. They're a simple pack, these basin dogs. Wouldn't believe that even *I* would harm a woman. I'm apt to do a sight worse, you know."

"I know," Channing said thinly.

"You do, don't you?" Santee said equably. "You have a rare habit of merciless honesty about people and life. So do I. No illusions. But it must be hellishly hard on a man with your scruples....Anyway, we'll take no chances." He raised his voice, ordering one of the gunnies in the next room to check the grounds, and the man tramped out.

Santee circled the chair to face Kristina. "Till now I've reasoned with you, Miss Nilssen, and very logically. A gesture doubtless wasted, since women are creatures of neither reason nor logic. However, I'll ask once more—"

"The answer is the same," Kristina said stonily, but it lacked conviction; she gave Channing a frightened glance.

"Yes," Santee said pleasantly, "which brings us back to that useful fact I mentioned. Follow me, Streak?"

"Channing?" Streak said gently, and when Santee nodded he moved away from the wall, jammed his gun hard in the small of Channing's back and cocked it. The metallic *snack* of the hammer made Kristina jerk erect.

"Have you ever watched a man—or even an animal—die with a torn spine, Miss Nilssen? To sever it clean would mean instant death, but there are ways of placing a bullet that mean extreme agony or permanent paralysis for the victim." Santee delivered the words as coolly and precisely as a pathological lecture.

Kristina leaned forward, gripping the chair arms. "Stop it," she whispered. "I'll give you anything. But stop it."

"Don't stop it, Streak," Santee said conversationally. "As you are till Miss Nilssen has put her signature on certain papers." He walked briskly to a cabinet and rummaged in a drawer, producing several folded documents.

"This—" he tapped the topmost paper—"is the deed to Spur. One of my men experienced in such matters removed it from Lawyer Wainwright's safe last night. This other is a quitclaim for your lease on old Brock's Strip. And a bill of sale for your cattle. Other necessary papers to facilitate transferral of property, as drawn up by a shyster friend of mine. We'll bring Brock around later."

"You've gone too far," Channing said softly. "That won't stand up—"

"The odd thing is—it will, horseherd. A man bold and imaginative enough can circumvent any law. The average man will break obscure statutes and the like, but is restrained from large crimes by his social conscience— which is mostly fear of punishment. The ordinary criminal is too hampered by limitations of caution and narrow greed to make a big, clean sweep. Even your land-grabbing cattle baron is basically a simple frontier lout who understands only blind force and a few clumsy extra-legal devices. Don't judge me by any of these; the big gamble is my forte, refined chicanery and judiciously applied force are my methods."

He's puffing his crop like a banty, Channing thought, yet he had to concede the truth, however one-sided, in Santee's cynical philosophy.

"See here—" Santee waved the papers—"Cholla, the county seat, is remote from our troubles. The authorities there will be ignorant of, even indifferent to, our little tableau here. Should the situation be referred to them, they'll be interested in nothing but the concreteness of these documents...as they'll be attested by a greasy-thumbed notary of my acquaintance."

"But signed under duress."

Santee merely smiled, dipped a quill pen in an inkwell in the cabinet drawer, and laid the papers on the arm of Kristina's chair. He extended the quill to Kristina; she automatically took it, painfully scrawling her name on each paper as Santee spread it out and placed his finger on the proper place.

Santee refolded the papers and tucked them in his coat pocket. He produced a cigar, carefully nipped the end with his gold cutter and lighted it. Against the bite of fragrant smoke, he squinted at Channing. "Yes…it would be awkward were both you and Miss Nilssen to swear she signed under duress. It might even hamstring *my* story, which will be that Miss Nilssen, sickened by the bloodshed, came to me and offered to sell out. Naturally I took advantage of the offer. I will say moreover that Miss Nilssen told me that she wished now only to get shed of this basin and everybody in it—a not unnatural woman's reaction under the circumstances—that rather than wait for the train she would ride to Cholla on horseback and there take the first train back to Minnesota. Thoroughgood is not likely to contest my story, though little matter; he can be taken care of precisely as Custis Thursday—as you two will be."

"That your idea too, Streak?" Channing asked quietly.

"Why, it was me beefed Thursday, bucko-boy. Didn't you guess that?"

Channing felt a cold sinking in his guts, though he'd known from the moment Kristina had agreed to sign that Santee could not afford to let either of them live. But he might at least save the Spur foreman…."You've done enough to Thoroughgood," he said quietly. "He caught a bullet last night."

Kristina gave a dismayed cry. Slowly Santee took the cigar from his mouth, studying Channing. "Dead?"

"Bad hurt. Shiloh Dawes was taking him in to the

doctor when I left. He came to long enough to say he was ready to quit."

"*Quit!*"

Channing, surprised at Kristina's sharply objecting cry, said, "He thought you'd want to."

"Ah, now I've had my eyes opened," she murmured bitterly. "Mr. Dyker opened them. To worse than dying."

Santee gave her a speculative regard, saying musingly, "Strange words...your hatred of violence was natural in a woman. Then—you're young, spirited, everything to live for, even with no cattle kingdom."

Her defiance was cold and stirring. "I've seen a lot of death, Mister Dyker. I have seen those dear to me kill and be killed. It made me afraid for a long time. Maybe, I think now, Kristina, you're selfish. It was for me I was afraid. I'm afraid still, very much. Only I think there will be no life worth living while things like you live. If I had a gun—"

"You'd shoot me? There's a little lady," Santee said dryly. "So Thoroughgood's lost the will to fight? Good, I'll ride to town presently and look in on him, show him these documents. They should be the final convincer, along with my story. And Lawyer Wainwright is a chicken-

hearted old fool who can be scared into keeping his mouth shut about the stolen deed...."

"One thing," Channing said softly. "Just how is she supposed to have learned what happened last night to the herd, to her crew, before she came to you?"

"Why, you told her, horseherd," Santee chuckled. "You solved that detail by blundering in here. You left Spur camp last night to ride to Spur headquarters, worried about her. But you found her safe—my story—and told her everything. She came to see me, you accompanied her. When she announced her intention of leaving the basin, you said you'd ride with her, and I saw no more of either of you. I've already had her few belongings brought from Spur; they'll be burned. You see? You both simply —drop out of sight." A salvo of thunder trampled on the heel of his words, trembling the house.

"Bob will not believe you," Kristina said tonelessly. "He knows us, Channing and me. He will not believe any of this."

"I think he will," Santee said blandly. "Thoroughgood is well aware of your aversion to violence. Channing says he believes you want to sell out now, and I saw your violent reaction before him that day in Sentinel when I told you of our kidnapping of Brock. As for Channing's leaving with you—my dear, a blind fool could see the man's infatuated with you. Oh, Thoroughgood will believe me...though he'd be near helpless if he didn't. Badly wounded. Nothing to fight for."

Kristina stood slowly, her fists clenched at her sides. She did not try to hide her fear. It strengthened her defiance. "Yes, you think of everything, Mister Dyker. Except one. Justice."

" 'A higher power than men's,' my dear?" Santee mocked. "You're snatching at straws in the wind, I'm a realist, and I'll take the chance." His tone became a brusque command. "Streak, get a couple of the men—"

"Santee." For the first time since Channing had entered the room, Costello had spoken. A heated eagerness flushed his sallow face. "Let me have them. Me and Bee."

Santee cocked an eyebrow. "You got brave of a sudden. You were shaking in your boots, minute ago."

Costello's flush deepened. "I have that much coming," he said sullenly. "Blowing his dirty—"

Santee cut him off disgustedly. "I've never doubted your ability to put a gun to an unarmed man's head—pull the trigger. That does take your kind of whiskey-guts, I suppose....Very well. Take Channing and the girl well away from the ranch. Find a cutbank to cave over the bodies, and it shouldn't take you long. The rain will wipe out any sign."

"We'll be back in no time," Costello grinned feverishly.

"I think not," Santee said gently. "No, Ward. Channing will be disposed of, and that's what you were waiting on. Afterward—you and your heel-dog keep riding. I don't want to find you here when I return from Sentinel."

SIXTEEN

They rode the narrow trail single file where it followed the bank of a tortuous gully, formerly dry and now roiling foot-deep with silted water. Channing headed the file with Costello behind him and then Kristina, Bee Withers bringing up the rear. On one side the gully, on the other a low-rising slope mantled with shaggy pine. The rain had thinned off to a fine drizzle which grayed the landscape to spectral outlines a few yards beyond a man's face.

Channing shivered, feeling the cold damp to his bones despite his high-buttoned slicker. The dread of death had long ago been absorbed into his daily philosophy; the impact of its present certainty did not shake his outward composure. But for Kristina?

He'd hardly dared admit to himself before now the

simple goodness and far more with which she'd touched
his life. There was a thing inevitable in the course of a
man's life and a woman's that nothing on earth had a
right to disrupt. It was this that shook Channing, and not
the death every man must taste, the furious and hating
knowledge that the best thing he'd ever know was ended before it had begun.

He lashed his mind for every possible way out; immediately, there was ncme. The pouring gully on one side
and the timbered slope on the other blocked a sudden
side-dash, even if his back hadn't been an easy target.

He looked over his shoulder at the three slow-pacing
figures behind—Costello and Kristina muffled in glisten-
ing slickers, Withers' grease-fouled denims shedding rain
nearly as well. Costello tilted the glinting revolver in his
right hand, reining his horse with his left. His eyes were
gleaming slits beneath a forward-tilted derby.

"No way out, Channing. How does it feel, death on
your neck? You made me feel it. Dogging me across the
territory." He laughed, a hysterical note in it. "Santee
was damned near right—I was close to praying for a
chance like this."

Channing looked ahead again. *No way out.* But Costello had Santee's absolute immorality without Santee's
guile or guts; Costello was all bluster, using an advantage that his uncle had set up. You could expect Costello
to make a mistake, and in his desperation Channing
knew he must seize the first opportunity.

The land began to mount, and the downstream flow of
the gully had subsided to a trickle as the party broke
from the crowding timber into a broad swath of clearing. Costello ordered a halt, and Kristina and Bee drew
up beside them.

Withers crossed his hands on the pommel and spat thinly over one shoulder. "She's flowin' light here, Ward. Nice high banks, pull one down easy. Won't have to drag the carcasses far, just roll 'em down the side."

Costello nodded, taking his eyes off Channing for a flicking instant. "It'll do. Tell you what, Channing...I'll give you a running chance. Kick in your spurs, head for the far end of the clearing. An interesting spectacle for your lady friend, eh?"

Channing looked at Withers with his slack grin, at Costello's sadistic intensity; lastly at Kristina. She raised her head, and though she seemed pathetically lost in a man's oversize slicker he saw something flicker through the unspeaking resignation of her face. He met her eyes, saying nothing because these two men would soil it. Knowing that he had to take the chance now.

Or never.

He reined away from the others and slammed his spurs in. Halfway across the clearing an arm of dense young trees, averaging six feet in height, extended from the wall of forest. He veered hard toward the heavy growth, body drawn together against the expected bullet. He strained low in the saddle, knowing Costello would never let him reach the opposite wall of the clearing. In a moment he would be carried past the thicket's sanctuary; it must be exactly timed....

Now. He freed his right foot from the stirrup, cocked his leg up, and launched his body sideways as the gun thundered less than a foot past the outmost edge of the thicket. Body balled up and hands shielding his face, he lit squarely on the springy topcover. Branches and twigs gouged his body as he plunged through. For a moment a tangled network of lower branches broke his fall, but they gave way and he landed amid the close-set trunks, free of foliage at their bases.

He heard Costello's yell of rage. On hands and knees he squirmed between the trunks, working toward the deep shelter of the forest. There was a burst of gunfire, lashing the spot where he'd fallen, then a sound of running feet.

Channing lunged to his feet, bursting through the dripping undergrowth heedless of the noise. Three more shots, one whipping inches from his head. The underbrush abruptly gave way to a wide swath of springy needle floor beneath towering pines and he ran low and soundlessly, dived over a deadfall and lay hugging the mossy trunk.

He heard the footsteps slow, the approach cautious now. He raised his head enough to see Bee Withers, head ducked, flailing through the brush straight in his direction.

He flattened out again. His heart thudded against the dank earth. He listened, heard Withers pause, apparently to scan the woods, and then swing slightly toward the left. His steps receded. From where Channing lay he glimpsed the man's gaunt back vanishing deeper into the forest.

With infinite care Channing stood and started back toward the clearing, calling on his tracker's lore and patience to approach without a shadow of sound. He could get away...but there was Kristina. And he had to get his hands on a gun.

He reached the clearing's edge, sank down behind a screening of leaves. Where the horses stood, Kristina still mounted, was Costello—gun in hand, staring fearfully about. Channing knelt and searched the loam for a pebble. He settled for a heavy, rotting pine-knot. He stood swiftly, hefting it in his palm as he waited for Costello to look away. Then he lobbed the knot in a high arc across the clearing with all the strength of his arm. It crashed in some bushes.

Costeilo made a bleating noise in his throat, whirling at the sound. He fired once. Then he advanced slowly. For a moment he paused, poking aside the thickets with his gun. He wallowed in, noisily beating his way.

Channing left cover and ran for the horses. Kristina gave a low cry, and he yelled, "Get back!" as he reached Withers' mare. The animal shied away and he leaped after it, yanking the saddle carbine from its boot. He swung around at the crashing of brush, levering the carbine; Withers had pounded into sight and was heading for him.

Withers began shooting wildly. Channing aimed from the hip as he turned, then, at the moment the rifle barrel hung steady and hip-braced, he shot. Withers folded at the middle. He clamped his arms across his belly, yet Channing knew he'd hit higher—a detached thought as he watched Withers twist in a graceless fall.

There was a rustle of soggy leaves where Costello had disappeared—and silence. Channing shot once, deliberately high. Costello's squeal was of abject fear, not pain. Channing was in pistol-range; Costeilo had the shelter, but abruptly he broke down and began to sob weakly like a weary child.

"Toss the gun out. First. You follow," Channing called.

"Yes, yes, don't shoot," Costeilo sobbed huskily. A pause, then the gun sailed from the bushes. Costeilo emerged, his hands raised, and slogged emptily across the sodden ground toward Channing. With the sharp draining of tension, Channing lowered the rifle.

At once Costello's arm blurred down; the Derringer cracked wickedly. The force of the near-quarter slug was weakened by the distance between them, but its hot, furrowing impact along his forearm numbed Channing's fingers on the rifle. *Damn fool, forgot that sleeve-rig!* The clear thought flailed against the blinding pain-flash.

He threw himself forward, and the hard slam of rising earth shocked his body to sentience. He heard Costello running, saw dimly his slicker skirts flapping. Awkwardly, frantically, he worked the carbine lever, bracing the stock against the ground as he swung up the barrel. The sights crossed Costello's body looming above; the gambler had to be close to make his remaining bullet certain.

The blasts of their weapons were almost one. Costello's gouged a muddy geyser; he jerked, seemed only to wobble in his run; actually he finished one pumping stride before he plunged down, skidding on his face in a puddle.

Channing lay a moment sucking in breath and hearing Kristina's voice but not her words. He did not have to look at Costello; he did not want to. He climbed to his feet and walked slowly over to Bee Withers. Withers lay face up; rain laved his open eyes and mouth.

He turned to Kristina as she came running up, just looked at her till she said his name. He said: "It's done. No more butchering. You hear me?" He stopped, realizing he didn't know what he was saying.

"Yes—yes." She took his arm and peeled back the slicker. It was a scratch, but he said nothing as she tore a strip from her petticoat and tied it around his forearm.

Timidly she touched his cheek. "Do you feel all right?"

He tried to remember his father's accusing voice, and could not. This was right, there was the difference. He had done it for Kristina, not for revenge. The numbness slipped away as he looked at her. "All right...."

SEVENTEEN

It was late afternoon when they rode into Sentinel. The rain had ceased, but the murky overcast had not lifted and early lamps burned in most windows. Kristina was exhausted, lurching slackly in the saddle as they rode stirrup to stirrup down the main street which was now a muddy channel wagon-rutted by long black pools catching yellow shimmers from the windows.

By the Stockman's Bar Channing pulled his horse around on a tight rein, seeing the five horses lined hipshot at the crowded tie rail, all branded Anchor. Kristina followed his glance. "No, Channing."

"Santee's got those papers you signed. If he gets them to Cholla, into the county records, you stand to lose everything."

"No," she repeated.

"You said yourself, there's a time to fight." He almost added, *and a time to die.*

"Please, not you. There are five of them, you have no chance. Spur I can stand to lose. But no more!" He sat motionless till she said pleadingly, "Come along, we must see Bob. Come along now."

They rode on without words. Channing dismounted by the doctor's office opposite Judd's saloon and assisted Kristina down, helping her over the slippery mud to the steps. They went into the waiting room. It was deserted, but the door to the inner office was open, and they entered softly.

Anne LeCroix sat in a chair drawn up to the table where Thoroughgood lay. He was sleeping, breathing evenly, and Kristina released a breath of relief. Anne's head was bent; she was dozing lightly, but now she glanced swiftly up at them.

"Channing. Oh, I'm glad to see you!"

"Where's Shiloh?"

Anne swallowed, her eyes wavering from his. "The doctor's out on a house call," she said almost inaudibly. "I—suppose this is Miss Nilssen?"

"Miss Nilssen, Mrs. LeCroix," he said tersely. Kristina nodded to the older woman, her sober glance moving then to Channing's tense face. She looked again at Anne, levelly and almost sternly. "Mr. Dawes is gone? He did bring Bob in?"

Anne bent her face against her palm; sobs shook her. "Yes, he's gone! Gone, Miss Nilssen!" Her voice was choked and muffled. "He thought he had to defend Bob, I suppose—or your damned ranch—"

"What happened?" Channing laid his words down cold and hard.

Kristina moved compassionately to Anne, bent and put her arms around the woman. Channing's tone was gentled by the pathetic incongruity of a woman he'd thought of as worldly and hard-shelled being comforted by Kristina, a young and barely sophisticated girl with a hatred of violence. "What happened, Anne?"

He listened still-faced as she told of the stranger who had come into her place late last night, demanding that Doc Willis fetch Santee to him—how she had sent Doc after Thoroughgood. She had not recovered from the shock of seeing Bob in this condition when Shiloh, convinced that the stranger had been brought to assassinate Thoroughgood, had gone into the saloon to face him out.

"He wouldn't listen to me, these men don't listen to a woman," Anne said with deep bitterness. "I asked Dr. McGilway to try talking him out of it...but as we started across the street, we heard the shot." Her voice went small and lost and she absently patted Kristina's shoulder. "Well, it was too late. Though I expect we couldn't have stopped him, and certainly not that Landers. McGilway and I carried the body over here, it's in a back room. Didn't want Bob to see...in his condition...."

"Landers," Channing said under his breath. He remembered the name and the man. Prescott, nearly three years ago—a street shoot-out. A rustler named Ory Thomason, one of the Hashknife outfit, later said to have quarreled with Landers over a split-up of loot, had cut down on the Tennesseean from an alley. Channing had seen it—Thomason wildly emptying his gun at Landers' back while the tall man turned almost casually. Nobody had seen his gun come out, but Ory Thomason was dead before he hit the ground. Landers was of a breed hired to do the lone and big and dirty-secret jobs. A man with ice in his veins had an edge, no matter what his opponent's skill.

Anne was looking at him wide-eyed. "Don't think of it, Channing. He's like nothing you've ever seen."

"I was thinking of Santee," he answered evasively.

"Oh...yes. He rode up an hour or so ago. Wanted to see Bob, had something to show him, he said. I told him if he came in here I'd scratch his eyes out. He laughed, said he'd be back, and went on down the street—to the Stockman's, I guess. But he has four of his men."

"He's still there," Channing said grimly. "You told him about Landers?"

"No. I thought if their meeting were delayed—you or somebody might come before he was sent after Bob." She added, "But I won't ask you to face him; I have a gun in case he comes." From her lap she lifted a little pocket pistol, concealed in the folds of her skirt.

Channing was silent a thoughtful moment. Both Shiloh and Anne had assumed that Landers would be sent to gun Thoroughgood, a tragic assumption that had cost Shiloh Dawes his life. It could be that he, Channing, was the man for whom they'd brought a special killer, shortly after that fiasco with Brock at the line shack. Couple that with the fact that Santee would have wanted to be rid of Channing for his nephew's sake. The thought automatically led to another, crystallizing into the germ of an idea. Landers himself might not know the name of the man or men he'd come hundreds of miles to kill; he was not the type to care, a job was a job....

"Landers'll still be at your place?" he asked Anne.

"Oh, he's there, large as any tin god; he's taken it over. Waiting for Doc Willis to return with Santee. I'd told him Santee was camped back in the hills, it would take time to bring him in...."

Chinning turned and walked slowly out to the waiting room, leaning his shoulder against the open outside doorway to stare bleakly across at the single rawboned nag hitched at Judd's tie rail. A foolish damned notion, probably unworkable. Still, if Landers had never met Santee face to face...like Santee himself—why not take a gamble?

He turned his head at Kristina's light footsteps; her contained face did not hide her worry. "I don't want you going across there!"

"Got an idea. See what you think of it."

She listened gravely till he'd finished and then said irrelevantly, "That Mrs. LeCroix—she loves Bob."

"Well, he'll be needing her now."

"Needing—who cares about his needs! Channing, I am trying....Do I have to say it?" As he started to speak, she turned away, pressing her hands to her temples. "A good girl is not to be shamed this way. You make me ashamed."

Almost roughly he turned her by the shoulders to face him. "Will you let a man say something—Kristina?"

EIGHTEEN

He had not intended to say anything, yet having said it he felt a lightening in him as he crossed the muddy thoroughfare to Judd's. The other day he had left a barrier of harsh words between them, shaming Kristina's pride by withholding his feelings. Regretting now his too-harsh and uncompromising self-respect that had not let him retract those words, knowing since the moment he'd realized her danger last night that he wanted no life without her, he had left her with the glowing certainty that no matter what happened now, all would be well.

She's still a child in some ways, he thought with the ingrained pessimism of experience. He was tense-muscled, pushing through the batwings of Judd's. But the Spur crew had lost stomach for further fight, Thoroughgood

169

was out of it…Shiloh Dawes was dead. It was up to him.

Brace Landers raised his shaggy head, his eyes bloodshot from sleeplessness as Channing came to the table and swung a chair out, straddling it, giving the snarling yellow cur only a glance before saying, quietly, "All right, Landers."

Landers' hand was arrested in mid-motion, reaching for a quarter-empty bottle. "Expected an older man."

"I'm not Santee Dyker. His man."

Landers' slaty stare was expressionless. "Took you a spell."

"Our camp's way back in the hills, took the barkeep a time to find us."

"How's Bee?"

Withers sent for him, Channing was on safe ground so far, with Withers out of the way. "Well. Sends his regards."

"Seen your face some'eres."

"Possible."

"Never fergit a face."

Channing tensed, seeing a dull glint of suspicion in the opaque eyes. Then realized that suspicion would be an automatic reflex with this man. "I was there time you downed Ory Thomason in Prescott Didn't think you'd remember…."

"Never fergit a face. You wasn't with the wild bunch."

"Not then. Was mustanging under the Tonto Rim."

This seemed to satisfy Landers. Golden glints raced along his glass as he raised it to the light, squinting at it.

"Like to do my talkin' with Dyker, cousin," he said softly.

"No need, the man you're to kill is in the Stockman's Bar. I can point him out."

Landers set his glass down gently. "Deal was fer a thousand cash, five hundred advance, same after the job."

Think fast. Channing held his face to utter calm before the gunman's probing stare. Then he remembered the moneybelt strapped beneath his shirt, holding the proceeds from the abortive mustanging venture. "Right here," he said lazily. He tugged out his shirt, opened the belt and counted out five hundred of the seven hundred and fifty-odd dollars it contained.

Landers pocketed the greenbacks without looking at them, downed one drink, sleeved his mouth and stood up.

"You show me that there bar."

Channing ted the way from Judd's with Landers stalking behind, the yellow dog trotting apace the gunman. Channing knew a cold and thorough hatred for the man which nullified his distaste for the savage deceit of the venture. He himself would have to face the guns of Santee's four hirelings the moment he set foot in the Stockman's. Landers, a strange face, would pass unrecognized. It was the only way.

As they pulled abreast of the Stockman's he turned to Landers. "Hold up. I,ll have a look." He walked on to the big half-frosted window and looked into the smoke-hazed interior.

The Stockman's had a certain tawdry dignity with its mahogany bar and brass foot rail and a reclining nude done in oils on the back-bar wall. The room was fairly crowded with merchants and townsmen, doubtless because the bad weather had decimated business, and this was their customary port of pleasure while most of the cowboys and rougher element frequented Judd's. Santee Dyker was seated at a rear table, dealing faro to three men in business suits, his eyes slightly squinted against wreathing smoke from his mouth-clamped Havana. Channing's eyes moved on, seeking Streak Duryea at the bar with three other men in range clothes.

Channing stepped back, almost colliding with Landers, who had moved silently up behind him. "How's it lay, cousin?"

Channing said low-voiced, "Your man's sitting at a table, left, rear of room, with three other men. He's about my size, thin, in his fifties. Graying blond hair, and he's wearing a light gray Stetson and a tan clawhammer coat." Channing paused deliberately. "He'll rile slow."

Landers slid out his horn-butted pistol, twirled the cylinder. "No law in this town, cuz?"

"No."

"Good, won't waste time choosin' him, no need for self-defense plea. Don't reckon no lily-innard counter-jumpers'll hinder me from ridin' out."

"That's your bet," Channing said softly. He moved back as Landers turned away, and when the batwings had swung to behind the man, he pivoted and went back down the street, walking fast. He felt no regret for Santee, a self-admitted murderer: only a strong revulsion for having to bring about his execution by this ugly deception. What Landers did not know was that the guns of Santee's four men would be turned on him the moment he fired. But if they didn't get him?

Channing reached the tie rail in front of Judd's. He tramped out into the muddy street and about-faced, watching the Stockman's twin doors. Landers had killed Shiloh. Sooner or later he would learn how Channing had duped him. It added to one thing: Landers had to be faced, and now. Channing slipped his gun from the holster.

From the Stockman's a shot hammered down the stillness. There was stunned silence, then a sustained outburst of gunfire.

The batwings sprang wide ahead of Landers coming out, his gangly frame crouch-bent with catlike grace as he pivoted smoothly and fired twice into the Stockman's barroom. Then he loped down the boardwalk toward his horse, the dog bounding behind.

Landers hauled up short on the walk under a porch awning. He was breathing hard; blood from a crease on his temple dyed his hair a deeper red and made a ragged trickle down his jaw.

His voice was deadly-gentle. "You didn't tell me he had gun-hangin' friends there, cousin." His gun dangled in his big fist at his side.

"You got handed some taffy, Brace," Channing murmured. "You just killed Santee Dyker. I'm the man. One you were supposed to gun."

Landers' breathing was a harsh sweep of sound. "You wasn't as smart as you thought, cousin," he whispered at last, and still he did not move, and Channing watched his face. When Channing saw the first break of decision, he started his move. He beat Landers' lift of arm by a fraction so that their shots did not quite merge. Landers' bloomed mud from the street as he buckled backward against the porch column. There was time for only fleeting astonishment to seize his face as he caught the second bullet. He rocked away from the column like a suddenly emptied grain sack and fell full length on the planking.

Channing sheathed his gun and took two steps forward. Then a bristling ball of yellow fury was streaking toward him, rising in a two-yard leap and slamming into his chest. Channing staggered, keeping his feet. He threw a forearm across his throat as the cur's fangs snapped for it. He felt the tearing pain in his arm simultaneously with the hot sear of a slug along his ribs. The dog's body jerked with the shot ripping squarely through it. Its falling weight carried Channing down to one knee before the jaws loosened on his arm.

A slug intended for Channing had killed the dog. His gun was already in hand, his eyes raking down the store fronts to the Stockman's. The man's hat rolled off with his sudden turn, exposing the bar of gleaming white in his hair as he quickly faded back through the batwings.

Channing sprinted down the street and lunged the swing doors with level gun.

And lowered it.

Brace Landers had done a full and bloody job of it. Santee was limply sprawled across the overturned table —beneath one trailing hand was a loose fan of cards. One of the Anchor men lay motioniessiy twisted on the floor. Another was sitting down against the bar, whimpering incoherently as he held his belly. The chunky man whom Channing recognized was leaning against the bar gripping a bloody shoulder, and he turned pain-glazed eyes.

"No fight," he said huskily. "Nothin' to fight for. Santee dead...."

"Tell it to your friends at Anchor, Elam," Channing said flatly. "Then clear out of the basin, the lot of you. I just want Streak."

Elam's head tilted tirediy against his chest. "Back way," he whispered.

Channing straight-armed two gaping merchants roughly aside as he went down the long room to Santee's crumpled body. He found the sheaf of documents, pocketed them. Then he moved to the rear door, stepped aside as he carefully turned the knob and abruptly flung the door wide.

A gun roared in the yard behind the building, gnawing a long splinter from the doorjamb. Then there was a rush of running feet. Channing went out the door as Streak left the shelter of a pile of stacked lumber, vaulted a hedge and scuttled across the adjoining yard. He wheeled at the corner of the next building, got off another wild shot before vanishing streetward between the buildings.

Channing catfooted down the areaway between the Stockman's and the adjacent mercantile store, reaching the sidewalk simultaneously with Duryea.

"Streak!" He made the name high and taunting, stepping
back within the areaway as Streak shot again, and again, wildly. Then Channing walked out, leathering his gun. Streak's fleeting grimace of triumph faded as his hammer fell on the loadless sixth chamber.

Channing walked straight for the Spur foreman. "Drop it, Streak...."

Streak lifted the clubbed gun—undecided. Then a gray courage sank across his lean face like a resigned shrug. He tossed the gun aside as he came on.

Channing sank under Streak's lunging straight-arm swing, brought his shoulder up into the man's midriff as he straightened, and the breath soughed from Streak's lungs. As Channing took a backward step, Streak bent with the pain, tried too late to rally. Channing hit him, driving him off the walk. Streak stumbled but kept his feet as Channing bored in relentlessly. A second blow arched Streak across the tie rail, bent at the waist. Channing whipped a down-chopping blow as though driving a nail with his fist against Streak's shelving jaw. The crosspole broke rottenly under Streak's weight and dumped him in the dirt He lit on his shoulder, rolled over once and was still.

Breathing gustily, Channing swung to face the muttering merchants clustering the walk. "Where's that prairie-dog jail? It was Duryea ambushed Custis Thursday."

The talk ebbed into silence.

Channing said softly, "Santee and Anchor've made their last tracks. One more time. The last. Where's your jail?"

A pudgy man toying with his watch chain hesitantly cleared his throat. "The log shack other side of the livery."

Channing bent, caught Streak by the wrists and dragged him semi-erect, then stooped to let the limp form collapse across his shoulders. He straightened in the same smooth motion and trudged to the jail. Nudging the heavy oak door open with his boot, he let Streak down on the floor. A wooden crossbar leaned against the wall. He closed the door, dropped the bar into its outside brackets with a hard, final slap of his palm. Holding kangaroo court on this one would be the sole pleasure of Spur people, them alone.

He turned down the street with the day's first thin shafts of sunlight topping the town's ramshackle outline washing against his tired and lid-narrowed eyes, and that was all, it was finished and it was ended, running into a many-figured blur in his mind, and there remained only Kristina. He forced his aching eyes wide and saw her, a small and proud-straight girl stumbling in her run down the mud-slick avenue, coming now to meet him.

T.V.OLSEN

SAVAGE SIERRA

CHAPTER ONE

FROWNING OVER an account book spread open on a rear counter, the sutler glanced up without much interest as Angsman entered the post store. Recognizing the newcomer then, Harley Moffat's bright swift eyes glinted with surprise and pleasure, not quite canceled by his dry greeting:

"Hello, you damned recluse."

"Harley."

Angsman paused in the cool mingled odors of leather and bolt cloth and foodstuffs, then came across the room, his moccasined tread noiseless and catlike. Angsman's towering and big-boned frame was dried to lean rawhide by desert heat and wind. He wore ragged duck trousers and a calico shirt long-faded to an indeterminate neutral color, a battered relic of a Stetson that was sweat-stained and curl-brimmed, and hip-length Apache moccasins with the stiff, upcurling toe, folded down at the knee. The light brown beard which slurred the outline of a stubborn jaw was bleach-streaked to a lighter hue than his sun-blackened face. His heavy brows were dust-filmed above sardonic, alert amber eyes which never changed, except for a fine deepening of the weather tracks at their outer corners, accenting a squint grown from the habit of scanning distances.

The two men shook hands as soberly and casually as though they had last parted a week, rather than six months, ago. Harley Moffat said then, "Well, I'm damned," standing back with hands on hips, a spare neat man with a benign ruff of sparse graying hair. He eyed Angsman over severely. "Figured you'd show up sporting a charro rig, plenty of braid, and spurs the size of cartwheels."

"Man don't go Mexican from half a year in Sonora,"

179

Angsman observed, leaning an arm and hip on the counter. "Besides, I'm not far short of broke, considering."

"Prospected?"

"Around the Madre foothills. Grubstake I bought of you before leaving took the last of my Army pay. That gone, I made do. Jackrabbits, cactus pears, berries, things I won't mention."

"You damned Injun. You look it." Harley Moffat shook his head in wonderment. "And nothing to show for it, eh?"

For answer Angsman drew a nearly flat leather poke from his pocket and laid it on the counter. The sutler picked it up and lightly hefted it, giving an expressive snort. "Six months breaking your back digging and panning, and for what? Damned little dust."

A corner of Angsman's mouth lifted faintly. "Weigh it out."

Moffat carefully spilled the contents of the sack onto a pan of his scales and counterweighted it. "Roughly three ounces, or about seventy-five dollars worth. Anyways, it'll send you off with another grubstake—I reckon?"

Angsman nodded, smiling at his friend's grimace of hopeless disgust. "Hell," Harley Moffat said then, "I gave you up years ago. Gold-grubbing, guiding the soldiers, living with Injuns, batting around the deserts and mountains…how many years of it?"

"Eleven."

"An' you're how old? Thirty-five, six?"

"Thirty-one last month."

"Look older. The life, I'd guess." Moffat gave a baffled sigh. "And you'll likely live to be ninety and never sick a day of it…you birds always do. Fiddlefooted, no ties, no ownin's, creature comforts an Injun wouldn't envy, and you thrive on it. Plain disgustin'."

"I could open a store. Ought to *give* me enough worries to put me under the ground inside ten years."

"You could do a sight worse, and the hell with you." The sutler's gaze shuttled above and beyond Angsman's left shoulder. "Oh oh," he said softly. Angsman turned his head enough to see the single rider pacing up the dusty street that passed up from Fort Stambaugh's parade ground between the adobe rows of enlisted men's houses.

"Jack Kincaid," Moffat said. "Been guidin' Lieutenant

Storrs on patrol, and it's payday. From the look of him, he had some whisky stashed away. Had, as I say."

Angsman knew Jack Kincaid: a thick bull of a man, composed of brute appetites, who had hunted Indians so long that he rode like one, with toes turned out and heels flailing. He could hold a trail like a hound on the scent; outside of that he was a surly misfit whose brain worked slowly and muddily, a fact which didn't trouble him so long as he could stay drunk, which was nearly always.

Kincaid dismounted at the rail and tied his whey-bellied roan, stood a fuddled moment inspecting Angsman's rawboned and gaunted paint already tied there and the pack horse alongside, then ducked under the tie rail and came onto the porch. He paused hanging to the doorframe, swaying unsteadily and blinking against the dim store interior after leaving the noonday glare. Kincaid's body was blocky and powerful, but lean-shanked; his Ute mother had bequeathed him his straight black hair and high cheekbones and the black bitter eyes, muddy now with liquor and the boiling resentments that surfaced to his mind with it.

He shuffled across to the counter and fell heavily against it, saying thickly, "Wan' a bottle."

"All right, Jack; back in there." Arms folded on the counter, Harley Moffat pointed with his chin toward the swing doors in the partition dividing his store and bar. "Be with you when I've finished here."

Jack Kincaid hammered a meaty fist on the counter. "Now, li'l man; wan' a bottle now."

"Jack," Moffat said testily but quietly, as though explaining to a child, "you can't just bull over people. Angsman was here before you."

"Let the sonofabitch wait."

Angsman felt the impact of the breed's black hating stare and barely glanced at him, not changing his own negligent pose, saying mildly, "Take care of him, Harley."

"No," Moffat said, his slight frame stiffening, "nobody's bulling over me or my friends in my place. What were we talking about? Your trip?"

"That's about talked out."

"Then we'll talk about the weather. When we settled that, we'll discuss the Indian situation—"

"Don' hear so good, storekeeper," Kincaid rumbled. "When Jack says he wan's a bottle, he don' fool."

Abruptly his thick ami swept out and knocked the scales with Angsman's gold spinning from the counter; his other hand leaped across to fist a handful of Harley Moffat's wilted boiled shirt.

Angsman shifted away from the counter, in the same effortless and unbroken movement slashing a rock-hard palm across Kincaid's wrist and breaking his hold, catching the stocky man by die neck. Pivoting to set his weight, he flung Kincaid away. The breed back-pedaled wildly for balance and slammed into a cracker barrel, upsetting it and crashing with it to the floor. He rolled at once to his feet, hand flicking down to a boot-sheath and coming up with six wicked inches of broad-bladed hunting knife. His eyes glinted almost soberly as he moved in on his quarry, this with relief at finding an object on which to vent his stored hatreds.

Angsman began circling out of his reach, baffled but not angry, not wanting to close with the man. You could only pity a man like Jack Kincaid, caught in lonely isolation between two races, too stupid and inflexible to relieve his dilemma except in an occasional drunken, killing rage; he'd had the bad luck to happen along at an infrequent time when the breed's withdrawn surliness had flamed into open grievance. Yet, too, Angsman felt the pressure of his own unreleased tensions, which built in the toughest loner after months of grueling hardship and solitude. He'd looked forward to a bath and shave and change of clothes, then a few pleasant days erf chatting and drinking with old friends. Within a few minutes of hitting the post he was confronted by a drunken, feisty dimwit ready to kill. He felt now a wicked pulse of eagerness that he suppressed; only cold wariness showed in his sidelong retreat. Actually his noiseless mincing shift of body carried him nearer Kincaid, like a big stalking cat.

Forced to a constant clumsy turning to face Angsman's long smooth circling, Kincaid's last shred of caution broke; he lunged bellowing like a bull, blade slashing down in a glittering arc. It didn't come within a foot of Angsman. He'd already leaped aside and was coming in low and fast; his knotted fist met Kincaid's belly beneath the right ribs. It was like connecting with a side of beef.

Kincaid merely gave a coughing grunt and fell back a step, then brought up his blade in a vicious underswing

...a fluid twist of body and the knife grazed past Angsman's shoulder. Still at close quarters he smashed his lifted forearm across the breed's thick neck muscles. Kincaid heaved forward like an axed steer and Angsman stepped smoothly from his path and pivoted on a heel, fist clubbing Kincaid across the jaw as the man blundered past.

Kincaid wheeled off-balance, sluggish and dazed, to face him. Angsman's stance was already set and he sank his fist into the pit of Kincaid's stomach. It stopped the half-breed cold; his hands dropped to his belly and the knife clattered on the floor. Angsman put his toe against it and skittered it into a corner. Deliberately, he picked his mark and slugged Kincaid in the throat.

Kincaid's knees melted and he slid retching to the floor. Still seething with a residue of anger, Angsman stooped and caught Kincaid by the belt and collar, hauling him bodily to his feet. He rushed him straight at the door, heels digging at the hard-packed clay for momentum, and pulled up suddenly at the threshold, heaving Kincaid's bulky weight up and outward. The half-breed's heels arched over his head in a flailing somersault, and he crashed on his back across the 'dobe porch, impetus bowling him down the steps till he thudded in a dusty sprawl against a tie-rail post.

Breathing a little harder, Angsman watched for a full minute as Kincaid fought to his hands and knees. Harley Moffat tossed out his hat and Kincaid picked it up without looking at them. He dragged himself upright leaning on the crossrail, elbows hugging his body and his lank greasy hair falling over his eyes. Catching up his reins, he stumbled around the rail to grab his saddle horn blindly; he heaved himself into the leather and swung off down the street.

Watching him go, Angsman felt Harley Moffat's baffled glance. "Funny damned thing. Don't recall seeing you in action before, 'cept for fun. Damn' tiger when you're het up."

Angsman said drily, "Price of survival," and switched the subject. "You mentioned him guiding out a patrol. Trouble?"

"Most always is, from time to time. Nothing like it was, now old Bonito's pulled in his horns. He was the last of the old-time broncho 'Paches, kind the bucks 'ud follow through hell and high water. Your friend Chingo broke reservation again; that's why the colonel had young Storrs on swarry. Chingo and his bunch left a plain trail swingin' southeast; burned a stage station and wiped out a couple settler families on the Gila. Hit and run; wasn't waitin' for the Army to find him, not with only a half-dozen braves, all feisty green youngsters. Anyways the patrol never got a sight of him. Figure he cut 'cross the border, maybe to Geronimo's old stampin' grounds in Sonora. Or could be," Moffat added wryly, "he heard you was down there and is lookin' to roast you head down over a slow fire...."

"He could be, at that." Angsman thought back to his first meeting with the broken-faced, bitter-eyed young war chief...three years ago when he'd guided a troop back into the Bailey's Peak country. Straight to a camp of reservation breakaways, a large band of Mimbre warriors and their families, led by El Soldado. It was a rare coup for the Army, that surprise attack on a well-hidden Apache camp in the dead of night. Will Angsman's knowledge of the country and the Apaches was directly responsible for the strategy and success. The Mimbres had rallied—a brief, savage and hopeless defense—and in the blind fracas that followed, Chingo's child-wife and infant son were killed.

That tragic night had branded the war chiefs body as well as his brain when, meeting Angsman in hand-to-hand fight, he'd received a defacing wound that had left him hideously scarred. The crippled band was rounded up and returned to reservation, but Chingo, crazed with grief and hatred, had soon broken out, heading up twenty braves to cut a bloody swath across the territory. But Will Angsman tracked him to bay a second time, guiding the troops that cornered him, and wiped out all but a remnant of his followers.

Chingo had guts and brains and heart; a born leader, a generation earlier he might have become another Victorio or Nana or Red Sleeve. But the days of the great war chiefs were long past, and something dark and warped in Chingo's mind, marred by youthful tragedy, caused all but a few of his own people to shun him as a man possessed. After Angsman had twice more led the troops that tracked him down, Chingo's consuming lust to find and kill the white scout had become the blind central goal of his life.

For Angsman there was no personality in their blood feud. Three times he had offered his free services to the Army and tracked Chingo down, because he saw the man's crazed depredations as a menace he'd unintentionally created. He saw Chingo's personal tragedy as part of the great tragedy of the Apache, betrayed and maltreated too many times. No way now to cut off these last flare-ups except by more bloodshed, and Angsman, with the fatalism of a solitary and wilderness-bred man, did his part without futile regret.

Harley Moffat's voice roused him. "Go on in the saloon, pour yourself a drink. Join you when I've cleaned up the dust that damned Kincaid spilled."

Angsman merely nodded because he wanted a drink, in fact, several. He crossed to the swing doors, parted them and entered the musty coolness of the adjoining barroom which smelled pleasantly of sawdust and stale whisky. He got a bottle of Moffat's best from a shelf under the backbar and had barely poured his drink when roistering voices from outside claimed his attention. A dozen thirsty troopers clamored through the swing doors, and he remembered then that Moffat had said it was payday. Angsman knew most of them, greeted them by name, and passed the bottle. When Harley Moffat came in and laid his poke of salvaged gold dust on the oak-plank bar, Angsman said soberly, "Harley, how drunk you reckon we can all get on half of that?"

The troopers laughed- and cheered him, but the frugal sutler showed a disgusted scowl. "Much a damned fool as ever, eh? Save out enough of six months' sorry earnings to buy a grubstake an' a new shirt, throw every remainin' cent into drink and cards before strikin' out again. When you goin' to get some sense, Will?"

"Reckon when I've seen the last side of the last hill…"

"I've a mind at times to go see it with you, ye damned tumbleweed," rumbled a deep brogue, and Angsman turned to face the man who had entered, a ruddy-faced trooper built like a squat barrel. They shook hands with mutual pleasure.

Angsman greeted him, "Terence Dahoney, when you end with the service, it'll be the millennium." He added, nodding at the dark patch where chevrons had been on Dahoney's faded blue sleeve, "Demoted again? Major couldn't find any new shavetails for you to field-break?"

"Admittin' nothing," Dahoney answered complacently, " 'ceptin' that B Troop's top noncom was by pure chance the center of an unseemly brawl back of Mr. Moffat's establishment Saturday night last—which the major him-silf, if you please, discovered. I'll have them stripes back inside three months. Meantime I'm secretary-orderly to the major as further punishment, him knowin' I'd rather be swampin' a damned stable."

"Or drinking Mr. Moffat's establishment dry, which project you're in time to help me begin, Terence."

Dahoney shook his head regretfully. "Afraid not, Wil-lis. There's a business a shade more serious afoot, which is why I'm here. From his window the major saw you ride in, this shortly before the two tenderfeet arrived—"

"Tenderfeet?"

"Aye, green as grass, and they're waitin' in the major's office. He sent me to fetch ye before the milk of Erin befuddles your senses. The Old Man is wearin' his best military bark, and I'm thinkin' the matter at hand may be urgent. Ye'd best not keep him waitin'."

CHAPTER TWO

After leaving Angsman's horses at B Stable, he and Terence Dahoney cut between the quartermaster's storehouse and the forage shed and then headed diagonally across Fort Stambaugh's parade ground toward the adobe headquarters building which constituted one side of the east sentry gate. Matching his stride to the brisk, swinging one of the stocky ex-sergeant, Angsman said again, curiously, "Tenderfeet?"

"Aye." Dahoney chewed out his words around the stub of cigar clamped unlit between his bulldog jaws. "A young lady and a gentleman...brother and sister, from the look of them; very like the grand toffs I once wheedled for coppers as a guttersnipe on the streets of Boston—from which city I'm thinkin' they hail. The major's askin' for you concerns them; that much I gathered, and no more...." He waved his cigar in a spare semi-circle as they neared the headquarters building. "They're provisioned for a desert trek, wouldn't ye say?"

Angsman nodded briefly, casting an eye over the two saddle horses tied at the weathered rail fronting the building. One bore a sidesaddle. Two pack mules were tied alongside, bulging tarp-covered packs diamond-hitched across their packs.

"Ye'll be at Moffat's later, Willis?" Dahoney asked as they ascended the steps.

"We'll split a bottle there, Terence."

They entered an outer office and circled an endgate to reach a closed door. Dahoney pocketed his cigar stub and rapped a panel with scarred knuckles, bawling briskly, "Mr. Angsman, sor."

Major Philip Marsden opened the door, dismissed Dahoney to his desk with a curt, "All right, trooper,"

187

and warmly shook hands with Angsman. "Come in, Will...good to see you."

He closed the door behind them, turning toward the man and young woman seated by his desk. "Miss Amberley, Dr. Amberley, may I present Will Angsman, the man I wanted you to meet."

Amberley rose and stepped forward with outstretched hand. He was a slight man in his middle thirties with a thin, sensitive face and gentle blue eyes behind iron-rimmed spectacles. His blond hair was receding above a high, rounded dome of forehead, and his smile, preoccupied and almost absent, was redeemed by a hint of warm shyness. In spite of a mild and scholarly appearance, there was something hard and capable about his wiry frame, this confirmed by his handshake. He wore a wrinkled and travel-stained corduroy suit, the trousers stuffed into high, laced boots, and his flannel shirt was open at the throat.

"Mr. Angsman," he murmured in a precise and pleasant voice. "Major Marsden says that you know the Territory better than any man."

"Except the Apaches."

"Including the Apaches." The major's contradiction was firm in spite of a faint smile. He seated himself in his swivel chair and leaned back, folding his arms across his faded blue blouse. He was a career soldier of fifty, lean of body and face, with a heavy shock of pepper-and-salt hair and a full cavalry mustache. His black eyes were alert and restless, tempered by humor, and there was about him an air of courteous gentility that could harden into steel, as Angsman knew. Stern in his way but not a martinet, Phil Marsden was no garrison soldier and so held Will Angsman's respect.

Angsman glanced now at the young woman seated board-straight in a crude chair by the desk, skirts drawn primly about her ankles. She was about twenty-five or six, he judged, rather thin but trim-figured, not pretty but certainly not plain. Her shining blond hair was parted in the middle and drawn to a chignon at the back of her neck, and she wore a fashionable gray cambric riding habit; a matching wide-brimmed hat sat on her lap. There was a pale delicacy to her smooth face and hands, and unlike her brother—for the identical configuration of their fine-boned features was obvious—she was suffering from the heat. Sweat finely beaded her face and wilted the high close collar of the once-crisp white shirtwaist beneath a close-fitting jacket.

Angsman thought with a faint, dour humor, she's got glassy-eyed from the heat, and she'd fall over in a dead faint before she'd twitch an eyelash. Yet that attitude, hinting at a defiant iron will, aroused his interest enough to let his gaze linger almost boldly on her face. Behind the inner strength reflected there, he felt, with the certainty of wilderness-keened senses, a nature as cold and unbending as ice.

She gave the faintest of cool nods, and Angsman slightly inclined his head, murmuring, "Servant, ma'am," before he put his back to the wall with an angular grace, folding his arms, hat in hand. Amberley motioned toward his chair, but the major said with a humorous lift of eyebrows, "Angsman doesn't use 'em."

Amberley seated himself. The major's swivel chair creaked to a forward tilt of weight as Marsden opened a box of cigars and extended it to Angsman, pausing in mid-motion. "Your permission, ma'am?"

Miss Amberley nodded coolly. Angsman accepted a cigar and Amberley refused, instead taking out a well-blackened pipe which he merely chewed meditatively. Major Marsden lighted Angsman's cigar and his own, then crossed his arms on his scarred desktop.

"Will, these people have their minds set on a trek into the Sierra Toscos west of the Paisano River. I can't dissuade them. Possibly you can."

Angsman scowled, exhaling a long streamer of smoke. "Bonito's country?"

The colonel nodded with a wry twist of lips.

For thirty years and more, Bonito, the ancient Chiricahua war chief, had been an ever-constant thorn in the side of the Army of the West. He had out-generaled the best officers put in the field against him by never fighting except on ground of his own choosing, with every strategical odd in his favor, a typical Apache stratagem to which Bonito had brought a high polish. When major Apache leaders like Cochise and Mangus Colorado had made their truces with the white invaders, Bonito had warned that the white-eyes' promises were written on wind. Warning unheeded and soon fulfilled.

Only recently, with all except a handful of renegades

driven to reservation, Bonito, the Apache who had never stopped fighting, halted his hopeless lifelong war against the whites. Even then he'd refused to surrender or even parley with his hated foes; heading up the last sizable band of non-reservation Chiricahuas, men and women and children, all their gear and animals, he had retreated into the far eastern Sierra Toscos, after serving warning through reservation relatives that should any white-eyed soldiers take the pursuit, they'd fare ill.

Of this there was little danger, as Major Marsden had drily observed. Standing departmental orders were that no band of the plains tribes, even hostile raiders, were to be molested by the Army patrols, except by direct provocation. A fact of which Bonito was fully aware, for he'd often turned it to shrewd advantage. His message was simply his proudly defiant way of saying he was through fighting. For the old-timers Bonito's action held a trace of nostalgic regret, for it marked the end of something. Henceforth young bucks primed with tiswin and windy stories from their elders might fire up occasionally, as Chingo had again done, but the old days were gone forever....

"As I understand the major," Amberley put in mildly, "the old chief's warning that he'll brook no trespass was directed at any who invade his stronghold with violent intent. However, our own purpose is quite peaceful."

"That so," Angsman murmured.

"Sir," Amberley rejoined sharply, "if I appear green, let me assure you that this isn't wholly the case. I am a professor of archaeology at Harvard University; my specialty is native American civilizations. My field studies have led me to many out-of-the-way places, including Yucatan, southern Mexico, and Peru. I know something of the aboriginal mind; it is my experience that if the natives are treated fairly and honorably, they respond in kind."

"Met any Apaches, professor?"

"No, sir; my field studies have been confined outside of the United States and its territories, but—"

"Your foreign natives, I'd reckon, had no previous dealings with the white man; the Apaches had a bellyful. Not exactly a hospitable folk, by any odds. Apache's a Zuni word, means enemy."

"Yes, I know."

Because few things irritated Angsman more than a greenhorn's smugness, he said harshly, "Then maybe you ain't green. Maybe you're just a plain damn' fool, Mister."

Miss Amberley stiffened angrily in her chair, and he added coldly, "Your pardon, ma'am." His glance held hard on Amberley's. "Man who puts a shabby premium on his own life may have his reasons. Out here, though, a woman's life means somewhat more."

Amberley's thin tanned face took on a swift ruddy darkening, but it was his sister who spoke first, in a tone the texture of ice: "I—we—are determined, Mr. Angsman. For reasons that you would never understand."

She's determined is what she nearly came out with, ran Angsman's startled thought. Her idea? His gaze shuttled to Amberley for confirmation, found in the hint of wry sheepishness touching his face.

Angsman said with slow bafflement, "Maybe, but I'll give it a try."

"James," she said brittlely.

Amberley breathed a deep sigh, looking from her to Angsman. "Perhaps, sir, you've wrongly concluded that our proposed trek into the Sierra Toscos is in the nature of a scientific expedition; if so, that is my fault through omission. Our only purpose is to find our younger brother, Douglas."

Major Marsden gestured with his cigar. "This is the interesting part, Will....Douglas Amberley's name had a familiar ring—then I remembered. A young fellow by that name came to the fort a year ago. Outfitted at Moffat's store, bought horses, told me he was planning a protracted trip into the eastern Toscos, and could I recommend a guide."

Though this was shortly before Bonito had retreated to that same country, it was ill-reputed by the few prospectors and trappers who'd ventured there as a waterless, barren hellhole. Even the Apaches, who could live on ground mesquite beans and cactus fruit, if necessary, had generally shunned it. Naturally, the major said, he'd tried to dissuade the young man; he wasn't over twenty-one, obviously Eastern and inexperienced. But the boy was adamant, and reluctantly the major had acquired for him the best guide available at the time, old Caleb Tree.

Tree was one of the last of the mountain men, crowding seventy now, irascible and mean and probably unscrupulous, but he knew the Apaches and the country as few white men did; and for enough money he'd undertake anything. Young Amberley had met his price without hesitation, and they'd struck west from Fort Stambaugh, equipped and provisioned for a lengthy sojourn in the wilds. The major could only assume they'd met with an accident—or fallen victim to Bonito's warriors when they made their unexpected withdrawal into the Toscos three months later.

"Your brother," the major concluded, "was absolutely silent about his purpose, Dr. Amberley. I hope you'll be more explicit. What in the devil was he after?"

Amberley hesitated. "Secrecy is hardly of importance now, of course....My brother had chosen my own profession, archaeology, as his life's work. Only—" Again Amberley hesitated with a brief glance at his sister, apparently weighing his words— "Dougjas was more restless than I. After three years of study at Harvard, he quit and went West. Two years earlier, at nineteen, he'd accompanied me to Mexico, to study the Toltec-Aztec ruins near Vera Cruz, an experience that had deeply fired his imagination. For months after he'd left Boston, we received no word—until a letter arrived, posted from Santa Fe...."

The letter had obviously been penned in high excitement. Douglas told how he'd toured the old Spanish missions of the southwest, poring exhaustively through their archives, examining hundreds of forgotten documents, for a shred of truth in the early Spaniards' belief that the puissant Aztecs, at the height of their power in Mexico, had established northern colonies in Arizona or New Mexico. An idea refuted by Prescott and other authorities, it had come to obsess Douglas.

He'd found nothing to confirm the theory, and was further discouraged by the present refusal of the Catholic Church to open certain stores of early Spanish records, secreted in missions and monasteries, to investigators. And so his youthful and restless curiosity was diverted by an unexpected discovery at a litde mission in a Pueblo village outside of Santa Fe. Here the Franciscan fathers had been most co-operative, and in their archives he'd uncovered an old manuscript penned here more than two centuries before by a Castilian grandee, Don Pedro de Obregon, then buried away to gather dust.

Obregon had been an exacting scholar as well as gentleman adventurer, and his fine flowing script offered easy translation. His account was of a journey that he and other soldiers-of-fortune had made in 1672, in an effort to find a trace of the legendary Cibola and its treasures, the golden lure which had first brought Coronado and his successors to this land.

Striking southwest from Santa Fe on the trail of one illusive but persistent rumor, Obregon and his well-equipped party of nine Spaniards and a score of Indians had crossed desert and mesa for weeks till in rugged country they struck a great mountain pass and swung eastward to follow it out. For days they moved deeper into the barren and desolate range. With their water running dangerously low and most of them ready to back-trail, they came to a stream of clear water. A little farther on, beneath the towering escarpment of a giant mesa, they found an incredibly wealthy vein of high-grade gold.

Their former goal utterly forgotten in this dazzling find, Obregon and his party drove their Indians mercilessly to erect a small stone fort against the bands of roaming *Querechos,* as the Spaniards had dubbed the Apaches. Then they began tunneling into the mountain from the rear of their fortress, tearing out great gold-rich chunks of ore, while a smelter was built close by. So rich was the vein that within a short time they had as much as they could pack out. Lacking molds, they poured the melted metal into improvised hide tubes to cool into heavy bars, loading these onto their sturdy Moorish ponies till the poor beasts staggered beneath the weight.

But the Querechos, by now gathering to one sizable band, were waiting unseen above the pass. Don Pedro de Obregon's party had no sooner abandoned their fort and struck upcanyon than the Querechos had surrounded and cut them off. The first volley of arrows had killed two Spaniards and four Indians; the remaining Indians fled in panic and were slaughtered like quail on the run. The surviving Spaniards kept the enemy temporarily at bay with their arquebuses, whose noise and smoke demoralized the surprised savages more than the whistling balls.

Slowly the Spaniards fell back to a trail which mounted the flanking pass wall to a high cave mouth. Because they refused to abandon their gold-laden animals, driving the terrified beasts up the narrow trail, two more Spaniards died before the survivors achieved the cave. From this position they easily defended the single narrow trail, though now the Querechos simply camped below for a patient siege.

They found water in the honeycombing of the caves, but their provisions, already depleted, soon ran out. A fifth man died in a quarrel over the last strip of dried meat. They killed their ponies for food, but the meat quickly spoiled. In desperation three of the remaining four decided on a break by night. The last man, Don Pedro de Obregon, listened in the darkness to their descent... heard them die at the hands of the waiting enemy.

A week later Don Pedro himself, nearly out of his mind with privation and shattered nerves, left the caves by full daylight and started the long trek back to Santa Fe. The Querechos, evidently believing this babbling survivor to be deranged, let him go. Of the nightmarish days that followed the Don had little memory. Somehow he'd crossed miles of mountain and desert wilderness to stagger, more dead than alive, into a village of Christianized Pueblos. These friendly natives bore him on by travois to Santa Fe and left him in the hands of the padres at the little mission of Tesque.

Rest and care brought Obregon gradually back to his senses. Broken in mind and body by his harrowing adventure, he didn't live out the year. On his deathbed he penned an account of the aborted mission; he set it down at the urging of his confessor, Father Garcia, to whom he had unburdened his venial conduct.

Young Douglas Amberley made the shrewd guess that the Franciscan Garcia had Don Pedro write his narrative, then himself withheld it from colonial representatives of the Spanish crown, with the intention of somehow channeling the wealth waiting in those far mountains into the coffers of the Church—for Obregon had included a detailed map and directions. Yet for unknown reasons the parchment manuscript lay buried for two centuries among other forgotten records.

Quietly, James Amberley now drew a folded paper from his pocket and handed it to Angsman. "There is the copy of Obregon's chart which Douglas sent me, together with description and directions translated from the Spanish."

Angsman unfolded the map and briefly scanned its painstakingly penciled lines and printed script, quickly identifying the meandering course of the Paisano River and other prominent landmarks. Obregon had other names for these, but had placed them with scrupulous accuracy. Was the half of the *derrotero* that charted the little-known country to the east of the river equally true? He felt irritation at his own stirring interest...treasure maps and lurid legends foisted off on greenhorns were a dime a dozen.

Curiously studying the chart, he noted a heavily marked cross underscored with the only words not rendered from the Spanish. *"Muro del Sangre,"* he murmured. "The Wall of Blood."

"That would be the location of the mine, according to the directions," Amberley interjected. "Cryptic bit of picturesque whimsy, eh? Touch of enigmatic poetry within the old boy's clear and factual prose. Seems to be descriptive, but I can't unravel its significance. Neither could Doug."

Angsman handed back the paper. "Did your brother say he intended findin' the mine?"

Amberley nodded soberly. "Starting from the nearest outpost—Fort Stambaugh. I wrote him promptly, advising against undertaking so hazardous a project alone in his inexperience. Suggested that he wait for me in Contentionville, where we could outfit and organize an expedition properly. Either he didn't receive the letter or, what's more likely, chose to ignore it. His next communication, and his last, was mailed from this fort—a brief hasty note. If he didn't return, his ownings were to be equally divided between his sister and me. That was all.

"I wanted to come West at once, but the Harvard trustees, academically conservative gentlemen, would not grant me a leave of absence, though a sabbatical leave was pending. I pointed out that Don Pedro's mine should prove an eminent archaeological find. They pooh-poohed the notion; my brother was irresponsible, as his quitting school demonstrated, and my judgment was overbalanced by concern. I pointed out that the conditions of Douglas' finding the Obregon manuscript certainly indicated its authenticity, while Don Pedro, penning it on his death-

bed, would have been in a passion to reveal the truth.
Vain argument. It wasn't till now that my sabbatical leave
came up—and Judith and I left as soon as possible."

Amberley's explanation of why he'd let a year drag by
after his brother's last message bore a false ring in its
painstaking detail; it occurred to Angsman that the man
might be covering a sense of guilt. But he said nothing.

Major Marsden leaned intently forward now, lacing his
fingers together on his desktop. "Well, Will—what's your
verdict? You know the Toscos."

Angsman scowled at his cigar. "Not that part of it, Phil,
not Bonito's country. Prospected west of the Paisano
River, that's all." He glanced abruptly at the Amberleys,
laying down his words hard and flat. "Might have been a
chance of finding your brother alive nine, ten months ago.
Not a year later, and not with the Chiricahuas dug in back
there. You waited too long. My advice, get back to
Boston, forget about it."

He said it with intentional brutality, hoping to drive a
wedge of sense through this wall of greenhorn ignorance.
But Judith Amberley said with no lessening of her inflexible coldness, "Mr. Angsman, I have a suggestion."

"Ma'am?"

"You have stated by inference that we are rash and
misguided fools, ignorant of the country and its dangers.
As bears on our ignorance, your surmise is accurate. We
would be helpless as children. You would not be. Therefore…will you be our guide?"

Her bluntness disconcerted Angsman, as he guessed
she'd intended it should, and now he shifted his shoulders
uncomfortably. "No, ma'am; I have not lived this long by
being a purple fool."

Her face pinkened beneath its pale gloss, but her tone
held even: "I believe that I can offer a reason that should
outweigh any objection."

"Yes'm."

"Money," she said laconically and flatly. "I will give
you a draft on our bank for the sum you name, in advance
of our leaving."

"No, ma'am," Angsman said quietly, stubbornly. "This
is a fool thing you propose, and I will not be party to
helping two people throw away their lives for no reason."

"I think, sir, that you are a coward."

Angsman pushed away from the wall and moved sound-lessly to the door, pausing to say, "That is your privilege," and then with a soft, sardonic, "Servant, ma'am," he was gone.

CHAPTER THREE

Following the awkward silence after the door closed behind Angsman, Major Marsden said courteously, but obviously supressing his anger, "I am trying to understand you, Miss Amberley."

"Judith, there was no call to pointedly insult the man!" James Amberley half-rose, Ins face deeply flushed. "Major, I must apologize—"

The major brushed aside his words with a curt, "Perhaps later, Dr. Amberley; I'd not approach Angsman now. He may well be in a mood to smash your jaw."

"No doubt," Judith Amberley said. "The man is a rude, unshaven boor. I see no reason to suppose him infallible— nor did I like his attitude or choice of words. I am sorry, Major, but that is my exact impression—and I am accustomed to speaking my mind exacdy."

"I at least respect your candor," the major said slowly. "Will was a little rough. But he is never irresponsible; I believe that his harshness was intended to dissuade you from what he summed up in no uncertain terms, and quite accurately." His pleasant courtesy restored now, he added, "Obviously this journey has been a trying one for you, Miss Amberley…"

She nodded, a faint concern in her cool smile, and now her brother studied her with genuine concern, seeing her face pale and drawn beneath a dew of perspiration. He knew her steel-willed checkrein on any display of feeling or pain, yet her cool, uncomplaining poise till now had been so convincing he'd forgotten that she was a soft and gently bred Eastern woman.

Marsden continued gravely, "My wife and I would be honored to have you both as overnight guests."

"We couldn't think of putting you to all that bother, Major," Judith said aloofly. Amberley inwardly damned her stiff-necked pride; too often she carried it beyond good sense.

But Marsden was convincingly insistent. The commandant's house had two large spare rooms ready for occupancy; his wife's home ties were in Boston, and she would be eager for news. Anyway, the major added smiling, it would do them both good to sleep on their illusions. His warm argument partly melted Judith's frosty reserve, and she managed a wan smile of agreement.

The commandant's house lay at the end of Officer's Row, and there Marsden introduced his wife, a plump and motherly woman who clucked solicitously over Judith and afterward hurried her off to a room where she might clean up and rest.

"I must see to our horses, Major," Amberley said. "And then, if you've a few minutes to spare, I hope you'll join me in a drink at the post trader's bar."

The major was agreeable, and they returned to the headquarters building where Marsden called out Trooper Dahoney and told him to take the Amberleys' saddle and pack animals to B Stable and see that they were unloaded and cared for. As Dahoney saluted and turned to untie the horses, the major ran an approving eye over them.

"You're a keen judge of horseflesh, I see, Doctor; a man wants animals with plenty of bottom for the desert."

"Yes...we outfitted just across the river from the fort, at Contentionville," Amberley explained as they swung into step, headed for the suder's. "I'm no stranger to wilderness jaunts. With Judith—it's another matter."

"She is a strong-minded woman, your sister," Marsden mused aloud, "but plainly unfit for the rigors of what you've planned." He hesitated. "I don't question her intelligence, but I must admit that her insistence on this dangerous and hopeless mission, more particularly her insistence on personally undertaking it, puzzles me. Your younger brother, after all, was a grown man...tackled his venture of his own will. She must think a great deal of him."

"Why," Amberley said absently, "you might call it an act of atonement, Major."

Realizing that he'd encroached on a highly personal matter, Marsden partly veered the subject. "I should say," he stated almost curtly, "that as the family head, you should assert your views over and above hers. She certainly can't carry the thing further without you. You'll pardon my bluntness, Doctor; I think the situation warrants it. That young lady must be brought to her senses."

Amberley smiled thinly. "You don't know my sister, sir...."

As they neared the sutler's, the swing doors of the saloon burst open and Will Angsman and a half-dozen troopers, loud with drink and argument, filed out, two of them with arms slung around Angsman's shoulders. All seven were out of sight between two buildings by the time Amberley and the major had reached the porch.

"What was that about?" asked the mystified Easterner.

"Let's find out," the major said, his eyes twinkling.

Inside the barroom, now deserted except for the sutler, Amberley was introduced to Harley Moffat, and then Marsden said: "What was the ruckus, Mr. Moffat?"

"Ah, Angsman's goin' to show the boys some Injun wrestlin' throws. Says if he can't flatten each in turn inside a minute, he'll pay for all the drinks. Reckon they'll conduct the show over behind the stables." Harley Moffat clucked his tongue resignedly.

A puckish smile touched the major's lips. "Suppose I'll have to break that up, but no hurry. We'll have a drink, Mr. Moffat, and you'll join us."

"By all means," Amberley said, smiling at the commandant's flexible disciplinary line; it left a broad latitude for release from the tensions, privations, and monotony of frontier duty.

The major now briefly mentioned Amberley's intended search for his brother, and Harley Moffat reinforced the other pessimistic reactions. "If you're set in your mind, sir, damn' pity you couldn't get Angsman as guide. If anyone could take you into hostile territory and out alive, that's the man. Otherwise...." Moffat clucked sadly.

Amberley nodded absently, curiously wondering about the man. All these Western men were hard and weather-scoured, yet they all seemed almost pale and soft compared to Will Angsman. Definitely a Southerner from his speech...or had been. It was difficult to tell much else; he guessed that even with his friends the man would be almost stoically reserved, blunt and brief-spoken. Yet he plainly had friends, and not only among the rough troopers. Though the major must be worlds apart from

Angsman—for it was a far cry from the rigid military echelons to Angsman's hard-bitten independence—Marsden plainly liked the man. He seemed utterly complete and self-sufficient; you could feel it in him, along with the incredible alertness and animal vitality in repose.

There came an unsteady shuffle of boots across the porch, and the major, glancing across the swing doors, murmured wryly, "I see that Mr. Kincaid is losing no time in disposing of his pay."

Harley Moffat swore softly. "Will Angsman threw him out once today—after he picked a fight." He raised his voice sharply as a thick-set, Indian-looking man blundered through the doors. "Jack, if you drink here, you mind your manners now."

Jack Kincaid stood in the center of the room swaying unsteadily, his bloodshot eyes moving almost furtively over the three men. He wiped his nose on his knuckles and lurched heavily to the other end of the bar. "Jus' gimme bottle," he muttered surlily.

Moffat silently set a glass and full whisky bottle in front of him. Kincaid slapped some coins on the bar, sloshed his glass full and settled down to morose, steady drinking. Amberley gave him a wondering regard, then swallowed his own drink.

As he and Major Marsden left the barroom, pausing on the porch, a group of four riders swung up the street. A strangely assorted quartet, Amberley saw as they drew near, but alike in their tacky civilian clothes, their worn, dusty and weathered appearance.

"These gentlemen seem to have ridden long and hard—"

"They always do." Marsden's reply was taut and harsh. "You have the dubious honor of viewing the worst gang of blackguards and cutthroats the border country has produced. Armand Charbonneau and his precious coterie. Damn—I'd hoped he'd stay in Mexico...."

As he spoke the major was moving off the porch, confronting the four as they reined to a dusty halt. The leader swung off his rawboned sorrel in a long agile movement that reminded Amberley of a snake uncoiling ...odd in a man so gaunt and towering. He was about forty, with a long axblade of a face darkened by wind and sun. His cocksure blandness was relieved by a great beak of a nose and a trim black mustache, a jutting jaw slurred by a ragged spade beard. His pale eyes were a flashing and luminous green, almost startling against his dark complexion. His long black hair was queued at the side, hanging past his collar. He wore a battered sombrero, a discolored and greasy deerhide coat, and frayed tight butternut pants stuffed into high jackboots. A twisted cheroot projected jauntily from a corner of his chalky smile.

He advanced with a gliding ease, throwing his arms wide, booming, "Ah, *mon ami* the major. 'Ow are you, my fran'?"

Marsden ignored the outstretched hand, his tone saber-keen: "This post is off-limits to you, Charbonneau. Has been since you smuggled that rotgut to reservation Chiricahuas last year."

Armand Charbonneau's brows rose in a deeply pained look; he spread his open palm against his chest. "You do not mean Armand, my fran'? Oh no, it is mistake, eh? I thought you 'ave hear bettair by this time. Armand nevair do such thing—"

"Not so anyone can prove it," Marsden cut in. "One of these days your cleverness will trip you up for fair —and I hope you're on this side of the big river when it happens. I'd hate to let the Mexican army have the pleasure of standing you against a wall." He paused, struck by a thought. "How the hell did you get past the sentry?"

"Ah, ha. If the major do not want his great fran' inside his so fine fort, he should not post the gate with green recruit, eh?" Charbonneau's broad shoulders shook with noiseless mirth. "I tal' him the major send for Armand and his fran's for the guiding. Is great joke, *non?*"

"Damn your gall, Charbonneau!" The major dashed his cigar to the hard-packed ground. "All right. Now you're here, have your drink. But you'd damn' well better be gone inside the hour!"

There was a cavalier and satirical elegance to Charbonneau's mocking bow. *"Merci,* my fran'. Come, *mes amis;* we toast Armand's good fran' the major in M'sieu Moffat's bad whisky. Come!"

The other three dismounted and silently followed the leader through the swing doors. Amberley, staring after them in fascination, swung to Major Marsden. "Why, Major, this man is fabulous!—a latter-day buccaneer to the hilt. Why don't you go on alone, sir; **I'd** like to stay a while...."

"Fabulous," Marsden snorted quietly, dourly. "You tenderfeet and your Wild West....All right, Doctor—but a word of caution. Just watch them, and no more. Under his dash and color, your swashbuckling friend is a snake."

With a curt nod, he strode away, cutting out of sight between the buildings where Angsman and the troopers had gone. Then Amberley jerked about, startled, as the swing doors parted suddenly and the dark, squat Kincaid leaped out backward onto the porch, crouched and poised, a long wicked knife in his palm. One of Charbonneau's men lunged out, his fists raised. He was a giant coal-black Negro, whose chest and shoulders swelled against his soiled shirt with the latent power of a young bull.

" 'Tol you next time we met I'd slit your gizzard, Armbuster," Kincaid hissed.

"That's the secon' time jus' now you call me Armbuster," the Negro rumbled, lumbering about in an effort to front the other. "You know my name's Ambruster. I'm gwine break you back fo' that, po' breed trash—"

"Turk!"

Charbonneau stood in the doorway, his voice cracking like a whip. "You want to get us all in the post guardhouse, eh? The major, he say drink, not fight. An' you, Jack, when 'ave we been bad fran's, eh? I think now you shake hands, we all drink on it."

Kincaid sullenly lowered the knife, rocking back on his heels. "I'll drink with you, Armand. But I don't shake hands with no nigger."

A rumble rose from Ambruster's cavernous chest.

Charbonneau flicked the ash from his cheroot. "Turk, get inside now. Armand does not fool. Inside!"

Suddenly the Negro laughed sheepishly, and it transformed his thick brutal face. Amberley had the startled thought, Why, the man's neither slow nor stupid—if this isn't the strangest....

Ambruster went in past Charbonneau, who now stepped out to slap Kincaid smartly on the shoulder. "Come on now, Jack." He poked Kincaid playfully in the ribs and flashed his white streak of a smile. "Get in there and drink."

Kincaid's surly face broke in a reluctant grin; he followed Ambruster. Charbonneau was about to swing after him when his curious gaze found Amberley staring open-mouthed.

"Beg pardon. Didn't mean to stare. But, by George, sir —yours is an iron hand."

For a moment Charbonneau seemed puzzled, then he gave an explosive laugh. "Merci, Mistair Dude. Ah, maybe you have a drink with Armand too? Eh?"

"Why—yes, thank you."

Charbonneau shouldered up to the bar between two of his men. "These *bon amis* are Will-John Staples and Ramon Uvaldes. Mistair—?"

"Amberley, James Amberley."

Will-John Staples shook hands readily, and his palm was thick and calloused. He was a short, barrel-chested young man in his early twenties with a round, mild face and eyes of a deep and dreamy brown. A tow cowlick hung over his ruddy forehead; he continually, absently tossed it back in a way that reminded Amberley of a stolid bull head-tossing at an annoying horsefly. He had the appearance of a thick-headed farmboy, seeming badly out of place with this hard-bitten trio.

Uvaldes was a lean villianous-looking man with a great knife scar cutting transversely across a narrow coffee-brown face. Without turning from the bar, he flicked a black lightning stare over Amberley and then looked away.

Charbonneau cocked ail elbow on the bar and tugged at his ear, facing Amberley with an appraising grin. "M'sieu, you are a gentleman, this is plain. Armand Charbonneau, who come of fine Creole family, does not mistake such things. Hah. Gentleman drink apart, *hein?* Come."

He flipped a bottle into one sinewy hand, scooped up two glasses with the other as Harley Moffat set them out, then jerked his head toward a round deal table in the corner. With half-amused curiosity Amberley followed him, taking the stool which Charbonneau indicated with a sweep of his hand. The air of someone at once raffish and dashing, engaging and knavish, that clung to him fascinated the Easterner. Maybe I'm the toad that the snake has mesmerized, he thought amusedly.

Charbonneau poured their drinks. "To the jade called

fortune, M'sieu; may she smile on us both." They drank, and Charbonneau grew voluble and expansive; obviously his favorite topic was himself. With gestures as eloquent as his colorful speech, he sketched a past of scandalous rascality.

"Such are the sad misdemeanairs of the black sheep scion of high-placed N'Orleans family, one in whose mouth the silvair spoon turn to tarnish," he concluded, grinning, and then his green eyes pronged abruptly against Amberiey's. "And now, M'sieu, what of you? You are no book-bound scholair merely, n'est-ce pas?"

"My work has entailed considerable travel," Amberley admitted modestly.

"Ha! This I knew." He refilled the Easterner's glass for the third time. "Tell me of your work, m'sieu...."

Afterward Amberley was never certain how it had come about, but there was Charbonneau with Douglas' map spread out on the table before him, asking penetrating and detailed questions in the most casually friendly manner.

Amberley tried to sort out coherent replies; his tongue seemed thick, and the room rotted like a ship's deck whenever he moved his eyes. He'd never had much stomach for liquor, even in his slightly rowdy undergraduate days, and he thought worriedly, Damned pleasant, chatting with this frontier chevalier, but I must stop drinking now. Judith will be furious....

He knit his brows befuddledly. "Wha' d'you say jus' then, Armand?"

"I say, smart boy with all that learning, like your brothair—he wouldn' kite off into the desert on the wild goose hunt, professair, eh?"

"Uh...yes, quite so."

"You need anothair drink, *mon ami*"

"No. Uh-uh. Mus' insist. Quite enough."

"We 'ave not drink to friendship." Overriding Amberlay's mild protest, Charbonneau poured another round. He raised his glass with eyes emerald-hard and glinting above its rim. "Doctair, I think we do each othair some good. You listen now to Armand, eh?"

CHAPTER FOUR

Angsman woke with a bad taste in his mouth. He rolled onto his back and inched to a sitting position in the hay, gently massaging his pounding head, wincing as the early sunlight seeping into the stable loft dislodged savage splinters behind his eyes. He found his crumpled hat beside him in the straw and clamped it on. As he climbed laboriously to his feet, holding a wall for support, he gave a ragged shudder and breathed gingerly against his bruised ribs where an over-sportive trooper had dropped on him with both knees during their mock brawl.

Bleakly he stared out the loading window of the loft, finding the morning tasteless and drab. Maybe it was only the dismal reaction of a hangover, yet Angsman couldn't recall feeling such a gray emptiness as filled him this morning. Thirty-one years of living…and nothing to show for it but his gun, saddle, scars, and empty pockets.

Yet these things had always been enough, along with the freedom and the desert life and the many friends he rarely saw. The pure freedom he wanted made necessary the shunning of any strong human ties. Maybe he was rimming a crucial summit in his life and seeing the other side desolate and aimless….

The hell with it.

He was letting his physical misery affect his mood, that was all; a bath and a solid meal would set him up again. Even so, breathing shallowly against his bruises and hangover as he moved to the loft traphole and descended the ladder, he resolved to go easier; he was no longer the green and resilient boy he'd been.

Down in the runway Angsman exchanged amiable insults with the stable sergeant while he rummaged through the pack of supplies for which he'd paid Harley Moffat the last of his dust and which he'd left in an empty stall. He dug out the stiff new shirt and trousers and headed for Officer's Row, answering casually to greetings of officers and enlisted men alike.

Though he'd slept through reveille and the sun was already high and strong in the brassy sky, the day was young. Breathing deeply of the air and sunlight and dust, Angsman felt more his usual self, even felt a mild pleasure on briefly reviewing his future plans. He had none in particular: loaf around the fort a day or so, cross over to Contentionvilie and renew some acquaintances, then strike out again. Probably north this time; it didn't really matter.

A scowl knitted his brows as his mind flicked back to yesterday in Marsden's office. He felt an obscure guilt at his indifferent judgment of those greenhorns. No concern of his, yet he hoped the Amberleys might now have the sense to go back where they belonged. On reflection, he couldn't blame the woman for countering his rudeness with an acrid insult of her own; no doubt her ultimate judgement of him was that he was a shiftless, useless frontier tramp. Which is close enough, he thought with a wry grin, and dismissed the incident from his thoughts.

Angsman tramped around the long building that housed the bachelor officers' quarters to the bathhouse at its rear. Five minutes later, standing under the shower and soaping his chest and shoulders, he glanced around as the door opened, seeing Terence Dahoney's broad bulk filling the doorway.

"I'm thinkin' that of us two, you're the wiser," Dahoney commented phlegmatically. "Today's that much a scorcher, I'd like to tell the major fie on his paperwork and the damned Army too, and join ye." He glanced over Angsman's lean white body with its startling contrast of deeply weathered face and neck and hands, and added, "That's why I don't. Look at the likes of you, ganted up like a deer-huntin' dog. The service at the least fills a man's belly."

"You've got pretty soft, Terence," Angsman observed. He waited for Dahoney's derisive snort, then grinned, "If you didn't come for a bath...?"

"The major sent me to find you, an' Trooper Wilcox saw you headin' for here."

"Now what the hell?" Angsman asked with a mild irritation.

"I dunno, Willis. Only that he's in higher dudgeon than yesterday. Ye'd best lose no time...."

Ten minutes later Angsman walked into the commandant's office, nodded to Major Marsden's grim and unsmiling greeting, and took his position against the wall, stirring his shoulders uncomfortably against the scratchy newness of his crease-stiff shirt and trousers, having discarded his other ragged clothes.

Marsden said flatly and without preliminary, "They did it. Kited off into the desert without a by-your-leave."

"The Amberleys, eh?"

The major stood, paced an angry circle of the desk and halted facing him. "Yes, dammit—stole off at first dawn before either Elsa or I were awake." He sighed and scrubbed his jaw with the flat of his palm, a gesture of weary disgust. "Let me start at the beginning. I invited the Amberleys to stay the night at our place. Then he and I went to the sutler's for a drink. As we were leaving, Armand Charbonneau and his gang of tough nuts rode in—"

"Charbonneau...." Angsman scowled. "Thought he'd have the sense to stay clear of Stambaugh after I uncovered his whisky-peddling last year. Didn't he head for Mexico?"

"He did, and stayed long enough to let the event cool. No case that'd hold water, and he knew it. Came riding in bold as brass, bluffed his way past the sentry. I told him to have his drink and clear out. Dr. Amberley was taken with the damned blackguard, stayed to size Charbonneau up. I'd warned the fool not to get cozy with Charbonneau, but—I got the rest of the story from Harley Moffat this morning."

The sutler had noticed that the professor was holding his liquor badly, and that the rascally Creole obviously had his nose to the wind and was straining at the leash. Busy serving drinks to Charbonneau's thirsty crew, Moffat had paid no great attention to the pair's low-voiced conversation, lost in the general hubbub. Then Charbonneau had abruptly called his pack to heel and they'd ridden away. Jack Kincaid had left with them, which had struck Moffat as odd, there being bad blood between the half-breed and Turk Ambruster, Charbonneau's right-hand man. Then the professor, weaving badly but navigating on his own, had left.

At the major's house, his wife had greeted Amberley pleasantly, without comment on his condition, and had shown him to his room. Judith Amberley was napping at the time. Later the major and his wife had enjoyed a tolerant chuckle over the incident, both agreeing to say nothing to the strait-laced Miss Amberley about her brother's unseemly behavior.

Later, as the Marsdens were retiring, they heard the Amberleys conversing in low tones in the sister's room. James Amberley had apparently slept off his liquor, and now, the major guessed, he and Judith were discussing their future plans. His first alarm hadn't come till this morning when Elsa went to wake the Amberleys for breakfast and found both of them gone.

Marsden had hurried to the stables, there to learn from the stable sergeant that the two Easterners had claimed their horses and pack gear an hour before reveille. Next the colonel had checked with the night sentry at the east gate, learning that the Amberleys had left the fort at first light and headed due east across the flats. Afterward, idly following their progress from the wall, the sentry had seen five horsemen, too distant to identify, canter over a low range of dunes and meet the Amberleys. The seven of them had ridden on together. Though curious, the sentry had made nothing of the incident, nor thought it worth reporting at the time. Finally on a hunch, the major had talked to Harley Moffat, finding his worst fears verified.

Angsman said softly, "Charbonneau, eh?"

"Who else? Amberley innocently mentioned his brother's mission, and at the mention of gold, Charbonneau became a wolf on the scent. In Amberley's state, he'd have needed little persuasion to fall in with our Channing rogue's suggestion that he and his crew were just the men to guide them into the Sierra Toscos and bring them out alive...."

Angsman rubbed his chin reflectively. "And he'd figure his past renegade dealings with 'Paches, some hostile, would get him past Bonito. Plenty risk even so, but the stakes'd be worth it."

"Yes, exactly; the point is those poor fools are lambs

ripe for the shearing—I should say slaughter, with that wolf-pack."

"Send a detail to bring 'em back."

The major snorted impatiently. "You know how the settlers resent the military, though our only purpose here is to protect them. In extreme cases when we've had to declare martial law, the stink invariably carries clear to Washington. War Department sends us strict orders to handle civilians with kid gloves. What in hell can I do? Hogtie our two lambs and bring them back at bayonet point? For unless I'm mistaken, you couldn't sway that Amberley girl otherwise. Has a mind like a steel trap —dominates her brother, if you noticed—and has some almighty intense reason to go ahead with this damnfool search, something beyond ordinary family affection." The major paused deliberately. "The point is, it's a free country, person can come or go at their whim. I work for that country; my hands are tied. Yours aren't."

"Wondered when you'd get to that."

"Will you do it?"

Angsman nodded wearily. "I'll bring your lambs back. Can't promise all the fleece'll be intact."

"Good," Phil Marsden said briskly. "Of course, the assignment's wholly unofficial, and this conversation never took place. You'll handle it as you think best...and accordingly, you're not merely on your own—the full responsibility for your action is on your head. Understood?"

"Pretty clear buck-passing, Phil."

"Sorry, Will. You know I'm strapped."

"Sure. I'll want one man, a good one."

"How about Mexican Tom?"

"The best, when he's sober. Where in hell is Tom?"

"Still on our guide payroll, and his wife still takes in laundry for the enlisted men. Tom, I regret to say, got drunk the other night and started shooting at the sky. Roused the whole post—thought it was a new uprising. To make a long story short, he's in the guardhouse serving a thirty-day sentence."

Angsman chuckled. "Same old Tomas...."

Marsden reached down his battered campaign hat and clamped it on. "Let's get him out."

Angling across the parade grounds and approaching the guardhouse, they heard the strains of a discordant but lively harmonica playing *La Cucaracha* drifting from the single barred window. The major spoke to the trooper on guard, who opened the barred door. Angsman followed Ate major inside, ducking his tall frame through the low doorway.

Tomas Ramirez was sprawled on his back across a bunk, one leg cocked up and the other trailing on the floor, his eyes closed. He tapped the harmonica on his wrist, pocketed it, and opened a black sparkling eye. He wasn't much past twenty, a squat brown gnome of a young man with a long lantern jaw which sagged in a lazy grin; he idly lifted a hand without otherwise stirring.

"*Buenas dias,* Willie. Heard you was on the post. Hey, you come to get Tomas out? We catch big drunk, eh?"

"You catch nothing from me but hell, Tomas."

Mexican Tom yawned and sat up, running one hand through his short curly hair, reached the other inside his cotton shirt and scratched his ribs. Angsman detected the wicked glint in his eye and was ready when Tom made a sudden grab at his wrist. Angsman sidestepped, grabbed his wrist and threw him face down across the bunk with a knee in his back. Both of them were laughing when Angsman released him and Tom bounded to his feet to pump his hand.

"You damned big kid," Angsman growled amiably. "When you going to grow up?"

"Hell, amigo, I got a whole life for that. Hey, you pretty fit for an old man. Come on, we catch that drink."

"Not so fast, Ramirez," the major said curtly. "I'm releasing you on conditions—one of which is, no drinking."

"Sure, big chief. It's what you say. Even so, by damn, is good to see you, Willie."

As they stepped outside, Marsden said, "You're under Angsman's orders, Tom. He'll explain the situation...." He extended his hand then, and Angsman took it. "Will, Miss Amberley should give you more trouble than Charbonneau. Go careful, and luck to you."

Angsman and Mexican Tom moved off toward the married enlisted men's row, Angsman quietly filling in the situation. Ramirez nodded in ready agreement. "I'm with you. Been honin' for excitement, and they ain't none to be had in this pesthole. Soon's I'm outfitted and say *adios* to my woman, we make the dust."

At the little Ramirez adobe at the far end of the row,

Mexican Tom assembled his gear while his pretty wife flailed him with a furious tongue, "*Madre de Dios,* before you are out of the *calabozo* almost, you ride off. …Ongsman, can you no leave my *bellaco* of a hosband with me a while, *por favor?* I will give him such a crack on the head…"

"Sorry, Lupe. I need him now." Angsman's quick eye traced a furtive movement. "Tomas, what'd you slip in that saddlebag?"

"Oh, nothing, amigo."

Angsman's hand dipped into the saddlebag and came up with a full pint of whisky. "None of that," he said roughly, and handed the bottle to Lupe. "Not this trip. I mean it, Tomas."

Mexican Tom spread his hands in abject mockery. "I am jus' one no-good bom, amigo." To which Lupe added her shrill, angry agreement.

They rode steadily across the mesquite-laced flats until, toward late afternoon, the plainly marked trail left by the Amberley-Charbonneau party mounted to low hills stippled by piñon and cedar. The heat pressed like a great blistered hand from a lemon-colored sky; the sun poured savagely against their right sides.

Will Angsman rocked easily to his paint's gait, his relaxed alertness a part of his thought and being. He breathed deeply of the hot air, already savoring the sense of release that came when he left the habitations of men. Unthinkingly his senses catalogued the smell of cedar, a chicken hawk dipping against the sky, the hooffalls of their mounts and pack mule, the quick-panted pushups of a lizard colorless against a rock.

Such notice was second nature to Angsman; he'd lived for a time with Apache friends, but mostly by himself. He'd devoured everything the Indians could teach him, then had struck out on his own, which was why he could beat the Apache at his own game. Even Indians moved in an interdependent society. Necessity of lone survival had left Angsman with the knowledge and senses and sure serenity of an animal uncomplicated by thought. Lately, though, he'd had the troubled conviction that for a man, life could never reduce itself to such simple terms….

Mexican Tom, pacing his short-coupled zebra dun alongside, mopped his sleeve across his brow. "Hey, amigo, we makin' pretty sorry time. You expect to come up on them *cabrons* next year?"

"The sign says we're matching their pace. They're not pushing fast in this heat, neither are we. Not much over two hours ahead, and we'll make up the difference after nightfall, when they strike camp."

"We take 'em then, eh?"

Angsman nodded.

"Figure they be a fight, amigo?"

"Try to surprise 'em. Never can tell, though."

"That's good by me."

Angsman returned the other's grin, feeling a stir of affection for this thoughtless, mañana-living youth, so like him in some ways, utterly different in others. Together they had guided for the troops more than once, working in easy co-ordination with a paucity of words, their mutual understanding as two men of action being complete.

Aside from this Tomas Ramirez was his good friend; he'd plumbed past his outward inanities to a bedrock nature of unswerving loyalty and steady strength under stress, marred only by his one great weakness. He didn't get stupidly, ugly drunk, as did Jack Kincaid; he simply became boisterous, then befuddled, and finally passed out. His wasn't a raw or constant craving for liquor, yet it temporarily bridged some fundamental flaw in his nature, and to that degree filled a genuine need for him.

Angsman uncapped his water and took a small swallow, afterward passing the canteen to Tom. Ramirez lifted it in wry salute, drank....

Toward evening, as the last stratified rose-gold of sunset died along the western hills, they halted for a brief rest and made a cold meal off the last of the beef sandwiches Lupe had packed. Again in the saddle as twilight thickened, they pushed steadily on, guided by the first gleam of stars. Angsman could not track by dark, but he'd seen the Amberley's map and knew their direction of route; he also knew that the desert flats and rolling, sparsely wooded character of the land clear to the Toscos foothills would enable the party to follow it up without detour. Now with the cool of night setting in, he held a rapid pace, alert for the first sign of a night bivouac.

Along the brief eddy of an air current he picked up a

faint trace of woodsmoke, mentioned this to Mexican Tom who shook his head. "Ain't arguin' with that Injun nose of yours, amigo. How far?"

"About an hour's ride."

Ramirez spotted the smoke wisping almost invisibly against the cobalt sky as quickly as Angsman. He answered Ramirez' half-seen questioning jerk of head with a sharp nod. Without words both men dismounted and ground-hitched their animals, working swiftly and silently.

They would separate here, Angsman whispered; he'd circle wide to come up on the camp from the south while Ramirez stalked the northern side. Each would work as near as possible, size up the layout from his own vantage, and pick his position. The signal to move in would be the hoot of a horned owl, and its reply.

The Mexican's assent was a mere nod; he settled onto his rump to slip off his boots while Angsman moved away on moccasined feet. He described a broad half-circle of the unseen camp, moving always nearer in a concentric line, till he made out the gently dipping bowl between a pocket of hills, filled with a ragged lift of scrub oak. The camp was concealed somewhere toward to the center of that grove, dense enough to hide their fire. Angsman could see only that fine banner darkly curling against the blue-black sky; next his ears selected faint camp-sounds from the other voices of night.

He went down the south slope of the bowl like a shadow, gliding noiselessly through the thorny brush encircling the oak stand. Shortly after he'd penetrated the first growth, flickering orange light grew against the darkness. Next the fire itself appeared through the tree boles...Angsman caught a sudden lift of angry voices. He achieved the low rimming edge of oak brush and there dropped to a crouch behind its leafy screen for a clear view of the camp.

He identified Charbonneau and his men—Ambruster, Uvaldes, a tow-headed stocky youth he'd never seen, and Jack Kincaid; following his habit, the half-breed was already the center of a flare-up.

James Amberley stood to one side with an arm thrown around his sister; Charbonneau stood with a slack negligence, yet defensively, between them and Kincaid. A knife flashed suddenly in the breed's hand, and Charbonneau moved like a striking snake. His fist made a meaty thud against Kincaid's bull neck, and the breed hit the ground on his hip and shoulder but rolled almost at once to his feet.

Charbonneau's three men were sprawled on the ground, indifferently watching while the leader and Jack Kincaid faced each other tensely. From the far side of the clearing drifted the deep hoot of a great horned owl. Nobody paid any heed, except for the dark, scar-faced Ramon Uvaldes. A cigarillo drooped from his thin lips, his eyes squinted against the smoke, and now his head lifted at the sound, twisting sharply at Angsman's low answering hoot.

Angsman was on his feet and moving forward as he replied to Mexican Tom's signal, moving quickly, because Uvaldes, sensing something amiss, had stabbed his cigarillo into the ground as he came swiftly up off his haunches, firelight glinting on his drawn pistol.

CHAPTER FIVE

The last rose-hued effect of the whisky had finally worn off, and James Amberley was fully and miserably aware of why he'd been so easily gulled into playing rabbit to Charbonneaừ's smoothly baited snare. The Creole had infused fresh life into his blasted hope of finding Douglas —an attempt that he felt must be made for Judith's sake, whatever the cost.

Not that Charbonneau wasn't possessed of a lethal charm to bolster his own self-argument…Amberley had the map and provisions for the trip and Charbonneau had a competent force of followers; why not join company? The good doctor had substantial funds; Armand and his men were presently at loose ends and could use this handsome payment for their services…in the event that they failed to find the gold, which, of course, all would share equally. A pleasant arrangement of business between gentlemen, *n'est-ce pas?* Of a certainty the good doctor, being a man of taste and discernment, did not believe the exaggerated nonsense of Armand's inherent duplicity that he guessed M'sieu the major had poured into his ears. It was true that the exigencies of frontier life did not breed archangels; but as to his personal honor, let no man cast slight on that of Armand Charbonneau, and was not a business arrangement an affair of honor?

Knowing few men outside of his own class, where honor was a thing taken for granted, Amberley was by nature trusting; moreover he had a myopic comic-opera view of the gentleman rogue. He'd muddily assured the Creole that he didn't doubt his integrity, but what of Bonito's Apaches, the necessity for a competent guide, and wouldn't Major Marsden object rather strenuously?

Charbonneau's deprecating gesture made nothing of these details. He spoke of his past fair dealings with the

216

Apache, the nature of which he failed to mention; and Chief Bonito would welcome Armand as a *sheekasay,* a great brother. As to a guide, *voila*—was not the finest guide in the territory, Jack Kincaid, standing not a dozen paces away; would not this fine guide gladly accommodate his bon ami Armand? Also it would be most simple to circumvent M'sieu the major, a good officer, but sadly given to exaggeration. Armand and his men would leave the fort now and camp not far distant; in the early dawn the professor and the ma'mselle would rise and depart, well before the major had arisen, and ride to join Armand and his men. They would all proceed together to the succor of the doctor's brother; was not the scheme the essence of simplicity?

Simple enough, Amberley thought bitterly now, and so was I....In his drunken state, deceiving the major had held a certain savor of forbidden fruit. Even when they had joined Charbonneau well beyond the haven of Fort Stambaugh's walls, the Creole's attitude had not markedly changed. But as the whisky wore completely off, the man's winning ways began to ring falsely. At last the muttered exchanges between the others had completely enlightened the Easterner....

Major Marsden's summing-up of this crew as cut-throats and blackguards had been only too accurate. Their talk was of nothing but the gold, and there was a fevered note to it. Whenever Amberley glanced at one of them, he met a silent and stony stare. These men would be of no help in their search, he knew then. They might even abandon them on reaching their destination or before—they needed only the map. Hard on the heels of that came a second cold realization: suppose they decided to kill them both in order to keep the secret of the gold, if any? Of course he'd heard that women could move in perfect safety among the worst of frontier desperadoes, but this was probably nonsense.

Judith too, though almost blind to everything but her purpose here, now realized their situation. She'd calmly shuttered any fear beneath the cold mask that Armored all her emotions, sitting primly beside James now, feet tucked beneath her outspread skirt as she examined a broken fingernail. Where her wide-brimmed hat hadn't shielded her neck and lower face, she was badly sunburned; dust deeply discolored her gray habit and laid its powdered grit across her smooth chignon. She'd almost fallen after dismounting, and he could only guess at the punishment she'd endured in her soft condition and on that damned sidesaddle. But it wasn't these details which agitated Amberley's deepening worry; Judith seemed to be simply wilting away in this dead, suffocating heat. She'd hardly touched her supper. Her face glistened with sweat; it formed dark muddy patches on her clothing; she kept swallowing hard, as though fighting sickness, and her eyes, at first unnaturally bright, were becoming faintly glazed.

"Judith—"

"Yes, Jimmy?" Her response was falsely quick and bright.

"Are you all right, dear?"

"Quite." The smile cost an effort; her throat muscles fought convulsively at her tight high collar. Good Lord, Amberley thought in alarm, she's roasting to death in that rig—and corseted up like a dowager, I shouldn't wonder.

It spurred him to sudden decision. Another time he might have let her stew awhile in her iron hotbox and iron pride. Yet taken with their present situation, the fact left him suddenly shaking with anger. He had to get Judith out of this...and his mind came to taut focus on the revolver he'd packed in his gear. Better chance of getting his hands on that than his saddle carbine. His gaze touched halfway across the clearing to his pack, and then he lounged casually to his feet.

"Sit down, my fran'."

Sitting tailor-fashion by the fire, Charbonneau spoke without troubling to glance up from the gun he was cleaning. Amberley felt his tight resolve harden, and with it a mounting wild stubbornness. He took a step toward his pack—

Suddenly glass broke on a rock.

Jack Kincaid had emptied a bottle he'd been steadily nursing for an hour, holding a black brooding silence. Flinging it away, he came to his feet, stumbling drunkenly, his mouth open and slack. His murky stare fixed on Judith as he started toward her mumbling, "Don't be skeered o' Jack, purty lady..."

Throughout the day the half-breed's attention had hardly left her. Amberley had been half-dreading this, yet for a frozen moment he couldn't quite believe it was happening. Then wholly without thinking he lunged at Kincaid. The breed shot rum a dully startled glance, growled deep in his throat and swung his thick arm as if swatting a fly. A hamlike palm clapped Amberley across the head and knocked him to the ground.

Dazedly he pushed up on his hands and knees. He straightened his askew spectacles, and the scene swam back to focus. Charbonneau was on his feet advancing toward Kincaid like a gaunt catamount. Amberley scrambled up as Judith rose uncertainly, putting his arm around her and drawing her back.

Charbonneau said patiently and without anger, "Let the Ma'mselle alone, Jack."

Kincaid hunched his great shoulders. "Naw...." He squinted rheumily. "Break you in half, Armand...."

The Creole glanced at the Amberleys, saying with a little shrug, almost apologetically, "No Western man do such thing, you comprehend. But Jack, he is not to blame. He is the pure animal—"

Kincaid growled again, suddenly stooping to tug at his boot. At once firelight flashed on a six-inch blade. Charbonneau moved swiftly, chopping a vicious blow to his neck. Kincaid went down, but came up almost at once. Amberley was obscurely aware that Uvaldes too had risen, his gun in hand. A voice that Amberley knew rapped out, "Drop it, Ramon!"

The scar-faced Mexican swung about; the pistol bucked in his hand as he shot twice at the bushes. An unseen gun blasted. Uvaldes, spun by an invisible blow, fell to his knees and toppled on his face across the fire. Glowing embers belched away from the smothering impact of his fall, and a dusting of sparks leaped and died.

There was still enough firelight to show young Staples and the giant Ambruster scrambling for their guns. Now a different voice said almost musically, "I wouldn', amigos."

Two men stepped from opposite flanks of the clearing, covering Charbonneau and his crew. Will Angsman moved in to place a moccasined foot against the sprawled Uvaldes' shoulder, roll him on his back. The body in its smoldering clothing was soft and limp and inert, and Amberley realized with a kind of distant shock that the man was dead.

The fire gathered back its steady outreaching glow,

sallowing every face, Matter-of-factly, while his companion covered them, Angsman moved among the desperadoes, collecting their weapons. He pitched these into the
bushes, afterward tramping over to Amberley,

"All right, professor? Your sister?"

"All…right," Amberley croaked. "My God—"

"Sit down, doctor, and take it easy," Angsman said
gently. His shuttling glance lay hard against Charbonneau,
and he tramped over to him. Incongruously in this shaken
moment, Amberley noticed with surprise that Angsman
was as tall as the gangleader; he'd thought of Charbonneau
as loftier because the man theatrically dramatized his
height, as he did everything.

Charbonneau grinned whitely, lightly resting his hands
on hips. "*Bonjour,* oldfran'…."

"Always a new iron in the fire, eh, Armand? Long-
looping, whisky-running…even a lost mine."

"Ah, yes, old fran'. But is legitimate business, no? Ask
M'sieu le doctair…."

"Get off the stage, Armand. There's your horses."

"I 'ave the agreement with M'sieu Amberley. I 'ave not
decide to break it."

"Long walk might help you decide."

Charbonneau's smile thinned. "Do not do that to me,
m'sieu."

Without turning his head, Angsman said softly, "Tomas
…hooraw them off," stepping back then to cover the
whole crew while the Mexican sheathed his gun and went
to loose the picket line that held the horses. With
Spanish epithets and lashing rope-end, he sent the gang's
animals thundering from the clearing and through the
brush, the sound of their going soon dying away. Grinning,
he re-tied the Amberley animals.

"Leave your gear, except for a canteen of water apiece,
Good twenty-five mile hike back to Fort Stambaugh—
only if I was you, I'd try Contentionville. Marsden wasn't
turning any cheeks, last I saw him." Angsman paused
gently. "If you have got any further objections you care
to state, go ahead. That's if you want to leave your canteens and your boots behind."

Charbonneau stood unmoving, still slack-poised, the
fireglow washing wickedly against his eyes. At last he
turned with the barest of shrugs, walked to the piled gear
and got his canteen. The other three sullenly followed his

example. Charbonneau, straightening with the strap of his canteen looped over a shoulder, let his glance briefly touch the dead Uvaldes, reserving his final look for Angsman. Then he turned wordlessly and walked from the clearing, the crew filing off behind him. Angsman stood with his head tilted, listening to the crackle of brush with their passage.

After a full minute he let his gun off-cock and sheathed it, turning to the Mexican. "Want to get our horses, Tomas?"

"*Como no?* Then I bury that countryman."

"Have a care of yourself out there."

"Bah. That Charbonneau and his curly wolves not waitin' around; they blunder like the bull. Such *cabron* never surprise Tomas." The Mexican slipped easily away through the brush on his sock feet.

James Amberley mopped his brow with a bandanna. "Angsman, I can't tell you...you saved our lives!"

"Like enough," Angsman agreed drily. "If they decided to chuck you both off along the way, you'd last about a day. Got to hand it to you, professor. It took some reaching, but you made it—worse damnfool than you were yesterday. Get some sleep, the two of you—we'll be starting back at dawn. Don't argue that, Miss; I'm not in the mood."

Judith had been staring at the dead man, her face white and pinched; she started as though his words had shocked her from a trance. But her instant reply was flat and toneless: "I do not propose to argue, Mr. Angsman. Your help was welcome, but you are no longer needed here. James and I will go on alone tomorrow."

"Reckon not, if you're tied to your saddle."

"If you touch me, sir, I shall scratch your eyes out."

A dead silence stretched out like a tenuous thread. ...Amberley had the queer feeling that he'd ceased to exist in the mute antagonism that crackled between these two. It struck him that he'd never seen two people as many worlds apart, yet with so similar a blunt head-on manner. Quite suddenly he would have laughed aloud if the situation hadn't been so deadly serious. Judith's stare mirrored open contempt and defiance; Angsman's showed nothing at all.

Amberley had no inkling of his thought till the scout

swung toward him unexpectedly: "Professor...you still want a guide, you got one from here out."

Amberley hadn't realized his own startled tension till he felt it wash out of him with his fast sigh of startled relief. "Gladly, sir—gladly." He added with a formal stiffening, minding Angsman's cold judgment of him, "Pleased that you changed your mind," and extended his hand. Ignoring it, Angsman swung away to stir the fire up.

CHAPTER SIX

"Stan' still, Angelito, you balky *chingado—*"

Mexican Tom fondly cursed the little gray mule as he diamond-hitched his and Angsman's gear to its back, and Angsman said without censure, "Easy on the mule-skinning lingo, Tomas."

Ramirez made a wry face, glancing at the Amberleys. "Sure, amigo, excuse it."

"By the way," Angsman murmured then, "you weren't committed to do more'n help me catch these greenhorns. Appreciate your joining up all the way. Can't have too many nursemaids."

"Por nada," Ramirez said cheerfully, adding with puzzled gravity, "Look, these...uh...Nuevo Ingles, they loco, eh?"

"That's it," Angsman agreed wearily. "Humor 'em, Tomas."

Mexican Tom covered his snicker by whistling *La Cucaracha,* and Angsman sent Judith Amberley a bleak glance. It hadn't been her blunt threat to fight him tooth and nail if he tried to force her return that had prompted his new decision. Irritably he'd told himself that letting her carry her search to its hopeless end was its own best means of punishing her blind, insensate arrogance; he couldn't let them go oh alone when his presence might mean the difference between life and death. But this excuse had a hollow ring.

Somehow the antagonism between them had narrowed down to a personal challenge: at their first meeting when with acid candor she'd accused him of cowardice and again last night when she'd deliberately baited him with her contemptuous dislike. Without putting it into words, she had flung the gage of challenge at his manhood and dared him to pick it up. Angsman wondered with wrathful

223

bafflement why he felt bound to prove anything to this headstrong and pampered woman, even committing his own life to whatever suicide pact she'd made with herself.

She was sitting beyond the dead fire, dabbing at her throat and face with a handkerchief she had soaked from her canteen, and now regarding her closely, Angsman forgot his anger—she was damned close to passing out. She appeared somewhat refreshed after a night's sleep, but the punishing heat of a new desert day was already taking its toll.

As he came up to her, she raised glazed eyes that held a residue of cold challenge; her prim chignon was undone, clinging in sweat-darkened strands to her cheeks, their feverish glow accenting her dead pallor. She was breathing quickly, partly through her mouth.

He said coldly, "That outfit belongs on a city bridle path. Likely to be your death here."

"I beg your pardon?"

James Amberley had finished tying his own pack on their animal, and now he came over with a frown of deep concern. "That's what I've been telling her. Jude, will you please listen? You can't continue another hour in that silly costume—convention be damned!"

"Nonsense, Jim." Her lips firmed thinly. "And I'll thank you not to swear."

Angsman said impatiently, "Got any spare duds like yours, professor?"

"Why yes, but I've put my pack together—oh, you mean—"

"Get 'em out. She can use one of the saddles Charbonneau left."

"How dare you!" The blood tiding against her sunburned throat showed a scarlet outrage even in her feverish weakness. "Are you—are you suggesting that I wear a *man's*—"

"You'll wear them, or we'll bury you before the day's out."

"Really, Angsman...." Seeing that neither of them was paying attention, Amberley let his shocked objection trail. Again a clash of will, standing staring at each other.

Angsman, hesitating, decided there was no way to put it delicately. "Miss Amberley, you're shut up in a furnace of your own making, and an airless one to boot. You breathe mostly through your skin, and it cools you. Yours hasn't a chance in—in what you're wearing. Body makes its own heat and sheds it. You're not shedding, only taking in." He hesitated. "And you can't take the days ahead, the country ahead, on any sidesaddle."

She glared at him, biting her lower lip, and glanced at her brother as if in angry appeal. But Amberley was already unfastening their pack, letting it slide to the ground. In a moment he returned with clean, folded clothing; wordlessly he laid it at her side and walked away. Angsman lounged over to his paint, occupied himself fooling with the cinch. For a full minute Judith Amberley sat stiff and unmoving. Slowly and painfully then, she gathered up the clothes and climbed to her feet, disappearing into the oaks that fringed the clearing. Amberley relaxed with a sigh of profound relief, took out his tobacco pouch and loaded his pipe, moving over to the guide.

"Angsman—" he began briskly, pausing to strike a match and puff his pipe alight— "let's be frank. You don't like us much, and all things considered, I can't blame you—"

"Not that."

"All right, but why change your mind? I'm grateful, certainly—but why?"

"Man doesn't want his eyes scratched out."

Wry amusement touched the Easterner's mild face. "I realize that you Western fellows resent prying...but I wish you'd tell me one thing: is the expedition so utterly hopeless in terms of our survival? I'm steeled for the worst, but I'd like to know."

Angsman frowned his hesitation. "Lot to consider. I've lived and foraged alone in country overrun with hostiles months at a stretch. To give you an idea what that means, even Ramirez thinks I'm crazy for doing it. Here I'll have you three to look out for. Add to that that the eastern Toscos are as wild and rugged a stretch as you'll find in the territory, and you got a catamount by the tail."

Amberley thought a moment. "It must be a large area, though...and the Apaches surely can't be everywhere at once."

"They move around a lot. Their camps are built to be broke up and on the move in minutes. And their scouts, their hunting parties, cover a lot of territory. Just enough of us to be easily spotted—just few enough to make a tempting target. Another thing—you show Charbonneau your brother's map?"

"He studied my copy, but if he has one, it's in his memory." Amberley paused wryly. "I see your meaning. He can get fresh horses and provisions at Contentionville and take up our trail...."

"And fast, with all that gold on his mind. By the way ...what's your slant on that, professor?"

"I'm not bloodless, Angsman," James Amberley said dryly. "I daresay my dry scholar's soul is somewhat taken by the thought of a large treasure waiting to be picked up—as is yours."

Angsman grinned faintly. "How about your brother?"

Amberley bit hard on his pipestem, spoke carefully around it. "Why...I'm not wholly certain of Douglas' reasons. We were similar in our tastes, and close enough in that way, but the twelve-year difference in our ages didn't invite confidences."

"Make a guess."

The suggestion plainly discomfited Amberley. "Rather difficult to explain....You've doubtless taken the impression from what we've told you that my brother was a rash and foolhardy boy. Rather, he was studious, a bit sensitive—and something of a weakling." He puffed on his pipe, embarrassed. "You might say this undertaking was a thing he had to do—to vindicate himself."

Angsman had been digging for useful information, and now from Amberley's cryptic and evasive reply, he realized that he'd touched crosscurrents that went far deeper, probably involving all three Amberleys.

The Easterner added awkwardly, "Don't think too harshly of my sister. I can state without prejudice that she has some splendid qualities, not the least of which is being eminently sensible, once she overcomes a narrow viewpoint. Yankee practicality, we call it."

Judith Amberley returned to the clearing, very straight and stiff and resolutely refusing to hide behind the bundle of clothing she held bunched at her side. The grimy habit was carefully wrapped, Angsman supposed, around a discarded under-armor of stiffened whalebone, suffocating basque, and numerous unmentionables. Though the oversize trousers and shirt and light jacket she now wore were comfortably loose and shapeless, she was plainly struggling to hide a deep mortification, as though she'd shed, with a set of iron conventions, some defensive coloration. Her face had regained color with her new well-being, and it was evident she'd rather cut out her tongue than admit it She walked to the open pack of her belongings, hesitated, then firmly dropped the bundle to one side. "You needn't trouble packing these things, Jim."

With this triumphant confirmation of her good sense, Amberley was prompted to say with completely untactful cheerfulness, "You know, in some warm countries I've been, women, uh—" At her icy glance, he blushed, muttering, "Rather becoming, though—"

She gasped, her martyred resentment flaming openly. "Oh? To be dressed like some painted saloon creature, or a—a circus performer? At least spare me that!"

Amberley sighed resignedly....

Through that day they continued across rolling and semi-forested country, then struck on over a vast, level *playa* whose white-hot dazzling brilliance stretched away to the first foothills of the blued saw-toothed sierra; this shimmered to distortion in the heavy heat waves. Impalpable dust rose as they plodded into its waterless desolation, and the sun broiled against their faces and backs all that day, and several more following. Restlessly scanning their back trail through his Army field glasses, Angsman saw the riders coming as distant dots on the playa late in the third day. He said nothing to the others.

Charbonneau had lost no time....

Moving onto the foothills, they fought through a jungle of mesquite, Spanish dagger, and cloudy white forests of yucca, until these gave welcome way to gentler open slopes of scattered manzanita and juniper.

On the seventh day, Angsman called an early halt, and while Tomas Ramirez and Judith Amberley gathered greasewood brush for a fire, he and Amberley pored over the *derrotero* spread out on a flat rock between them. Angsman traced a calloused finger along a wavering line that bisected the chart, which was now frayed and grimy and discolored by a brown waterstain. "Obregon's landmarks have placed out right as rain so far...and that should be the Paisano River. Far as I've ever been. From there on, this better be damn' well right."

"Hasn't the old Don's accuracy so far proven anything to you, Angsman?"

"Don't make the rest of it gospel. The man admitted he was out of his mind on the return trip."

Amberley shook his head. "You're quite an agnostic."

"What's that?"

"Word recently coined by a British scientist named Huxley. Means one who suspends belief until all the evidence is in."

"We'll see," was all Angsman said.

He glanced at Judith Amberley who was occupied in building a fire as he had shown her, arranging sticks to make a small concentrated blaze. He had to admit she was bearing up far better than he'd expected, performing homely camp chores without complaint. She had begun to harden past the first raw experience of aching muscles, blisters, and sunburn; after struggling for a time with the dusty matted tangle of her long hair, she'd cropped it off close to her head. The skin of her nose and cheeks was peeling. With her man's clothing, it made her seem slight and boyish and urchin-like, and the outward change had thawed a little of her chilly reserve. She had unbent from time to time to ask questions about the desert and its fierce teeming life.

Yet the upshot of it was that Angsman understood her less than before. She was a strange woman, at once woodenly reserved and candidly forthright, never revealing more than a little of herself at a time. He'd wondered whether the core of her was empty or sound; her incredible adaptability had answered him. Judith Amberley contained untapped reserve adequate to meet the demands exerted by even her iron will. It deepened the puzzle; she seemed to be all driving tensions, without a trace of womanly softness, and he could wonder now whether there might be depths to her no man had touched.

The thought was disturbing. Lately, some restless dissatisfaction which he recognized as a threat to his cherished independence had nagged at him, and he warily wondered whether Judith Amberley had somehow become tied up in his struggle with himself.

Suddenly his mind was emptied of everything but his alert senses. A strengthening downcurrent breeze bore the faintest trace of burning curl-leaf...hardly any smoke. That was Indian; and without a word he walked to the pyre of creosote twigs, scattered it with a sweep of his foot. Before she could form an angry response, he said curtly, "No fire. We've got company."

Amberley glanced up from his chart. "What?"

"Stay here, and stay quiet. Tomas, we'll have a look.'"

Amberley came to his feet in alarm. "You aren't leaving—!"

"No danger yet. Don't know of us, or they wouldn't be thinking about supper."

"Not Apaches?"

"I'll let you know," Angsman said sardonically, already rummaging into his saddlebag for his field glasses. He looped them around his neck by the thong, glancing at Mexican Tom waiting with his old Springfield slung under his arm. The two men scaled the shallow ridge above their bivouac and followed its wide summit south, holding to the slope below skyline. At the southern extremity of the ridge a large bluff rose like a flinty fist, this sheering steeply off above a brush-filled valley.

Angsman flattened himself atop the crumbling scale of the bluff, easing along on his elbows till he could get an all-over view of the valley. Sunset crowned its western end with pink and gold, and he analyzed light conditions for chance of sunflash, afterward training his glasses on the telltale smudge of smoke and moving down to its source. Though dense brush almost concealed the camp, he could make it out enough to be certain. Bellying up to his side, Mexican Tom grunted, and Angsman handed him the glasses. After a moment Ramirez murmured: "How you make it, amigo?"

" 'Pache. Small party. Came from the south, or they'd have crossed our trail."

"Por que?"

"Quien sabe? Renegades up from Sonora maybe, on their way to join Bonito. Only way to be sure is wait till morning, see how they head out."

Back at camp Angsman told the Amberleys what he had seen, adding that from now on the three men would divide a night watch between them. Shortly they would reach the Paisano River and definitely hostile country. This night Mexican Tom and Amberley would split the watch while Angsman caught a few hours' sleep, then returned to keep lookout on the Apache camp.

Soon after midnight Amberley ended his nervous vigil and woke both Ramirez and Angsman; while the

Mexican took up his post, Angsman moved off through
the night toward the bluff without haste. The Apaches,
believing that the spirits of their dead roamed the darkness and must do so undisturbed, wouldn't break camp
till first light.

At full dawn he watched them move out through the
brush toward the eastern valley, cutting straight for the
heart of the Toscos. So they were heading for a rendez-
vous with Bonito...well, it didn't greatly worsen their
position, at least for now. This band was holding roughly
parallel to their route, but well to the south, probably
along an old Apache trail.

As they crossed an open break in the dense mesquite
and chaparral, Angsman trained his glasses in turn on
each rider. He counted five fiercely alert warriors, all
heavily armed...probably fresh from the latest skirmish in the hereditary war between Mexico and Apacheria.
Traces of faded warpaint showed on dark faces. Now
Angsman held on the sixth rider, feeling a thin backwash
of surprise. This was a woman, small and slight of stature
in a dirty and tattered cotton dress. He had the fleeting impression that she was Indian but not Apache—perhaps a captive—and then she passed from sight.

Angsman caught the last rider in his sights now, and
seeing the heavy barrel-chested figure naked save for
warband, a muslin loin cloth and hip-length moccasins
of white deerskin, seeing the broad ochre-smeared face,
he knew cold recognition....

Chingo.

Angsman lowered his glasses as the file of riders
vanished through a steep cut in a ridge. His breathing was
slow and even, but he felt the heavy thud of his heart
against the bare rock. Till now he had augured a slim
chance for their survival in Bonito's country...for the
wily old Chiricahua would not fight except on his own
terms, and if possible, Angsman had meant to give him
no good chance. But that chance had just been narrowed
by a deadlier concern than either Charbonneau or
Bonito....

The Amberleys were still asleep when he dropped
back into camp. Ramirez gave his grim face one searching
glance and said softly, "What is it, amigo?"

"Chingo," Angsman murmured. "On his way to Bonito
all right. When and if he learns that I'm with this party—"

Mexican Tom whistled. "Man, this is not good."

"Not a word to the Amberleys. No need getting up more worry. If we're lucky—"

"Amigo, I'm scared that keepin' Chingo from smelling out anyone he hates much as you is gonna take more luck'n any of us got."

CHAPTER SEVEN

That night they reached the muddy wide millrace of the Paisano River where it cut down a shallow dip worn through lava. Here they crossed easily, pitching camp on its far bank. While the bitter light held, Angsman carefully consulted the Obregon chart, and afterward left the camp and ascended a lava ridge fifty yards away.

From this height he had his first view of the country east of the Paisano...a broken and desolate infinitude of mesa and canyon and naked rock. He was searching for a key landmark, and with a flicker of excitement he found it...a freak white streak that zigzagged like petrified lightning down the blue-black basaltic wall of a towering mesa to the northeast. The old Spaniard's chronicle had stressed that unusual formation; if he was further correct, beneath it would begin the huge pass that would lead through the Toscos to their goal.

Back in camp he told of his find in a few words, seeing Judith Amberley react to the news as a parched man would to water.

The next two days were pure hell, fighting their way across a treacherous upheaval of broken lava, slashed by tortuous canyons and ridges, toward the white-streaked mesa that had seemed amazingly near. The region was like a great raw cinder consumed by the burning eye of the sun arcing its fiery glance above. Nothing flourished here but the tough cholla and the spiked wands of ocotillo...no moving life except snakes or lizards which basked trailside in the sun and slithered from sight. They made painfully slow progress, covering most of the terrain on foot, fighting their skittish animals every yard of the way. Angsman called frequent halts while he went ahead to scout the best route along rimrock or canyon floor.

232

On the night they camped at last beneath the looming south wall of the mesa, everyone rolled exhaustedly into their blankets without food or talk, except for Angsman. Inured to the bitterest hardship, he held a watch most of the night, cutting Tom's and Amberley's to an hour apiece. Standing vigil on a basaltic height of land, he could see into the vast black gulf of the pass not two miles to the north, its high rims awash with moonlight, marking the last leg of their journey...*Obregon Pass,* he thought, for the old Don deserved that much testimonial.

By late dawn they were picking a cautious way down a rugged slide into the great gorge. Angsman didn't have to warn the others to go easy. A furnace-blast of heat reflected by the sheer high walls beat fiercely against animals and riders, holding them to a snail's pace. It was anything but easy going, for the flat canyon floor, nowhere less than a hundred feet in width, was strewn with massive jagged boulders and smaller rubble fallen from the crumbling rim two hundred feet above. Again and again they had to climb laboriously over a huge slanting slide where an entire section of rimrock had collapsed. Occasionally the walls were bisected by huge cross-hatching canyons which had flooded the pass with shallow ridges of alluvial sediment.

By now Angsman's main concern wasn't the Apaches nor the brutal heat that was wearing down each one of them...their water was running dangerously low. Ramirez had packed a water keg on the mule Angelito, shielded from the sun by other gear—this in addition to an extra canteen apiece. But they had found only one muddy spring since leaving the Paisano, and their remaining water was swiftly eked to a limit by the canyon's raw heat and glare relentlessly drying the tissues of their bodies.

At dawn of their third day in Obregon Pass, James Amberley carefully checked Don Pedro's directions against the distance that Angsman had computed they'd covered. "It seems fairly certain that we're very close to Muro del Sangre..."

"Whatever that is," Angsman observed sardonically.

"In any case the pass should end there...can't miss that." Amberley scanned the map once more, gave a weary shake of head, and pocketed it. He looked a far cry from the casually immaculate Easterner he'd been. His ragged blond beard was bleached lighter than his sun-blackened face, and his corduroys were shapeless with sweat and wear, colorless with dust. Judith in her brother's spare clothes looked as disreputable. She was thinned to gauntness, her lips cracked and blistered, and the fine slim planes of her face now seemed bony and angular. Her movements were mechanical with the dull-ness of exhaustion. Angsman uncapped the last canteen of rancid liquid and passed it around, only pretending to drink as it came back to him...and in saddle again, they plodded on.

Less than an hour later Angsman felt a faint tension in his mount, seeing the animal's ears prick up. "We're near on to water, I reckon."

"But where is it?" came Judith's husky query, to which Mexican Tom answered, "Senorita—if Willie say water, it is there."

"Not me. Paint here. He's never lied yet."

Soon the other animals caught the smell, quickened their drooping pace. Ahead the canyon took a majestic, sweeping curve, and they almost stumbled onto the stream. It cut transversely down from the upper pass, fanning out here in a broad shallow flow, then vanishing into a side canyon. It was the purest of water, cold and sparkling and crystal clear.

Angsman studied the surrounding cliffs while he held the mules and horses, letting them drink a little at a time, this while his companions stretched out on the low bank, drinking and bathing their faces and drinking again.

"Come on, amigo! The water, she's fine," Mexican Tom whooped at Angsman. He whooped again as, hunkered down, he scooped his sombrero full and poured it over his head. Water darkly stippled his dusty clothing, glistened on his brown laughing face and matted his shining black hair to his head. Then his expression changed queerly, fixing intently on something between his feet. His cupped hands darted down and brought up a double handful of the streambed.

"Madre de Dios," he whispered. His mouth hung foolishly open as the water streamed off his head. "Pa-tron de oro—*gold!*"

Amberley, bellied down, squinted at the pebbly bottom

of the stream. "Good heavens," he murmured. "There's a fortune right under our noses—"

"Catgold," Angsman suggested. "Pyrites—"

"Ain't no catgold, amigo; ain't no flash-in-the-pan strike, either! Por Dios, take a look for yourself!"

"While you hold the horses," Angsman said calmly.

Swearing under his breath, Mexican Tom reluctantly left the stream to tend the animals. Angsman threw off his pack and dug out his prospector's gear. He stooped beside the water, aware of their fascinated concentration as he panned up a little sand and gravel bearing a flicker of sunny color, stirred it in an expert curving and rocking motion. He coaxed up sun-caught flecks of heavy metal, thinking incredulously, There's twenty dollars worth of yellow in this pan....

He showed none of the keen excitement that bit into his usual cool perspective. It was no time for anyone to become infected with gold fever. "Middling good strike."

"Middling—! Gold washes down, not up, *compadre*. This stuff, she's just float. Up higher they must be solid veins an' outcrops. We all rich, Santa Maria!"

Angsman said softly, "May be time later to think about gold. Want to go kiting after it now, amigo?"

Mexican Tom met his hard stare a long moment, sullenly let his own gaze fall. "Ain't no need you should ask that, hombre. I stick."

"Gold—and Don Pedro's stream. We must be close to the old Spanish diggings," Amberley said excitedly.

Angsman scooped up a handful of the pan's contents and examined it. Gold washed any distance from its source became polished by abrasion of rocks and gravel ...these flakes were rough. The presence of much broken quartz indicated a source lode rather than placer deposits, he guessed...and damned highgrade stuff.

"I'd say so," he answered Amberley, and came to his feet then, assessing the surrounding terrain in detail, for this had to be journey's end. Obregori Pass ran at a gradual upslant for another half-mile, its main trunk terminating at the scarp of an almost sheer, flat-topped mesa. Toward its end the high cliffs tapered low, and studying the gray rimrock, Angsman saw a suspicious detail. It moved and was gone.

"Don't look up. We're being watched."

"Apaches?" Amberley whispered. "Then they know about us—"

"Have for some time. No enemy of Bonito's ever surprised him. He'd keep his scouts flung out wide, handpicked to a man."

The scientist stared a helpless question.

"We pick a spot, and fast," Angsman said quietly. "My guess, if we stay in the open, we won't live out another day."

"More likely, another dawn," Amberley muttered.

"Mostly they don't fight at night—has to do with their religion." Angsman smiled faintly. "Only they got their agnostics too, professor, so you could be right. One thing, Bonito won't attack till he's sniffed us out thoroughly, made sure of winning. With good cover and a lot of luck, there's a chance."

"What you propose, sir, is that we run and hide, like frightened rabbits." Judith Amberley's still-parched throat gave a shrill shrewish edge to her words. "We did not come all this way to crawl into a hole and hide—"

He met her hot, bitter stare, understanding her exhausted tension. He said matter-of-factly, "We need time to plan. This is roughly the place, but we haven't a notion of where to start looking. Got to figure out what that Muro del Sangre is—assuming Douglas and the guide got that far—then study how to scout it out. Large order, that, and we got to stay alive to fill it. Set up a base camp, work out from there."

Amberley smiled wryly. "We're in your hands—as usual."

"I'll have a look. Tomas, keep a sharp watch."

On foot, Angsman cut across to the broad branch canyon into which the stream poured. He moved into it, working downstream along the left bank which was a shelving ledge two yards wide between cliff and water.

Shortly he halted by a small ravine which penetrated back several yards till it widened into a large bowl, roughly oval in shape, and boxed in by sheer walls which sloped gently off toward the bottom. At one end the cliff formed a high bulge, like a protective overhang, above a deep cleft along its base. Angsman nodded his satisfaction—with one man mounting guard at the narrow mouth, an approaching enemy should be quickly spotted. The cliff overhang would shield them from the rim, with a scattering of giant boulders for additional cover. Except for a drawn-out siege, this cul-de-sac was ideal; they had plenty of food and there was abundant water nearby. To one side a large patch of grass flourished in the lava soil—enough to last their animals a while.

The lowering sun had already gilded the rimrock to a muted gold, and Angsman wanted to set up permanent camp before darkness. Returning, he told the others of his find, adding, "Tomorrow I'll scout to the end of Obregon Pass...see what I can find."

"By the bye, Angsman," Amberley commented gravely, "rather nice gesture of yours, naming the pass after the old boy. Didn't suspect you of that much sentiment."

Angsman regarded his serious face a long moment, unable to decide whether he'd been treated to a specimen of greenhorn humor.

Amberley took the first guard shift by the ravine mouth, sitting on a low rock with his rifle across his knees, keeping a drowsy attention on the canyon beyond, from which drifted the murmurous glissando of the stream. Behind him Judith and Angsman and Ramirez slept circling the meager warmth of a small fire which created a weird dance of light and shadow along the rugged walls.

Amberley's nervously excited thoughts were shaded by disappointment at Angsman's flat insistence on investigating the terrain alone. By George, the man was as bull-headed as Judith...insisting that the others needed a few days' rest, bluntly stating that they'd only be in his way. Angsman had yielded only once, in his reluctant agreement to guide them, and since that time there had been absolutely no arguing with the man. Damn it, he, Jim Amberley, was no amateur in the wilderness. His archaeologist's soul was itching to be present if Angsman should uncover the old Spanish mine.

A backwash of guilt nudged his conscience, thinking of how Judith's single-minded concern was with finding their brother. Yet, knowing himself, he could only be honest. He'd traveled to the corners of the earth without ever, in a sense, leaving his ivory tower. Amberley liked people, found them fascinating at times, but always as objects of his analytical curiosity; he'd always shunned personal involvement.

Maybe that secret shame of his own lack of responsive warmth had let him timidly permit a younger sister to assume the dominating role in their little family circle after the deaths of their parents in a train wreck ten years ago. That had been a mistake, and so, perhaps, was his failure to argue her out of this hazardous and hopeless search. But he didn't think so—

Suddenly he came alert...a dislodged pebble had plopped into the stream.

Something was moving up the black canyon gulf, hugging the wall at a dozen yards' distance, picked out by the faint light of a crescent moon. It came on silently in a prowling crouch. Shocked from his bemused revery, Amberley could only stare. Without thinking now, he brought his rifle to his shoulder, firing hastily.

The shot cascaded a pulse of flinty echoes from the cliffs; the figure scurried away upcanyon toward the pass, quickly swallowed by the darkness. And now Amberley's blood ran cold at the sound that drifted back...a moaning wail which climbed to a raging, maniacal scream. Angsman and Ramirez had already scrambled out of their blankets with guns in hand; the sound froze them in listening attitudes...then it died away.

"Mother of God," Ramirez whispered, crossing himself.

Angsman stepped forward, clamping a rough hand on Amberley's arm. "What was it? You see it?"

"Apache, I think. I shot—"

"Too damn' fast," Angsman declared roughly. "That was no 'Pache."

"She was no 'Pache," Mexican Tom echoed in a shuddering whisper. "Ain't nothing alive make no sound like that. Ths is place of the dead, *los muerto*...."

Amberley said hotly, "I tell you it was a man, Apache or not!"

"Not an animal," Angsman slowly agreed, frowning. "You might have waited a little, professor."

"Lost my head," Amberley confessed lamely. "Had my mind on other things. Startled the devil out of me."

Judith had moved to her brother's side, and he could feel her uncontrollable trembling. He shared her sudden fear...of a thing neither one of them had considered. "Jim," she breathed. "Was it—do you think—it could be—"

"No."Amberley shook his head, trying to convey certainty against his memory of that chilling scream, and he thought now fervently, *I pray God it wasn't.*

Angsman eased the rifle from his nerveless fingers, saying quietly, "I'll take over, professor. Rest of you try to get some sleep. Better stick here till daylight; no point batting around in the dark. If there's any sign, it'll be there come morning."

CHAPTER EIGHT

When dawn spread its roseate glow across the gray rimrock and lanced scarlet arrows of first sunlight across the paling sky, Angsman left off guard duty and woke Tomas Ramirez, telling him to keep a close lookout.

"Sure, amigo." With daylight, Ramirez had recovered his lazy poise; he dexterously struck a spark into his tinder-cord with flint and steel *eslabon,* blew it to glowing life in his cupped hands and ducked his head to light the cornshuck cigarette he'd rolled. "Gonna follow up that crazy laugh?"

Angsman nodded.

Ramirez lunged a deep drag, exhaled it almost reluctantly, glancing at the sleeping Amberleys. "You think it's maybe their brother an' he eat some loco weed?"

"Tomas, I don't know. Hell of a thing."

"Yeah. Well, I nursemaid pretty good. Get along, amigo; give a yell, you need help."

Angsman left the box ravine and swung up the branch gorge. Where the pebbly bank of the stream gave way to patches of soft sand, he found the marks of splayed bare feet, and thought wryly, A real wild customer. Then, leaving the gorge where it debouched into Obregon Pass, he came to a dead halt. Angsman wasn't a man easily disconcerted, and now he was held utterly motionless.

The facing wall of the giant flat-summitted mesa that ended the pass was, as he'd noted, of common red sandstone, though unusually smooth and straight, as though the elements had vied to crack and erode its tough substance and had only succeeded in polishing it to what, at this distance, was a softened gloss. The first rays of dawn, streaking across the heights, so angled their red glow against the smooth sandstone that instead of being absorbed or diffused it was flung back brilliantly, almost

240

hurtingly, against the watching eye. Along the crest it flamed like red-hot iron. But the really striking effect was in the way the livid glow moved slowly downward, transforming the dull crimson stone beneath. It sent ahead big globular feelers that were actually the mounting surnrise gradually highlighting the faint swells and irregularities, creating the fierce illusion of a great bleeding wound streaming bright rivulets down the mesa flank....

This, Angsman knew, could only be Muro del Sangre ...the Wall of Blood. He was seeing it as Pedro de Obregon the grandee had first viewed it more than two hundred years ago, in an awed scholarly reverence that he'd rendered in riddle, so as not to violate some sensitive, if morbid, chord set to quivering in his poetic soul. Angsman, not at all a poet, understood his sensations exactly.

The effect was transient, and even as he watched, the sharp glow faded and was soon gone, leaving only a mundane wall of red sandstone under a hot mounting sun. Somewhere.beneath that wall should lie the old Spanish mine...and with it, if he was lucky, a clue to Douglas Amberley's fate.

Moving upcanyon toward the mesa, following the bank of the stream, Angsman found more bare footprints. Their prowler had come this way. Angsman kept a watchful surveillance on the cliffs, knowing he'd make a choice target for an Apache scout.

He wondered if there was a bare chance that Amberley might be right, that Bonito might not trouble them while their intentions remained obviously peaceable. The old chief had brought his people here to avoid trouble, not to seek it. Still there was no cut-and-dried pattern into which the motives of an Apache—or anybody else— would fall. A lot might depend on how near they were to Bonito's rancheria. For on reflection, Angsman thought that Bonito probably had a permanent camp somewhere in this mountain stronghold. To feed and water a band of upwards of fifty bucks, squaws and children, taken with all their animals, was obviously the ancient chiefs main problem in selecting his retreat. And Apache or not, providing for such a band in this barren and near-waterless range would require a special place. He made a mental note to find and size up the camp for a better idea of what they might have to face—especially with Chingo in the vicinity....

Angsman felt a vast wash of relief when at last he turned into a feeder canyon with high sheltering walls, just beneath the looming height of Muro del Sangre. The stream issued from this canyon, and the footprints, scuffed and re-crossed along its bank, indicated that the intruder had often come and gone this way.

Suddenly, turning a sharp angle in the canyon, Angs-. man came to a halt. He had found the old fort built by Don Pedro and his companions.

It was a narrow, low-built structure with thick walls constructed of flat stone slabs and longer flat slabs laid above these to form the roof which wasn't over four feet across...crude but damned substantial. Evidently it had been originally built into a long deep notch in the canyon wall, but numerous landslides from the high rim had partly filled that notch. They had crushed most of the stone roof and cascaded inward. Peering through a low entrance, he saw that the interior was choked by boulders and debris, leaving only a dark cubbyhole toward the front. The old mine was sealed off for good....

Gun in hand, Angsman ducked inside. Sunlight pouring through the jagged wall interstices showed this to be the home...or lair...of their wild man. A circle of black-ened stones held the ashes of a cookfire, and scattered about were the bones of small animals, broken for the marrow. Angsman sheathed his gun and settled on his haunches to study the dirt floor, fouled with excrement and other filth. A dull gleam of half-buried metal caught his eye. He unearthed it with a root of his boot, picked it up. A battered and useless canteen, with a gaping hole in its side.

Angsman carried it out to the light and knocked the dirt off to examine it carefully. Deep scratches in the in-tact side formed the plain initials *D. A.* Douglas Amber-ley...?

The identity of their prowler might be narrowing down, he reflected cautiously...if you assumed that an acci-dent had left young Amberley deranged, a cackling mad-man who kept alive by scavenging for rodents, who holed up in this filthy burrow like a wild beast. But there was also old Caleb Tree who'd guided the boy...and one of them must be dead.

The other was likely worse than dead.

Angsman went over the ground now with infinite care, but found no more signs on the stony ground. The tracks had led into this canyon, so he must have returned to this lair last night—where had he gone from here? No telling, for he probably roamed the area freely, unmolested by the Apaches who would recognize his madness and shun him. Somehow he had to be run to ground and taken alive...

If he'd been frightened off by Angsman's approach, he could only have retreated up the feeder canyon to its source on the rim above...or to its dead end. The latter possibility was worth following up.

As Angsman proceeded along the narrow ledge bordering the stream, the canyon narrowed, confining the water as it gushed down the mounting slant into a deep and roiling torrent; its echoes chattered together in a thin roar between the high walls. There were flecks of heavy color here which indicated that the gold in the lower stream had not been carried from the old mine diggings, but from still farther up—a second rich lode.

Now the canyon widened toward its end—a box canyon. Here was the source of their clear cold stream, swirling out from a broad placid pool, fed by an underground stream as he'd thought. The gold ore must have washed from the rim somewhere above this point. Angsman peered briefly into the pool, finding it dark and still and sullen, as though bottomless.

He retraced his steps to the old fort, there pausing to debate whether to wait for the prowler's return.... decided against it. The wild man's absence at this early hour suggested that he'd resolved with mad cunning to avoid his lair for a time; there were other side canyons where he might hole up. Tracking him down would require time and patience. Just now Angsman felt a strong curiosity to test Pedro de Obregon's veracity further—so far the old Don hadn't missed a turn.

According to Obregon's account, after leaving the fort his gold-laden *conducta* had been attacked by Indians. The men and animals had retreated up a trail to an opening in a maze of caves. Since gold meant nothing to the Apaches, a fortune in gold bars must still be intact somewhere in those caves. As he recalled Don Pedro's description, the entrance lay just below the rim on the south wall of Obregon Pass, approximately two hundred *pasos,* or double steps, downcayon from the base of Muro del Sangre.

Emerging from the feeder canyon, Angsman kept a wary watch on the cliffs while he mentally counted his steps, working back down the pass along its south wall. Having paced off the distance, he craned his neck back to scan the cliff. A broad shelf projected about thirty feet below the rim, and above it a glimpse of what might easily be mistaken for a dark shallow pit in the rock. That must be the cave...but there was no trail, only a sheer hundred foot drop to the canyon floor. Still, the wall was rotten with age and erosion, its base heaped with tons of rubble. A whole section of wall could have scaled off and collapsed at any time...and with it the trail.

Discovering that he was ravenously hungry, Angsman decided to join the Amberleys for breakfast. His finding of Doug's canteen in the wild man's lair was no pleasant detail, but they needed to be prepared for the worst. So far both of them had borne up well. Angsman had to smile, thinking of how Amberley's scientific enthusiasm would be fired by his news of finding the mine. Might have to hogtie the man to keep him in camp now. He'd be like a kid in prospect of a new toy. With his lifelong urge to see beyond the next hill, Angsman could understand that, and he thought with a wry grin, Likely neither of us ever finished growing up. Amberley lacked his own tough streak of independence, and his occasional absent-mindedness was annoying, but he'd showed adaptability, solid courage, and a keen mind. Angsman felt a curious liking for the man.

Returning to the branch canyon, he was about to swing into it when he came to a halt, hearing now a faint and distant sound, a chink of iron on stone. It came from downpass to the west—and shod horses meant white men.

Angsman settled into immobility behind a shoulder of rock that partly blocked the gorge mouth and waited. His dusty clothing might have been part of the sun-blasted rock. A chuckwalla lizard wriggled from a fissure a yard away, sensed his presence and promptly shrank back, bloating its body to wedge itself immovably within the crack. A hawk wheeled concentrically against the sky, dipped and vanished beyond the rimrock. It was very hot. A ragged trickle of sweat glided down Angsman's ribs.

The four riders rounded the sweeping turn in the pass, coming at a thirsty run for the stream. They flung themselves from their saddles and bellied down to drink—all but Charbonneau. He knelt holding his reins and drank from his cupped hands, then stood hipshot and alert, letting his horse drink while he scanned the surrounding rocks.

"Hold them horses, mes amis, or they founder themself."

"Armand," Big Turk Ambruster croaked, "this heah look like gold...and they's a lot of it." His shining black fist rose with a handful of stream gravel. "My Gawd—*gold!* We gwine be rich!"

Charbonneau was unmoving for a moment, watching the excited scramblings of his men. Then he too was on hands and knees, with clawed fingers gouging at the streambed.

Angsman rose now, cocking his Colt as he stepped out to sight. The crisp metallic sound froze Charbonneau and Kincaid and Ambruster, caught on their hands and knees in the water. Only the blond kid named Will-John Staples seemed to take no heed, pawing frantically at the gravel and laughing and crying at once.

"...We gonna have it now for sure, Lucy, that big farm and all—"

"Shut up, boy," Turk Ambruster rumbled.

Will-John's jaw fell stupidly, seeing Angsman; he climbed to his feet, mud and gravel slipping from his fingers. The others came upright too, all four watching Angsman with a kind of wary calculation as though they and not he held the gun, wondering whether they could take it and kill him and keep the secret of this gold.

"While you're thinking about it, get your hands high."

Sullenly they obeyed except for Charbonneau; recovering jaunty arrogance he drew a cheroot from his vest pocket and lighted it without haste. Angsman tilted his gun an inch downward and shot into the mud, spattering the Creole's boots. "Hear that all right, Armand?"

"Armand's hearing is pairfec'," the Creole grinned cockily, but he raised his hands. "My memory's pretty good too, 'specially for old Spanish maps. She's a free

country, hein? Nothing to say we don't stake the claim
here."

"Nothing to say I don't drop the four of you now.
Can't find a good offhand reason I shouldn't."

"Because you are one damn' fool, you will not. come,
my fran'; leave us alone, we leave you alone. By the
way, you 'ave find the Spanish diggings, eh?"

Angsman said gently, "You're movin' on, Armand."

"Ah, oui?"

Angsman gave a backward nod, saying flatly, "We're
camped in there. You're a sight too close for our comfort...see that big slide yonder? You can get up the
cliffs that way. Advise you camp back a piece from the
rim—I see one of you stick his head over it, he's dead."

Charbonneau slowly sank to his haunches, lowering
one hand to get a handful of gravel. He studied it
thoughtfully. "Plenty rough flakes. Means this drift stuff
has not wash' far. We follow this stream, and—"

"You're way off, Armand. I followed the stream. Got
an underground source. This stuff fell from the rim and
got washed down here. Up there's where you'll find the
lode."

"But the old Obregon mine—"

"Buried up under tons of rock. You'll never open it."

Charbonneau straightened to his feet, motioned curtly
to the others. They mounted, the Creole briefly wheel-
ing his horse toward Angsman. His green eyes were
opaque and flinty. "The bargain, she work two way,
M'sieu—stay clear off from us! A man is dead for a
long time."

"Just so you don't forget it."

Drawn by Angsman's shot, the Amberleys and Ramirez now hurried up. Charbonneau murmured ironically,
"Ma'mselle," touched his cheroot to hatbrim and cantered away. At the long broken slide indicated by Angsman the four men dismounted and began its ascent,
leading their animals.

"So they found their way here," Amberley mused
worriedly. "Will they make trouble?"

"Not unlikely, without they find what they're looking
for up there."

CHAPTER NINE

Angsrman spent the remainder of that day prowling the canyons and sub-canyons that opened in a complex maze off the big pass. He'd picked up fresh trail of their wild man below the mine canyon, but it soon petered out on bare rock. Through that day he saw no sign of wild man or Apache. The cliffs seemed to brood in the sun-shimmering stillness, waiting out the human intrigues that disturbed their ancient peace, in the serene knowledge that they would endure unchanged long after these human invaders had gone to dust.

So Angsman thought, and smiled dourly at himself. It was the sort of profound fantasy that came to grip a man who had lived alone too long in vast barren silences that hadn't been intended for a lone man. He realized, with the unsettling sadness that came when a man faced some great change in his life, that this might be his last foray into such places. He'd lived alone too much, that was the long and short of it. He'd lived with the Indians and had recognized the great good of their simple and natural lives.

But he wasn't an Indian in heart or thought, and it was high time he faced it squarely. He was a maverick civilized man whose thoughts were turning more and more back to the society he'd repudiated. A man needed certain things—a wife and children and home—and he felt a strange ache, seeing in memory the green Virginia farmstead of his boyhood.

The following morning, up again with first dawn, Angsman returned to the old mine diggings on the slim chance the wild man might have returned. He was patiently scouring over the stony floor of the feeder canyon, when the noise began, startling him to poised alertness—a low roar of rock grinding on rock. At first he thought of a landslide, but the sound kept up with a steady, measured rumble, drifting down from the heights to his straining ears.

With mounting puzzlement he listened, fixing the source of the noise. He left the feeder canyon then and moved down Obregon Pass toward the slide where Charbonneau's gang had ascended to the cliff. Achieving its rim, Angsman glanced downward at a faint halloo. He saw Ramirez and Amberley, also attracted by the rumbling, leaving their canyon on the run. Angrily he waved them off, grimly waiting till they'd turned reluctantly back.

Then he struck back due south from the rim, moving at the tireless Apache jogtrot. He crossed one bare, canyon-riddled ridge and then a second, afterward threading through a forest of gigantic rubble. The roar was deafening now. He moved warily up near a lip of crumbling granite, seeing below it a round pocket set between the twin prongs of a horseshoe-shaped ridge.

Now he saw with little surprise the meaning of that steady, far-reaching rumble. It was an *arrastra,* such as the early Spaniards had used for breaking down gold-bearing ore. In the center of the pocket was a shallow pit floored with flat rocks, an upright beam set in its center. From this extended low crossbeams to which were lashed heavy rocks; as the upright post revolved, the rocks were dragged circularly around the pit, crushing the ore.

Also projecting from the upright about four feet above the ground was a long pole, to which was applied the motive power, usually a mule or horse. But this arrastra, Angsman saw with a coldness touching his spine, was powered by a man.

An Indian boy was pushing at the pole, his wrists lashed to it, feet digging at the stony earth. He was naked to the waist in the broiling sun; blood streamed from a dozen cuts on his lean coppery back and soaked his cotton drawers. It took plenty of muscle to even budge the arrastra, and the young Indian was faltering now, the long sinews of back and shoulders shuddering with his effort. But he was given no chance to rest.

Jack Kincaid paced the relentless circle with him, cursing hoarsely between pulls on a bottle in one meaty fist. In the other hand he held a thorny mesquite branch, and whenever the Apache broke stride, the branch curled viciously around his bare torso.

Stretched prone on his belly on the superheated rock, Angsman scanned the camp. It was a permanent site, for they had built brush lean-tos and heaped their gear beneath these. Four animals including the two pack mules were hobbled nearby, skittish and wild-eyed with the strange roar. A great raw excavation showed on the ridgeside where chunks of ore had been torn out.

Young Will-John Staples sat cross-legged on the ground by a lean-to, twanging on a Jew's-harp, keeping time to the turning arrastra. He was bareheaded, and his broad simple face was sweat-shining and distorted by a queer fixed smile...

There was no sign of Armand Charbonneau or Turk Ambruster.

They must have located the lode almost at once, for constructing the arrastra would have taken at least a day. The labor that had gone into it meant a rich strike, for only heavy-larded ore would satisfy these greed-crazed men.

At least it must have driven Kincaid and Staples crazy; evidently they had somehow captured a careless young buck, and now meant to torture him to death. For a warrior, such an end, measured not by its torment but by the humiliation, was the worst possible death. Angsman felt little compassion for the Apache who would have shown his enemies none. The Apaches had their own code and followed it pretty scrupulously, more than could be said for most of those who adjudged them bestial savages. Only cruelty and tenderness had nothing to do with ethics as the Apaches conceived them. Among those of the desert, beast or man, a cruel dying was accepted as matter-of-factly as the cruelty of life; it changed a man in fierce and subtle ways in his dealings with those not of his own people.

Entirely another motive prompted Angsman's sudden decision to help the Apache youth. So far Bonito had not moved against either party of whites. When the Apaches learned what had happened to this boy, the wary truce would certainly be ended, thanks to these fools. Saving the youth might also save Angsman and his companions.

He could handle Kincaid and Staples easily enough

...he had no idea how far away Charbonneau and Ambruster were, but he wasn't waiting.

Gently Angsman nosed the barrel of his rifle over the liprock. His weapon was a '73 Winchester repeater, capable of getting off fifteen shots in as many seconds. He settled his sights on Jack Kincaid's wide chest, then tilted them a little aside, and fired. Splinters flew from an arrastra crossbeam. Kincaid stopped in his tracks, his jaw falling slack. Angsman sent two more shots into the dust at his feet and Kincaid retreated, wildly back-pedaling; he tripped and fell and then lunged on his hands and knees toward the shelter of a lean-to. Angsman aimed carefully and snapped one of the slender supporting poles, collapsing the brush roof. With a deep-throated bawl of rage, Kincaid floundered away. The guide turned his attention to Will-John Staples who had grabbed for his rifle, leaning against a nearby rock. A spray of bullet-gouged sand stung his reaching hand, and he snatched it back.

Laying his shots down with systematic coldness, Angsman drove the pair to their feet and toward the far slope, egging their uncertain confusion into a direction of flight. They deserted their camp then in a scrambling ascent of the rock-strewn slope. Angsman left his own position, catfooting along the circular ridge crest where it joined the twin prongs, holding to shelter of scattered rocks. He wasn't a dozen yards from Kincaid and Staples as the panting pair topped the ridge, now swinging frantic glances to place their enemy. And then Angsman fired from his fresh position.

" 'Paches!—they're all around us!" Kincaid bawled. He tore off down the outer ridge at a blind angle, heading for the cover of a deep distant wash, and Staples loped at his heels.

Angsman bounded down the long slope to the camp. The Apache's body sagged limply against the pole. Angsman reached his side, drew his knife and slashed the lashings on the captive's wrists. The boy's legs gave way and he fell. Roughly the guide hauled him to his feet and half-flung him into a drunken run toward the slope...

Angsman worked back a half-mile toward Obregon Pass, mercilessly prodding the Apache ahead of him, halting finally in a nook between two sheltering rock slabs. The Apache fell to the ground, and Angsman sank on his heels facing him.

"Habla espanol?"

The youth gave no sign that he understood. He was heaving great gasping breaths, and blood still trickled from the long raw weals seared across back and chest and belly. There was no fear, no expression in his thin dark face; only the black eyes smoldering their unquenchable hatred and contempt. Angsman was fully aware of his sick humiliation at being snatched alive from a disgrace worse than death.

Speaking haltingly then in the slush-tongued Apache language Angsman said: "I use the tongue of the People badly, as you see."

The buck's hating stare betrayed no surprise; his mouth briefly worked, spat gummy saliva at Angsman's feet. The guide's tone held quiet and even. "I have killed Apaches, but as a man against men. I have not dragged brave men to death in the dirt, as a dog dies. There are two bands of *pinda-likoye* in your country. This you know well. You know it was not my white-eyes who did this thing. When you see Bonito, tell him of that, and of who saved your life and then spared it."

Then, because he knew that the disgrace of being captured and used like a draft beast would follow this youth through all his days, he added quietly: "The *Shis-in-day* are a proud people, and the pride of a people is a good thing. But a man feeds on the pride of himself, not that of others. The scars of the body are nothing; it is only the scars within that eat out manhood."

Without more words Angsman left him, feeling the Apache's burning stare hold to his back till he was cut off from sight over a ridge. Swiftly then Angsman mounted a jagged buttress and flattened against its contour, there to take up a patient watch. His hope that his rescue of the young Apache would keep the Chiricahua from their throats was admittedly a slim one. He intended to track the youth to Bonito's rancheria and assess the odds they must face. And there was Chingo to consider. If he and his Mimbrenos had been heading for this rancheria, and this seemed certain, they had long since arrived.

One thing about those odds. They were bad.

Presently the Apache emerged from the nook, fresh-
ened by a brief rest, and set off at a painful jogtrot toward the southeast. Angsman left cover and followed him,
calling on all his trail craft to hold the Chiricahua's track
unseen. They moved on deep into midday, far into steadily heightening country.

Toward early afternoon, Angsman, about to skirt a
thicket of catclaw, pulled swiftly back. A sentry was
moving up on a bluff to hail the youth below. They
passed a few words, and the boy went on. Having reached
the outer line of lookouts, Angsman holed up to wait for
nightfall. He made a meager supper off jerked beef
strips he carried in his pocket, chewing them to a fibrous
pulp and washing it down with a few swallows from his
canteen. It was the crudest of fare, and the sun beat
with blistering violence into the boulder field where he'd
laid up out of sight of a chance hunting party or lone
scout; sweat soaked his shirt and pants and pooled in
his moccasins, and out of habit he conserved his water.

Once he caught sight of eight mounted warriors cutting the dust down a dry wash, headed for Obregon Pass
—to avenge their young tribesman, he supposed. Charbonneau and his gang were in for it, and perhaps his
own party. But Charbonneau would come first, and the
wily Creole wouldn't kill easily; he'd hold the Indians
off at least till night, and then they'd pull back till dawn.
It gave Angsman time to use.

After dark he left hiding and descended into a canyon
where the moon's soft rays did not penetrate, following
its twisting course two miles west, knowing this would
place him well within the heart of the guard perimeter.
With heightening caution he left the canyon where it debouched into a valley and scaled a gently sloping ridge.
Distantly he saw campfires pinpointing the night, and
now he set to working in at a wide circle, holding his
route below the ridge lines. When the first faint sounds
of the camp grew ahead, he proceeded with utmost care,
halting motionless several times when a fitful breeze
arose so that his scent wouldn't alarm their horses.

Achieving the last ridge, he waited a long time before
moving up onto it, alert to the smallest sign of a nearby
sentry. The moonlight bathed the vast valley below in
silvery relief, showing grass and forest. Down there

would be abundant water and small game—this was Bonito's last-ditch stronghold.

The encampment was set off below this ridge. Angsman studied it through his field glasses. This was a typical Apache camp, with a half dozen small fires tended by women. The sizable remuda was confined in a makeshift corral of brush and rope, situated to the near side of the cluster of jacales. Angsman counted these, and made a rough count also of the grown warriors he could see— thirty or more men of all ages. Another eight with the bunch he'd seen earlier. A few outpost guards. The women were about half as many as the bucks, and there weren't many children. A band of about seventy souls, all told. The camp appeared quite haphazard and dis-organized, and Angsman knew how deceptive was this impression: it could be broken up and on the move in a matter of minutes.

Idly now he moved his glasses across it, lingering on details. He focused briefly on one thick-set warrior and moved away, then came back swiftly with belated rec-ognition. The man had just moved into the firelight; it clearly etched his broken flat face. Chingo, squatting now by a single fire with his five bucks—and the woman. Chingo and his hostile handful were no doubt enjoying a vacation, flushed with successful raiding in Mexico, but he and his Mimbrenos held warily apart from the Chiricahuas; the Apache tribes freely united only on the warpath, their ordinary relations strained and uncertain at best.

Again Angsman curiously studied the lone woman of their group, on her knees adding wood to the fire. She was slender and young. He couldn't tell much else from here.

For fifteen minutes he mentally catalogued the camp, afterward pulling back off the ridge to begin his cir-cuitous return trek. He traveled a good ten miles by full moonlight, then halted to catch a few hours of sleep. He guessed that by now his companions would be deeply concerned, both by his failure to return and by the rat-tle of gunfire when the Apaches went after Charbon-neau. Anyway they were safely forted, and there was Ramirez to handle any emergency. By setting out again before midnight, he should reach base camp shortly after sunrise…

He shook away a last faint, nagging worry for them, and slept.

CHAPTER TEN

James Amberley piled more greasewood on the fire, watching its leaping blaze wipe back the night shadows banking the rough high walls of the bowl. He and Judith sat cross-legged by it, and now he glanced sidelong at her shadowed profile. In those last days, he reflected, the habit of silence had grown on them both. It was the savage, lonely quality of this country. It touched wellsprings in you that were deep and primitive, something not quite smothered by effete civilization. But the effect was an unsettling and half-fearful one; you had to be an Indian or a man like Will Angsman to take nature on its own terms—straight, and without Ralph Waldo Emerson's philosophical chasers.

This was Angsman's element, but even so Amberley was worried. After Angsman had waved off Ramirez and him when they'd started to investigate the mysterious grinding roar, they'd had no hint of his whereabouts. Ramirez had solved the noise: it was made by an old-time arrastra, sometimes still used in Mexico. But then came the rifle shots that had ended it...Angsman's no doubt, but why had he shot, and why hadn't he returned? Following his order, they'd stayed where they were, waiting out a nerve-wracking day. Then at early twilight had come more shots, an erratic flurry of firing that seemed to tell of a pitched battle. Soon it was finished, and they could only guess at what had happened.

Of course none of this necessarily meant that Angsman had come to harm. He was not, after all, unreliable, but uncommunicative, with an intense self-reliance that made him unpredictable and difficult to understand. Yet this was so integral a part of the man that you couldn't condemn it Quite likely none of them would be alive now but for Angsman. In his own element, he was a man you couldn't help but like and admire.

Still Amberley wished with increasing unease that Angsman would return, for a new and immediate problem had come up. Mexican Tom had started to drink.

Ramirez had furtively produced the square brown bottle from his pack for a long thirsty pull shortly before supper. Later, bright-eyed and boisterous, he hadn't troubled to conceal his tippling, even brashly offering Amberley a drink. The Easterner had controlled his anger because in Angsman's absence they were wholly dependent on young Ramirez, and nothing could be served by antagonizing him. Yet aside from a heightening gaiety to stress his usual cheerful manner, the liquor hadn't appeared to greatly faze Mexican Tom, and he'd stowed the half-empty bottle away in his gear before moving jauntily out to the ravine mouth to take up the night watch...

Quietly now, Amberley said: "A penny for your thoughts, Jude."

She sighed. "Hardly worth a copper, Jim. Only that I'm beginning to wonder—at last—if any of this is worth it. It's this country, I suppose. It's so big and naked and cruel that you can't look on the face of it and afterward be dishonest with yourself."

Amberley almost started in surprise. Her words had been spoken casually, but they'd hinted at a self-yielding of which he'd never believed his iron-willed sister to be capable. "Why," he said carefully, "that's rather odd, old girl."

"Coming from me," she said a little sharply. "Why don't you say it emphatically? Do you have to always be so—so pliable?" She broke off and laid her hand on his, saying contritely, "I'm sorry, Jimmy."

He said quietly, almost stiffly, "I've done what I felt I must, Jude...like you."

"Oh, I know...it's just that in all this empty silence, a person is thrown back on his own thoughts. Lately I've thought longer and harder than I ever could in my snug Boston cocoon. I don't regret coming here—it was a thing I had to do—"

"I understood that from the first. It's why I gave you barely a token argument."

"I know. You see a good deal more than I've ever

credited you for....What I *do* regret is dragging two others, Angsman and Ramirez, into our situation. I baited Angsman quite deliberately into helping us, you know. Then, I didn't care how he felt, so long as I got what I wanted. Now—whatever his opinion is of me—it probably falls short of the bitter truth."

Amberley was silent an embarrassed moment. Then he said hopefully, "We're all alive and well till now—that's something. I'm sure Angsman will come back soon. And don't forget that prowler I scared off two nights ago. Angsman says that he is probably a white man. If so—well, we all called you foolish for insisting on what seemed a hopeless quest. Now, maybe we're the fools."

"Oh, Jimmy," she whispered. "If that *was* Doug—"

"If it was Doug, we'll find him. And make him well. You and I together—"

Behind them a boot grated on gravel. Amberley broke off, looking back over his shoulder. He felt a quick cold panic and stifled it with an effort, then came slowly to his feet. Judith rose with him, her fingers closed tightly on his arm.

Charbonneau stood facing them spraddle-legged; in his wolf-lean face, something harried and fierce and implacable warned Amberley to make no sudden move. Behind the Creole came a shuffling of feet, and Jack Kincaid emerged into the firelight, his dark broad face wary and sullen, pushing the staggering Ramirez ahead of him. The hulking Ambruster brought up the rear, supporting Will-John Staples. The blond youth slumped against the giant Negro, his head bent on his chest and shirt soaked with blood.

Charbonneau stepped forward to lift Amberley's pistol from its holster, ramming it in his own belt. "Sit down, doctair."

"What do you—"

"Do w'at I say, mon ami." The tone was flat and wicked, and Amberley obeyed, drawing Judith down beside him. Kincaid gave the young Mexican a shove that sent him sprawling at their feet.

Ambruster effortlessly bore Will-John's sagging weight to the fire and stretched him out on the ground, propping up his head on one of the Amberleys' blanket rolls. Charbonneau knelt by the boy and opened his shirt, removing a dirty compress. Blood welled cleanly from a hole high in the pale skin of his left chest. The blond youth's eyes were closed and his breath a harsh rasping; convulsive shudders wracked him.

The gravel-voiced Ambruster rumbled with an odd gentleness, "How he doin'?"

Charbonneau cuffed his hat awry on his head, rocking back on his heels. "He ain't good. Me, I think he don' make it. The damn' young fool." He spat sideways, glaring up at Kincaid. "You too, Jack."

Ambruster growled, "Be plenty time later for fetchin' down blame, Armand. Best we look to helpin' this boy."

"Oui. Fetch some water from the stream."

Charbonneau expertly cleaned Will-John's wound while Ambruster rummaged through Amberley's duffle and found a fairly clean shirt which he tore into strips for bandages. Amberley settled a bitterly accusing stare on Tomas Ramirez, who refused to look up, sitting with his head hung between his knees.

Then the Easterner's attention was diverted by Jack Kincaid, sitting off to the side in black silence, his hot murky stare fixed on Judith. If he makes a move toward her, I'll kill him, Amberley thought with cold decision. I'll get my hands on a gun and kill him. Beyond that silent promise, he warily decided to offer no resistance. Charbonneau could have killed him and Ramirez at once, had that been his intention.

Ambruster supported Will-John half-upright as Charbonneau affixed the bandage tightly around his torso, then eased him back and covered him with a blanket. Charbonneau then began to untie a bloody rag wrapped around his own wrist.

"Did you kill Angsman?" Amberley blurted point-blank.

Charbonneau glanced up with a grunt. "Why you think so, eh?"

"I don't believe you'd dare come here otherwise."

Charbonneau laughed shortly. He washed his flesh wound with clean water, fumbled a dry bandanna from a coat pocket with his good hand, caught an end of it in his teeth, wrapped it tightly around his wrist as he muttered a brief explanation.

They had found gold in the heights above, he said, a whole ridge larded with highgrade ore, and had built an arrastra to crush it out. But before they set to work,

Charbonneau decided to try locating the rancheria of
Bonito, which from the Apache signs he'd found, must
be nearby. He had once sold repeating rifles to the
Chiricahua leader, and hoped that by this past relation
he might somehow dicker the old savage into letting
them work their claim unmolested. The fact that Bonito
hadn't as yet made a hostile move had emboldened him
to make the try.

Early this morning he and Turk Ambruster had set
out to find the rancheria, working in a wide circle toward the south. Having no success, they had started
back when they heard the distant roar of the arrastra.
Charbonneau's first fury at Kincaid and Staples for dis-
obeying his orders had changed to sudden concern when
he heard the whipcrack of a rifle, then the abrupt halt
of the device. Urging their jaded animals toward camp,
they'd found Staples and Kincaid cowering in a wash.
Sorting out their blurted explanations, Charbonneau had
learned that in his absence a young Apache buck spying
on their camp had rashly ventured too near; a chunk of
crumbling scale had broken off and tumbled him down
the slope practically into their arms.

Charbonneau came to his feet now, awkwardly knotting the bandanna. His voice was flat and angry: "It
was prime chance to show the Apach' our good faith, eh?
But do these stupid cochon think of that? Non! Jack,
who get drunk soon as I leave, now hitch the Apach' to
the arrastra and 'ave the big fun making of him the mule
to grind the gold. The Will-John go along, being not too
bright as you comprehend; also he is not right in the
head since we find the gold. It is maybe fifteen minute
'ave pass, someone start shooting down into the camp
and drive our stupid ones off. When we come back with
them, the Apach' is gone. Someone 'ave cut him free."

Amberley said tensely, "The Apaches?"

Charbonneau had finished tying his bandage; it freed
his good hand for an expressive angry gesture. "Non, the
Apach' would 'ave kill' our stupid ones, n'est-ce pas?
And where is Angsman?"

Amberley shrugged coldly. "Gone since early this
morning."

Charbonneau spat his anger. "That is w'at I figure.
M'sieu Angsman is brought to our camp by the arrastra.

It is he who free the Apach'. He think that will help him and you."

Understanding now, Amberley said slowly, "The Apache brought his friends back—they attacked your camp. Those were the shots we heard a while back...."

"Oui. But Armand think this may 'appen; already I 'ave move our camp a distance away. They find us, but at least we are holed in the rocks, we fight them off till dark. We kill no Apach', but Will-John is hurt bad; me, I am only scratch'. I know it is up with us; man can't fight the dirty Apach' on his own ground. We must try to get away in the night when the Apach' not fight...."

A faint grin curled his bearded lips. "We 'ave to sneak out on foot, leaving the horse and the gear. This is not good, so Armand get the idea—why not come to this place which mus' be the fine fortress, for 'ave not my clever fran' Angsman chosen it? Here will be water and food. Here too will be gold. Not so much as up above, but that is now lost, eh? Armand is ver' sad for this. If your so-fine guide 'ave not let that Apach' go alive to tell his friends, it would not 'appen."

Amberley cleared his dry throat, saying coldly, "You'll kill us then, I suppose."

The Creole took a twisted cheroot from the waning supply that had bulged his vest pocket, eyed it regretfully, then bent and picked up a burning twig from the fire. "I tal you, my fran' "—he puffed the cheroot alight, squinting at Amberley through the smoke—"Armand is not the saint. But I like you, this was not the fake, nor am I the ravisher of fair ladies." He gave Judith a slight courtly bow. "It is ver' simple...be good an' you live a while. The Mex, too." Chuckling, he rooted Ramirez in the ribs with a boot. "We expect trouble coming in here. The Mex, he is pretty sorry guard; he is sleep' like the babe in arms...."

He broke off, glancing irritably at Kincaid, who was rummaging noisily through Ramirez' pack. With a grunt of satisfaction he came up with the half-empty bottle, yanked its cork with his teeth. "Figgered that greaser'd been drinkin' something fierce," he announced, tilting it to his lips.

With a savage oath Charbonneau dashed his cheroot to the ground and took three swift steps, snatching the bottle from Kincaid's hand. A flick of his arm and it sailed into the darkness, shattering on an unseen rock. "That 'as cause us grief enough!"

Kincaid pivoted in a half-crouch, hand darting to the bone-handled knife in its boot-sheath. The cocking of Charbonneau's pistol froze him in mid-motion, its muzzle less than a foot from his head.

"Lemme break his goddamn breed neck, Armand," the Negro rumbled. "Been nothin' but trouble, him. Missed more sign'n he's found. Gwine git us all killed yet...."

The half-breed hissed, "You try it, Armbuster," but he was careful not to move.

"But no, Turk," Charbonneau said gently. "Jack is but the animal, the big dumb animal. The rutting swine can be tamed, eh? Jack will be a good boy now. Eh, Jack, w'at you say?"

Kincaid barely nodded.

"This is ver' good of you," Charbonneau purred. "Go out now and mount the guard. I think with no whisky you keep the sharp eye."

Kincaid muttered, "Ain't no 'Paches gonna foller us at night."

"Not the Apach', you stupid cochon. Angsman. He is out there someplace, he may return tonight. He will come like the shadow." Charbonneau grinned wolfishly. "Keep the ver' sharp eye, my fran', or he see you first. The slaughtered pig does not rut good."

Kincaid picked up his rifle, paused momentarily with a sweep of hating black eyes that touched them all in turn, lingering lastly on Judith Amberley. His eyes narrowed, squinting almost shut, and he licked his lips. Abruptly he swung away and vanished noiselessly down the ravine.

Charbonneau let his pistol off-cock and slapped it into his holster. "So. Now we all sleep sound, I think...."

Amberley woke with the first gray seep of false dawn, struggling half-upright in his blankets by the dead fire. With some vagrant sense of unease, he rubbed his eyes and swung a sleep-drugged glance around the camp, then settled it swiftly to his sister's blankets. These were bunched in a wadded heap on the scuffed ground. She was gone.

"Judith!" It left his throat in an agonized croak as he came to his feet. He thought of Kincaid, and even as

the thought formed he was charging down the rocky corridor to its mouth. Kincaid was not on guard. Amberley plunged into the canyon and up the shelving stream bank. He stumbled twice, almost falling into the rushing current.

Where the canyon debouched into the broad span of Obregon Pass, he brought up in his tracks, straining his eyes against the dim half-dawn stillness. *"Judith!"* The stony echoes mocked his thin shout, and then he sank down against a rock, rubbing a shaking hand over his face.

No great trick for the half-breed to stalk soundlessly into camp while they slept, and how he had taken her away without a noisy scuffle did not matter. It was done. The man was an utter animal, without restraint or moral sense.

"I should have known—I should have known!" Amberley groaned aloud, smashing his clenched hand against a rock. The sharp pain shocked him to the need for practical action.

Hurrying back to camp, he found the others awake. Ramirez was staring at the ground with a deep sickness in his face. Ambruster was bending above Will-John Staples who was babbling deliriously to somebody named Lucy about the farm they would buy.

"Hush up, boy." Ambruster's harsh bass was curiously gentle, deep and soothing. "You gwine open you wound with all that thrashin' 'bout, then you really have somethin'…"

Charbonneau was on his feet, scowling and assessing the situation, swearing with a savage tonelessness as he lighted a cheroot.

"Got to help me," Amberley panted. "My sister— Kincaid—"

The Creole blew smoke, his scowl deepening. "I 'ave seen, M'sieu. Do not tal me more. It is ver' bad thing. I would 'ave shoot Jack las' night if I know w'at is in his dumb-ox head. But now it is done. The poor little lady. But she is the lucky one, maybe. W'atever he do to her—my fran', it is nothing to w'at the Apach' do to Jack when they find him…."

"My God, man—-you mean you won't—?"

"Do w'at, eh?" The Creole's voice softened then. "I am ver' sorry for this, professair. Now it is daylight, the Apach' will kill any of us they find. They are waiting out there. In here is cover, is food and grub. We stay here a long time and hold off the Apach'—in time maybe find the way out." His fierce frown fixed on the cheroot smoke wreathing up in the still dawn air, avoiding Amberley's unbelieving stare. "It is too late, or I would go. Now, is hopeless. We only get ourself' kill'."

James Amberley was a man of logical bent, and the relentless logic of the Creole's words wasn't to be argued. Without replying, he pointed to his pistol in Charbonneau's belt. The Creole silently handed it to him. Amberley holstered it and went to his gear. Dug out a pasteboard box of rifle cartridges and rammed it in his coat pocket. He picked up his rifle, found his hat and tugged it on, left them without a backward glance.

Emerging into Obregon Pass, he began the hopeless task of scanning for sign. In his sweating concentration, he barely glanced at Tomas Ramirez as the youth shuffled softly to his side, extending one of the two canteens he held. After a moment Amberley took it, slipping the strap over his shoulder. His cold eyes met Mexican Tom's dark ones, seeing the somber stunned sickness there.

"Better get back with them," Amberley told him coldly. "Safer there."

"It is my doing, no?" Mexican Tom said softly. "If I am not drunk and asleep when they come, this would not 'appen."

Amberly did not answer, his face held stiff and unrelenting. More softly then, Ramirez said, "I am the tracker, you are not."

Amberley released a deep sigh of assent, saying brusquely, "Let's not waste time."

"It may be the long trail. I think the horses would be good to have. It is for you to say."

Briefly Amberley studied the dark young face, feeling a faint shock now, seeing there all the resigned fatalism that Ramirez' conquered and downtrodden people had learned in three centuries. He was ready to die to expiate his mistake, and fully expected to do so.

Amberley gave a slow, weary nod. "Get the horses, Tomas."

CHAPTER ELEVEN

True dawn had streaked the sky when Angsman topped a rugged promontory on his last leg off the heights down to the complex of gorges toward the end of Obregon Pass. He halted to alertness, hearing the faint drift of shots from far below. Evidently Charbonneau's crew had retreated into these canyons to make their last-ditch stand. With the new day, the Apaches had taken up the fight once more, and Angsman considered their plight without pity. They had pushed their greedy gamble too far, and must pay a grim piper.

Then, moving across a craggy rim before the last drop into the canyons, he paused curiously. A line of riders, like a file of ants, showed briefly to view on the floor of a distant shallow wash, then were cut off once more. That would be the raiding party, evidently headed back toward the rancheria. He supposed that those shots had accounted for the last of the Creole and his men, and tonight there would be a celebration in the lodges of the *Be-don-ko-he.*

Still, a faint worry for his own companions was revived in Angsman's thoughts. Though he had no doubt of Ramirez' ability to deal with any emergency, it had now been twenty-four hours since he'd left the base camp. Anything might have happened in that time.

An hour later he was nearly to Obregon Pass, swinging out of a rocky defile into the broad wash where he'd seen the riders. From the sign, they had both come and gone this way. And then, moving on, he heard the first faint sounds of a man in agony, and steeled himself. He turned a sharp bend and found Jack Kincaid. They had taken him alive.

He was stripped naked and lashed upright against a giant *bisnaga,* facing it. His wrists were bound together by a length of green rawhide circling the barrel cactus, hugging his arms around its spiny hulk in a fatal embrace. Other rawhide strips anchored his chest and waist. These had shrunk rapidly in the oven-blast of the mounting sun. His legs were splayed out and quivering, feet digging great furrows in a last terrible effort to push away from the barb-tipped spines. They had pierced his body in a hundred places, face and trunk and limbs, and blood, dried and fresh, covered him from head to foot and made a dark mire around his feet.

Like all Apache methods, this one was as exquisitely lingering as it was certain. Yet the bubbling moans were ebbing away, and only the convulsive quiver of tortured flesh showed a residue of life. Angsman had cut the last rawhide strip and eased Kincaid slowly off the excruciating barbs and onto the ground when the clink of shod hoofs on stone alerted him to horsemen moving up the wash. He had the startled thought that at least two of Charbonneau's crew still lived, and now he picked up his rifle and faded back to the turn, blending motionlessly against the bank.

Then Amberley and Ramirez rode into view, halting their skittish horses. Amberley half-fell out of his saddle and walked over like a man in a trance to the bloody, naked form. Angsman stepped out then, and Amberley lifted his glazed stare, whispering, "My God."

Mexican Tom dismounted, his dark eyes strangely haunted, and then realizing that Judith wasn't with them and that Amberley appeared in a state of near-shock, Angsman rapped out, "What's happened?"

Ramirez told him, giving himself the weigjit of blame. Angsman, listening with his head bent as he studied the ground, didn't censure him by a word. The thing was done, and Ramirez' voice held a misery to which nothing could be added. He himself shared blame, Angsman knew, for failing to return to camp yesterday. It stood to reason that Ramirez would have a bottle he hadn't found stashed somewhere.

The sign was badly scuffed, but enough remained to show how Kincaid, dragging Judith with him, had been surprised and wounded by the waiting Apaches, who then, satisfied with the double coup of bloodily revenging their young tribesman and taking a white woman captive, had headed triumphantly back for the rancheria.

He briefly explained this, and as his words struck through Amberley's grieving stupor, the Easterner said, "She—she's alive then? But merciful God—"

"On a far raid, they're likely to rape and kill," Angsman said thoughtfully. "This close to their camp, they'll take her there. She'll be slave to the buck that took her. Mostly they don't fancy white women. But they're like us, exceptions to every rule."

Amberley stared at him, white-faced. "Are you out of your mind?"

"What I'm pointing out," Angsman said thinly, "is she's alive and well...for which you can thank the Apaches. The rest is up to us."

"I—I'm sorry, Angsman. I should have known. But is there a chance?"

"Man can only try, professor."

"Going to be hell finding that Chiricahua camp, amigo," Mexican Tom said soberly. "This, she's a hard place to track."

"I found it yesterday—that's why I didn't make it back. I saw the bunch that has Miss Amberley swing southeast an hour back, following this same wash."

"Did you see her?" Amberley asked eagerly.

"Spotted 'em from that big bluff over east." Angsman swung his arm in a spare gesture. "Too far to more'n barely make 'em out. I came back here as the crow flies, but I was on foot, covering damn' rough terrain. Too rough for horsebackers. These 'Paches are mounted. So they're swinging wide, but along an easier trail. I got the lay of the land though, and we can follow 'em faster their way. See you brought the horses." He nodded toward his and Judith's mounts tied to Ramirez' dun by lead ropes.

"Yes—we hoped we'd run into you—and find her, of course." Amberley dragged his reluctant gaze down to the now-silent body of Kincaid. He shuddered. "What about—?"

"We'll be back this way—I hope." Angsman moved to his paint and swung into saddle, his face grim and tight. That hope was damned slim. Even if he could get into the rancheria alive, there wasn't only Bonito to face out. There was Chingo, who wouldn't rest till either he or Will Angsman was dead. But there was no choice left now....

It was high noon when they approached the first wave of barrier ridges that guarded Bonito's valley. Against Amberley's chafing impatience, Angsman had held them to a steady, unhurried pace. Their horses were well-rested, and had to be conserved against future need.

He had no clear-cut plan for effecting Judith Amberley's rescue, for only one thing was certain: there was no possibility of taking the girl alive from an Apache camp by stealth or force. Whatever hand was dealt him had to be played boldly and openly.

As the three men rode up from a last dusty wash into sight of the first ridge, Angsman raised his hand for a halt, surveying its bare summit. As the others ranged up beside him, he said quietly, " 'Pache sentry up there who's seen us by now, or I'm a liar."

"Do you see him?" Amberley demanded.

"No. Just the first likely place on this horse trail." He paused to isolate his next words. "You'll be staying here, the both of you. I'm going on alone."

Against their strenuous objections, he made his patient, reasoned argument. It wasn't a question of courage or even of duty. Three armed men would draw lightning; a single man stood the best chance of bluffing himself alive into the camp. Angsman was the logical one, knowing the customs and the language.

Ramirez' silence was his reluctant agreement; Amberley gave a slow and painful nod, and then, as Angsman started to dismount, the Easterner reached out to grip his arm. "Angsman—" he swallowed hard—"whatever you have to do——don't fail her."

Angsman stepped to the ground, tossed his reins to Ramirez, and leaving his rifle in its boot, tramped the fifty yards to the base of the ridge. He halted there, feeling the first crawl of strong tension as he watched the sun-scorched ridgetop. Nothing moved in the heat-dancing stillness. He unbuckled his pistol belt and let it fall, drew his hunting knife from its sheath and discarded that. He raised his voice in the Apache tongue: "I come as friend today, as I came yesterday to one who was whipped by the pinda-likoye who's now died for that thing."

His words trailed into the waiting silence, and Angsman let it run on for a half-minute before he spoke again,

now with a taunting edge: "My weapons are on the
ground. Does the Be-don-ko-he fear that one man, alone
and unarmed, will rout the People like frightened rabbits?"

A lean dark form glided up to view, his rifle ready but
only half-raised. The buck's tone was low and contemptuous. "If a great noise could frighten the People,
they should fear you, white-eyes who fights with his
mouth." He spat briefly. "What do you want here?"

"I'd speak to Bonito. Today a white-eyed woman was
brought this way by your warriors. I would speak of
her."

"How do you know of this?"

"The woman was stolen from my camp by the bad
pinda-likoye. We found his body. Your warriors took
the woman."

"You followed them quickly."

"I knew of your camp."

"You lie, white-eyes. Only the Apache knows of this
place."

"I found it yesterday—and spied on it by darkness.
Tell Bonito not to post boys for sentinels."

The Apache was momentarily silent; a hint of grim
respect touched his voice: "The woman is yours?"

Angsman said "Yes," without hesitation, because the
Apache would appreciate the simple and direct. The
sentry's glance flicked above his head. "And the two
others?"

"They'll wait my return." He gave the words just enough
bold assurance.

Abruptly the Apache left the ridgetop, descending with
an easy grace, and then he motioned Angsman to
precede him. They entered a deep notch that cut through
this ridge and two more. The last ridge tapered off, ending the notch, and the rocky ground dissolved into a
grassy gentle slope as they descended to the valley.

Approaching the rancheria, its sights and sounds and
smells washed through Angsman's senses with the not-
unpleasant memory of other camps...the smoke of
greasewood fires, the smell of roasting muleflesh, the
nopal drying, the grazing remuda tended by adolescent
boys, the children running and playing among the
pyramidal brush wickiups. A curious throng began to

follow apace as Angsman and his guard moved toward a centrally placed jacal.

He did not see Judith Amberley...nor Chingo. Angsman held his face tight and his muscles loose, swinging easily ahead of his guard. He had only his patience and nerve and wit and his knowledge of these people; if they weren't enough, he would die a worse death than Jack Kincaid, for there would be warriors here who knew him. He could run no bluff; his speech must be as true as it was careful.

Two men stood by the jacal, quietly talking; both ignored the approaching hubbub until Angsman's guard spoke to one of them. Though he'd never seen the Apache leader, Angsman knew that he was facing Bonito.

Almost diminutive in stature and further bent and withered by age, he was far from impressive at first glance. An ordinary warband confined his straight gray hair, and he wore a faded calico shirt and hip-length moccasins. His only adornment was a shiny, worn object hanging from his thin, sinewed neck by a rawhide cord—it was, Angsman realized wonderingly, a saint's medallion. Because Bonito was nothing if not all Apache, this one ironically displayed token—or trophy—bore strongly home to the white scout that within this shabby ancient little man lay an enigmatic depth of character that only a fool would take lightly.

He glanced briefly at Bonito's companion, the same youth he had rescued from Charbonneau's camp yesterday. The smooth young face was stony, his eyes unblinking as they met Angsman's.

Bonito listened to the sentry's words, his face a shriveled and unchanging mask. But his eyes were alert black lightning, flickering from Angsman to the sentry and back again. Then, as he seemed about to speak, a barrel-chested brute of a man shouldered roughly through the crowd. It was Chingo.

The renegade Mimbre chief was a squat dynamo of energy, restless and quick-motioned, with a vibrant and violent nature to match. His broken face contained none of the Apache's impassiveness, being as mobile as it was cruel. His side-shuttling glance at Angsman was brief in its searing hatred; his sudden speech raged with his feeling:

"I know this white-eyes. He is Ongs-mon, a guide for

the pony soldiers. He has killed Apaches with his own hand. Give him to me, Bonito. Long before I've finished with this one, he'll scream for death."

Bonito's reply was a thin and papery husking: "Chingo's thoughts are as easily read as fresh mule droppings. It is a personal thing, your hatred for this white-eyes. Why?"

Chingo scowled at this perception. "This spittle of a coyote led the pony soldiers to one of El Soldado's camps. They surprised us. My woman and my son were killed." He touched his scarred face. "This, Ongs-mon did to me himself. I swore an oath that I'd watch him die through many days and nights, that the end would come at night and his bones be scattered so that he'd walk forever between the living and the dead and find no rest." His barely suppressed passions flamed impatiently. "Now I'll do it…give him to me!"

"This is the one who took me alive from the white-eyed camp a sun ago," Bonito's young companion muttered, not looking at Angsman.

"Bonito is chief here, not Chingo," the old chief husked softly. "I will judge." In Spanish, he said then, "Did you think that by aiding Tloh-ka you could pass safely among the Be-don-ko-he?"

"I did not think this," Angsman answered in Apache. "I meant to show that my white-eyes had come in peace."

As though he hadn't heard, Bonito piped gently on, "You thought this because you know that Tloh-ka is the son of my son."

"I did not know this," Angsman answered steadily, feeling that he stood on the shakiest ground with this wily and inscrutable old man.

Abruptly Bonito reverted to Apache: "No white-eyes I've met speaks our tongue, not even as badly as you. You have lived among the Shis-in-day."

"Yes."

"Yet you've guided the pony soldiers against us."

"This thing is true."

"You have killed Apaches."

"Yes." He felt the wicked silence of the watching Indians draw around him like an invisible net.

"Why have you come to this land, Ongs-mon, you and your white-eyes?"

Angsman began to talk quietly, starting from his meeting with the Amberleys in *Nantan* Marsden's office, carefully omitting no detail. The telling took a long while, because he spoke only in Apache, wanting to make each listener understand perfectly that his mission here was a peaceful one. Time and again he stumbled and paused in the effort to convey his thoughts without the subtle nuances of a tongue he'd never wholly mastered. Being uncivilized, his listeners were people of an abiding patience, also accustomed to long ceremonial tales, and there was no interruption. Then Chingo, champing with un-Apache restlessness, burst out, "The white-eyes' tongue splits many ways, and none are straight. When has Bonito listened to a white-eyes?"

Bonito husked tonelessly, "In this, at least, he speaks truth: he and his companions did not come for *pesh-litzog,* the yellow iron, for our scouts have told us that they found some and left it. It is Sha-be-no's white-eyes who want pesh-litzog and who whipped Tloh-ka. It is Ongs-mon who saved Tloh-ka. I have bought guns from Sha-be-no in the past; I know him. He's treacherous as a snake. Since these things are true, why should Ongs-mon lie about the rest?"

"I would put a question to Bonito," Angsman said quietly.

"I will think on whether to answer it."

"I've told you of the two white-eyes, a young one and an old one, who came to this land a summer gone, and of the strange one who wanders the canyons like a wild beast. What can Bonito tell me of these things?"

They had not seen the two white-eyes, Bonito said. They had come here before the Apaches. Perhaps they were dead and their bones scattered by coyotes. Unless —Bonito paused with a good storyteller's drama, and Angsman found himself holding his breath—unless the wild man was Angsman's old one. One of Bonito's warriors who knew him had said that this old one was once a guide for the pony soldiers. They did not know how he came to be here or how his madness came on him. They hadn't harmed him, because he was already *tats-an,* though his body lived on. With scarcely a pause, Bonito's reedy murmur continued, "If you leave this land alive, you will lead no other white-eyes here."

"I will promise this."

"You'll tell none of the yellow iron here, for which white-eyes lust as starving wolves for a strayed buffalo calf."

"This too."

"You will guide no more pony soldiers against Apaches —any Apaches."

In a breath-hung instant Angsman knew how much hinged on his reply; he said steadily then, "This I will not promise."

"*Enju.* You are a man....Bring out the white woman."

A big young warrior with a bluff, scowling face thrust to the front of the throng. "The white woman is mine. I ran her down and made her captive; I claim her by this."

"Who expects Matagente to lightly surrender such a claim?" Bonito's tone hinted at dry irony. He made a spare motion that broke up the throng and spread it out, clearing off a space of hard-packed ground.

Laboriously the old man picked up a stick and shuffled off a slow wide circle, drawing a ring roughly fifteen feet in diameter. Then he motioned to two warriors, took their knives and laid these in the center of the circle. As the medicine man began intoning a ceremonial chant above the knives, Bonito droned quietly, "Is the meaning understood, white-eyes?"

Angsman nodded; it was the Blood Right. He would fight a duel with Matagente in the Apache fashion, for possession of the white girl.

CHAPTER TWELVE

Chingo made his loud and abusive protest. Bonito's answer was soft and dry as the rustle of dead leaves, with an irrevocable note of warning: "Matagente is of my following; his claim I've judged and decided. If the white-eyes wins against Matagente, he and the woman leave my camp alive. Then take your quarrel to him, Mimbreno. It's no concern of mine. I have spoken."

Chingo moved back to the edge of the crowd, standing scowling and spraddle-legged with arms folded, a bull-chested and dominant figure. His eyes were glazed with his frustrated hatred. He plainly feared that young Matagente might kill Angsman, cheating Chingo of the goal that centered his savage life. Bonito's reasons were equally clear: he'd evidently declared publicly that his life-long battle with the white man was ended; he was making his word firm by releasing both these white-eyes on condition. At the same time he must observe tribal justice by Matagente's claim. To Chingo, a younger upstart war chief of another tribe, he was deliberately giving short shrift, emphatically settling any doubt as to whose was the voice of command here.

The crowd gave way as a squaw approached, pushing the stumbling white girl ahead of her. Judith Amberley's dirt-smudged face was discolored by a great swollen bruise on one cheek. Her short pale hair was matted with dirt, and her blouse was torn. Her whole slender body was slack with exhaustion and brutal treatment.

Seeing him then, she stared in unbelieving recognition. A half sob started in her throat. Almost imperceptibly Angsman shook his head; she must show no weakness. At once that still cold pride masked her face; he knew then that the iron fiber of her was untouched by what she had endured.

"Let the white-eyed woman watch," Bonito said. He turned a slow glance of grave impatience on the medicine man, who brought: his muttered incantations to a hasty close.

While Angsman shed his shirt, Matagente moved into the center of the ring and stood flexing his long arms, preening for the young squaws. Watching him carefully, Angsman decided that he was not too bright and that this was Matagente's sole disadvantage. He was bigger than most of his fellows, as lean and sinewy as any. Like all Apache youths, he'd been trained from childhood for the deadliest games of close-fighting his youth meant that he would think and act swiftly if not brilliantly.

Each slightly crouched, the knives on the ground between them, neither wanting to make the initial move that might give his opponent an opening. Angsman made it then, bending and scooping up his knife, leaping back before Matagente could move. He saw the brown face jerk with surprise at this unexpected reflex in a white man, one who lacked Matagente's youth by a good ten years.

Now the Apache did move, quickly dipping up his knife and pivoting away to escape Angsman's side-arcing slash at his belly. Angsman pressed him close, feinting low and then high, and Matagente, placed on a sudden defensive, retreated awkwardly. A ripple of laughter went through the crowd, and Matagente didn't like it. A soundless snarl twisted his lips and now he recovered, still retreating but with the delicate, foot-mincing shift of a trained fighter.

Angsman moved in faster; with a sudden sweep of blade he drew a fine red line across Matagente's chest, barely moving away in time. It left Angsman briefly wide open and the Apache came swiftly inside his guard, his knife arcing up and inward. Angsman grabbed his wrist, stopping the fatal thrust cold; with a savage twist he locked that arm behind Matagente's back. It might have diverted Matagente for the split-second needed for Angsman to counter-thrust, but the Apache had presence of mind enough to seize Angsman's arm as it pulled back. They strained chest to chest, Angsman fighting to turn steel into Matagente's neck, the Apache striving to free his immobilized knife-arm.

Angsman abruptly hooked his left leg around Matagente's right one and threw him, their locked bodies crashing to earth together. The white scout was on top now, his weight inching his blade nearer by straining degrees toward the Apache's throat. Matagente's body was a taut arch of resistance, tensed muscles coiled like powerful springs against every inch of his coppery hide. He succeeded in rolling them both on their sides.

Thinking always a step ahead of his slower-witted enemy, Angsman relentlessly drove his knee into Matagente's unprotected groin. Matagente twisted with agony, doubling up his knees to protect himself, and the pain galvanized him to a burst of power. He wrenched his locked arm around in front, though Angsman kept his hold.

For a time they grunted and rolled and strained, with neither gaining an advantage; their struggles carried them back to their feet. Deliberately then Angsman shifted to a wrestling position and hip-threw Matagente, at the same time releasing him. The Apache somersaulted in mid-air and hit the earth on his back with a jolting impact that knocked the wind from him. He rallied at once, kicking blindly upward, his moccasined toe slamming Angsman's hand. The knife arced from it, hit the ground and skittered among the feet of the onlookers.

Matagente bounded to his feet with a hoarse shout of triumph, moving slowly in against his opponent. Angsman shot one baffled glance at the dust-moiled spot where his knife had vanished and started a circling retreat. But there was small room for evasive tactics in this closely cordoned circle, and he had to constantly watch Matagente against a sudden charge.

There was a sudden flicker of movement—the sunflash of his knife in the dust, skidded into the ring by a sly kick. His swift glance found the face of the boy Tloh-ka, standing almost at the front of the throng. That face, not wholly disciplined in its youth, held a half-defiant vindication: whatever he owed the white man was paid in full.

Matagente, puffed with certain victory, had missed this byplay; he edged in for the kill, biding his time for a certain thrust. Suddenly Angsman darted low and past him, diving under his belated downstab of aim, hitting the ground and rolling over twice; his outflung hand closed true around the knife hilt.

Matagente's large bluff face sagged as he saw his enemy coming upright and armed; he started a desperate lunge, bearing down on Angsman before the white scout had his balance set. Angsman dug in his heels and drove in low and fast, his head butting solidly against the Apache's middle. He caught Matagente by surprise, smashing the breath from him and flopping him on his back, arms and legs thrashing wildly.

In an instant Angsman had dropped above him, his knees pinning Matagente's shoulders while his free hand caught the other's knife-wrist. He laid his knife along the Apache's corded throat muscles.

"I give you the choice, Be-don-ko-he," he grated. "Now—"

Old Bonito's calm words were very low. "Do you choose, Matagente?"

"I—choose."

Slowly Angsman rose and stepped back; Matagente rolled onto his belly and got a knee under him, rising painfully. The pain was not physical. He turned the bald venom of his hurt on Angsman. He spat at the white man's feet and flung his knife into the spittle, spun on his heel and stalked away through the crowd. Another enemy who would not forget, Angsman knew then, thinking coldly, I should have killed him....

There was a sudden flurry of confusion from the far side of the camp where the remuda grazed; the crowd broke apart, and Angsman saw a pony streaking away toward the near ridges that ended this side of the valley. A small form lay flat against its back, clinging like a burr.

Chingo voiced a fierce and raging command to his men as he spun and ran for the remuda; his five men joined him on the run. In less than a minute, the seven were riding away in hot pursuit of the escaping one.

"This is a lucky thing for you, white-eyes," old Bonito droned matter-of-factly. "While the Mimbreno is chasing down his woman, you may leave in safety. Take the white woman and go, nor come again to the lodges of the Be-don-ko-he."

After watching Angsman and the sentry vanish into

the notch, Amberley and Ramirez could only lay up in the mouth of the wash and wait. James Amberley's nerves were pulled taut, and his eyes ached with the strain of staring across the heat-shimmering flat at the notch. His clothes were drenched with sweat; he could feel it pooling soddenly in his boots. He tried not to think of how thin Angsman's chances really were....

"Hssst!"

The Mexican gripped his arm. Amberley heard the fast tattoo of a running horse coming up the notch and behind it what sounded like other riders in bunched pursuit.

He and Ramirez were hunched side by side behind a low barricade of rocks that partly blocked the end of the wash, and now Mexican Tom lifted his rifle from his knees and laid it across the rocks, sighting on the notch. Mechanically Amberley followed his example.

The first rider broke into sight—a small brown figure clinging bareback to a running pinto. It streaked across the flats toward the draw, covering half the distance before a half-dozen mounted bucks thundered out of the notch. And then the pinto stumbled and went down on its knees, recovered footing and lunged away. The mishap had tumbled the rider off.

It was an Indian girl, Amberley saw, climbing to her feet dazed but unhurt. She shot a glance at her horse sidling away, then at her pursuers. She began a hopeless, stumbling run toward the wash. One buck drew ahead of his fellows, grinning broadly as he quickly overhauled her.

Amberley, being a scholar and gentleman, didn't hesitate. He shot hastily at the buck and missed. The Apache wheeled his pony up short and so did his companions. The girl stopped in her tracks uncertainly. Amberley dropped his rifle, scrambled over the rocks and ran toward her, ignoring Mexican Tom's frantic, "Profes', you goddamn fool—!"

The girl shrank back now, and seeing her startled fear, Amberley slowed to a fast walk. "We're friends—" he started to call. Then the first buck, seeing a lone white man, gave a delighted whoop and kicked his pony forward.

Amberley reached the girl and pushed her behind him, tugging at his holstered revolver. The Apache thundered down on his easy prey, his slender lance poised for the thrust. Ramirez' Winchester roared. The slug wiped the buck from horseback; he hit the ground like a broken bundle of rags and rolled to a dead stop.

His cautious fellows had held back; now they broke apart, sliding to the ground and fading out of sight like dust on the rock-littered flat. Amberley put his head down and ran, dragging the girl with him. They had almost reached the rocks when the Apaches opened fire. Ramirez rapidly emptied his magazine to give them a covering fire. Amberley felt a blow in the foot that almost crossed his legs in mid-run. Then they were up and over the rocks, tumbling breathlessly down beside Ramirez.

Mexican Tom thrust the Winchester into Amberley's hands and snatched up the Easterner's rifle, saying flatly, "Reload, man. Santa Maria, I think you shake down a hornets' nest on our heads."

Amberley, staring at the shot-off heel of his boot, glanced up in honest surprise. "I couldn't let them—"

"Sure, sure. Load the gun, profes', eh?" As he spoke, a buck lifted part of his body to view, ducking back with a taunting laugh as Ramirez' shot puffed rock dust from his shelter.

"This is fine game for 'Pache," Ramirez observed, rocking back on his haunches, his long brown face shining with sweat. "Well, we ain't so bad off for now. Ain't gettin' behind us without they cut across the open, makin' damn' fine target. They stuck there, we stuck here. Willie and the senorita stuck in the rancheria, and that ain't good."

Amberley turned an ashen face toward him. "Good Lord."

"Yeah. You shouldn't of been so quick to help this siwash gal, profes'. Me havin' to shoot one won't help our compadres none."

The Apaches did not shoot again, and Amberley supposed that ammunition was fairly dear to them. He glanced out once at the dead Apache, his body splayed grotesquely across the rocks and dark blood dyeing the tawny dust by his head. Amberley didn't look again, settling down to a bitter cud-chewing of self-recrimination. Then he realized that the girl was crowded tightly against him.

Mildly embarrassed, he noticed the curious plaiting of her black hair, the sturdy Apache moccasins and leggings, and the shapeless dirty cotton dress that didn't wholly conceal her youth and lithe slimness. The black eyes in her thin brown face met his with no fear now, only a deep wonderment. She smelled of grease and sweat and woodsmoke, distinct odors that badly impregnated his own clothing, he knew. He shifted uncomfortably away, muttering.

"What you say, profes'?"

"I said, what the devil will I do with a runaway Apache female!"

Ramirez briefly studied her, frowning. "I don't think this one she's Injun."

"What the devil?"

Ramirez spoke rapidly in his own language. She murmured a short reply, and he grunted. "She's Spanish, like I guess. Not much Injun blood. Mebbe none."

"I know something of your language," Amberley snapped. He was deeply irritated because he had a professional pride in his ability to identify the Latin-Indian peoples. Damned fascinating to look for traces of original Aztec or Incan bloodlines, as well as the more recent Spanish infusions. Yet now he'd been misled by first appearance, for in spite of the girl's natural darkness and deep tan, her features obviously weren't Athapascan.

Haltingly he questioned her. He learned to his vast relief that Angsman had fought and won a duel for Judith's freedom with the buck who had captured her. The girl hadn't seen more, because she had used this distraction for her first chance at escape. Of course with these warriors laid up by the notch, Angsman and Judith would have to leave the valley by another way and skirt around the notch to get here...which would explain their delay in coming.

The Apaches began shouting insults in Spanish, and Ramirez returned them with interest. Meanwhile Amberley questioned the girl further. She was the only daughter of Don Luis Valdez y Montalvo y Salazar y Torres, a wealthy hacendado of southern Sonora. While returning to her father's estate from a visit to relatives in Hermosillo, her small wagon party was attacked and wiped out by this same renegade band.

It appeared that the young war chief Chingo had at

once conceived a strange passion for her, she reminding him of another who'd been his child-bride. Though she'd been subjected to terrible hardship in the weeks that followed, she hadn't been ill-treated or otherwise molested. Chingo, a very strange Apache, had seemed to be waiting for her heart to soften toward him. He had used her kindly, and yet sensing something mad and twisted in the man, Pilar Torres had come to fear Chingo more than any of them.

"You're quite safe from him now," Amberley told her gently.

Her large black eyes were solemn. "I cannot say why I believe you, senor, only that I do. It must be that you're as good as you are brave."

"Oh," Amberley blushed.

A sudden crunch of gravel down the wash at their backs brought their heads around. Amberley's breath exploded from his lungs in full relief. It was Angsman and Judith. Crouching low, the two moved in to drop at their sides.

"Jude," Amberley said urgently.

"I'm fine, dear. Tired and bruised and mauled. But otherwise fine, thanks to our friend...."

Angsman gave a brief nod toward the Spanish girl. "Your idea, professor?"

"What else could I do? She's not an Apache, Angsman."

"So I see. Odd she ran, though."

"What do you mean?"

"Mostly women taken by Indians, white or not, don't run away. Lot of 'em refuse to leave the tribe, offered a chance. Figure what they'll have to face with their kinfolk'll be a sight worse."

"The poor child," Judith said softly.

"Time we thought about pulling out of here."

"To where, amigo?" Mexican Tom asked wryly. "That cabron Charbonneau is holed up in our good place."

"We'll dicker with Armand," Angsman answered grimly. "With what he's going to face, I'm thinking he'll listen."

CHAPTER THIRTEEN

When the girl Pilar mounted behind Judith Amberley, the five people began their slow retreat down the wash, Angsman and Ramirez bringing up a rear guard. Angsman knew that Chingo and his men would follow, well out of sight. An Apache wasn't supposed to attack until all odds ran his way, but trying to graft hard-and-fast rules on the behavior of a maverick like Chingo was to run yourself up a blind alley. The young Mimbreno's mind and motives were too twisted and unpredictable, and he had three good reasons not to rest until he'd settled with this party of white-eyes: Ramirez had killed one of his handful of loyal followers, Amberley had snatched away his prize captive, and Angsman, his blood enemy, was one of them.

The shadows had lengthened when they dropped wearily off the rugged heights before the final swing down to Obregon Pass. On a rare wide stretch of rolling dunes and flats where they could see for a mile in any direction, Angsman called a brief halt, to give horses and riders a safe breather.

Almost at once Chingo and his followers appeared on a distant bare ridge and likewise dismounted. Five of them dropped from their mounts and hunkered down to rest and watch, but the sixth man felt frisky. He abandoned his loincloth and exposed his hindquarters, strutting back and forth as he made obscene and taunting gestures at the whites.

"What *is* he doing?" Judith Amberley burst out. A little later she turned away, her face scarlet. "Well—*really!*"

Angsman rubbed his chin thoughtfully. "That my Winchester you're hefting, Tomas?"

281

"Si, amigo. She's a repeater, and I was usin' her to pin down them cabrons back there—you want her?"

"No. I was wondering where's your old Army Springfield. Singleshot, but it's got a mite better range than my long gun."

A broad grin of understanding broke Ramirez' long face. "I get her." He went to his horse and got the battered rifle from its boot. Angsman took it, checked the load, then stretched out on his belly behind a low flat rock. He laid the barrel across it and began to place his aim, calculating windage and angle. He drew a slow breath, held it, and squeezed off his shot. The cavorting buck, standing sideways, leaped as though stung; he ran a few queer, bucking steps, holding his buttocks, then rolled wildly on the ground.

Mexican Tom whooped his delight, and Angsman rose to his feet with a faint grin, handing back the rifle. He would have tried for Chingo, but couldn't identify the war chief at this distance. The lucky long shot had its immediate effect; the Apaches realized they weren't quite out of rifle range and scrambled back over the ridge, dragging their horses and their floundering fellow with them. That, Angsman judged with satisfaction, should pull Chingo off for a while. He had already lost one man, and another would be riding no warpaths for a time. His force was cut to three, very un-Apache odds.

An hour later they left the last heights and followed a branch canyon which brought them to the terminus of Obregon Pass below Muro del Sangre, here pausing to debate their next move. Both Amberleys were cool to Angsman's idea of joining forces with Armand Charbonneau; they'd had altogether enough of that unscrupulous gentleman, Judith declared flatly. Angsman pointed out that Charbonneau and his crew were forted up in their own choice cul-de-sac, the best place he'd found to withstand an attack.

Sooner or later, he added, Chingo would be raging down on their trail. It might take time for the Mimbreno to recruit help from his hostile fellow Apaches, Bonito's tribesmen, but eventually he could probably persuade a number of the younger Chiricahua bucks to foflow him. They would be champing restlessly from months of inactivity in the rancheria, their savage spirits hardly allayed by the little hunting available here. A small party of whites in their own country was their natural prey. Old Bonito had restrained them so far, but Chingo could wear through that thin checkrein by persuasion and by wondering aloud whether all Chiricahuas were women.

James Amberley frowned. "But I thought Bonito more or less agreed..."

"Bonito's quit fighting. That goes for those who'll follow his lead. But every Apache warrior's his own man, professor. Even the hereditary chiefs are really sort of sage senior advisers. Most times the rest will follow 'em, if only because most people like to be led. But Bonito's not even a hereditary leader. He's a war chief, an ordinary warrior with extra status on a war party: that's when he gives orders and the rest listen. To his people, Bonito's come to mean a good deal more—a sort of living symbol of what they once were—and he's a sound leader in his own right. But he's got no legal power as tribal law recognizes it. Chingo's descended from old Tah-zay, a famous Mimbreno chief; he's got that edge. Also, the younger bucks looked up to Bonito because he was the most warlike of 'em all. Now he's hung up his fighting spurs, he's going to lose something in the eyes of the feisty ones. Chingo may be a mite crazy, but he's smart enough to know all this."

It was a long speech for Angsman, and now he paused before adding pointedly: "We got a couple days' grace maybe, while he's rallying his young men. But he'll come sure as sunrise. When he does, we'll be sitting ducks, unless we do two things: we find a good fort and we throw in with Charbonneau. That's three more guns, and we'll need 'em all."

Amberley sighed. "Your argument seems unassailable, and 1 suppose there's no alternative?"

"Just one, professor."

"What's that?"

"We use the time that's left to pack up and clear out," Angsman replied flatly. As he spoke, his gaze veered hard and direct to Judith Amberley. She flushed, but he knew from the immediate stubborn set of her thin, smudged and sunburned face that on this point she wouldn't yield a jot.

"Not," she said clearly, coldly, "until we have learned of Douglas."

Angsman merely nodded, then gigged his horse down

the pass. By now the muted glow of sunset was shedding its refulgence across the rim, dyeing the walls to a soft gray-blue, and deep shadows began to fill the canyon vales. Enough light remained to make out shape if not detail, and now Angsman caught a shadow of movement in the mouth of a side canyon.

Instantly he spurred his mount sideward toward it, and a dark form sprang up and started a hobbling run. Angsman let his horse out, plunging recklessly into the canyon and bearing swiftly down on the figure. It wheeled to face him; he glimpsed a snarling face half-hidden by a tangle of white hair and beard, thin arms raising a heavy knob stick.

Angsman reined his horse to a skidding halt, roughly swinging the animal so that its shoulder slammed the man's scawny chest, knocking his light body spinning. He sprawled face down and didn't move. Angsman vaulted to the ground and threw his reins. It was their wild man, for sure. Angsman stooped above him, wary that he might be shamming, and then saw the blood trickling from a deep cut in the man's scalp where his head had struck a rock in falling. He turned the wild man on his back. It took him a full five seconds to identify positively Caleb Tree, the old guide from Fort Stambaugh.

Behind his filthy matted hair and beard, Tree's bony features were ravaged by privation—and something worse. His feet were bare, horny and calloused, and his bare arms and legs were withered sticks, the weathered skin taut across bone and tendon. Only tattered dirty rags remained of his clothing.

The others moved up slowly, and Amberley murmured, "Good God." The others said nothing, watching Angsman feel for pulse and heartbeat. He looked up at Judith Amberley, answering the question in her strained dark gaze.

"He's alive—Bonito had it right."

"Caleb Tree," she whispered.

Angsman nodded, dropping his gaze to the unconscious man. Whatever hope there was of discovering Douglas Amberley's fate lay locked in the maniacal brain of this half-starved bundle of bones and skin, and looking at him now, Angsman thought that hope was pretty thin. He did not voice his pessimism, coming now to his feet.

"Best we don't move him. Make him comfortable as
you can and keep a sharp eye on him. Crazy man is
wilier than most. Rest of you stay here while I see friend
Armand."

Mexican Tom stood hipshot, thumbs tucked in his belt
and his Springfield slung in the crotch of his arm. "Better
you don't go alone, amigo."

Angsman shook his head. "You stay. This calls for
talk, and I talk Charbonneau's language. No love lost,
but we understand each other from way back."

He left them, hiking downcanyon through the pooling
shadows, following the stream a half-mile and swinging
with it into the branch canyon. He paced noiselessly up
the pebbly bank to where the dark mouth of the cul-
de-sac yawned, lifting his voice:

"Charbonneau!"

No answer. From here Angsman could see the orange
wash of firelight bathing the inner wall of the ravine,
and he said in a normal tone and drily, "All right, Armand. I'm alone. One man come to scare hell out of
you."

A tall lean form detached itself from a bulge of shadow and came forward, halting a cautious dozen feet away.
The faint light laid blue glints along a rifle barrel.

"One thing I nevair figure you for, Angsman, is a great
fool."

"You're a sight too smart to shoot before you hear
me out, Armand."

"That is very true." The Creole's white grin was
wolfish. "Not till I know whether there's anythin' in it
for Armand, eh? We figure you are dead...the othairs
too."

"No thanks to you we aren't. Kincaid, though...."

"You?"

" 'Paches."

Charbonneau lowered the rifle with an expressive
shrug. "He was a fool. What 'appen?"

Angsman explained, and then Charbonneau doubled his
long legs and settled on his haunches, rifle across his
knees, thoughtfully stroking his beard. "Thing about a
deal is, a man has something to give, something to get.
You need our fort, our guns. W'at you got to give,
Will?"

Angsman sank down facing him. Idly, he scooped up

a handful of sand and sifted it through his fingers, saying softly, "Use your head, Armand. The Taches know you're here. Bonito paid you back for that whipped kid when his braves got Kincaid; that score's settled. He wants no more trouble with whites. Fact remains that when Kincaid and Staples whipped Bonito's grandson, they cut clean any understandings you and him had once. You're on your own now with Chingo set to rampage. We'll be camped on your doorstep, and when Chingo's through with us, he'll just be cutting his teeth. Afterward there'll be you. None of us'll leave the Toscos alive that way." He added wryly, " 'We must hang together, or most assuredly we shall hang separately.' "

"Huh," Charbonneau grunted. "Ben Franklin, ain't it? You know, Will, I'm of good family in N'Orleans. Called myself an educated man, once. Never thought of you as one, though."

"We'll compare family notes sometime," Angsman told him drily, feeling a faint irritation. He had never hinted of his past to any of his Western acquaintances, and he realized that in some obscure way he might have been on guard against doing so. Maybe he'd used up the reason for that self-restraint. The thought passed fleetingly across his mind, and then he said: "We're three able-bodied men; with your three, that's six. A sight better odds. How's it to be, Armand? I haven't got all night."

Charbonneau shifted on his heels to get out a cheroot, placed his thumbnail to a match and paused. "You say Chingo pull' back?"

"For the time."

"Good—so I don't give them red niggers no target." Charbonneau snapped the match alight; its saffron flare highlighted his roughly debonair features as he lighted his cheroot. Puffing, he said, "Three and two makes five, Will."

"How you mean?"

Charbonneau was silent a moment. He tossed the match away with a deep sigh. "The kid, Will-John...he die this morning." His tone became musing. "He was a fonny kid...a little crazy in the head with wantin' to make his fortune. Just an Ohio farm boy, you comprehend, who leave his girl and come to the great West where a man can make money overnight, enough to buy a fine big farm where he can be proud to bring his Lucy. But a kid like that, not very bright, slow like an ox, what is there for him anywhere but the hard labor?"

"Or making a big fast killing by throwing in with cut-throats?"

Charbonneau's shoulders heaved in a chuckle. "You anticipate me, mon ami. Maybe I feel sorry for the kid, maybe them big brown eyes remind me of a poodle my

grandmere give me once. Anyway, I like him, I take him on. Figure first big job that comes off, I send him packin' back to his Lucy with a bonus. Enough to get marry, buy that farm, raise a brood of towheaded slow-witted brats." The cherry-coal of the cheroot glowed brightly as he drew on it. "An' now all that is left of poor Will-John an' his dreams is buried under a pile of rock back in this cul-de-sac. Damn' fonny how things work some-time…I kind of like that kid."

"I know how heartbroken you must be. It a deal or not?"

"Ah oui, why not? I am feel' generous; 'ave my next-to-last cheroot, we smoke on it."

"We don't have to smoke on it," Angsman told him curtly. "It's a truce, Armand. If we get out of this, I'll be watching my back with you. That's one thing never changes where you're concerned."

CHAPTER FOURTEEN

Two days passed in the cul-de-sac. The time of grace left before Chingo made his move was narrowing, if Angsman was right...the Mimbreno might have already assembled his force and was waiting on the chance that he might catch one or all of them in the open. But Angsman doubted it: Chingo had none of the infinite patience of his people. His great nemesis was his own seething energy; it couldn't be bridled for long.

Meanwhile, with five men to alternate the guard duty, they were all left with a good deal of time on their hands. Charbonneau, Ambruster and Tom Ramirez used it to gather some of the float gold that enriched the nearby stream, working out daily from the cul-de-sac. They thoroughly covered the branch canyon and even worked a short distance up Obregon Pass, but none of them ventured too far. The three men panned for the yellow metal from dawn to dusk; all were exhausted but feverishly exuberant at the end of the second day. Already each had a heavy poke containing several hundred dollars worth of dust.

Strangely, Angsman found himself unaffected by their fever. True, though he'd found prospecting a fair means of grubstaking his long desert sojourns, it had never been an addicted lust with him as with some prospectors. Still under ordinary circumstances he'd have availed himself of this opportunity, as would any normal man. He supposed that his present indifference was part of facing this turning point in his life and not being yet certain of what direction it was taking.

He spent the hours studying himself, on his past and present, on life in general, and mostly on the people around him with whom he'd become peculiarly involved. He guessed that one other who might be changing was

James Amberley. The staid Easterner was plainly entranced with the Spanish girl he had rescued; he spent hours sitting with her out of earshot of the others, quietly talking. Angsman wondered amusedly what a man like Amberley, scholarly and reserved to shyness, in whose life there had obviously been no woman except his mother and sister, could find to speak of with a young girl...but he seemed to be having no trouble.

With the pliancy of youth, Pilar Torres had swiftly recovered from her harsh and frightening weeks as the prisoner of renegade Apaches. She still wore the ragged dress and Apache moccasins, but through some woman's wizardry she no longer resembled a thin, frightened waif. She was quite pretty with her vivacious play of dark eyes and smiling lips, and often the soft trill of her laughter welcomely broke the grim quiet. Because she was quick of wit and speech and fully understood their danger, Angsman had guessed that her high spirits were due to her escape from Chingo. Later, becoming more aware of her bright-eyed attention to the professor, he concluded that Pilar had a private happiness of her own.

Of this, Angsman guessed that Judith Amberley had taken a dim view from the outset. But she had occupied herself in caring for Caleb Tree, rarely leaving his side. Something obsessive in her tender concern worried Angsman...she had hardly eaten or slept for two days and nights. How far did she intend carrying this thing?

The old man had taken complete leave of his senses, spending hours in raving delirium, becoming so violent that he had to be held down. Angsman guessed that the head blow Tree had taken only partly explained his condition. They'd found a badly healed scar on his scalp which must have been inflicted months ago. Afterward, already aged to senility and living like an animal, he'd received none of the proper care and rest which might have restored him. Angsman hoped for Judith's sake that Tree might come to his right senses, at least briefly. It might be better if she never learned the truth, but how could a man judge? It was certain that she couldn't go on with the blind spot of Douglas' fate gnawing in her mind.

A few years back when the Army, constantly in the field against the insurgent Apaches, had required a large contingent of civilian scouts, Angsman had been chief of scouts at Fort Stambaugh for a time. He'd made it his business to know his men, Caleb Tree among them. The ancient mountain man had always been irascible, reserved to taciturnity, and it was said that he'd had liaison between gun-runners and Sioux-Arapahoe in the Dakota campaigns, though nothing was proved. Such talk was current through the army echelons, and Major Marsden had passed it on to Angsman as a word of precaution, Angsman had decided that Tree was capable of nearly anything, but was too shrewd to be caught out. He was thoroughly reliable aside from that; his knowledge of the territory he'd ranged from the early fur-trapping and trading days was second to none.

From this meager knowledge and Tree's near-incoherent ravings now, Angsman had tried to piece together what might have happened after he and young Amberley had left Fort Stambaugh. But the old man had only carped on happenings that were now frontier legend, confirming what Angsman had supposed: Tree's past contained dark spots that no man in his right senses would reveal.

Pondering all of it as he sat off to one side on the evening of the second day, Angsman decided that only time could fill out the answers. He glanced at the others, picked out by flickering firelight. Ramirez was on guard at the entrance of the cul-de-sac. Caleb Tree's sleeping form was bundled in blankets by the fire. He'd been resting well for some hours now, his wasted chest rising and falling with steady breathing. Amberley and Pilar sat away from the others, their voices bare murmurs. Turk Ambruster was carrying on an awkward conversation with Judith, while Charbonneau sat cross-legged by the fire; his teeth clamped a dead stub of cheroot while he scowled over the contents of his gold poke which he had spilled out on a blanket, muttering under his breath in French.

Gold fever's really got Armand, Angsman thought narrowly. There's another it'll do to watch....

"...But Mr. Lincoln freed the slaves, Mr. Ambruster," Judith was asserting earnestly, as she sat facing the big Negro, her knees drawn up *to* her chin.

"Yes'm," Ambruster rumbled patiently. "But that didn't make no never mind to a black man in the south, even after Genril Lee surrendered. You don't write off

folks' feelin's by signin' no paper. You was a 'Bolition-
ist, ma'am? Lots of Massachusetts folks was."

"My father was," Judith smiled.

"Sure, you'd of been a little gal then. What I'm sayin',
you folks never saw they ain't no easy answers. Us people wasn't ready for freedom when it bust on us overnight. They was carpetbaggers who used us while we went
plumb wild. An' that rec'nstruction was hard on the
white South'ners, made 'em bitter. You ast how I wound
up out here with a renegade bunch. Details ain't so important as the whys an' wherefores. Easy to set blame
without thinkin' it through. We's all to blame, come down
to it. Hope I ain't offended you, ma'am."

"You are an intelligent and discerning man, sir, and
I'm afraid that my ignorance is an insult to you."

Ambruster smiled widely. "No, ma'am, I'm pleased for
your interest. I been playin' a mean dumb bad actor
so long, I just—"

"Turk." Charbonneau spoke flatly, without looking up.
"How you think it looks, eh, you talkin' to this white
ma'mselle?"

All the diehard arrogance of a dead way of life tinged
his words, and Judith replied angrily, "How dare you!
I will speak to whomever I please, and so will he!"

"No, ma'am," Ambruster rumbled softly, coming to
his feet. "Things as they are, Armand's right. Was right
nice talkin' to you...man could forgit for a little
while. Anyways I got to look to my horse."

"I will not press you, sir, but you are always welcome
to speak to me."

"Thank you." Ambruster turned away toward the niche
where their horses were tethered on the patch of grass.
He paused. "Figgered oncet I had a bellyful of knowtowin'
to white folk, servin' em, only—" he hesitated "—anythin'
I can ever do fer you, miss, you whistle." He walked
quickly away.

Judith sighed, then bent above Caleb Tree, tucking
the blankets closely under his chin, afterward rising to
her feet and walking over to where Angsman sat with
his back propped against a rock, legs outstretched and
crossed, slacked at complete rest with the negligent ease
of a big cat. She settled her own back to the rock a few
feet away, her face softly brooding. "How terrible. You

would think that among outlaws, at least, a man might enjoy freedom from the barrier of his skin color."

Angsman said nothing, and she added sharply, "Of course you're Southern."

"Don't bait me, lady," he murmured. "Your Pa was likely a merchant. Mine owned a big Virginia farm— owned four slaves. We lost everything when McClellan went through to Richmond. Took years to recover. Man can't wipe his memory clean like a kid's slate. As your friend said, there's no easy answer."

"Then," she said icily, "you think—"

"Tom Ramirez is my friend. I've lived with Mexicans, Indians. That answer you?"

"I'm sorry," she said wearily, pressing a hand to her temple. "I'm tired and upset. This danger...caring for the old man...and then Jimmy and that girl—"

"Different when it touches you, eh?"

"Certainly not," she snapped. "Anyway she's really a Spaniard, not a Mexican. But she's been with those Apaches. You haven't lived away from society so long that you've forgotten how people talk."

"That matter?"

"It does, and don't deny it. You have to live with other people, however you dislike their thinking."

"And with yourself."

"That is no answer."

"It is for me."

"It's selfish."

"Leastways I don't try living someone else's life."

"What a cruel thing to say!"

"Sorry. None of my business."

"Perhaps it is. You've certainly earned the right to know." She was silent a moment, biting her lip. "Try to understand. Though Jimmy's older than me, I've had to look after him constantly since our parents died. Somebody had to...he's so impractical. He paid no attention to girls when he was younger, and he's always been tied up in his work. Now he's swept quite off his feet by this girl. It simply won't work. Can you blame me for being concerned?"

"Boston's a long way off. No reason anyone has to know about the Apache business. He met her in the southwest—that's all."

She laughed bitterly. "How very simple. A strange little waif of a girl—"

"The daughter of a grandee. Her people likely set foot on American soil before yours did. She'll stand head and shoulders in Boston society—even be the rage of your class for a time."

"Rather good, for a desert-dweller," she said mockingly. "But her religion does place strong conditions on marriage. You see? That's the sort of thing poor Jim never thinks of."

Angsman smiled. "I've talked some to this little lady. Have the feeling that won't make a jot of difference to her."

"But she's only a child—Jim is thirty-four. At least fifteen years difference. Oh, it's impossible!"

"Wouldn't know. Never made up other people's lives as I went along. Too selfish, I reckon."

She stiffened icily, then relaxed with a sigh. "Perhaps you're right. Perhaps I am only making excuses to hold onto him at any cost. There were only the three of us …and Douglas is gone. And yet I lost him because—" She shook her head, her eyes haunted. "Never mind. At least it should have taught me a lesson. Perhaps I'm generically a meddling fool."

"You can be too hard on yourself too."

Her glance was quick and a little surprised. It was the first gentle word he had given her, Angsman realized with a faint nudge of shame. The desert hardened and roughened a man farther than skin-deep; whatever wells of gentleness remained were almost buried.

"Strange—I just realized that you hadn't breathed a word of your past until you mentioned your father's farm —in Virginia. Is that all?"

He shrugged bleakly. "The rest isn't important."

"Perhaps it is."

He turned his head and met her eyes fully, saying after a moment, "Maybe sometime I'll…."

They heard a low moan over by the fire. Caleb Tree had elbowed himself to a sitting position, and was staring vacantly about. "Where's this child at?" His faded eyes came to sharp focus under a frosty rim of brows. "That you, Angsman?"

"Me, Cal." Angsman went down on one knee by the old man while Judith on his other side pushed Caleb

Tree firmly back. He glared at her. Angsman shook his head slightly and she drew back, biting her lip.

"Hoss, who's thet thin biddy?"

"She's cared for you mighty close, Caleb," Angsman said gently. "Been out of your head a long time."

"Know that," Caleb Tree grunted testily, gingerly passing a scrawny hand over his white hair. "Took a knock on the head. Was quite a spell ago. Some of it comin' back. Not all. What'n hell happent?"

"Remember Doug Amberley?" Angsman studied Tree's face as he spoke.

Just a couple of days' rest seemed to have begun restoring the old man. The second head injury he'd sustained might even have helped his memory and sanity —Angsman had heard of such things. Anyway he was rational enough for the moment. This might be a good time, while his recollection remained murky, to try to catch him off-guard on any subterfuge he'd attempt.

Caleb Tree swept the circle of intent faces with a shuttling glance, coming back to Angsman's. "Amberley. Young cub I brought here. I 'member. A little, leastways …ain't too clear."

"The kid's dead, Cal."

Judith gasped, and Angsman ignored her, watching for Tree's reaction. Tree's eyes narrowed. "Could be so, hoss," he murmured.

He wouldn't be baited into self-betrayal, Angsman knew then, and told himself, Go easy now. Aloud he said quietly, "How much you remember?"

Haltingly, pausing many times to knit his white brows, the mountain man told them of bringing Douglas Amberley to this place, of finding the old Spanish gold diggings and making camp there. Of sighting the cave entrance high on the pass wall, where the Obregon party had taken refuge…and of finding a way to reach it. "My stick don't float no further, hoss—she's hung on a snag. Cub wanted to look in them caves…all I know."

Angsman told him, "Take your time," his glance touching Judith then. She was gnawing her lip, hands clasping her knees with white-knuckled fingers. "You sure about the cave, old timer? I spotted it myself. But if there was ever a trail up there, it's gone."

"Wagh. Know that." Tree hesitated, frowning. " 'Member now. Didn't come to it from blow. Follered thet big slide up to the rim, let ourse'f down by rope. Wa'n't nohow easy, but...." He broke off, a fleeting wariness touching his seamed face in its filthy tangle of white hair and beard. Angsman knew then that Tree's own words had surfaced some troubled memory. Angsman gave him no chance to backtrack, pressing it mercilessly: "Let's have it...then?"

Tree's tongue rimmed his cracked lips. "Wagh," he grunted irascibly. "Tryin', hoss. Give an old man time."

"What happened?"

Tree's white head stirred in vague negation. "Damn this child's liver an' lights if he kin recollect...."

Whatever Tree's reason for being evasive, Angsman knew that at last they had pinpointed something certain. "Reckon we can make it down to those caves same way you did," he said softly.

To that Tree said nothing, closing his eyes. Shortly he seemed to be asleep.

"Tomorrow, Angsman," Judith Amberley's voice was coldly even, "you and I will go together."

About to flatly state that he'd go alone, Angsman hesitated. Getting to the caves could prove dangerous, but she'd never settle this thing with herself until she saw whatever was to be seen with her own eyes. He nodded curtly. "Get your sleep. There'll be some hard climbing."

Angsman was not sure what woke him...it might have been a mere shadow of sound. He came awake at once, every sense alert, as was his habit. A crouched form was half-bent above him, and he had an instant to register a wicked flash of firelight on knife before he rolled, sidelong and away, his legs tangled in his blanket. The tail of his eye caught the last of that livid steel arc as it ended in his ground sheet, ripped savagely through the tough tarp, yanked free. A wiry form veered away in a hobbling run.

Angsman lunged from the ground, tearing a foot free of his blanket, landing with a grunt on his side as his hand closed around a bony ankle. With surprising strength Tree dragged him a foot before turning with a curse, his knife lifted. Angsman twisted savagely and Tree's light frame turned in the air and fell on its back. Angsman reached for a higher grip, took it in a fistful of Tree's ragged shirt. His other hand caught a skinny wrist, twisting till the knife fell free. He kicked free of his blanket and got up, dragging Tree into the ruddy glare of the fire.

Mexican Tom, drawn by the commotion, hurried up from his guard post. "All right, Tomas. It's under control." Angsman glanced at the others rolling out of their blankets, and again at Tree. His ancient shrunken body was hunched in a tight crouch, bearing the force of his hate against them all.

His attempt on Angsman's life merely confirmed suspicion: Tree's memory had fully returned with its knowledge of what they would find in the cave. He'd shrewdly feigned weakness and sleep, waiting till they slept to make his break, not knowing about Ramirez on guard outside the cul-de-sac. He had stealthily filched a sleeper's knife to make his try for the guide before his escape, knowing that only Angsman could track him down later.

Angsman hefted the knife lightly in his palm, saying, "Think this is yours, Armand," before tossing it to Charbonneau. The Creole snaked it deftly out of the air by the hilt, sheathed it with a cool nod. "Feisty old *bastard,* ain't he?"

"This child 'ud of killed you, Angsman!" Tree shrilled suddenly. "I'd 'a sliced your sweetbreads outen your goddam plew!"

"That's right, Caleb," Angsman said slowly. "So you're going with us tomorrow. Might be you can show us what you're afraid we'll find up in that cliff."

CHAPTER FIFTEEN

On foot the three of them left the cul-de-sac shortly after first light—the scout, the woman, and the old mountain man. They headed up Obregon Pass, hugging the right wall. Here a litter of heavy boulders fallen from the rim would lend plentiful cover at a moment's notice. Angsman was held back by Judith, helping her over the roughest places. Caleb Tree hobbled ahead of them, his tattered trousers flapping around his thin muscle-knotted shanks, his calloused feet impervious to the flinty ground.

Angsman had left him tied hand and foot last night after the attempt at escape, drawing the ropes mercilessly tight. At first barely able to walk, the old man was now swinging briskly along. He hadn't uttered a word since last night.

"I feel guilty," Judith whispered. "Look at him... poor old man. I can't help feeling—"

"Don't," Angsman cut in quietly. "Don't deceive yourself. He's tough as rawhide, in mind and body. He's only watching for a chance to get out of this with a whole skin, even if he has to kill both of us to do it."

"As he probably killed Doug!"

"We don't know that. Best to go slow." He was considering the possibility that Chingo and his bucks might come before they returned to the cul-de-sac; if that happened, they would be cut off from the others. Angsman had flatly argued against Amberley's first insistence on accompanying them. No sense to jeopardize any more lives. If Chingo came, the cul-de-sac would have to be defended. And, Angsman had pointed out, there was Pilar. The reminder had clinched Amberley's reluctant agreement.

Reaching the broad slide where the cliff had long ago

collapsed, they started upward. It was a rugged climb to the rim, and all three were breathing heavily when they reached it. Swinging east along the cliffs, Angsman held them to a cautious advance. The rimrock was weathered and rotten, and from the debris below, it must have often scaled away in great chunks...the slightest jar might start a slide.

They halted above the flinty ribbon of ledge. It lay about thirty feet below the rim. Angsman had been prepared for the difficult descent of an almost sheer drop, for so it appeared from the bottom. He saw now that the rim actually sloped off at a steep angle down to a slight shelf above the cave mouth. He had come lightly geared and provisioned, taking only a canteen of water and a pocketful of jerked beef, together with his pistol and rifle, some candles Amberley had thoughtfully packed, and two ropes coiled over his shoulder.

The descent to the ledge should be relatively simple— the danger lay in the badly eroded rim and the wall immediately below the rim. It appeared that this whole upper cliff had become badly faulted; a slight disturbance might cause it to plunge at any time.

Of this he said nothing, slipping the ropes from his shoulders and uncoiling them. Holding an end of each, he let them snake down to the ledge. Their fifty-foot lengths reached with plenty of slack to spare. He hauled them up and selected a huge rough-sided boulder back off the rim, knotting an end of each line securely around it. He tied one opposite end around Judith's waist, the other beneath her arms, then tested the knots. The tying up had taken a good deal of slack, but enough remained to make the ledge.

"Go down backward," he told her. "Don't think about it and don't look down. Think of doing a Sunday promenade walking backward." She smiled, and then he said a little awkwardly, "Don't be frightened. There's me, and just in case, the boulder."

Her gray eyes were steady. "I won't be frightened."

Keeping a watchful eye on Tree, Angsman braced himself on the rim and gripped the rope two-handed, gradually letting it out as she went over the rim, her feet feeling out each step of the rough slant. She tightly fisted the upper rope and kept her eyes up, not looking down as Angsman must. He felt the sweat start on his forehead, seeing her framed against the dizzy drop. She reached the shelf above the cave, let herself carefully over it, and Angsman lowered her slowly the last few feet.

On the ledge Judith pried the knots loose with the tip of her knife, freeing herself from the ropes. Angsman murmured, "Well, Caleb, you too old to shinny down?"

Tree sent him a stare of bleak hatred, then snorted softly, grabbed both ropes and clambered down the slant with a kind of stiff agility that made Angsman smile. When Tree had nearly reached the ledge, he himself made a swift descent, dropping to Tree's side in a few seconds.

Judith had already moved into the cave mouth, peering against its darkness, and he moved over to her, shoving Tree ahead of him. He took one of the short thick candles from his pocket, struck a match and hand-cupped the flame. The wick took it easily in the musty still air, and now with its sickly washback of shadow, he saw a deep cavern penetrating back into the cliff. Propelling Caleb Tree ahead, he picked his way over the rubbled floor, Judith's fingers tight around his arm. The tunnel walls had an angular jaggedness, and Angsman guessed that it was a mere fault formed by an ancient convulsion, later hand-hewn to its present rugged proportions by some prehistoric tenants. The work must have involved years of patient labor, breaking and chipping with crude flint tools; only the rottenness of the rock would have made it possible. To those primitive people, the result had no doubt been worth it: a secure fortress-home against the dangers of their savage world.

At long intervals, internal faults similarly hewn into negotiable passages intersected the main tunnel, sometimes penetrating it through floor or ceiling, so that the place was a labyrinth. Angsman swore under his breath; it could make their search near-hopeless. A man could spend days trying to trace out this maze and never find his way out. Which was why he'd brought Caleb Tree— as a last measure he could force the old man to talk. For now, there was no danger of becoming lost while they held to this main shaft...might as well follow it out.

Now it cut hard to the left on a flinty downslope, and they groped along cautiously, the saffron flame bathing out the walls ahead, those behind slipping back into oblivion. Angsman had thought he was inured to every sort of harsh exigency, but for an outdoorsman, this business of crawling through the ground like a damned mole was different. Something about it laid a suffocating tension against a man. Maybe it was some aroused racial memory of a time when men had believed in trolls that lived in the recesses of the earth. For a while he had to fight the urge to scramble up to sunlight and fresh air.

Shortly the roof and sides of the tunnel sharply rose, and they stepped into a vaulted round chamber, this obviously hollowed out by human hands. The candlelight played over a high roof of reddish brown crumbling rock, with odd patches of deep blackening. Soot and smoke above the sites of cooking fires, he guessed, and then held the candle lower. Judith gasped—the light played on the partly intact skeletons of animals, horses from their skulls. The slaughtered ponies of Obregon and his party, but where was the gold they had carried here?

"Angsman," Judith whispered.

"Wait," he said slowly. "Can't be a dead end...." He circled the chamber, holding the fight near the floor. With his toe he unearthed a half-buried object—a stone metate. And other relics. A flint arrowhead, a fragment of yucca matting, shards of broken pottery on which the black-on-white paint designs seemed almost fresh. And something else—bits of whitened stone, soft and crumbling to the touch. He blew the dry powder of what had been human bone from his hand and straightened up.

Time had almost stood still in this place, yet that fact lent a sense of incredible ancientness. Ages ago people had been here. They had birthed and lived and died, leaving some of their possessions almost intact, and yet their own substance was now dust a man could blow from his palm. It had an effect both serene and unsettling, giving a man the kind of thoughts he couldn't stay with for long.

Caleb Tree's voice, cracked and dry and broken by hollow echoes, startled him. "Wanta find young Amberley, do you, hoss?"

Angsman eyed him narrowly, wondering at his sly, humorous calm.

"Oh, please," Judith whispered. "If you know anything…."

"Know a sight, missy. Studyin' on whether to tell you." Tree stroked his dirty beard with a malicious grin, and Angsman supposed he was savoring his peculiar advantage here in some twisted way.

"Caleb," he said quietiy, "don't push it now."

"Don't you, child. Fer I'll tell you this: *thout old Cal, you ain't gonna find a billy-be-damned thing. I fixed that."

His faded eyes alight with childish pleasure cut swiftly from one to the other. Abruptly, then: "I done my studyin'. Looka here." He hobbled across the chamber to a large slab tilted against the wall, seemingly inset there. He seized on it, saying testily, "Lay hold, hoss."

Angsman joined him, and together they dragged the stone outward at an angle till it tilted and crashed on its side. A low black maw was exposed. Tree grunted, muttering, "Ain't got the stren'th I had when I laid that thing agin it."

"After you," Angsman said softly.

Tree bared his yellow teeth in a grin and ducked into the opening. Angsman reached his hand to Judith and she took it, following him at a low crouch through the tight burrow. They emerged into a second chamber larger than the first, of which their entrance was one of several passages intersecting it. A draft caught the candle flame; it guttered low and Angsman cupped his hand about it, holding his breath till its sallow flicker grew.

Tree was chuckling softly; there was a tense mad fiber to the sound that made Angsman's spine crawl. Judith pressed trembling against his arm as he held the candle low. The light caught on a dull yellow glitter. Gold bars stacked against a wall. A fortune in bullion deserted by the Spaniards in their last desperate try for escape. Ten full *cargas* of six bars each, molded in the old Spanish way to cylinders two and a half feet long and six inches thick.

Tree knelt by the stacked metal, his clawed trembling hands fumbling across it, shaken by his quiet chortling. Angsman watched him a cold moment, then turned away, moving deeper into the chamber.

Judith, clinging to him, screamed softly.

The skeleton at their feet was that of a man. The

grinning empty-socketed skull was still encased in a hel-
met of hammered brass; the fleshless ribs still wore a
corroded steel breastplate. Rotten leather harness clung
to it here and there. Beneath the pelvic bones lay a
straight sword of what had been Spanish steel, partly
drawn from its metal scabbard and rusted there as the
arrested motion of a long-dead hand had left it.

"One man," Angsman said, his voice hollow and quiet,
"was killed here, when they fought over their last provisions. The old Don told it straight all the way."

He moved farther along the wall. Judith's breathing
was steady in his ear, but he could feel her leashed tension biting at his own nerves. And then they found the
second skeleton, twisted as it had fallen in its dying
sprawl. In this deep dry air, the bones of dead men
looked much the same till they began falling to dust,
whether they were fleshless a year or two hundred years.
But this one's clothing was still whole, faded and sunken
against the skeletal ridges and cavities.

Judith said tonelessly, "I gave Doug that belt...for
his birthday." She seemed to be standing in a shocked
trance, and then she sank down on her knees with a low
moan. Angsman reached a hand to her shoulder...he
stiffened with a swift backward glance.

Caleb Tree was gone.

Angsman stooped and jabbed his candle upright into
the sand floor. He crouched there, his gun in hand, listening—he heard nothing. Tree had slipped silently away
into one of the converging tunnels, and now Angsman
knew why he'd shown them the chamber which he'd
painstakingly blocked off: to provide this momentary
distraction.

Angsman dug out another candle and lighted it, thinking coolly against his sense of warning urgency. Tree
would try escape by the way they had come, rather than
risk losing himself in another passage. Quickly Angsman
told Judith his intention of finding Tree, and to stay
where she was. He was leaving a candle, and he wouldn't
be gone long. She did not look up or reply.

He catfooted to the low connecting shaft and entered
the next chamber. It was empty. He crossed quickly to
the main tunnel and started up it. Tree, half-animal,
would probably feel his way through the darkness with

a sure-footed instinct. Angsman moved on carefully, shielding his candle against a chance draft.

Ahead, he heard a pebble rattle. It set up a small clamor of echoes.

He increased his pace, heart pounding. If Tree could reach the rimrock and pull up the ropes, they'd be hopelessly stranded. Also Angsman had left his rifle up there for the descent to the ledge, and Tree could be thinking of that. He might attempt to bargain for his life and the gold.

Daylight rimmed the jagged walls up ahead, and Angsman dropped his candle and scrambled up toward it. He could see the ropes dangling past the cave entrances, saw their telltale little jerks as Tree went up. Angsman lunged the last few yards to grab, too late, at the ropes. A sudden yank whisked them upward.

Stepping onto the ledge he saw Tree on the rim hauling in the lines. The old man gave a burst of crazed laughter. Angsman swung up his pistol, and Tree scrambled swiftly from sight. In a moment he appeared again, pointing the rifle downward. He was breathing hoarsely, his sunken eyes burning behind the tangle of his white hair.

"Greaser stand-off, hoss. You ready to make medicine?"

"No deals—"

"Eh, this child figgered so—want all that yaller gold to yourse'f!"

"Not me, Caleb, you. You killed that boy to keep the secret. I get you back to Stambaugh alive, you'll hang for it."

"Ain't that the truth," Tree jeered softly. "Big if, child. Lessee now. No deal, no gold, an' you'll hunt ol' Caleb down like a dog."

"That's the way of it."

"How you gonna get outa thet hole, child?"

"You forgetting the others? By tomorrow at the latest, Amberley'll be worried enough to come after us. There's other ropes in camp, Caleb."

"Ahuh." Tree's yellow grin was savage. "And you'll be a-hyperin' on my trail." The strain of his growing madness strongly edged his soft words. "Cain't let thet be, hoss."

He stepped backward from view. Angsman stood a

puzzled moment, waiting in the sun-blasted stillness. Till he heard the faint grate of rock on rock. Then he knew. Tree meant to start a slide, to seal off the cave. *"Caleb!"*

No answer except Tree's panting grunts as he heaved at a heavy boulder. Angsman saw it tilt out above the rim, and he stepped quickly into the cave mouth.

The massive chunk crashed into the ledge lip, then bounded out and downward. The whole cliffside shuddered and then came a massive ominous rumble. It confirmed his earlier guess. This entire section of wall was faulted, hanging by a hair over a vertical drop where the lower cliff with its old trail had scaled off. Loosened rubble began cascading down.

He cupped his hands to his mouth and shouted, "Caleb! This wall's rotten—you'll bring the whole rim down!"

If Tree heard, he was too far gone to heed. Again his hoarse panting, the grate of heavy rock. A second chunk slammed into the ledge, striking farther inward where it tilted down into the tunnel. The rock angled in with a sudden leap past Angsman, missing him by a couple of feet, then ground to a stop.

The ground trembled. Again the angry rumble.

"Caleb!" His shout was drowned in a thunderous roar. Above it he heard Caleb Tree's thin wail...caught in his own trap. Angsman was already retreating deep into the tunnel at a lunging run. He tripped and fell. Then lay hugging the floor as the rimrock avalanched onto the ledge, breaking and spilling over it and into the cave. Pieces of the cave roof fell. The bellow of the ruptured cliff drowned all other sound, but he felt flinty fragments strike his back and legs. As the roar dwindled off, he heard a huge chunk crash not a yard from his head.

Then he was lying quietly in a choking rock-dusted silence. Slowly he opened his eyes, blinking at their sudden sting. He was in utter darkness. He pushed himself up on hands and knees, got to his feet, felt for a wall. He leaned against it, coughing, fighting for breath, till the dust began to settle.

Only then, cold realization flooded him. He and Judith were trapped behind tons of fallen rock.

CHAPTER SIXTEEN

Angsman stood quietly, letting his first panicked knowledge that they were sealed off in a vast catacomb wash away. Methodically he dug out his third and last candle, cupped a flaring match to it. The flame was steady, picking out the clotting slide of rock and debris where the cave mouth had been.

He made his way deeper into the tunnel, paused where he'd hastily dropped his second candle, searching on his knees till he found it. The air should last a good while, long after their last feeble illumination burned out and left them in darkness. Remembering his sensations during those few moments of black silence, it was a thing he didn't want to contemplate.

Now Judith's sobbing cries drifted faintly to his ears, calling his name, and he realized with a shock what her state of mind must be. He called to her, telling her that he was all right, to stay where she was. Groping down the treacherous slant he reached the first chamber and crossed it to the shaft, ducking quickly through. She ran into his arms and he held her tightly, waiting for her hysterical sobbing to ebb away. Then he told her the truth, as gently as he could.

She stepped back slowly and sank to the floor, staring at her clasped hands in her lap. "We'll die, then. It doesn't matter—nothing matters."

"Watch that talk," he told her sharply. "Start that, you're dead already."

"I am dead already," she whispered. "Don't you see— I've found what I had to be sure of—that I killed Doug."

Angsman carefully pinched out his candle, glanced at the first one's steady flame, then kneeled facing her. Took her by the shoulders, shaking her gently. "Listen to me...listen, dammit! Tree killed your brother. Caleb

305

Tree. For the gold. And he's done for. Down at the bottom of that cliff under the rockslide he started—"

He broke off. Her eyes dull and glazed and she was shaking her head back and forth with a pettish little frown that reminded him of a rebuked child in a sleepy tantrum. "You don't understand," she said with soft insistence. "That was only at the beginning. It began a long time ago...in Boston. I really killed Doug. This had to be. It's my punishment, don't you see?"

Angsman hesitated only a moment. Then slapped her, and hard. Her mouth fell open and she stared at him in a vaguely shocked way. Her hand lifted halfway to her cheek. He shook her savagely. "Lady, I came a hell of a ways with you and your owl-brother for no pay but wearing and worrying myself near to death. I've killed a man, walked into a hostile 'pache camp, tangled with a feisty buck, got that lunatic Chingo breathing on my neck, holed up in a dead-end ravine, got a cliff pulled down over my head, sweated and swarmed over half the damned country for you, and I'm as much in the dark as when we started on this damnfool junket. Now by God, you're going to tell me what's sticking in your craw!"

His harsh rage, only half-feinged, aroused her at once as he'd intended it should. The pained anger in her face faded to a slow understanding. She gave a weary nod. "All right...it can't make any difference."

"It could make a hell of a lot."

He was forcing the shaken girl to a harrowing limit, Angsman knew. But she'd come this far merely to confirm some bleak horror that had haunted her for too long. If she turned from it now, she was lost. She'd go on living with a sick fantasy till it finished her. Under the circumstances, the thought held a wry irony. But in the desert a man came to a hard fatalism concerning life and death. You had no choice as to dying, but there were two ways to finally face it. One way summed up whatever dignity there was in being human.

Judith's words came with halting reluctance, and he began to piece out the truth he'd half-suspected. After her parents were killed, Judith had firmly assumed a responsible role toward her orphaned brothers. Both were quiet-natured and flexible, a fact which had aroused her warm concern. Their backbones had to be stiffened for facing life. Discipline was the answer. But James was already a man, eight years Judith's elder. Though he'd acceded with a mild annoyance to her authority, he was matured enough to be more amused than deeply affected.

With young Doug it was different. Yet, sensitive and shy and indrawn, he'd suffered in silence. For his own good, she'd ordered him about relentlessly, checking every detail of his comings and goings. She'd blinded herself to the changes in them both as the years passed —she becoming a cold and petty tyrant, he turning sullen and more withdrawn.

Then, at nineteen, he'd suddenly rebelled. Against her furious protest, he had gone off to Mexico with Jim. When they returned months later, Judith found that she had lost all control over Douglas. He took to staying out late hours with rough companions or worse; he became cocky and impudent, deliberately mocking her efforts to re-assert authority. One night when he'd come in somewhat the worse for drink, she was waiting for him. He'd taken the tongue-lashing in glaring silence. Then all his pent-up resentment had burst out. He'd cursed her for a meddling old maid; worse, she was cold and sexless, a man in skirts. He'd said other things that had horrified and disgusted her, and then, trembling in cold rage, she had ordered him to leave the house. He'd leave, Douglas promised, and damned if he'd ever come back.

They heard no more of him until six months later, when Jim received the letter from Santa Fe. It had been a long boastful burst of enthusiasm over his finding of the Obregon map and manuscript, without a single mention of Judith. By now sick with regret and self-loathing, she had realized that the worst thing she could do was interfere further in his life, though Jim told her frankly that Douglas was attempting a thing foolhardy and dangerous.

She had known only too well why Douglas had been driven to this suicidal quest. Despite his bitter repudiation of her, she had succeeded in making him feel like a callow, spineless child. He needed desperately to prove himself to her and Jim and most of aU to himself....

As the months went by without word, their worst fears became near-conviction, and with it Judith's aching remorseful feeling of guilt had deepened. For nearly a year she had lived on the edge of apprehension, torn between her desire to learn the truth one way or the other and her fear of widening the break between Douglas and herself if he turned up alive and well. Then Jim's sabbatical leave had come up, and Judith had desperately goaded him into coming west. He'd told her quietly that she was jeopardizing her life for a hopeless needle in a haystack. And yet, understanding, he had offered no objection, and they made the trip.

And now, Judith said in a dull and hopeless voice, she knew the truth. Douglas was dead, and she had killed him.

In the dead silence Angsman rose to his feet. "Stay here," he told her, and crossed past the remains of the conquistadore to the second skeleton, kneeling by it. He pulled out one of the candles and lighted it, holding it low for a careful inspection. There was a round clean hole in the base of the skull where the bullet had gone in. This was what Caleb Tree had known they'd find, the proof that he'd shot Douglas Amberley from behind.

Later, no doubt, Tree had planned to come back with enough mules to pack out the gold. He'd sealed off the main tunnel shaft against chance discovery before he returned. Then, in some way they'd never know, he had sustained the head injury that had turned him into a raving animal. Alone and lacking proper treatment, he had never entirely regained his senses. Even toward the last that was true, Angsman knew, remembering the maniacal frenzy that had cost his life.

Tree had evidently stripped the body of any weapons or useful gear. Frowning, Angsman searched the pockets. He found only a hand-tooled wallet and a leather-bound notebook. Both were dry and cracked, but their contents were preserved perfectly. The wallet contained identification papers and a folded, frayed copy of Obregon's map. Thumbing through the notebook, he realized that it was a journal, with only a few blank pages toward the end. The rest was filled with a tidy, close-written script in pencil, each entry scrupulously dated.

Angsman pocketed both articles, pinched out his candle and stood up, turning his attention to the grim, practical need of dealing with their predicament. There might be another, unknown exit from the caves, for they had penetrated deep into the cliff. But the next step had to be taken carefully; if they went batting blindly about through this maze of tunnels, they'd only lose themselves hopelessly. At least here he had an approximate idea of their position.

He studied the candle on the floor for a slight waver of flame that might betray a draft from one of the converging corridors. There was none, yet there had been a draft before, carried in through the many tunnels. It could only mean that their one possible exit had been choked off....

Steady now, Angsman told himself. He picked up the candle and moved to the nearest tunnel mouth, peering into it. Then to the next. Came to a dead halt, holding his breath. There was no mistaking the sound...running water purling its faint echoes up the rocky shaft. He glanced at Judith on her knees staring dully at the floor. He said sharply, "Snap out of it...follow me."

The tunnel was cramped and twisting, winding angularly downward at a treacherous pitch. Angsman held their advance to a wary crawl. The sound of rushing water steadily grew. Dropping down and past a sharp bend, they came on it suddenly. An underground stream whose swirling blackness was penciled by the wan glimmers of candle-shed light. The wax cylinder was a mere stub now, singeing Angsman's fingers. He set it down and lighted another, studying the swift current. It cross-angléd this narrow tunnel and poured into a second.

It jogged a half-forgotten detail in his mind, and instantly other facts jigsawed into place. Cautious excitement gripped him. He had carefully oriented their advance into the main tunnel from outside, hazarding at the distance covered, noting their left-angling descent at one point. The chamber they had left lay deeply inward, well below and to the left of the former cave entrance. They had continued due west on the continuing downslant of this tunnel. If his rough computing was correct, they were now close to the deep feeder canyon that contained the old Spanish mine, not far from its east wall and almost level to its boxed end. There lay the deep spring-fed pool where their gold-bearing stream had its orgin. And maybe the outlet of this subterranean channel.

It was still guesswork, and it would mean taking a

dangerous chance. If he were wrong, a drowning death fighting for life would be faster and cleaner than remaining in the caves till they suffocated.

"Can you swim?" he asked suddenly.

"No," Judith murmured dully. Then raised her head sharply, giving him a puzzled look.

He briefly explained, holding the candle low above the water. The flame barely wavered. "Some free air in the water. Not enough to feed these caves. It'll go bad soon enough."

"Could it be any worse?" she whispered.

"You want to live?" he demanded harshly.

A long moment of silence before her almost inaudible sigh. "Strangely, I do. Why do we hold on to life so?"

"You better want it more than that." He paused. "Even if I'm right, it'll be mean going every foot of the way."

"I want it. Will, I want to live."

"All right."

"Can you—swim?"

"Haven't seen that much water since I was a kid, except a muddy river now and again. There was a fine old swimming hole on the farm...tell you about it another time."

He flattened on the stony bank and sank his arm into the stream. Its numbing chill took his breath away. Two feet down he touched a pebbly bottom. He lowered himself into the roiling current now, feeling its powerful tug along his legs, then helped Judith to descend. She caught her breath at its icy shock. He led the way down the tunnel, holding her hand tightly, the candle picking out their way.

The water deepened steadily and the rock roof closed down to little more than a foot above their heads. The current was less confined by this deeper channel, its force somewhat weakened. Only this saved them from being swept from their feet as its sullen surge pressed upward from knees to waist. The stream bed underfoot was slick and loose-pebbled, and Angsman felt a knotted tension against the moment when they'd either lose footing in the current or be unable to touch bottom.

The water rose nearly to chest-heigjt as they angled around a stone abutment, and then Angsman halted. The channel ran a straight pourse ahead for perhaps ten yards, coming to a dead end where the roof tapered gently down to meet the water. He barely made it out by the unsteady flame, and then he twisted back a glance at Judith. Her teeth were chattering uncontrollably, and her face was bloodless. She was standing shoulder-deep in churning water, and he could feel her tight-braced effort to keep footing as she gripped his hand in her own.

"The last lap," he said softly. "Well know in a minute."

"It's elemental at least." She tried to smile. "Life or death. Don't let go of me, Will. Whatever happens."

"I won't. But it's likely we'll be swimming now. You can't, and I'm no great shucks. I'll keep you up...but don't fight me."

He slipped his arm around her waist and they took the last steps, and then his feet flailed into an abrupt drop-away. The candle spat out...darkness then. Judith's small scream ended in a splutter. *"Don't fight!"* He shouted it in her ear, shifting his hold to her shoulders, treading water one-handed and riding the current. It swept them toward the tunnel end they couldn't see. Judith's fingers taloned into his arm with her tense panic, but she did not struggle. In a moment he would be forced to dive... how deeply, he didn't know. If the stream did not break through the outside, or if it emerged at too great a distance, or if the last passage was too narrow....

It's elemental at least, Judith had said. With that wry flicker of thought he said quietly, "We're about there. Take a deep breath—hold it."

As he spoke, he strained his eyes downward...saw a rippling refraction of daylight break beneath the water.

He dived deeply and strongly toward the pale illusive glitter, knowing it was deeper than it seemed and somewhat wider. The current was tightly confined in its final thrust, and it caught them helplessly as a pair of corks. Angsman felt a bruising blow as his hip struck a jagged rim, and then they were swept through. Shafting sunlight blazed down into the open water. Tlie current turned them head over heels with a final playful nudge, and they were free of it, and he struck upward, his lungs bursting. He broke suddenly to sunlight and air, and they were out; they were free.

CHAPTER SEVENTEEN

They sat on the sun-wanned rock by the pool to rest and catch their breaths. Angsman thought of the wallet and journal; he took the soaked articles from his pocket, pressed them on the rock to remove most of the water, then handed them to Judith. She gave them a listless glance and dropped them at her side.

"I'd look through that journal."

"So that I can read first-hand his feelings for me?" she asked bitterly. "No, thank you."

"You going to face all of it or not?"

She was silent for a full minute, then said wearily, "You're right. But I don't think I can bear to. You read it, please. If there's anything important…"

Angsman picked up the journal and leafed through it slowly, carefully separating the wet pages. He gave a sharp look. "You know he had a girl?"

"Douglas?" She was plainly startled. "He never said a word—but I gave him no reason to confide in me, did I?"

Turning the pages slowly, frowning over each, Angsman pieced out the story of young Amberley's first and only romance. Florence Leighton had been a common waitress in a cafe frequented by Douglas and his wild crowd. A sensitive young girl, it appeared, who had given him the sympathy which he'd found neither in the prison of his home life nor the roistering company of his hard-drinking friends. The early entries were full of Florence, with only a bare mention of his sister—this with a tight and bitter comment that he wouldn't dare bring this working girl to his home.

Angsman flipped on through the pages, coming to the entry relating die final quarrel with Judith. Far from being a bitter note, it contained a burst of wild, boyish

312

exuberance. At last he'd found the courage to make the break and was now free to be his own man. No more of meeting Florence in secret like a skulking coward, no more of loafing off Jim's bounty. He would strike out on his own to the West, land of fresh opportunity; he'd make an archaeological find that would win him wealth and fame and make him worthy of Florence's love.

A man had to pause and smile a little at such romantic idealism. It belonged only to youth, and it touched a mature man with a brief unsettling sadness. The rest of the journal was a straightforward and factual account of Doug's search, his finding of the Obregon *derrotero,* his journey with Caleb Tree into the sierra, finding the Spanish gold diggings—and that was all.

"Doug," Judith whispered, staring blindly at the pool.

"Now you know," Angsman said quietly. "None of it was on your account. All he did was for her."

Judith heaved a deep sigh, shaking her head. Absently she picked up a pebble and tossed it at the pool. "Things aren't that black and white. I played my part, and you know it. I can't escape that, Will."

"Just so you don't try."

She looked at him questioningly, and now he scowled, palmed a pebble and threw it after hers, watching the concentric ripples spread outward. "Once I gave a green second lieutenant some bad advice that helped get a cavalry patrol massacred. Inexcusable carelessness. Point is, I did it with the best intention. I like to think that what I learned has helped keep some good men alive since." He paused thoughtfully. "Once you've made a mistake, you can't take it back. But you can live with it, because it'll hurt you enough to make you live better."

"You—did that? And you seem so sure—"

"Damned carefully sure."

They talked on a while, quietly, and slowly then he saw the wonder of a great budding change in her. It was as though in fronting herself and her guilt, she had found another self she hadn't known existed, a warm and knowing person thawing through her lonely armor. And suddenly she said bluntly, "Will—you came of a good home —a gentle upbringing. Why did you leave it for this?"

He shrugged. "Reasons."

"Who was she?"

It startled him, and then he smiled dryly. "No girl.

The reason I left was not a very good one, I guess. I hated the stuffy boy's academy Pa packed me off to. Hated being caught in the tight social conventions of the Southern gentry. Thought I was in a trap. I wanted freedom, all I could get of it—ran away from home to find it. Of late I've figured that what I really hated was responsibility—but I gave it a shape of noble rebellion. A kid does that."

"You sound as though it's worn awfully thin."

"Lately, it has."

She sighed, looking into the pool. "Is it wrong for me to suddenly be so happy? Poor Doug. Not even a Christian burial...."

Angsman lifted his glance to the red-walled mesa far above. "Why, I'd say he had the biggest monument in the world. And the one he came to find."

He was silent then, thinking of how they had started this journey poles apart, as a prim Boston lady and a ragtag-and-bobtail frontier loafer, and of how events had moved them toward some middle ground. Somehow he'd become a nostalgic ex-Virginia gentleman, and Judith was learning to be more than a mere lady.

She said nothing for a time, gazing at the pond with a faint, secret smile, and now she drew up her knees and hugged them, and laughed softly. "I'm still alive, Will. I've done my mourning for Douglas, a year of it, and now it's over. I'm alive and I'm a woman.

Of that fact he'd been strongly and uncomfortably aware for some moments. It was not only that the wet bulky man's trousers and shirt now clung with a loving fidelity to the long slender legs and the two pointed breasts they had indifferently denied, but also that the trim body was drained at last of its icy tensions, softened and relaxed in all its lines.

Unbidden their eyes locked now, and he saw the beginning of a different tension in her, warm-breathing and softly swelling. Her hand moved hesitantly along the rock, and his covered it. They were sitting close, and now they came suddenly together. Some minutes passed, broken only by occasional intervals of breathless murmurs ending impatiently in long heady silences. When they drew apart at last, her eyes were shining with a new, breathless wonder. "Will...oh Will." She laughed shakily. "Your beard scratches."

"Beards can be shaved." He added wryly, "I've taken on a lot of rough edges. Some of 'em won't wear off so handily. Can't see myself in a tie and white shirt."

"I'm trying, but neither can I." Her tone was teasing and gently sober. "Suggestions?"

"I got a letter from my brother Joe six months ago. He said that Pa's changed in his mellowing years. Used to be a hard old devil—"

"Are you sure that your running away was all your fault?"

"Well, we scrapped a lot. Mother always took my side, but you didn't argue with Pa."

"I see a certain similarity...but go on."

"It seems Joe is busy making quite a name for himself in state politics. Pa and Mother are getting on... need somebody to run the farm. Anyway, Pa wants me to come home."

"A gentleman can live with considerably less formality on a farm than in a city, can't he? I've always liked the country."

He said slowly, "It's all pretty sudden."

"I'm not so sure. Will, you didn't do all you've done for us simply because I injured your pride."

"I expect not."

"Is that all?"

"I'm not very eloquent."

"But you are. This way...."

When they arrived back at the cul-de-sac, Ramirez was standing guard at its mouth, impassively ignoring Charbonneau and Ambruster panning the stream. Lately Mexican Tom had walked a straight and sober line, following Angsman's orders to the letter, and the guide felt a kind of wry affection, knowing that Ramirez was fighting all of his irresponsible instincts in holding to his duty while the others gold-grubbed. Because he knew what gold fever could do to a man, Angsman realized how deeply Tom's previous defection had affected him.

Amberley and Pilar came out then, and all of them gathered to listen to Angsman's terse telling of what had happened. Amberley, however, was plainly flabbergasted by the change in his sister. Angsman drew him aside and they talked quietly for a few minutes.

Amberley's thin face broke in a broad, relieved grin.

"Now you've enlarged on the situation somewhat, I understand. You and Judith, eh? Wonderful, old man. Congratulations." He thrust out his hand, and Angsman took it, lifting an eyebrow.

"Wasn't sure how you'd take it, professor."

Amberley laughed heartily. "When two people strike sparks from one another, as you did from the first, it's certain that there's more than meets the eye. Now that her mind is cleared of that morbid nonsense, whatever stood between you has been cleared away." He coughed, a shade embarrassedly. "A man's quality shows under stress, Angsman. I've seen yours. Why should I be anything but pleased?"

Angsman said slowly, "Professor, I owe you an apology."

"Oh." Amberley blinked, adjusted his spectacles, and grinned boyishly. "I know. You thought of me as rather a strait-laced fool, an absent-minded bookworm who couldn't see ahead of his nose. In some respects the indictment holds water. Pilar has helped me to understand a good deal that I hadn't, about myself and other people." He coughed again. "We're going to be married, as soon as her family knows."

"Congratulations to you, professor."

"Jim, old man, Jim." Amberley paused soberly. "I'm sorry about Doug, of course, but it only confirms what I'd believed certain. After all we've been through— frankly, for Judith's sake, I'm too relieved to feel sorrow. We've both lived with it too long."

"He took a long chance when he struck out here— reckon he knew that. And figured the risk was worth it, if it was for something he believed." Angsman took out the journal and handed it to the Easterner. "It's all in there, Jim. Your brother died with a purpose."

"It's certain that he hadn't been living with one. It's a good thing to know. Thank you, Will."

Charbonneau sauntered up, chewing a twig in lieu of a cheroot. "Reckon you'll be packin' out now, eh, mes amis?"

"We've got what we came for, Armand. You?"

The Creole's bearded lips twisted wryly around the twig as he took out the poke of gold dust that sagged his pocket, hefting it "Man don't nevair get enough of

this, my fran' Will." He sighed profoundly. "I suppose
we got to get, though, before Chingo come...."

They assembled their camp gear hurriedly, loaded
their pack animals, heading out from the cul-de-sac and
the canyon in a tight group to swing eastward up
Obregon Pass. Pilar Torres rode the lineback dun that
had been Will-John Staples's. Angsman moved fifty yards
ahead on scout, and Ramirez pulled back an equal distance
to the rear; the other three men flanked their mounts to
either side of the two women.

Angsman had expected Chingo's move before now, and
he knew that their situation was still far from secure.
Chingo had now had nearly three days to gather a band
of young bloods behind him. And though he would un-
doubtedly take a long chance to satisfy his thirst for
revenge, he was still an Apache. So Angsman, wary of
ambush, was scouting out a wide lead on his companions.
The Apaches could be following behind, on flank beyond the rim, or holding ahead of their party...wait-
ing.

Even if Chingo wasn't yet ready to make his move
they were still in the heart of the savage Toscos, with
long days ahead. He'd have plenty of time and a hundred
ideal points ahead to set up an ambush. Overtaking a
party of mounted whites and skirting ahead of them
would be no trick at all; in the long pull an Apache buck
on foot at his tireless jogtrot could easily distance the
strongest horse. Their horses, rested and fresh now, had
to be conserved for the grueling trip that still lay ahead.

As they moved on into the late afternoon, the floor of
the pass became more rugged with its litter of fallaway
rimrock. Because this stretch was ideal for ambush, Angsman slowed pace and made frequent dismounts to check
the ground. He paid particular attention to a sandstone buttress hard by the right wall, a perfect lookout
point for an Apache scout

Tramping over to it, a glance told him that someone
had laid up here shortly before. The sandstone was
pitted and rotten, with a slight abrasion on its surface
where a man had leaned his sweaty hand. A faint sift-
ing of loosened sandstone grains covered the spot,
still clinging there from moisture.

It meant that Chingo had already laid his deadfall

ahead, and that by now his scout had reported their approach. No time to lose...the Apaches wouldn't attack after dark, and it was nearly dark now_p The impatient Chingo would not wait on tomorrow_e

Angsman signaled the others to halt and rode back to them, told what he'd found, and pointed out a natural breastwork of rock he'd already noted under the rim. As Apaches would always try for the horses first to put their enemy afoot, they herded the animals back into a deep protective niche in the wall behind the breastwork. Charbonneau grunted, "W'en you think it come, mon ami?"

"When he knows his ambush failed," Angsman said flatly, "and that'll be shortly, because he'll know how close we were."

The men deployed at yard intervals behind their shallow barricade, Angsman placing the two women toward its rear behind larger rocks after seeing that each was armed with a pistol. As he turned back to join the men, Judith clutched his arm, her eyes wide and strained.

"Suddenly I want to live...so much that it frightens me."

"We're not dead yet."

Pilar spoke swiftly, and Judith looked questioningly at Angsman. "She says she'll die before going back to Chingo. Says that you should save a shell too."

Judith moistened her lips. "She should know best...."

They waited in the gathering shadows as the afterglow faded to the first soft touch of dusk, making the light uncertain. This, Angsman knew, would be the ideal moment for Chingo. A minute later he saw the first dark forms slip noiselessly up the pass, flitting from rock to rock. Afterward he caught only brief glimpses, and knew they were coming on at a belly-crawl, slithering almost unseen among the rocks.

Chingo was depending on this first skirmish line of five excellent stalkers to work as close as possible, then rush the barricade and engage the whites at close quarters, Angsman guessed. This would provide momentary diversion necessary for the rest to close the final charge...

"Do you see them? I can't," came Amberley's panicked whisper.

"Yes. Keep your nerve, hold your fire, or you'll be

shooting at shadows. Chingo'll want to finish it in one rush, before dark. If that fails—"

He broke off, swinging his rifle quickly toward the right, as a lean form leaped up and sprang for their barricade in long bounds. At the same instant, the other stalkers leaped to sight, charging in a spread-out line. Angsman's rifle roared; the first buck went down in a lunging sprawl. Charbonneau's shot crashed on the heel of his, and Amberley and Ambruster and Ramirez all fired at once. A second man was spun by a shoulder hit, and a third went down with a shattered leg.

The last pair successfully hurdled the barricade, one of them springing on Angsman who tried too late to bring his rifle to bear point-blank; the buck's rush bowled him over.

The other warrior, clearly aware of the white man's protective devotion toward his women, leaped clear past the men and went after the two girls. He reached Judith and caught her by the hair, striking her pistol aside, evidently intending to use her as a shield and pull their attention to him—

Big Turk Ambruster had already dropped his rifle and was lunging after the buck, reaching him an instant after he'd seized Judith. His hands caught the buck's throat, wresting him bodily away from the girl, and they fell together. The warrior fought futilely against the giant's strangling grip. Then a knife flashed in his choppy fist; a moment later the blade was sheathed to the hilt in the big Negro's belly. Ambruster coughed and stiffened ...put a last crushing effort into his hold.

The first buck, a mere boy, was tussling on the ground with Angsman; the white scout mercilessly used his greater weight and strength to pin the Apache and disarm him—-drew the knife in a quick slash across his throat.

The din of gunfire had filled the pass with crackling echoes. Ramirez and Charbonneau and the Easterner, heeding Angsman's advice as to Chingo's strategy, had held their posts, and now their steady fire had broken the main wave of charging Indians..Amberley had been diverted for only a moment by the second buck's attack on the girls, and then seeing Ambruster take the situation in hand, he crouched shoulder to shoulder with the others, matching their fire.

Angsman gave a swift glance at Ambruster now, saw the giant body slumped silently across his dead opponent. Catching up his rifle then, the scout scrambled to the barricade. No more Apaches reached it, though two came close. Charbonneau brought down one at three yards' distance, and the other floundered away on hands and knees, lung-shot.

Already the main body was falling back, carrying wounded fellows, a few rear flankers covering their retreat. In a minute they were gone, fading like ghosts into the lowering dusk.

Three warriors lay sprawled and silent beyond the barricade. Two more lay dead inside it...and Turk Ambruster was dead. A reek of burned powder stung the air.

Mexican Tom turned slowly from the breastworks, his rifle slipping from his fingers, a queer, puzzled expression on his long face. "*Por nada,*" he whispered. Angsman caught him as he went down, then saw the clean-welling hole high in the boy's chest.

Ramirez' lips stirred, and Angsman bent his head low to catch the faint whisper: "That meke up a little for my mistake, amigo?" He tried to grin and died in the effort.

CHAPTER EIGHTEEN

Until full dusk closed down, the three men crouched by the barricade, watching and listening. At last their tight vigilance unknotted, and then Amberley rose shakily, his face pale in the dim light, and slipped back to the women. Their voices were dazed murmurs in the silence.

Charbonneau shifted a cramped leg, afterward taking out his poke of gold dust. He poured some of the grains into his palm, muttering under his breath as he held them up near his eyes, studying them with a kind of fevered intensity. Angsman regarded him with a thin weary disgust.

"Armand."

"Ah?"

"Keep a watch."

"Sure, sure," the Creole murmured irritably. He returned the gold to the sack, pocketed it, and picked up his rifle. Angsman left him then, moving back to where Judith knelt by the blanket-covered bodies of Ambruster and Ramirez. Her head was bowed, her lips moving in prayer. She looked up with tears penciling bright streaks on her face.

"Mr. Ambruster died for me, Will."

"It's what he had to *do*," Angsman said gently.

They had been damned lucky. Rarely was an Apache outfought on his own ground, especially under conditions so favorable. The Apaches had outnumbered the whites, two of them women, by three to one. And they had failed. Only because of Chingo's seething impatience, Angsman's thinking always a step ahead of him, and their successful downing of the two who got past the barricade, had the encounter turned on a hair's balance.

It would badly shake the warriors' confidence for a

time, but their next reaction would surely be a vengeful rage. What had promised to be a casual slaughter had turned into a humiliating fiasco, with a serious toll in dead and wounded—a thing these young bucks' seething pride couldn't bear. And the enraged Chingo would be goading them fiercely on to settle the account.

After losing two fighting men like Ramirez and Ambruster, Angsman knew that they could not last another charge. And that charge would come at first light, always the Apaches' favored hour of attack. A few hours' grace while darkness held. They could not kill all of the Apaches, and that left one alternative: kill their whetted thirst for fight and drive them off. It had to be done before they recovered from the first failure.

And there was only one way to do it.

He stood a thin chance of bringing it off. If he failed, Angsman knew, they were as good as dead.

Moonglow shed a silvery cast of almost daylight brightness across cliff and canyon, except for the deep pockets of shadow to which Angsman clung, making his way down-pass. He picked his way in sure-footed silence across the tortured bare rock, where etched contrast of light and dark gave a weird effect of crossing the scarred face of a dead world.

He carried only his knife and Ramirez' old Springfield. Once within shooting distance, he'd need only one long shot. If he missed, there would be time only for a fast retreat, and afterward a hopeless wait till dawn.

The main obstacle was the Apache sentry, and a knife was the quietest and surest way. If he failed to surprise the man and bring him down in silence, or if there were more than one, it would be all up in a minute: that was the calculated risk. In his mind Angsman cursed the moonlight. It would highlight his moving form at every break in the banked shadows. The sentry, standing his watch in immobile alertness, need only fire one shot, and even if it missed, it would alarm Chingo's camp.

He couldn't even be certain that the Apaches had bivouacked in the pass, though that was the logical place. He hadn't yet caught a glimpse of firelight; or telltale sound. Ahead lay only a silvered panorama of gilded spires and black swales, craggy and desolate and forbidding even by the softening influence of moonlight. Angsman moved with every sense straining to alertness.

He came to a dead halt, crouching with rifle braced against his hip. Something detected, or only sensed, pinpointed his attention. Carefully he laid the rifle on the ground, slipped his knife from its sheath and glided toward an abutting boulder by the left wall. As he started up a slight incline to reach it, a dark form detached itself from shadow and sprang like a cat, a knife flashing in its fist.

Angsman pivoted aside, ducking low; the savage knife-thrust missed him, and then the hurtling body struck him head on, and they rolled downward in locked battle, thrashing in the moiling silvered dust. Angsman rolled atop his opponent and pinned him. He felt the Apache's blade tear his shirt and glide coldly along his ribs, and then he caught the wiry wrist. The Apache grabbed Angsman's right arm below the elbow.

Moonlight struck the buck's upturned face for one straining instant. The sentry was Matagente. Angsman knew then that the Apache had seen his approach and had deliberately given no alarm, waiting to take his white enemy by knife and finish their quarrel as it had begun, to wipe out the black shame in his mind.

Matagente hissed his fury and heaved wildly upward, rolling them down the last of the incline, he on top now. He fought with all his strength to turn his knife into Angsman's chest. Handicapped by Matagente's leaning weight, Angsman felt his own straining resistance slowly give way. He tried to throw them sideways and only succeeded in bringing the blade nearer his chest. Deadlocked in this spot with his back pinned in a hollow, he knew that his only chance was to get in the first cut.

His knife and arm were cramped against his belly by Matagente's pinioning hand, and now he forced it upward, feeling the buck wince as the keen tip drew a bloody line up his bare stomach and chest to his throat.

With a final furious effort, Matagente thrust all his weight forward and down, driving his blade home. Angsman's desperate wrench on his wrist deflected the knife from above his heart, and then it sank deeply between his ribs. At the same moment Angsman's knife touched Matagente's throat, and then he jerked it in a side-slashing motion. A single gurgling sigh escaped Matagente, the hot wetness of his blood drenching Angsman's arm, and now with a last convulsed shudder his muscles relaxed. Angsman rolled his limp body aside.

Angsman sat up slowly, gripping Matangente's slippery knifehaft in both hands, wrenching it free. The pain surged high in his right side, and he set his teeth against it, letting its first savage agony ebb away. Afterward he shrugged out of his shirt, tore off his dirty bandanna and made a plug and compress, tying the shirt tightly over it around his chest.

The fight had carried through in a grunting, panting near-silence. Now he had only to last on his feet till he got above the camp, provided there were no more sentinels. Recovering his rifle, he moved on with dragging steps. It seemed much later that he saw the first tawny wash of flamelight bathe the cliff beyond a gentle bend in the vast cleft.

He made slowly for a crumbled slide of giant rubble off to his right where the bend began. He began to climb it next to the shadowed wall, pausing frequently to rest. He was drenched with sweat and sparks flailed behind his squinted eyelids; every slug of heartbeat against his ribs brought knifelike pain, and the breath soughed in and out of his lungs as though he'd finished a hard run.

Working to the highest point of the slide, Angsman flattened out on its crest, heedless of flinty surfaces gouging his legs and belly. He rested for a panting minute till the distant firelit scene beyond the bend took sure focus in his swimming vision.

It was a small fire that faintly limned the dark lean forms around it, these hunkered down or standing, all fixing a common attention on the squat barrel-chested figure of Chingo. He was speaking volubly and swiftly, matching speech with his dynamic gestures, holding their fascinated stares. Even in this moment, Angsman could feel the drama and tragedy of it: behind Chingo's strange madness lay both brilliant cunning and born leadership. Except for the thing that festered in him, nullifying his native abilities, he might have influenced frontier history for better or worse.

Now he must die, because it was the only way to turn back the others.

An Apache did not run scared, though he'd take sensible flight on those rare occasions when he was surprised by overwhelming odds. His was the ultimate in physical courage. But the supernatural and its grim omens were another matter. A leader was believed to possess strong medicine that would protect him against injury and death. If that medicine went bad, his followers understood that the only course open was instant flight. A strong lieutenant might rally them after a time, but here was only one leader: Chingo.

Laboriously Angsman drew up his rifle and laid the barrel across a rock, painfully shifting his body to settle into his aim. The flickering light was uncertain and Chingo was stalking dramatically back and forth, haranguing his men...he took one long step that brought him nearly to the fire. It played over his coppery body naked except for breechclout and high moccasins. He stopped pacing now, pausing with lifted arm in a moment of dramatic emphasis.

Angsman cautioned himself that it was down-slope shooting...he allowed for it in taking his sights... squeezed off his shot. Chingo was rocked hard on his heels, and in reflex flung back a foot to brace himself, holding erect. Then he toppled forward full length, his still-raised arm falling in the fire. Flying sparks showered his body.

The bucks were utterly frozen for a moment; as the clapping shot echoes died off, one of them rallied enough to bend and turn the leader over. Then he straightened with a wild shout. The dusky forms began scattering off from the firelight, and Angsman waited to see no more.

He pulled down off the slide at a scrambling run, falling twice. At its bottom he headed back at a stumbling weary trot. The others, tensely waiting, would know the meaning of that single shot, followed by no others: either he or Chingo was dead. Though he'd ordered them to remain where they were, very likely they would come to meet him. Angsman hoped so, because he doubted that he had enough to make it back....

CHAPTER NINETEEN

While darkness held, they waited in hopeful uncertainty, and when no Apache attack came at dawn they knew that Angsman's one-man sortie had paid off. To make sure, Armand Charbonneau trekked down pass to where the Apache bivouac had been. Shortly he returned to confirm it: the Apaches had apparently pulled back for good. The body of Chingo was gone, and Charbonneau had displayed himself boldly to any concealed sniper. No bullet or arrow had answered his rashness....

It was Amberley who, after the rifle shot had come, had left shelter and moved cautiously down the pass. For all they knew a sentry might have shot Angsman; he might be badly hurt and unable to get back. Two hundred yards up the pass he'd found the scout's sprawled form, and afterward toted him back to the barricade across his shoulders. There Amberley had expertly cleaned and treated the wound. The sting of carbolic revived him, and against Judith's objection he sat upright while Amberley affixed a bandage.

Matangente's last ferocious try had not inflicted so deep a cut as Angsman himself had supposed; its force was deflected by the glancing slash along his ribs before it entered between two of them. No vital organ had been touched. His strength had been sapped from loss of blood pumped away in his effort to reach the slide, then by his stumbling retreat. He got some restless sleep, and by morning was running a slight fever; he felt clear-headed enough.

Against Judith's concern now, Angsman insisted that they move on at once. The Apaches would shun them for a while, it being plain that their medicine was stronger, but while they remained here their presence would be an angry goad to the young bucks. A few wild ones

326

might take the bit in their teeth. Also they'd want to re-cover the bodies of their dead from this place.

Within the hour they were packed and saddled, mov-ing on with Judith flanking Angsman; Pilar Torres and Amberley brought up the rear. Charbonneau took the lead, riding well ahead.

Through the shimmering dead heat of the long day, they were held to a slow pace. Angsman's brains seemed to boil moltenly in his head. He was drenched with sweat, and every hooffall of his animal over uneven ground brought stabbing pain. As the day wore on, he felt a hot trickle under his shirt and knew that his wound had opened again. It patched a slow stain against his shirt, and he was glad it was on the side away from Judith. He held straight in the saddle, giving the rest no hint of his condition, and feverishly wondered if this day would ever end.

In spite of which he kept a watchful eye on Charbon-neau. The Creole rode leisurely ahead, occasionally with a lanky leg cocked around his saddle horn. From time to time he took out his gold pouch and spilled some of its contents into his hand. Once he took out another that had been jammed out of sight inside his shirt. No doubt Ambruster's, relieved of his dead body when they'd buried the Negro and Ramirez this morning be-fore setting out....

It was a natural thing to do, but knowing Charbon-neau, Angsman's unrelaxed suspicion was heightened. There was something feverish and obsessive to the way the Creole kept poring over the gold dust. That lust had destroyed plenty of good men; Charbonneau already had the moral fiber of a rattlesnake. For hours, too, the ebullient Creole had held a strangely brooding silence. Angsman steadily watched the back of his lean head with its greasy queued hair beneath a battered slouch hat, wondering exactly what was passing through it.

At dusk they made an early halt at a good camp site in the flanking boulders. Here, Amberley said firmly, they could rest for a day or so until Angsman recovered some strength. He helped the scout to the ground, and eased him over to a low rock where he seated himself. By now he was so intent on Charbonneau that he wholly ignored Judith's shocked scolding when she saw his bloody shirt, and she broke off in a hurt silence. Charbonneau casually heaved the packs off their animals. Then as, without a word, he started rummaging through Angsman's own things, the scout reached awkwardly, wincing, for the gun holstered at his right hip.

Instantly Charbonneau wheeled erect, his gun in fist. "I wouldn', mon ami...you 'ave no chance. Pull the gun slowly an' throw it away—you too, professair—that is it."

As Amberley mechanically obeyed, he could only stare for an uncomprehending moment, then got out, "What's the meaning of this?"

"Ask your so-fine guide. Armand is through with the talk, through with the waiting."

"What do you mean?" Judith whispered. "What do you want?"

Charbonneau had Angsman's pack open, and now he stooped without taking his eyes off them, came up with a heavy leather sack in his fist. "This for now, Ma'mselle...." He shoved it in his coat pocket.

"But that's Ramirez' gold Will is saving for his widow—"

"Of this I would not worry, Ma'mselle...eh, Will?"

Angsman, watching him steadily, said nothing, and then Judith cried, "Will, what does he mean?"

"He wants all the gold," Angsman said softly. "The lode back in those cliffs—the *cargas* the Spaniards left in the caves—all of it."

Charbonneau's shoulders heaved with a fevered chuckle. "W'at I tal' you, Ma'mselle? That Will, he don' miss nothin'."

"Besides him, the four of us are the only ones who know...and we've got the only copies of the old map."

"My God," Amberley said tonelessly, "he wouldn't— not women—"

"A transplanted Southerner, once a gentleman," Angsman murmured. "A frontier man now...seems like everything would go against it. In his right mind, it would. And he'd take our word not to tell anyone about the gold. But he's lost his right mind, Jim. Look at him."

Charbonneau's faint grin faded; his eyes burned like coals as he tilted his gun an inch to bear on Angsman. "You *Americain* cochon—"

"Charbonneau, listen," Amberley pleaded, spreading his hands. "Listen, man. The Spanish gold is buried in those caves for good. You can't get the rest with the Apaches back there. Bonito won't tolerate any more gold-seekers; he told Will as much. Without those considerations, how do you expect to mine and transport it out—alone?"

"Ahh...always he is the logical scholair, my fran' James. Ah. But Armand 'ave a little upstairs, too. The Bonito, he is ver' old *sauvage,* n'est-ce pas? He will live only a little while. Then his people, they will not 'old out longair; they will come in to resairvation like good Apach'. Armand will then return, with the mules, the dynamite and the quicksilvair, the tools; he will blast and sluice and dig; alone he will take out the fortune of Croesus—and share with no one. Ha!"

A muscle twitched in Charbonneau's jaw as he talked; sweat glistened on his face and the gun he held trembled. Angsman thought, Gone completely out of his head with it. It'll kill him sure before he's done...but too late to do us any good.

Now the final decision was taking wicked shape on the Creole's gaunt face, his gun lifting to center squarely on Angsman's chest. For a wild moment Angsman felt his thoughts thread out against a blank wall, and then he thought coldly: Delay him...buffalo him.

He glanced quickly at Pilar, spoke in swift Spanish, to the effect that it was a fine day without rain in prospect.

Charbonneau, knowing only the crudest Mexican argot, scowled and half-lowered the gun. "Eh? W'at you say?" Swiftly he wheeled, covering the Spanish girl. "Wa't you tell her?"

"She doesn't savvy Yankee. I was telling her you mean to kill us. To say any prayers she knows."

"You lie!" Charbonneau strode forward, black fury boiling in his face. He stopped in his tracks with a dreamy and relaxed smile. "Ah-ha. You try to throw Armand off the guard, so one of you make the try for me." He laughed harshly, suddenly raised a foot and set it against Angsman's chest with a brutal thrust that drove him sideways off the rock. He fell on his back with a grunt of pain.

Charbonneau roared. "Ho, look at you, the great white scout; weak as a 'ousecat. Look at all of you!" He spun on a heel, swinging his gun in a wild arc toward the others. "A Yankee scholair too absent of the mind to find his way outside a book...his silly love-struck sistair...a goddam greaser girl likely *enceinte* with an 'alf-Apach' brat for all her lies." He spat sideways. "I should not 'ave to waste the bullet on such dumb useless cochon; they nevair find their way out of the mountain without you—"

As the Creole's attention had partly veered from him, Angsman doubled his knees and inched his prone body forward a few cautious inches, fighting the pain of it. Even as Charbonneau swung back to him, he straightened his legs in a savage kick. His feet struck the Creole above the ankles, knocking his feet from under him. He fell to his knees with an explosive curse. "*Sacre*—"

As Amberley lunged at him, Charbonneau surged to his feet, hissing his inarticulate fury. He swung his gun in a short savage arc. In mid-lunge, Amberley tried to halt and fling up his arms, but the muzzle caught him across the temple. He fell without a sound.

With straining haste Angsman had already rolled on his belly, then came up on his knees, floundering to reach and grab Charbonneau's belt. He strengthened his hard tug with a backward heave of his body. Yanked off-balance Charbonneau fell solidly atop him, and in the crushing pain of it, Angsman's senses momentarily blacked away. Charbonneau's curses were a distant roar in his ears, and then he could see again, felt the Creole's weight straddling him. Charbonneau's lips peeled off his teeth as he held the pistol an inch from the scout's face, cocked it. Angsman caught his wrist in both hands and twisted the gun sideways.

Slowly Charbonneau forced it back against his weak hold, and Angsman put out a last weary effort, watching the barrel slide into line with his right eye. Beyond it lay Charbonneau's blood-swollen face, and over his shoulder then Angsman saw Judith stoop quickly, come up with a pistol in her hand. She pointed it at Charbonneau's back, and Angsman tried to shout, *Hammer it back!* but the words were a strangled gasp. Then he saw the pale horror in her face and understood her hesitation.

Pilar did not hesitate. She snatched the gun from Judith, held it at arm's length in both hands, double-thumbing the hammer. The shot was like a flat hard blow.... its echoes trailed into a stunning silence.

Angsman used his last strength to roll away Charbonneau's limp body, turning it face down. The bullet had emerged from his face, but the hole where it went in was small and clean.

Judith sank to her knees, burying her face in her hands, and Angsman lay on his side, panting, resting a moment so that he could move to her and tell her it was all right. Amberley groaned and tried to sit up, and Pilar pressed him back, saying calmly, soothingly, "Rest a little, Jaime; do not try to move...everything is fine."

Long days afterward, four people halted to rest their horses on a last long rise of land. The squat adobe shape of Fort Stambaugh still lay distant on the flats, but it seemed very near now. Behind it the Pinos River crawled like a sinuous brown snake down to the shabby sprawl of Contentionville. Here at last lay the first links with the civilization to which they were coming home.

Home. The word had a strange sound in Will Angsman's mind, but it was a good one.

He helped Judith to dismount, watching her face. It was sun-darkened and thinned and dust-filmed, and she was very tired, he knew, with a deeper exhaustion than she'd ever known. Still, she summoned a smile for him, and he decided that she was quite beautiful. He thought this, knowing another man would think him a fool, and not caring.

He uncapped his canteen and handed it to her, and she drank deeply. Lowering it then, she surprised him looking off toward the hot, lonely wastes they had crossed. Aware of her sober gaze, he grinned, took the canteen and drank.

"You were thinking that this was the last time for you...out there," Judith said quietly.

"That's done with."

"But it gave you something good, that life. Something I'll never know. Perhaps a disciplined toughness—to face anything." She bit her lip, glancing at her brother and Pilar who stood off a little distance by their horses, their voices quiet murmurs. "I always prided myself on being strong. Then, after facing what I had to, about Doug, I'd thought that I could bear up under anything. Yet a little Spanish girl of nineteen showed me for a weak, preening—"

Angsman put an arm around her, shook her gently. "Anyone can take buck fever. You saw Pilar cry later on…she's not so hard as all that. All she's been through would toughen someone for anything, if they lived through it."

"But I failed you, Will, when you needed me most—"

"Failed to kill a man? You don't want to think like that. Right or not, a thing like that marks you where it doesn't show. She'll have to live it for a long time. I know."

She nodded and was silent. He sensed the lingering trouble behind her still face, and wondered if she were still brooding on it. But she said softly, "I saw the look in your face a minute ago. Will, are you sure that you'll never want to go back? Perhaps for the gold?"

"That's blood gold, Judith. Killed everyone who touched it, from Obregon through Charbonneau. I've already burned both maps—Doug's and Jim's. We've got Ramirez' gold, Charbonneau's and Ambruster's…it'll all go to Tom's wife, Lupe. Let the rest stay where it is —it'll be found again." He shook his head bleakly. "In some ways the Apaches show a damn' sight more sense than us."

He saw the wistful question still touching her expression, as though she thought that a part of him she'd never know would remain here. He considered that, looking back toward the hazy line of far sierra. No… why should it? A man was himself the holder of the parts, of all he'd been and seen and done; if he didn't regret any of it, he would lose nothing, for the best of it would stay with him.

"No regrets," he told her gently. "Let's get on. We'll make the fort before nightfall."

Mounting again, they put their horses down the long slope.

ABOUT THE AUTHOR

T.V. Olsen was born in Rhinelander, Wisconsin, where he lives to this day. "My childhood was unremarkable except for an inordinate preoccupation with Zane Grey and Edgar Rice Burroughs." He had originally planned to be a comic strip artist, but the stories he came up with proved far more interesting to him than any desire to illustrate them. Having read such accomplished Western authors as Les Savage Jr., Luke Short, and Elmore Leonard, he began writing his first Western novel while a junior in high school. He couldn't find a publisher for it until he rewrote it after graduating from college with a bachelor's degree from the University of Wisconsin at Stevens Point in 1955 and sent it to an agent. It was accepted by Ace Books and was published in 1956 as *Haven Of The Hunted.*

Olsen went on to become one of the most widely respected and widely read authors of Western fiction in the second half of the twentieth century. Even early works such as *High Lawless* and *Gunswift* are brilliantly plotted with involving characters and situations and a simple, powerfully evocative style. Olsen went on to write such important Westerns novels as *The Stalking Moon* and *Arrow In The Sun,* which were made into classic Western films as well, the former starring Gregory Peck and the latter under the tide *Soldier Blue* starring Candice Bergen. His novels have been translated into numerous European languages, including French, Spanish, Italian, Swedish, Serbo-Croatian, and Czech.

The second edition of *Twentieth Century Western Writers* concluded that "with the right press Olsen could command the position currendy enjoyed by the late Louis L'Amour as America's most popular and foremost author of traditional Western novels." Any Olsen novel is guaranteed to combine drama and memorable characters with an authentic background of historical fact and an accurate portrayal of Western terrain.

His novel *The Golden Chance* won the Golden Spur Award from the Western Writers of America in 1993.

Made in the USA
Charleston, SC
20 December 2013